The Dedalus Book of Austrian Fantasy 1890–2000

Edited and translated by Mike Mitchell

Dedalus

Dedalus would like to thank the Kunstsektion of the Austrian Bundeskanzleramt in Vienna and East England Arts in Cambridge for their assistance in producing this book.

eastengland|arts

Published in the UK by Dedalus Ltd, Langford Lodge, St Judith's Lane, Sawtry, Cambs, PE17 5XE
email: DedalusLimited@compuserve.com
web site: www.dedalusbooks.com

ISBN 1 903517 13 3

Dedalus is distributed in the United States by SCB Distributors, 15608 South New Century Drive, Gardena, California 90248
email: info@scbdistributors.com
web site: www.scbdistributors.com

Dedalus is distributed in Australia & New Zealand by Peribo Pty Ltd, 58 Beaumont Road, Mount Kuring-gai, N.S.W. 2080
email: peribo@bigpond.com

Dedalus is distributed in Canada by Marginal Distribution, Unit 102, 277 George Street North, Peterborough, Ontario, KJ9 3G9
email: marginal@marginalbook.com
web site: www.marginal.com

First published by Dedalus in 2003

Translation and compilation and introduction copyright © Mike Mitchell in 2003
See acknowledgements for copyright for individual stories.

It has not been possible to find all the copyright holders and we would be grateful to hear from any not yet contacted.

The right of Mike Mitchell to be identified as the editor and as the translator of this work has been asserted by him in accordance with the Copyright, Designs and Patents Act, 1988.

Typeset by RefineCatch Limited, Bungay, Suffolk
Printed in Finland by WS Bookwell

A C.I.P. listing for this book is available on request.

Acknowledgements

The editor would like to thank the following for permission to use copyright material

Ilse Aichinger, 'Where I Live' from *Wo ich wohne. Erzählungen. Gedichte. Dialoge* © S Fischer Verlag, Frankfurt/Main.

Gerhard Amanshauser, 'The Unmasking of the Briefly Sketched Gentlemen' from *Der gewöhnliche Schrecken. Horrorgeschichten*, ed P Handke © Residenz Verlag, Salzburg.

H C Artmann, 'In the Gulf of Carpentaria' from *Die Anfangsbuchstaben der Flagge* in *Gesammelte Prosa* vol 2 © Residenz Verlag, Salzburg and Vienna.

Martin Auer, 'The Trouble with Time Travel' from *Phantastisches aus Österreich* ed Franz Rottensteiner, © Suhrkamp Verlag, Frankfurt/Main.

Rudolf Bayr, 'Something to be Said for the Rain' from *Ich habe nichts als mich*: Professor Dr. Friedrich Harrer.

Theodor Csokor, 'The Kiss of the Stone Woman', 'Shadowtown' from *Ein paar Schaufeln Erde* © Langen/Müller, Munich.

Jeannie Ebner, 'The Moving Frontier', 'The Singing in the Swamp' from *Protokoll aus einem Zwischenreich*: Jeannie Ebner/ Verlag Styria, Graz.

Erich Fried, 'An Up-and-coming Concern' from *Fast alles Mögliche* © Verlag Klaus Wagenbach, Berlin, 1975, new ed 2000; also in Erich Fried: *Gesammelte Werke*, Verlag Klaus Wagenbach, Berlin, 1993.

Barbara Frischmuth, 'Journey to the World's End' from *Traumgrenze*: the author.

Anton Fuchs, 'Ebb and Flow', 'Flow and Ebb' from *Nächtliche Begegnungen*, Bibliothek der Provinz, Weitra: Frau Lotte Fuchs.

Marianne Gruber, 'The Epidemic' from *Protokolle der Angst*: the author.

Marlen Haushofer, 'Cannibals' from *Schreckliche Treue* © Claassen Verlag, Munich.

Fritz von Herzmanovsky-Orlando, 'Signor Scurri' from *Maskenspiel der Genien* © Langen Müller, Munich.

G F Jonke, 'My Day' from *Beginn einer Verzweiflung* © Jung und Jung Verlag, Salzburg.

Florian Kalbeck, 'The Toad' from *Das Basler Träumebuch*: Frau Judith Por-Kalbeck.

Michael Köhlmeier, 'Snitto-Snot', 'The Thief' from *Der traurige Blick in die Weite* © Franz Deuticke Verlag, Vienna, 1999.

Paul Leppin, 'The Ghost of the Jewish Ghetto' from *Alt-Prager Spaziergänge*: Dierk Hoffmann.

Peter Marginter, 'Funeral Meats' from *Leichenschmaus*: the author.

Leo Perutz, 'Pour avoir bien servi' from *Herr, erbarme Dich meiner* © Paul Zsolnay Verlag, Vienna, 1985.

Jakov Lind 'Journey through the Night' from *Seele aus Holz*: the author.

Barbara Neuwirth, 'In the Sand', 'The Furnished Room' from *In den Gärten der Nacht* © Suhrkamp Verlag, Frankfurt/Main.

Georg Saiko: 'The Dream' from *Sämtliche Werke in fünf Bänden* vol 3 *Die Erzählungen* © Residenz Verlag, Salzburg and Vienna.

Karl Hans Strobl, 'The Head' from *Unheimliche Geschichten* © Langen Müller, Munich.

Peter von Tramin, 'The Sewermaster' from *Taschen voller Geld* © Böhlau Verlag, Vienna.

Hannelore Valencak, 'At the World's End' from *Erzählungen*: the author.

Franz Werfel, 'The Playground' from *Erzählungen aus zwei Welten* vol 1, S Fischer Verlag, Frankfurt/Main; Alma Mahler-Werfel.

I would particularly like to thank the Österreichische Gesellschaft für Literatur for funding a stay in Vienna to allow me to gather material for the new, expanded edition of this anthology. MM

The Editor/Translator

Mike Mitchell is one of Dedalus's editorial directors and is responsible for the Dedalus translation programme.

He has translated some thirty books, including *Simplicissimus* and *Life of Courage* by Grimmelshausen, all the novels of Gustav Meyrink, three by Herbert Rosendorfer and *The Maimed* by Hermann Ungar.

His translation of Rosendorfer's *Letters back to Ancient China* won the 1998 Schlegel-Tieck German Translation Prize.

Contents

Introduction

'It is a sad but incontrovertible fact that the world stands in profound ignorance of the phenomenon of Austria.'

Since Fritz von Herzmanovsky-Orlando wrote those opening lines to his anarchic comic novel, *Maskenspiel der Genien* (Masque of the Spirits) at the end of the 1920s, much more has become known of Austria than 'the mistakes contained in a few tourist guides published abroad.'

Freud was already on his way to becoming a household name even then, but the other figures who are now widely associated with the cultural florescence of the turn-of-the-century Habsburg Empire were almost unknown outside Austria: Mahler, Schoenberg, Klimt, Kokoschka, Schiele, Wittgenstein, Mach, Schnitzler, Hofmannsthal. Now the whole concept of *fin de siècle* Vienna is so well-known that it is an effective tourist attraction vigorously promoted by the Austrian Tourist Board.

However, Herzmanovsky-Orlando's lament, as far as it was intended to be taken seriously (and there is a serious concern lurking deep beneath the comic-grotesque surface of his novel), does not refer to these cultural icons of a golden age that was brought to an end by the First World War. For him, the 'phenomenon of Austria' was an essence, a mode of being that found expression in the Habsburg Empire or, rather, in *his* vision of Austria as a state where the elemental forces embodied in the myths of antiquity still managed to survive behind a grotesquely bureaucratic surface.

These two disparate elements are brought together in one of Herzmanovsky's pictures (he was also an artist of some stature): 'Austrian customs officials supervise the birth of Venus'. They are also present in the story included in this

11

anthology, 'Signor Scurri', in the soldier who, when invalided out of the army, was given 'The Sea', just as others were given the more traditional barrel organ or tobacco shop. Herzmanovsky's novel is set in an imaginary buffer state between the German, Slav and Latin areas of Europe, a concept that has reappeared on the political menu of the real world since the collapse of the Soviet Union and Yugoslavia. This state combines an anarchic vitality with the most rigidly formal of constitutions, which is based on the rules of *Tarock*, a popular Austrian card game. Hence its name: Tarockania.

Another more widely known fantasy version of Austria, and conceived at about the same time, is *Kakanien* (Cacania) in Robert Musil's novel, *The Man without Qualities*. The name derives from a combination of the initials *K. K.* standing for 'Imperial and Royal' and seen everywhere in the old Empire, and *Kacke*, crap. Musil's country might be regarded as the negative to Herzmanovsky's positive, since in Cacania the dead hand of bureaucracy tends to stifle rather than protect positive forces, although it does allow Musil to examine potential realities as a counterweight to the actual world.

A third example of these fantasy states is the Dream Realm in Alfred Kubin's novel *The Other Side* (Dedalus 2000). The Dream Realm is a state founded somewhere in the middle of Asia by Klaus Patera, a fabulously wealthy school-friend of the narrator. Its buildings have all been transported from various parts of Europe, none being later than 1860. The narrator never meets Patera, who remains a mysterious force at the centre of this kingdom where time has stopped, guarded by a punctilious and impenetrable bureaucracy. This combination of mystical force and rigid bureaucracy relates the Dream World to Herzmanovsky's and Musil's creations, though the atmosphere of Kubin's country reeks of decadence and decay.

Probably the best-known literary evocation of the bureaucratic spirit is the castle in Kafka's novel of the same name. There, whatever authority resides within the castle is surrounded by an impregnable wall of bureaucracy. Yet however mean, spiteful or stupid the subordinates seem to be, those qualities do not reflect on whatever is at the centre, which remains powerful but unknowable. These features are illustrated here in the little parable 'Before the Law'. The intimidating figure of the doorkeeper cannot diminish the radiance of the light pouring out from the door he guards so effectively. Paradox becomes an existential mode of being.

These fantasy images of Austria such as Tarockania or Cacania are not merely nostalgic recreations of the multinational Empire which was wiped from the map at a stroke in 1919, though there were also many of those. There is a quality of paradox underlying them all, and in this they hark back to the Monarchy's increasingly desperate search, as the 19th century proceeded, for a unifying *idea* to justify a state which held together so many disparate nationalities. Immediately after the 1848 revolution a distinguished historian, J. G. Helfert, pointed out that for most citizens of the Empire there was a distinction between *Heimat*, the region to which they felt an emotional tie, and *Vaterland*, the state to which they owed loyalty, and he proposed a vigorous programme of education to inculcate an attachment to the *fatherland*. As far as they were ever carried out, Helfert's ideas did not have any great success; until the end of the Empire the loyalties of its subjects were focused mainly on the *person* of the Emperor, rather than on the state he represented. This ambiguity the inhabitants felt as to where they actually belonged, can perhaps best be seen in the fact that the state had no real name. Although commonly referred to as 'Austria', that was only the name of two tiny medieval dukedoms that form the north-eastern corner of the present state. Its official designation was: *The Kingdoms and Countries represented in the Imperial Diet*. Not a name to engender a strong feeling of belonging.

The contrast between the ceremonial splendour of the centuries-old Habsburg Empire, with the apparently permanent Francis Joseph at its head, and the shifting sands of increasingly disaffected nationalities on which it was based, has something baroque about it and, indeed, the baroque is an important part of Austria's cultural heritage. Baroque art has a splendour which is undermined by the fact that its all-too-palpable physicality is not important in itself, but as a symbol

13

of a transcendental, spiritual world. Life is not something independent, self-sufficient, but merely a pale image of another, more real world. Life, in the words of the title of Calderon's play which the Austrian Grillparzer also used, is a dream.

To the baroque inheritance and the awareness, often unconscious, of the insecurities beneath the glittering surface of Imperial society must be added the researches of a school of psychologists, of which Freud is only the best-known, which laid bare the powerful urges and desires beneath the surface respectability of the personality. It was also in Vienna that Ernst Mach, the scientist whose name has been perpetuated in the term for the speed of sound, concluded, when he was looking for a solid foundation on which to base his science, that the self as an independent, ordering entity was 'irretrievably lost'. The literature which sprang from this background was one which casts doubt on the apparently solid surface of reality, which questions the meaningfulness of human activity, which is always ready to admit that the opposite might just as well be true. It is a literature that is a fertile ground for the fantastic.

It is this which distinguishes Austrian literature from German. A culture which emphasises the potential as much as the real, which has a taste for the humour of paradox, is one which does not take a too earnest view of itself. German literature takes itself, the world *and* the supernatural far more seriously. There was a fashion, in the first twenty years or so of the twentieth century, for literature of the supernatural in the manner of E. T. A. Hoffmann and Edgar Allan Poe in which some Austrian writers, in particular Karl Hans Strobl, were prominent. But more characteristic Austrian fantasy tends to emphasise the puzzling coincidences, parallels and paradoxes of this world, revealing it as less solid than we would think. A good example of this is Leo Perutz. He was a mathematician and his novels are finely calculated equations of chance, coincidence and mystery. It is a style which is less well-suited to the restricted length of the short story, but 'Pour avoir bien servi' has a typical twist at the end which turns its whole basis inside out, revealing the apparently clear relationships as a construction of the narrator's imagination.

As part of Austria's baroque heritage death, too, is seen not as the end, the negation of life, but rather as a continuation in another sphere. Dying is often shown not as an abrupt event, but a slow transition of which the character and the reader gradually become aware. A good example is Csokor's 'Shadowtown' where the characters only gradually realise they are dead and where death is like 'a safe, dark cave, which will protect me as I fall asleep.' In Hofmannsthal's 'Sergeant Anton Lerch', the whole subtle transformation of mood through the day is a prelude to Lerch's unexpected and unexplained death. In Max Brod's story the 'first hour after death' is a period of adjustment to a continuation of existence on a more spiritual level. The personification of death in the extract from Rilke's novel, *The Papers of Malte Laurids Brigge*, is not a mere literary device. For Rilke, the depersonalisation of death was the ultimate sign of the loss of individual substance in life, which he experienced particularly strongly in Paris.

In Kafka's story, 'Gracchus the Huntsman', death is an intermediate state, neither the one thing nor the other, since the hero's funeral barge 'went the wrong way,' leaving him 'on the great staircase leading up . . . sometimes at the top, sometimes down below, sometimes to the right, sometimes to the left, always in motion.' But this is the state in which most of Kafka's characters find themselves: Gregor Samsa is a man who has metamorphosed into an insect, but still retains human feeling; Josef K. in *The Trial* has been arrested but does not know what he is accused of, nor by what law; K believes he has been appointed surveyor to the castle, but cannot convince the administrators of the fact; the man from the country in 'Outside the Law' spends his life at the gate to the Law, hoping to be granted entrance, and the country doctor in the story of the same name does not belong in the country area he serves. This sense of not belonging doubtless had its roots both in Kafka's relationship with his father and in his situation as a Germanised Jew in the increasingly Czech city of Prague, but in his writings it is raised to an existential plane. (The cryptic references to his own name in the names Kafka gave to his characters has frequently been commented on; *kavka* in Czech and *graculus*, in Latin, related to 'Gracchus', both mean 'jackdaw', for example.) These stories, which have been called 'parables from which the first term is missing,' present man as a displaced person in the scheme of eternity. For many readers they express the *condition humaine* of the twentieth century and this doubtless explains Kafka's worldwide popularity since the end of the Second World War.

Like a number of the writers included in this anthology – Brod, Leppin, Perutz, Rilke, Werfel and Ungar – Kafka lived in Prague which, in the early part of this century, came to rival Vienna and Berlin as a centre of German literary life. But the figure with whom Prague, with its brooding castle, crowded ghetto and mysterious atmosphere, is most closely associated is Gustav Meyrink, who went to live there as an adult. An elegant dandy around whom legends naturally accumulated (he once supposedly challenged the whole of the officers' corps to a duel), he began writing while recovering from tuberculosis in 1901. His popularity was established by his short stories (*The Opal and Other Stories*, Dedalus 1994), in many of which his fantasy has a sharp satirical edge, attacking all kinds of narrow-mindedness, especially military, religious and scientific.

The story included in this anthology, 'The Master', is an example of Meyrink's combination of the grotesque and the occult, with which he became increasingly concerned. He joined many occult groups, only to be disappointed at their spuriousness, and spent much time investigating, and often exposing, mediums; at the same time he edited a number of occult texts and, despite his frequent disappointment in the practitioners, clearly believed in the existence of occult forces. He later claimed his novels and stories should be judged by spiritual rather than aesthetic criteria.

Paul Leppin was a disciple of Meyrink and the figure of Nicholas, who flits in and out of *Severin's Road into Darkness* (Dedalus, 1997) is a tribute to him. However neither that novel, despite its subtitle of 'A Prague Ghost-Story', nor the piece in this collection, 'The Ghost of the Jewish Ghetto', is a story of the supernatural in the traditional sense. Rather, they evoke the atmosphere of decadence associated with *fin de siècle* Prague which captures young men in the clutch of its 'ghostly' tentacles.

It is perhaps worth pointing out that Prague as a city of decadence and mystery, where the Golem walks or a whore becomes a kind of succubus, is a German image. For most Czechs of the period, Prague was the vital symbol of a people who were about to take what they regarded as their rightful place in history.

Brod and Werfel belong to the next generation of writers, which made Prague the most important centre of Expressionism in the Monarchy. Although both later abandoned the exaggeratedly expressive style, they remained concerned with a renewal of the spiritual side of man which was fundamental to Expressionism and which informs both the stories in this anthology. Brod's 'The First Hour after Death', first published in 1916, goes beyond Expressionism in its addition of humour to satire and spirituality. It creates a future world which has been at war for so long it is regarded as the natural condition of mankind. The apostle of this acceptance, the minister, is confronted with the spirit of a being from another sphere, whose punishment for his sins is to be sent for an hour to our – lower – world. What makes the story particularly attractive is that the ghost, who temporarily converts the minister away from his rationalistic relativism, is a comic figure who has great difficulty adapting to the physical conditions of this world.

At the beginning of his career Werfel was primarily a poet, and there is something of the expansive gestures of the writer of *Der Weltfreund* (The World-Friend) in the texture of 'The Playground'. There is also something post-Freudian about its dreams within dreams, especially the first section recreating the hero's relationship with his father. What Werfel takes from Freud is not, however, psychological analysis so much as archetypal relationships which he transforms into poetic symbols. The central section, on love/sex, is probably a working-out of some of the guilt Werfel felt at his relationship with Alma Mahler-Gropius, who was already pregnant with his child before she left Gropius for Werfel in 1920, the year in which 'The Playground' was first published.

Another Jew from what is now the Czech Republic who wrote in German was Hermann Ungar. Like the short piece, 'The Reason for It', the two novels (eg *The Maimed*, Dedalus 2002) he completed before his early death are stories of degradation descending to the grotesque and macabre narrated with an unemphatic, bleak matter-of-factness which only serves to intensify the monstrousness of the events.

Much closer to Freud was the oldest writer represented in this anthology, Arthur Schnitzler. He trained as a doctor (his father's profession) and continued to practise for some years after his initial success as a writer. His interest in psychology was scientific as well as literary (he had been an assistant in the clinic of Freud's teacher, Theodor Meynert). Freud, six years his senior, even felt a superstitious thrill at the similarity between them. In a letter congratulating Schnitzler on his sixtieth birthday, he wrote:

I have plagued myself over the question how it comes about that in all these years I have never sought your company . . . The answer is this much too intimate confession. I think I have avoided you from a kind of awe of meeting my 'double' . . . whenever I get deeply interested in your beautiful creations I always seem to find, behind their poetic sheen, the same presuppositions, interests and conclusions as those familiar to me as my own.

Schnitzler's style is, in general, a finely nuanced social and psychological realism, and the suggestion of the supernatural in the story in this anthology is used to highlight the psychological analysis, rather than out of sensationalism. The hero of 'Flowers' feels the ghost of his former lover is taking possession of him through the flowers that come to him after her death. In fact, it is his belated pangs of conscience for his heartless treatment of her that give the memory its hold over him. His release from the spell, when his healthy, uncomplicated current mistress throws the withered stalks out of the window, has much of the moral ambiguity that abounds in Schnitzler's work. Life wins over death, health over sickness, but also, so it seems, egoism over moral sensitivity.

Schnitzler's characters tend to live for the moment. Ethical values which suggest a longer-term commitment usually crumble when faced with immediate demands. In some younger writers of the generation that followed Schnitzler and Freud, writers who appeared in the 1890s, this developed into an extraordinary sensitivity to mood and atmosphere, which threatened to dissolve the personality into nothing more than the focus for a multitude of separate impressions, which was all that was left of the 'self' in Ernst Mach's philosophy. Rilke's early poems are products of this subjective impressionism, which in his *New Poems* of 1907–8 he attempted to overcome by concentrating on objects from the world outside. *The Papers of Malte Laurids Brigge* is a product of that period of what has been called the 'crisis of subjectivity', when Rilke learnt, from his association with Rodin, for whom he acted as secretary for a time, to 'see' the external world, rather than the reflection of his own soul in it.

The main representative of this 'impressionism' in this anthology is Hugo von Hofmannsthal. He astonished the Viennese with his delicate, almost perfect lyrics published in the early 1890s when he was still at school. They reproduce moments of intense harmony with the beauty of the world, a beauty which he was aware was fragile, that could easily be shattered by contact with social and political realities, with ugliness and squalor. The problem of this aesthetic mode of existence runs through his short verse plays, which show a clearer awareness that it might come into conflict with the demands of ethical values than one finds in Schnitzler, who appears to record the problem without taking sides. Around the turn of the century Hofmannsthal went through a crisis of confidence in the ability of language to express what he really wanted to say, caused to a certain extent by his own facility, which is almost paradigmatic of twentieth-century European intellectuals' difficulties with language.

His short story, 'Sergeant Anton Lerch', was written in 1899, three years before the 'Chandos Letter', in which he described his crisis of language. Although the hero of the story is not one of the aesthetes of Hofmannsthal's early verse plays who shut themselves off from the world outside, there are parallels in the intensely experienced inner world and the squalor outside. Lerch sets off with his cavalry troop on reconnaissance during the Italian campaign of the year of revolution, 1848. An apparently trivial incident during a highly successful series of operations turns his thoughts away from reality and into a day-dream of a future where he can mould his life to his own, rather crude desires. From then on the narrative hovers with remarkable sensitivity between the real and the unreal until the sergeant comes face to face with his own double. His death at the end (summarily executed for insubordination) is crude reality breaking in on a state of mind which he cannot or will not relinquish; it is left to the reader to decide the balance of daydream, trance or supernatural, but that is one of the factors which make the story so powerful.

As well as these writers, who represent the main streams of literature in Austria in the period before and after the First World War, there were a number who used the supernatural and macabre in a more direct manner as a means of arousing horror. The best known of these, Karl Hans Strobl, was probably as responsible as anyone for the spread of the influence of Edgar Allan Poe in the German-speaking world. Between 1900 and 1920 he initiated something of a fashion in the ghost/horror story, at which many writers tried their hand. Strobl himself brought out numerous anthologies and collections of his own stories. He is generally not seen as a serious writer, but 'The Head', which presents incidents during the French Revolution from the point of view of a head which has been cut off from its body by the guillotine, is a masterpiece of the macabre genre.

Paul Busson was another once popular writer who used

elements of the supernatural, including folk beliefs, in his novels. The short story, 'Folter's Gems', published in 1919, is a good example of the influence of Edgar Allan Poe. The 1929 *Guardian* review of Hermann Hesse's *Steppenwolf* quoted Busson's novel *The Rebirth of Melchior Dronte* as a typical example of German novelists 'overdoing the exploitation of the macabre in fiction.'

Perhaps the best example of this type of story, however, is Csokor's 'The Kiss of the Stone Woman', written in 1915. Csokor was a dramatist, the main representative of Expressionism in Vienna, who also wrote a number of short stories. 'The Kiss of the Stone Woman' is his only foray into the Gothic, which was probably written as a stylistic exercise or in the hope of being able to sell it. What raises it above the others is the trace of Expressionism in the style. His deliberate choice of active vocabulary, especially verbs, for what are really static objects – trees, houses, churches etc – invests the whole setting with a dynamism and sense of threat which is not unlike the effect of distorted backgrounds used in the German Expressionist films of the time (e.g. *The Golem* or *The Cabinet of Dr Caligari*).

*

The small state created in 1919 by the Treaty of St Germain had never attracted the loyalty of the majority of Austrians, who either looked back to the days of the Monarchy, or wanted to be part of a greater Germany, which the treaty expressly forbade. The authoritarian state, set up by Dollfuß in 1933 and continued by Schuschnigg after Dollfuß's murder by Nazis, attempted to remedy this by combining all conservative elements in a Patriotic Front. Despite the signal lack of impact this made on the population in general, when Hitler invaded in March 1938 it was because the Austrian government was about to hold a plebiscite which was expected to result in a majority in favour of Austria's continued independence. When the Nazis held their own referendum a month later, however, the result was a 99.5 % majority in favour of union with the German *Reich*. There were many reasons for the *size* of the majority, but there is no doubt that a substantial portion of the population welcomed the German troops and their *Führer*.

The one certain and, as it turned out, permanent cure for the Austrians' wish for union with Germany was to have that wish granted. As the Second World War came to its inevitable end, they embraced with fervour the Moscow Declaration of 1943 in which Austria was designated 'the first free country to fall a victim to Nazi aggression.' This allowed the state to bask in the status of 'liberated victim', which to an extent it was, and sweep the crimes committed by the many willing collaborators in the country under the carpet. Amnesia as to what happened between 1938–1945 became official policy. A history of Austria published with government support as late as 1970 stated that 'The Second World War . . . was not an Austrian war. Austria as a *state* did not participate in it;' its only sections on the Nazi period are headed 'Austrian victims' and 'Austrian resistance'.

As far as literature was concerned, there was, in the immediate aftermath of the war, no shortage of calls for a complete break with the past and the development of a new culture of critical awareness. It soon became apparent, however, that what the public at large wanted, after decades of instability, culminating in the horrors of the Nazi dictatorship and the destruction of the war, was a return to the familiar, the tried-and-tested. Official cultural policy, too, started to look backwards rather than forwards, to the policies of the authoritarian state of the 1930s, which itself had propagated the 'Austrian idea' developed in the latter days of the Habsburg Empire.

Continuity, then, rather than innovation was to be a major aspect of Austrian literature in the post-war years. Although Austrian writers such as Ilse Aichinger were associated with the German *Gruppe 47*, no similar critical forum developed in Austria. When a radical group, including H. C. Artmann among others, did appear in the 1950s, it was aesthetically rather than politically or socially radical, its method a critique of language rather than of politics or society. This was also true of the loose grouping around the *Forum Stadtpark* in Graz, which dominated avant-garde Austrian literature in the 1960s and later. It was only in the mid-1970s and 1980s that a substantial literature which dealt critically with contemporary society emerged, with writers such as Franz Innerhofer, Elfriede Jelinek, Michael Scharang and Josef Winkler.

Although, in comparison to its size, Austria seems to have provided a surprisingly large number of important writers to post-war literature in German, it was in painting that Austrian artists enjoyed the greatest international success through the group known as the Vienna Fantastic Realists, to whom might be added Friedensreich Hundertwasser (whose 'Bleeding Houses' is used on the cover of this anthology) and Gottfried Helnwein. Rudolf Hausner's portraits of himself as Adam, the representative of humanity, and Helnwein's pictures, painted with almost photographic realism, of heads bound in bandages with metal forks and similar implements over the eyes, nose or mouth are immediately recognised throughout the world. The post-war rediscovery of Freud's psychoanalysis was one stimulus to these painters who plumbed the subconscious to give expression to fears, longings and obsessions in the guise of myths, daydreams and fantasies painted with masterly precision.

This combination of unreal or surreal subject matter with a realistic style also characterises some of the best Austrian writing of the post-war years. In literature the rediscovered Kafka, banned like Freud under National Socialism, was an equally important inspiration in producing stories which seem to work as parables, yet do not dictate to the reader what truths they illustrate.

Examples of this are Jeannie Ebner's 'The Singing in the Swamp' and 'The Moving Frontier' and Ernst Fuchs's 'Ebb and Flow' which inhabit a mythical world beyond history and yet reflect on contemporary concerns. Ilse Aichinger's 'Where I Live', on the other hand, has a very precise location, which, however, turns out to be not as stable as we assume our everyday world to be. But it is the protagonist's unhesitating acceptance of the dislocation which encourages the reader to look for meaning in the surreal events and places her close to figures in Kafka. A similar type, not uncommon in post-war German literature as well, whom one might describe as 'by Oblomov out of Kafka,' is the protagonist of Rudolf Bayr's 'Something to be Said for the Rain' who takes to his bed as a kind of training for his 'one long, last look' before he takes his leave of the world.

Fantasy is also a vehicle for explorations of the conscious and subconscious mind. Two stories look at suicides from almost opposite perspectives. In Barbara Frischmuth's 'The Journey to the World's End' a young woman's suicide by drowning becomes a journey under water in the course of which her experiences, her hopes, desires and fantasies are revealed as she gradually takes her leave of the world. In Barbara Neuwirth's 'The Furnished Room' we learn little about the woman who moves in there, but her alienation is reflected in the objects and furnishings that come to life around her. Death as a journey rather than a single point is the subject of Hannelore Valencak's 'At the World's End', though it relies on more classical forms. Two suicides meet on the banks of the Styx in a Rilkean soulscape.

Subconscious desires of a more violent nature are laid bare in two stories in which cannibalism surfaces in a railway carriage, Jakov Lind's 'Journey through the Night' and Marlen Haushofer's 'Cannibals'. While Haushofer reveals the secret desires triggered off by the presence of an apparently innocent, scarcely pubescent girl, Lind's unrepentant cannibal is more an extremely vivid concretisation of the secret fears of the victim.

In Florian Kalbeck's 'The Toad' the account the madman writes in his own 'defence' develops inexorably into a megalomaniac vision of himself and his like freeing the world of the people he sees as 'toads'. The parallel to recent history is hinted at in the doctor's final comments.

In two pieces the bizarre events have the surreal qualities of a dream. George Saiko's fantasy in which the insides of the protagonist's body and his internal organs are at the same time the city of Paris complete with buildings and monuments, people, trains and traffic, is entitled 'The Dream'. Günther Kaip's 'Novak', on the other hand, narrates its dreamlike happenings with a certain comic élan but as if they were normal, everyday reality. The increasingly surreal events narrated with the straightest of faces in Gert Jonke's 'My Day' result in grotesque humour.

More traditional types of Austrian fantasy are represented by Peter Marginter, whose witty and sometimes grotesque inventions mark him out as the successor to Fritz von Herzmanovsky-Orlando. Peter von Tramin's 'The Sewermaster' takes up the menacingly macabre atmosphere of Karl Hans Strobl. Michael Köhlmeier, who has had great success with his retelling of Greek myths, is represented by two stories from his amusing and inventive collection of pastiche folk tales.

A more modern variant of fantasy, science fiction, has also attracted Austrian authors. There are suggestions of it in the creation and repair of the human body by industrialised processes that form the background to Marianne Gruber's 'The Epidemic' and Erich Fried's 'An Up-and-coming Concern', though both use the futuristic setting to examine the age-old relations between the sexes. More straightforward science fiction, with a sardonic twist on time travel, comes from Martin Auer. Gerhard Amanshauser and Peter Daniel Wolfkind both use the appearance of a Quatermass-like alien growth to undermine the basis of what we accept as normal reality. Another strand of science fiction appears in Barbara Neuwirth's miniature 'In the Sand', in which the traveller describes a strange unknown civilisation. H. C. Artmann's 'In the Gulf of Carpentaria' appears to belong to the same genre, but is revealed as a resumé of a Hollywood film of that type, with, of course, a further twist at the end. The exuberance of Artmann's imagination, which includes playing with genre in a wide variety of ways, could be called baroque, making him perhaps the best representative of traditional 'Austrian' characteristics carried into the post-war world.

Flowers

Arthur Schnitzler

I've just spent the whole afternoon wandering round the streets, with white snowflakes floating down, slowly, noiselessly, and now I'm back home, and the lamp is burning, and my cigar is lit, and my books are beside me, and everything is ready for me to enjoy a cosy evening . . . But it's all to no avail, I can't stop my thoughts continually coming back to the same thing.

She had long since been dead for me, hadn't she? . . . Yes, dead, or even, as I put it to myself with the rather childish grandiloquence of the betrayed lover, 'worse than dead' . . . And now, since I learnt that she is not 'worse than dead', no, simply dead, like all the others out there, lying beneath the earth whenever spring is here, and whenever the sultry summer comes, and whenever the snow is falling as today . . . dead without any hope of returning – since then I have realised that she did not die for me a moment sooner than for everyone else. Grief? No. It's only the usual frisson we feel when someone that once belonged to us sinks into the grave while their whole being is still quite fresh in our minds, down to the light in their eyes and the sound of their voice.

There was certainly much sadness when I discovered she had been unfaithful to me; . . . but how much else there was as well! My anger and sudden hatred and disgust with life and – yes, that too – my hurt pride. I only gradually came to realise I felt grief as well. But then I could relieve it with the comforting thought that she was suffering too. I still have them all, all those dozens of letters, sobbing, begging, pleading for forgiveness; I can read them whenever I want! And I can still see her in that dark English dress with the little straw hat, standing on the street corner in the twilight whenever I came out of the house . . . and watching me walk away . . . And I can remember her at that last meeting, standing there with her big, wondering eyes and round girlish face, that had become so pale and haggard . . . I didn't even shake hands with her when she left, when she left for the last time. And I watched her from that window as far as the street corner and then she disappeared, for ever. Now she can never return . . .

It's the purest chance I know about it at all. It could have been weeks, months before I heard. I haven't seen her uncle for a good year now, he only rarely comes to Vienna, and I met him this morning! I had only spoken to him a few times before. The first time was that skittles evening when she and her mother had come along as well. And then the next summer; I was with a few friends in the garden of that restaurant in the Prater, the *Csarda* it was called. And her uncle was sitting at the next table with two or three other old gentlemen, in unbuttoned mood, almost merry, and he raised his glass to me. And before he left, he came over and told me, as if it were a great secret, that his niece had a crush on me! And in my half-tipsy state I found it odd and funny, piquant almost, that the old man should be telling me that there, to the sound of the cymbalom and the shrill violins – me, who knew it only too well, who still had the taste of her last kiss on my lips . . . And then this morning! I almost walked straight past him. I asked after his niece, more out of politeness than interest . . . I didn't know what had become of her; the letters had stopped coming a long time ago; only flowers she still sent regularly, reminders of one of our most blissful days; once a month they came; no message with them, mute, humble flowers . . . And when I asked the old man, he was quite astonished: You didn't know that the poor child died a week ago? It gave me quite a start. Then he told me more. That she had been ailing for some time but had been bed-ridden for scarcely a week . . . And what was wrong with her? . . . 'Some emotional disorder . . . anaemia . . . The doctors never really know.'

I stood there for a long time at the spot where the old man had left me; I was worn out, as if I had just made some great effort. And now I feel as if I should regard this day as marking the end of an era in my life. Why? – Why? It is not something that concerns me closely. I no longer had any feelings for her, I hardly ever thought of her any more. Writing all this down has done me good: I am calmer. I am starting to enjoy the comfort of my home. It's pointless to go on tormenting myself with thinking about it . . . There'll be someone, somewhere who has more cause for mourning today than I have.

I have been out for a walk. A fine winter's day. The sky was so pale, so cold, so distant . . . and I am very calm. The old man I met yesterday . . . it seems as if it were weeks ago. And when I think of her, her image appears in my mind's eye in strangely sharp, complete outline; only one thing is missing, the anger that until very recently accompanied the memory. It has not really sunk in that she is no longer in this world, that she is in a coffin, buried . . . I feel no pain at all. Today the world seemed quieter. At some point I realised that there is no such thing as joy or sorrow; no, we twist our faces in expressions of desire or grief, we laugh and cry and invite our souls to join in. Just now I could sit down and read profound, serious books and would soon penetrate all their wisdom. Or I could stand looking at old pictures that used to mean nothing to me, and I would respond to their dark beauty. And when I call to mind people who were dear to me and whom death has taken away, my heart does not ache as it usually does: death has turned into something pleasant; it walks among us and means us no harm.

Snow, white snow piled high in all the streets. Little Gretel came to see me and suggested it was time we finally went out for a sleigh ride. So there we were, out in the country, flying along the smooth bright tracks with a jingle of bells and a pale grey sky above us, flying along between gleaming white hills. And Gretel leant against my shoulder, watching the long road stretching out before us with bright eyes. We went to an inn that we knew well from the summer, when it was surrounded by greenery, and now looked so different, so lonely, so completely unrelated to the rest of the world, as if we had to discover it afresh. And the stove in the lounge was glowing so hot that we had to move the table well away because little

Gretel's left cheek and ear had gone quite red. I just had to kiss the paler cheek! Then the drive back, in the semidark already. How Gretel snuggled up to me and held both my hands in hers. Then she said, 'Today I've got you back again.' Without having to think about it at all, she had found the right words, and it made me happy. Perhaps the crisp, frosty air out in the country had relaxed my senses, for I felt freer and easier than I had during the last few days.

Once again recently, while I was lying half asleep on the sofa, a strange thought crept over me. I felt as if I was cold and hard. Like someone standing without tears, without any capacity for feeling even, beside the grave into which a loved one had just been laid. Like someone who has become so hard that not even the shudder at an early death can placate him . . . Yes, implacable, that was it . . .

It has gone completely, completely. Life, pleasure and a little love has swept away all those silly ideas. I'm back amongst people once again. I like them, they're harmless, they ramble on about all sorts of cheerful matters. And Gretel is an adorable, loving girl, and so beautiful when she stands there by the window with the sunbeams glistening in her blond hair.

Something strange happened today . . . It's the day she used to send me flowers every month . . . And the flowers arrived, as if . . . as if nothing had changed. They came with the early morning post in a long, slim, white box. It was still very early; my eyes and my brain were still drugged with sleep. I was already opening the box before I became fully aware of what it was . . . I almost jumped with fright . . . and there they were, tied up with a delicate gold thread, carnations and violets . . . They lay there as if they were in a coffin. And as I picked up the flowers, my heart shuddered. I know why they still came today. When she felt her illness coming on, perhaps even a presentiment of her approaching death, she sent her usual order to the florist's. She did not want me to go without her tender gesture. Certainly that must be the explanation for the package; it's quite natural, touching even . . . And yet, as I held them in my hand, the flowers, and as they seemed to tremble and droop, I could not help but feel, against all reason and determination, that there was something ghostly about them, as if they came from her, a greeting from her . . . as if she still wanted to tell me, even now, when she was dead, of her love and her – belated – fidelity. Oh, we do not understand death, we never understand it; creatures are only truly dead when everyone else has died who knew them . . . Today I handled the flowers in a different way than usual, more tenderly, as if I could hurt them if I held them too tight, as if their gentle souls might start to whimper softly. And looking at them now on the desk in front of me in their slender, dull green vase, I seem to see them bow their blossoms in melancholy thanks. With their fragrance I inhale the whole sorrow of a futile yearning, and I believe they could tell me something, if we could understand the language of all living, not just all speaking beings.

I refuse to fall under their influence. They are flowers, nothing more. Greetings from the other side, but not a call, not a call from the grave. They are flowers and some shop-assistant in some florist's tied them up mechanically, wrapped a little cotton-wool round them, put them in the white box and posted them off. And here they are, what is the point of brooding over them?

I spend a lot of time in the open air, take long walks by myself. When I am with other people I feel no real relationship with them, the links have all torn. I even notice it when my dear, blond girl is sitting in my room chattering on about . . . that's just it, I have no idea what she's talking about. When she leaves, the very moment she has gone she is so distant from me; as if she were far away, as if she had been swept away for good by the current of humanity, as if she had disappeared without trace. It would hardly surprise me if she never came back.

The flowers are in their vase of shimmering green glass, their stalks reach down into the water and their fragrance fills the room. They still give off a scent, even though they have been in my room for a week and are slowly starting to wither. And I have come to understand all sorts of nonsense that I used to laugh at, I can understand people holding conversations with natural objects . . . I can understand people waiting for an answer when they talk to clouds and springs; here I am, staring at these flowers and waiting for them to start to speak . . . No, no, I know that they are speaking all the time . . . even now . . . that they are constantly speaking, sorrowing, and that I am close to understanding them.

How happy I am that the frozen winter is coming to an end. There is already a hint of the approach of spring floating in the air. Time passes in a strange way. I live my life as usual, and yet I sometimes feel as if the outlines of my existence were less sharply defined. Even yesterday is blurred, and everything that lies just a few days in the past takes on the character of a hazy dream. It keeps on happening when Gretel goes, and especially when I don't see her for a couple of days, that I feel as if it were an affair that is long since over. When she comes it is from so far away! Of course, once she starts chattering on, everything is back to normal and I have a clear sense of immediacy, of life. And the words then are almost too loud, the colours too bright; and just as the darling girl vanishes into some indefinable distance the moment she leaves me, so abrupt, so fiery is her presence. Moments of brightness, of vibrancy used to leave an after-image, an echo within me; now sound and light die away at once, as if in a dim cave. And then I am alone with my flowers. They are already withered, quite withered. Their fragrance has gone. Up to now Gretel has ignored them; today for the first time her gaze rested on them a while, and I sensed the question rising within her. Then, suddenly, some hidden qualm seemed to stop her asking it; she said not a single word more, but took her leave of me and went.

They are slowly losing their petals. I never touch them; if I did they would crumble to dust between my fingers. I feel an inexpressible sadness that they have withered. Why I have not the strength to put an end to the ridiculous spell they cast, I don't know. They are making me ill, these dead flowers. Sometimes I can't stand it any more; I rush out. And then in the middle of the street a thought grips me, I have to come back, have to check that they are all right. And then I find them, tired and sad, in the same green vase I left them in.

Yesterday I stood there and cried, as one would cry at a grave, and I wasn't even thinking of the girl from whom they actually came. Perhaps I'm wrong, but it seems to me as if Gretel too feels the presence of something strange in my room. She has stopped laughing when she comes to visit me. She doesn't talk so loud, not in that fresh, lively voice I was used to. Also I am tormented by a constant fear that she might ask me; I know that I would find any question intolerable.

She often brings some needlework, and when I am working at my books, she sits quietly at the table, sewing or crocheting, patiently waiting for me to put the books away, stand up, come over to her and take her needlework out of her hands. Then I take the green shade off the lamp she was sitting by, and the whole room is flooded with warm, soft light. I don't like it when it's dark in the corners.

Spring! My window is wide open. Late in the evening I was looking down into the street with Gretel. The air around was soft and warm. And when I looked towards the street corner, where the lamp casts a faint light, there was suddenly a shadow. I could see it and I couldn't see it . . . I knew I was not seeing it . . . I closed my eyes. And suddenly I could see through my closed lids; there was the wretched figure, standing in the faint light of the lamp, and I could see her face with an eerie clarity, as if it were illuminated by a yellow sun, and I saw her pale, careworn face with her large, wondering eyes . . . Then I walked slowly away from the window and sat down at my desk; the candle was flickering in a breath of wind that came from outside. And I sat there motionless; for I knew that the poor creature was standing, waiting at the street corner; and if I had dared to touch the dead flowers, I would have picked them out of the vase and taken them to her . . . Those were my thoughts, perfectly lucid thoughts, and yet at the same time I knew they were irrational. Then Gretel too came away from the window and stood for a moment behind my chair, and brushed my hair with her lips. Then she went, leaving me alone . . .

I stared at the flowers. They are hardly flowers any more, just bare stalks, thin and pathetic . . . They are making me ill, driving me mad. And it must be plain to see; otherwise Gretel would have asked me; but she feels it too, she sometimes flees as if there were ghosts in the room. Ghosts! They exist, they do exist! Dead things playing at life. And if flowers smell of decay as they wither, it is only a memory of the time when they were blooming and fragrant. And dead people return as long as we do not forget them. What does it matter if she can no longer speak – I can still hear her! She doesn't appear any more but I can still see her! And the spring outside, and the bright sun streaming over the carpet, and the scent of fresh lilac coming from the nearby park, and the people walking past below who are no concern of mine, is that life? I can close the curtains, and the sun is dead. I can ignore all those people, and they are dead. I close the window, the fragrance of the lilacs is not wafting around me any more, and the spring is dead. I am more powerful than the sun and the people and spring. But memory is more powerful than I am, it comes when it will and there is no escape. And these brittle stalks in the vase are more powerful than all the lilac scent and spring.

I was bent over these pages when Gretel came in. She has never come so early before. I was surprised, amazed almost. For a few seconds she stood in the doorway; I looked at her without saying hello. Then she smiled and came closer. She had a bunch of fresh flowers in her hand. Without a word she came up to the desk and laid the flowers before me. The next moment she grasped the withered ones in the green vase. It felt as if someone were squeezing my heart, but I was incapable of saying anything; and as I was about to stand up to grab the girl by the arm, she looked at me with a laugh. Holding her arm aloft as she carried the withered flowers, she rushed round the desk to the window and simply threw them out into the street. I felt as if I ought to follow them . . . But there was the girl, leaning against the window-sill, her face towards me. And the sun was streaming over her blond hair, the warm, living sun . . . And a rich scent of lilac coming from across the road. I looked at the empty green vase standing on the desk; I was not sure how I felt; freer, I think, much freer than before. Then Gretel came over, took her little bouquet and held it up

33

to my face: cool, white lilac . . . such a healthy, fresh scent, so soft, so cool, I wanted to bury my face in it. Laughing, white, kissing blooms: I knew the spell was broken. Gretel was standing behind me running her hands wildly through my hair. You fool, you darling fool, she said. Did she know what she had done? I took her hands and kissed them . . . And in the evening we went out into the open air, out into the spring. I have just come back with her. I lit the candle; we had a long walk and Gretel was so tired she has nodded off in the armchair by the stove. She is very beautiful as she smiles in her sleep.

Before me is the lilac in the slender green vase; down below in the street − no, no, they disappeared from there long ago. The wind has already scattered them with all the other dust.

The Master

Gustav Meyrink

Leonhard sits in his Gothic chair, motionless, eyes wide, staring into space.

The flames blazing up from the twigs in the small fireplace send the light flickering over his hair-shirt, but the immobility surrounding him allows it no purchase, and it slides off his long white beard, his furrowed face and old man's hands so deathly still they seem part of the brown and gold of the carving on the arms of the chair.

Leonhard is staring at the window. Outside, the ruinous, half-tumbledown castle chapel where he is sitting is surrounded by snowy mounds the height of a man, but his mind's eye sees the bare, narrow, unadorned walls behind him, the squalid pile of bedding and the crucifix over the worm-eaten door, sees the jug of water, the loaf of bread he baked himself from beech-nut flour and the knife with the notched bone handle beside it in the corner recess.

He hears the huge trees crack under the hard frost and sees, in the harsh, sharp-edged moonlight, the icicles glittering on the branches groaning under their burden of white. He sees his own shadow stretch out through the pointed arch of the window and join the silhouettes of the fir-trees in a spectral dance over the sparkling snow as the flames leap up and down; at other times he sees it shrink to the figure of a goat on a blue-black throne with the knobs on his chair forming a pair of devil's horns above pointed ears.

An old, hunchbacked woman from the kiln, which is down in the valley hours away across the moor, hobbles laboriously through the trees, pulling a sledge with dry wood. Startled, she gapes at the brilliant light, uncomprehending. Her eye falls on the devilish shadow on the snow and she realises where she is, that she is outside the chapel where, according to legend, the last scion of a cursed line, immune to death, lives out his empty life.

Seized with horror, she crosses herself and hurries back into the forest, knees trembling.

In his mind's eye Leonhard follows her for a while along the path. It takes him past the fire-blackened ruins of the castle beneath which his childhood lies buried, but he feels no emotion, for him everything is present, beyond suffering, clear as a shape formed out of coloured air. He sees himself as a child, playing with bright pebbles under a young birch-tree, and at the same time he sees himself as an old man sitting watching his shadow.

The figure of his mother appears before him, her features twitching as always. Everything about her is in a constant quiver of restlessness, only the skin on her forehead is unmoving, smooth as parchment and stretched tight over her round skull, like an ivory sphere imprisoning a swarm of thoughts which buzz like flies to get out.

He hears the constant rustle of her black silk dress, never silent for a moment, filling the castle with the exasperating whine of millions of insects, finding its way through every gap in walls or floorboards, robbing everyone, man and beast alike, of their peace. Those thin lips, ever ready to snap out a command, hold even objects in thrall; they seem to be permanently on the alert, not one of them daring to make itself comfortable. She only knows of what goes on in the world outside from hearsay and thinks that searching for the meaning of life is a waste of time, merely an excuse for idleness. As long as the house is filled from morning till night with pointless, ant-like scurrying around, needless moving of things from here to there, feverish activity to the point of exhaustion and sleep, wearing down everything and everyone, she believes she has fulfilled her duty in life.

No thought ever reaches fruition in her mind. Hardly has one entered her head than it is transformed into hasty, pointless action.

She is like the second hand on a clock, forever jerking

forward and imagining, in its insignificance, that the world would come to a standstill if it didn't keep twitching, three thousand six hundred times an hour, twelve hours a day, grinding time to dust and impatiently waiting for the placid hour-hand to give the signal for the bell to chime.

In the middle of the night her obsessive restlessness often drags her from her bed and she wakes the servants: the interminable rows of flower-pots on the window-ledges must be watered at once. She cannot say why, it is enough that they 'must' be watered. No one dare gainsay her, everyone is struck dumb, since to reason with her is as hopeless as trying to fight a will-o'-the-wisp with a sword. None of her plants take root as she repots them daily, birds never perch on the castle roof; driven on by a deep-seated instinct they crisscross the sky, wheeling this way and that, up and down, now appearing as dots, now broadening out into black, fluttering hands. Even the sun's rays are eternally atremble, for there is always a wind hustling the clouds to blot out their light. The leaves and branches are swirled and ruffled from morn till eve and fruits never ripen, the May breezes themselves blow away the blossom. All around, nature is sick from the restlessness in the castle.

Leonhard sees himself, twelve years old, sitting at his sums, pressing his hands hard over his ears so as not to hear the slamming of doors, the constant up-and-down of the maids on the stairs or the shrill of his mother's voice. But it's no use, the numbers turn into a herd of tiny, spiteful, writhing goblins, run through his brain, through his nose, in and out of his eyes and ears, making his blood boil and his skin burn. He tries reading. In vain, the letters dance before his eyes like a blurry cloud of midges.

'Have you still not done that exercise?' He starts at the sound of his mother's voice, but she doesn't wait for an answer, her watery blue eyes are already flitting from one corner to the next to see if she can spot a trace of dust. Non-existent spider's webs have to be brushed off, pieces of furniture moved, carried out and brought back in again, wardrobes taken apart to make sure there are no moths, table legs are screwed off and on again, drawers fly open and shut, pictures are rehung, nails torn out of the walls to be hammered back in an inch to the left or right, objects are seized with a frenzy, the hammer-head flies off the shaft, rungs of the ladder break, plaster trickles down the wall – fetch the plasterer at once! – cloths get stuck, needles slip out of hands and hide in gaps in the floorboards, the watch-dog in the courtyard breaks loose, comes rushing in, its chain clattering behind it, and knocks over the grandfather clock. Little Leonhard immerses himself in his book again and grits his teeth, trying to get some sense out of the curly black pothooks chasing each other across the page. He must sit somewhere else, the chair has to have the dust beaten out of it. He leans on the window-ledge, a book in his hand – the window-ledge has to be washed, has to be painted white. Why is he always in the way, and has he finally done that exercise? Then she sweeps out. The maids have to drop everything, quickly, follow her and get shovels, axes and sticks in case there are rats in the cellar.

The window-sill is half painted, the chairs are all minus their seats and the room is a scene of devastation. Dull, unbounded hatred of his mother eats into the boy's heart. With his every fibre he yearns for peace. He longs for night to come, but even sleep does not bring the desired rest, confused dreams split his thoughts in two, chasing but never catching each other. His muscles find it impossible to relax, his whole body is tensed, waiting for a lightning order to perform some pointless task or other.

His daytime games in the garden are not the expression of childish exuberance, his mother decrees them mindlessly, like everything she does, to interrupt them the next moment. To her, persevering with one thing for any length of time looks like inactivity, which she feels she must fight against as she would fight against death. The boy does not dare leave the castle, always stays within earshot. He feels there is no escape; one step too far and a loud command from the open window will shackle his foot.

Little Sabina is a peasant girl a year younger than Leonhard who lives with the servants. He only ever sees her from a distance, and if they do manage to talk for a few brief moments, they speak in rushed, disjointed phrases, like people on passing ships calling out a few hurried words to each other.

The old count, Leonhard's father, is lame in both legs. He spends all day in a wheelchair in his library, always just about to start reading, but even there he has no peace. At regular intervals Leonhard's mother appears and her restless fingers root around in the books, dust them and clap them together, sending markers fluttering to the floor. Volumes which are here today are on the top shelf tomorrow, or piled up in mountains on the floor if the wallpaper behind suddenly has to be brushed or wiped down. Even when the countess is occupied in other rooms, that only increases the mental confusion and torment of the nagging suspense that any moment she might unexpectedly reappear.

In the evening, when the candles are lit, little Leonhard creeps in to be with his father, to keep him company, but they never talk. It is as if there were a glass wall between them, making understanding impossible. Sometimes the old man excitedly leans forward and opens his mouth, as if he had suddenly made up his mind to tell his son something important, something with far-reaching consequences, but the words always stick in his throat, he closes his lips and just mutely, tenderly strokes the boy's burning forehead, and even as he does so his gaze flickers towards the door through which interruption might come at any moment.

The boy has a vague sense of what is going on inside his father, that it is the fullness, not the emptiness of his heart that ties his tongue. Once again he feels the bitter hatred of his mother rise in his gorge. In his mind he perceives an obscure connection between her and the deep furrows and distraught expression on the old man's face in the cushions of the wheelchair. A wish that his mother might be found dead in her bed one morning quietly surfaces inside him, adding the agony of waiting to the constant torment of inner unrest. Secretly he observes her features in the mirror, looking for any trace of illness, watches her as she walks, hoping to discover the signs of incipient debility. But the woman remains as fit as a fiddle, never shows the slightest weakness, indeed, seems to draw new strength the more the people around her grow jaded and infirm.

From Sabina and the servants Leonhard learns that his father is a philosopher, a wise man, and that all the books are full of wisdom, so he resolves, in his childish fashion, to acquire wisdom. Perhaps then the invisible barrier separating him from his father will fall, the furrowed brow be smoothed, the bitter old man's face become young again. But no one can tell him what wisdom is. He turns to the priest, but his orotund, 'The fear of the Lord is the beginning of wisdom' only succeeds in confusing him more.

One thing he is absolutely convinced of is that his mother does *not* know, and it slowly begins to dawn on him that everything she thinks and does must be the opposite of wisdom

One evening when they are alone together for a moment, he plucks up his courage and, abruptly, haltingly, like someone crying out for help, asks his father what wisdom is. He sees the muscles in his father's clean-shaven face straining with the struggle to find the right words for the mind of an inquiring child. His own head is almost bursting with the effort of trying to understand what his father is saying. He realises why the sentences coming from the toothless mouth are so hurried, so fragmentary. It is his father's fear of interruption by his mother, his concern lest the sacred seeds be corrupted by the corrosive matter-of-fact aura she exudes. If Leonhard should misunderstand them, they could easily send up poisonous shoots.

All his endeavours to understand are vain. Already he can hear the loud footsteps bustling along the corridor, the curt, shrill commands and the terrible rustling of her black silk dress. His father speaks faster and faster. He tries to catch his words, to store them up so he can think about them later, grabbing at them as if they were knives whistling through the air, but they slip from his grasp, leaving bloody cuts.

The breathless utterances: 'the longing for wisdom itself is wisdom' – 'search for a fixed point within yourself, my child,

40

that the world cannot reach' – 'regard everything that happens as a lifeless painting and do not let yourself be touched by it,' pierce his heart, but it is as if they were wearing masks he cannot penetrate. He is about to ask another question, but the door is already flying open. One last piece of advice – 'let time run off you like water' – floats past his ear, then the countess rushes in, a bucket topples over on the threshold, a flood of dirty water pours over the tiles. 'Don't get in the way! Make yourself useful!' The words echo behind him as, filled with despair, he dashes down the stairs to his room.

The images of childhood fade and once more Leonhard is looking at the white forest in the moonlight outside his chapel window and it is no clearer, nor fainter than the scenes from the days of his youth. To the adamantine clarity of his mind reality and memory are equally lifeless, equally alive.

A fox trots past, lean-limbed, silent. The snow spouts up in a glittering puff where its bushy tail touches the ground, its eyes glow green in the darkness of the trunks, then disappear in the undergrowth.

In his mind's eye Leonhard sees scrawny figures in shabby clothes, vacant, expressionless faces, different in age and yet so strangely similar, hears names whispered in his ear, unmemorable, everyday names, which scarcely serve to distinguish their bearers. In them he recognises his tutors, who come and then go after a month. His mother is never satisfied with them, dismisses them one after the other without knowing, nor asking herself the reason. All that matters is that they are there and then gone again, like bubbles in seething waters.

Leonhard is a youth with down on his lip and already as tall as his mother. When he stands facing her, his eyes are on the same level as hers, but he always feels compelled to look away, not daring to give way to the constant prick of the urge to fix her vacant stare and pour into it all the searing hatred he feels for her. Each time he chokes it back and the saliva in his mouth tastes bitter as gall, his blood feels poisoned.

He pries and probes within himself, but cannot find what makes him so powerless in the face of this woman with her restless, bat-like zigzag flight. A chaos of ideas is swirling round inside his head like a wheel spinning out of control, each heartbeat washes another scum of half-grasped thoughts into his mind and washes it away again. Jostling and shattering against each other, plans that are no such thing, contradictory ideas, aimless desires, blind, ravenous cravings emerge from the turbulence of the depths, which immediately suck them back in again. Screams suffocate in his breast, unable to reach the surface.

Leonhard is in the grip of a wild, howling despair which grows stronger with each day. His mother's detested face haunts him. A ghostly apparition, it stares out from every corner, leaps up at him from every book he opens. He is incapable of turning the page, for fear of seeing it again, does not dare look round in case it is behind him. Every shadow congeals into the dreaded features, the sound of his own breath is like the rustle of her silk dress.

His senses are as sore and tender as an exposed nerve. When he is in bed he does not know whether he is dreaming or awake, and when sleep finally does overcome him, her figure rises up from the floor in her nightgown, wakes him and screeches in his ear, 'Leonhard, are you asleep already?'

Now he is convulsed by a new, strangely hot sensation, which constricts his breathing, pursues him and drives him to seek out Sabina, without really knowing what it is he wants from her. She is grown up. Her dresses come down to her ankles and the rustling of her skirt arouses him even more than that of his mother's.

Understanding with his father is impossible now, his mind is completely clouded by madness. At regular intervals the old man's ghastly groans interrupt the hustle and bustle of the house, hour by hour they swab his face with vinegar, push his wheelchair here and there, torture the dying man to death.

Leonhard buries his head in the pillows so as not to hear. A servant plucks at his sleeve. 'Quick, for God's sake come quick, the old count's almost gone!' Leonhard jumps up, doesn't know where he is, how the sun can be shining, why it isn't deepest night if his father is dying. He staggers, telling himself with numb lips that it is all a dream, then hurries over to the sickroom. Wet towels are hanging up to dry on lines stretched right across the room, baskets block his way, the wind is roaring in through the open windows, making the white linen billow; from somewhere in the corner comes the sound of the death rattle.

Leonhard tears down the clothes-lines – wet washing smacks onto the floor – flings everything aside and forces a way through to the wheelchair from which the eyes, as the final curtain falls, fix him with a blind, glassy stare. He collapses to his knees and presses the unresponding hand, damp with the cold sweat of death, to his forehead. He tries to cry out, 'Father!', but the word will not come, it has suddenly been expunged from his memory. It is on the tip of his tongue, but the next moment, seized with terror, he has forgotten it, choked by a mind-numbing fear that the dying man will never regain his senses if he doesn't call out that word to him. That word alone has the power to call the fading consciousness back over the threshold of life, if only for a brief second. He tears his hair and beats his face. A thousand words bombard him, only the one word, the word he is seeking with all the fervour of his heart, refuses to come, and the death rattle is growing weaker and weaker, halts, starts again, breaks off – for ever.

The jaw drops. The mouth stays open.

'Father!' Leonhard cries. At last the word has come, but the man to whom it is addressed will never move again.

Uproar on the stairs, screaming voices, running steps echoing up and down the passages; the dog starts barking, interspersed with howls. Leonhard pays no attention, all he can see and feel is the terrible calm on the rigid, lifeless face. It fills the room with a radiance which illumines, envelops him. A dizzying sense of a happiness he has never known lays its hand on his heart, an intimation of an unchanging present beyond past and future, a mute rejoicing in the discovery that all around is the pulsation of a force in which he can take refuge, as if in a cloud that makes him invisible, from the restless maelstrom of the house.

The air is filled with brightness.

Tears are pouring down Leonhard's cheeks.

He starts as the door opens with a clatter. His mother comes tearing in. 'No time for crying now. Can't you see we're rushed off our feet.' Her words cut like a whiplash. The orders come tumbling out, the one countermanded by the next, the maids sob and get thrown out, in frantic haste the servants carry the furniture out into the corridor, panes of glass rattle, medicine bottles smash. 'Get the doctor' – 'No, no, the priest' – 'Stop, stop, not the priest, the grave-digger, tell him not to forget his spade' – 'and to bring a coffin too, with nails to nail it down' – 'and someone go and open up the chapel, prepare the family vault – 'At once, right away!' – 'And where are those candles that should be burning? And why is no one laying out the corpse? Do you have to be told everything ten times over?!'

With a shudder Leonhard sees how the frenzied witches' sabbath of life does not even pause before the majesty of death and step by step wins a hideous victory. He feels the peace within him vanish like the morning dew.

Slavishly obedient hands are already being laid on the wheelchair to bear the count away. Leonhard tries to intervene, to protect the dead man. He spreads his arms, but they drop back feebly to his sides. He grits his teeth and forces himself to look his mother in the eye to see if there is the slightest hint of sorrow or grief there, but not for one second can he hold her shifting, restless gaze. Like a monkey's, her eyes are constantly on the move, flitting from corner to corner, up and down, from ceiling to wall, from window to door with the zigzag flight of a demented blowfly, revealing a creature with no soul. Pain and passion bounce off her like arrows off a whirling target, she is a giant insect in the form of a woman, a woman possessed, embodying the curse of aimless, pointless toil on earth. A spurt of dread paralyses Leonhard. He stares at her, horrified, as if she were a creature he were looking at for the first time. There is nothing human about her any longer, she appears to him as an alien being from some hell, half goblin, half vicious animal.

The idea that this is his mother turns his own blood into a noxious substance, eating away at his body and soul. His hair stands on end in a sudden onrush of horror at himself that drives him out: anywhere as long as it is away from her! He rushes into the park with no idea where he is going, what he is doing, crashes into a tree and falls on his back, unconscious.

Leonhard is staring at a new image crossing his inner vision like a fevered dream: the chapel suffused with candlelight, a priest muttering at the altar, a scent of withering wreaths, an open coffin, the dead count in his white cloak of office, his waxy yellow hands crossed over his chest. A glint of gold on dark pictures of saints, black-clad men standing in a semicircle, lips mumbling prayers, cold musty air coming up from the floor and an iron trapdoor with a shining cross propped open: the square, yawning hole leads down into the crypt. Muted chanting in Latin, sunlight coming in through the stained-glass windows, dappling the drifts of incense with patches of green, blue, blood-red, an insistent, silvery ringing from the ceiling, the priest's hand in its lacy sleeve waving the aspergillum over the dead man's face. Suddenly there is movement: twelve white-gloved hands bestir themselves, lift the bier from the catafalque and close the lid; the ropes go taut, the coffin sinks into the depths, the men descend the stone steps. Then a dull echo from the vault, the crunch of sand, solemn stillness. Grave faces emerge silently from the crypt, the trapdoor descends, the lock snaps shut, dust swirls up round the edges, the cross is now horizontal. The candles gutter, go out; once more the light comes from the pine twigs in the fireplace; altar and pictures are replaced by bare walls, the flagstones covered with soil; the wreaths crumble to dust, the figure of the priest dissolves into air. Leonhard is alone again.

Since the death of the old count, the servants' quarters are in turmoil. They refuse to obey the pointless commands, one after the other they pack their things and leave. The few that are left are insolent and insubordinate, only do the most basic tasks and do not come when called.

Lips pinched, Leonhard's mother still rushes from room to room, but without her train of helpers. She tugs clumsily at the heavy wardrobes, hissing with rage, but they refuse to budge, the cupboards seem to be screwed to the floor, drawers resist, won't open, won't close. Everything she takes in her hand, she drops and no one picks it up. There are hundreds of objects lying around, debris piles up forming insurmountable obstacles no one clears away. The bookshelves fall off the wall, engulfing the room in an avalanche of books, making it impossible to get to the window to close it. It bangs in the wind until the glass breaks and the rain pours in. Soon everything is covered in a grey blanket of mould.

The countess is seized with fits of insane fury, hammering the walls with her fists, gasping for breath, screeching, tearing up anything she can lay her hands on. Her impotent rage at the fact that no one obeys her any longer – she cannot even use her son as a servant since he fell down and has to hobble round with a stick – finally robs her of the last shreds of reason. She spends hours muttering to herself, grinding her teeth, giving angry shouts, scurrying along the corridors like a wild animal.

But gradually a strange transformation takes place. Her features take on a witch-like air, her eyes a greenish shimmer, she seems to see spectres, suddenly listens, open-mouthed, as if someone were whispering to her, and asks, 'What? What? What must I do?'

Little by little the demon inside her unmasks itself as her mindless urge to be busy is replaced by a conscious, calculating malice. Now she leaves the things around her in peace, does not touch anything. Dirt and dust gather everywhere, the mirrors are clouded, the garden choked with weeds, nothing is in its right place, even the most essential utensils are impossible to find. The servants offer to clear away the worst of the mess but she forbids it with a peremptory 'No!'. She is quite happy that everything is in chaos, the tiles falling off the roof, the woodwork rotting, the fabrics mildewed. She gloats inwardly as she sees those around her suffering a new kind of torment, an unease mounting to desperation, in place of the old restlessness that made their lives a misery. She no longer says a word to anyone, gives no orders, but everything she does is done with malice, to spread fear and terror among the servants. She pretends to be mad, creeps into the maids' bedrooms at night, sending jugs crashing to the floor with a shrill cackle of laughter. Locking the door is impossible, she has removed every key in the house, now there is no door she cannot fling open with one heave. She doesn't bother to comb her hair, it hangs down in tangled knots, she eats as she walks, she doesn't go to bed any more. Only half dressed, so the rustling of her clothes will not warn people she is coming, she steals through the castle in felt slippers, suddenly appearing like a ghost, now here, now there.

On moonlit nights she even haunts the chapel. No one dares to go there any longer. There is a rumour that the ghost of the dead count walks.

She will accept no help, what she needs, she takes. She knows full well that her silent, lightning appearances arouse greater fear among her superstitious servants than a show of imperiousness. They only talk in whispers, never a loud word, they all have guilty consciences even though there is not the slightest reason.

But the main object of her machinations is her son. With insidious cunning, she uses every occasion to exploit her natural dominance as his mother and increase his feeling of dependence. She plays on his nervous fear, his feeling he is never unobserved, whipping it up into a delusion of constantly being caught in the act until he is oppressed by a permanent sense of guilt. Whenever he tries to speak to her she just screws up her face in a mocking sneer so that the words stick in his throat and he feels like a criminal whose iniquity is branded on his forehead. His vague fear that she might be able to read his most secret thoughts, that she might know about him and Sabina, becomes an alarming certainty when her penetrating gaze rests on him. At the slightest sound he desperately tries to look innocent, and the harder he tries, the less he succeeds.

A secret longing ripening into love draws Leonhard and

Sabina together. They slip each other little letters with the feeling they are committing a mortal sin. But the tenderer shoots of affection are poisoned by their sense of perpetually being followed and wither, leaving them in the grip of boundless animal lust. They station themselves at the junction of corridors where they cannot see each other but where one of them will spot the countess if she comes and can warn the other. Thus they talk and, afraid of losing precious minutes, speak frankly, openly putting their feelings into plain words and fanning the flames of desire even more.

But they find they are more and more restricted. As if the old woman suspects what is going on, she locks up the second floor, then the first. All that is left to them is the ground floor, where the servants are coming and going all the time. Leaving the castle grounds is forbidden and there are no hiding places in the park, even at night. If the moon is shining, they can be seen from the castle windows, if it is dark, they risk having the countess steal up on them.

Their passion grows impossible to curb the more they are compelled to repress it. The idea of openly disregarding the barriers between them never enters their heads. From earliest childhood they have been too deeply imbued with the conviction that they are completely at the mercy of a demonic force with power over life and death for them even to think of looking each other in the face in his mother's presence.

The meadows are scorched by the torrid heat of summer, the ground is parched and cracked, the evening sky is aflame with sheet lightning. The grass is yellow, numbing the senses with the sultry smell of hay, the walls quiver in the heat haze. Leonhard and Sabina too are so hot with desire their whole being revolves around one thing alone. When they meet they can hardly stop themselves falling upon each other.

Then comes one feverish, sleepless night with wild, lascivious waking dreams. Every time they open their eyes they see Leonhard's mother peering in, hear her stealthy footsteps at their doors. It hardly registers with them, seems half reality, half delusion, they cannot wait for the morrow when they are finally going to meet, regardless of the consequences, in the chapel.

They stay in their rooms the whole morning, listening at the door with bated breath and quaking knees for signs that the old woman is in some more distant part of the castle.

Hour after hour passes in agonising torment, midday sounds. There! A noise like the clink of keys in the interior of the building gives them the illusion of safety. They dash out into the garden. The chapel door is ajar, they push it open and slam it to behind them so that the bolt snaps shut.

They do not see that the iron trapdoor leading down into the crypt is propped open by a wooden strut, do not see the square hole yawning in the floor, do not feel the icy air coming out of the funeral vault. Like beasts of prey, they devour each other with their looks. Sabina tries to speak, but all that comes out is a frenzied babble. Leonhard rips off her clothes and throws himself on her. Panting, they seize each other in a vicelike grip.

In their intoxication they lose all sense of their surroundings. Shuffling steps feel their way up out of the crypt; they hear them clearly but they make no more impression on their consciousness of what is happening than the rustling of leaves.

Hands appear in the opening, take a grip on the stone flags and pull up.

A figure slowly emerges from the floor. Sabina sees it first through her half-closed lids, as if through a red veil. Suddenly awareness of the situation strikes and she lets out a piercing cry. It is the gruesome old woman, the terrible creature who is everywhere and nowhere, rising from the ground!

Leonhard jumps up in horror. For a moment he is paralysed as he finds himself staring into his mother's face, twisted in a malevolent grimace, then fury breaks out in a wild, foaming torrent. He kicks away the wooden prop. The trapdoor comes down with a crash on the countess's skull, sending her tumbling down into the crypt. They hear the dull thud as her body hits the ground.

Rooted to the spot, they stare at each other without a word, eyes wide, knees trembling. To save herself from falling, Sabina slowly crouches down and, groaning, buries her head in her hands. Leonhard drags himself over to the prie-dieu. His teeth are chattering audibly.

Minutes pass. Neither of them dares to move, they avoid each other's eyes. Then, under the whiplash of the same thought, they both dash out into the open and back into the house, as if the Furies were at their heels.

The setting sun transforms the well into a pool of blood, the castle windows are ablaze with fire, the shadows of the trees turn into long, thin arms with fingers inching their way across the lawn to stifle the last chirping of the crickets. The breath of twilight dulls the radiance. Night falls, blue-black.

With much shaking of heads the servants speculate as to where the countess might be. They ask the young master; he just shrugs his shoulders and looks away so they won't see how deathly pale his face is.

Lantern lights bob to and fro in the park. The servants scour the banks of the pond and shine their lanterns over the water; black as asphalt, it throws back the light. A sickle moon is floating on the surface. Startled marsh-birds fly up from the reeds.

The old gardener unleashes his dog and combs the woods round the castle. Now and then the sound of his voice calling can be heard in the distance. Each time Leonhard starts, his hair stands on end, his heart misses a beat. Is that his mother crying out under the ground?

Midnight. The gardener still has not returned. The servants are oppressed by a vague sense of impending disaster and crowd together in the kitchen, telling each other spine-chilling stories of people who mysteriously vanished to reappear as werewolves, digging up graves and feeding off the bodies of the dead.

Days, weeks pass. No sign of the countess. It is suggested Leonhard should have a mass said for her soul. His response is violent. He refuses. The chapel is emptied of its furnishings, only a gilded, carved prie-dieu is left in which he sits for hours, brooding. No one else is allowed to enter the building.

Some say that if you look through the keyhole you can often see him lying with his ear to the floor, as if he were listening for sounds from the crypt.

At night Sabina shares his bed. They make no attempt to conceal the fact that they are living together as man and wife.

The rumour of a mysterious murder reaches the village, will not die, eats its way instead farther and farther out into the country. One day a spindly, bewigged official drives up in a yellow carriage. Leonhard remains closeted with him for a long time, then the man leaves. The months pass and no more is heard of him, yet the malevolent whispers in the castle continue. No one doubts that the countess is dead, but she lives on as an invisible ghost, everyone can sense her malign presence.

The servants give Sabina black looks, think she is somehow to blame for whatever has happened; conversations abruptly break off when the young count appears.

Leonhard sees what is happening, but behaves as if he hadn't noticed, puts on a frosty, peremptory manner.

In the house nothing has changed. Creepers climb up the walls, mice, rats, owls nest in the rooms, tiles are missing from the roof, exposed beams rot and crumble. Only in the library is there some semblance of order, but the books have gone mouldy with the damp and are scarcely legible any longer. Leonhard spends whole days hunched over the old volumes, laboriously trying to decipher the smudged pages covered in his father's jerky scrawl. Sabina must be at his side all the time.

Whenever she is not there he falls prey to an agitation almost beyond control; he doesn't even go to the chapel without her any more. But they don't talk to each other. Only at night, when they are in bed together, he is seized with a kind of delirium and, in an endless tangle of gabbled sentences, he spews out everything he can remember from the books he has devoured during the day. He knows the reason for this compulsion. It is his mind desperately struggling to stop the terrible image of his murdered mother taking shape in the darkness, to drown out with words the hideous, resounding crash of the trapdoor which keeps on echoing in

51

his ear. Sabina lies there motionless, rigid, not interrupting, not even with a single word, but he can feel she is not taking in anything of what he is saying. He can tell from the empty look in her eyes, permanently fixed on one distant spot, what thought she cannot get out of her mind.

He squeezes her hand; it is minutes before he feels her fingers return the pressure, and it does not come from the heart. He tries to plunge them back into the riptide of passion, to return to the days before the happening and make them the starting point for a new life. Sabina responds to his embrace as if in a deep sleep and he feels a horror of her pregnant womb, heavy with the fruit of murder.

His sleep is leaden and dreamless, but it does not bring oblivion. He sinks into a boundless solitude in which even the dread images are lost to view, leaving only an agony of suffocation, a sudden blackout of the senses such as someone might feel who, eyes closed, is expecting the executioner's axe to fall with the next heartbeat.

Every morning when he wakes up Leonhard resolves to break out of the torture chamber of this memory. He recalls his father's advice to find a fixed point within himself, then his eye falls on Sabina, he sees how, desperately trying to smile, she only manages to twist her lips in a contorted grimace, and once again he sets off on a headlong dash to escape from himself.

He decides to change his surroundings and sends all the servants away, keeping just the old gardener and his wife. The only effect is to make his solitude with its lurking menace even more profound, the ghost of the past even more alive. It is not a guilty conscience for the murder that is plaguing Leonhard. Not for one second does he feel any remorse, his hatred of his mother is as intense as the day his father died. What is driving him to the edge of madness is her invisible presence as a formless spectre he cannot exorcise standing between him and Sabina. All the time he feels her horrible eyes fixed on him, he cannot rid himself of the scene in the chapel, which is like an ulcer festering inside him.

He does not believe the dead reappear on earth, but that

they can live on in much more terrifying form, without visible shape, as a malign influence which neither lock nor key, curse nor prayer can keep out, that is something he learns from his own experience, something he can see every day in Sabina's behaviour. Every object in the house awakens the memory of his mother, there is nothing that has not been infected by her touch, that does not hourly summon up her image in his mind. The folds in the curtains, a pile of crumpled washing, the grain in the panelling, the lines and spots on the tiles, everything he looks at resolves into her face. His similarity to her leaps out at him like a viper from the mirror, making his heartbeat run cold for fear that the impossible might happen, that his face might might suddenly turn into hers, a gruesome legacy that will remain with him to the end of his days.

The air is filled with her stifling, ghostly presence, the creak of the floorboards sounds as if it comes from her footsteps. Neither heat nor cold drives her away; whether it is autumn, a cold, clear winter's day or a mild, sickly spring breeze, it only touches the surface. No season, no outward change affects her, she is constantly striving to take form, to become more clearly visible, to assume permanent shape. The secret conviction that one day she will succeed, even if he cannot imagine how it can happen, is like a huge boulder pinning him down.

Help, he realises, can only come from his own heart, for the outside world is in league with her. But the seed planted in him by his father seems to have withered and died. The brief moments of relief, of peace he felt then, refuse to return, however hard he tries to revive them. The most he can do is evoke the superficial impressions, which are like artificial flowers, lacking scent and with ugly wire stalks. He tries to breathe life into them by reading the books which form the spiritual bond between himself and his father, but they remain a labyrinth of abstractions which set off no vibrations inside him.

Strange things turn up as he delves into the jumble of tomes with the ancient gardener. Parchments covered in symbols, pictures of a goat with a man's face, devil's horns at the temples and a golden beard, knights in white cloaks, their hands folded in prayer and crosses on their breast that are not formed from an upright and a horizontal bar, but from four running legs, bent at the knees, the satanic cross of the Templars, as the gardener reluctantly tells him, then a small, faded portrait, his grandmother, to go by the name embroidered underneath in coloured glass beads, with two children, a boy and a girl, sitting on her lap. Their features seem strangely familiar. For a long time he cannot tear his eyes from them and a dark suspicion surfaces in his mind: these must be his parents, even though they are clearly brother and sister. The sudden unease in the old man's expression, the way he avoids his eye and obstinately ignores all his questions about the two children only serve to strengthen his suspicion that he is on the track of a secret that concerns him.

A bundle of yellowing letters appears to belong with the picture since they are in the same casket. Leonhard takes them, resolved to read them that very day.

It is the first night for a long time that he has spent without Sabina. She feels too weak to sleep with him, says she is in pain.

He walks up and down in the room where his father died. The letters are on the table. He keeps going to read them then puts it off, as if under some kind of compulsion.

A new, indistinct fear announces itself. It is as if someone were standing behind him with a drawn dagger, throttling him. He knows that this time it is not his mother's ghostly presence that makes him break out in a cold sweat, it is shadows from a distant past that are bound to the letters and are waiting to drag him down into their realm.

He goes over to the window, looks out: all around a breathless, deathly hush. There are two bright stars close together in the southern sky. They seem strangely alien, the sight troubles him, though he cannot quite say why, arousing a foreboding of some cataclysmic event. They are like shining fingertips pointing at him.

He turns back to the room. The flames of the two candles on the table are waiting for him, motionless, like two ominous messengers from the world beyond. It is as if their light comes from a long way away, from a place where no mortal hand can have placed them. Imperceptibly the hour draws nigh. Softly, like ash falling, the hands move round the clock.

Was that a cry downstairs in the castle? Leonhard listens. Everything is quiet.

He reads the letters. His father's life unrolls before him, the struggle of a free spirit who rebels against everything that goes by the name of law. He sees a towering Titan bearing no resemblance at all to the dotard he knew as his father, a man who will stick at nothing, a man who openly proclaims that, like his ancestors, he is a knight of the true Order of Templars, who glorify Satan as the creator of the world and for whom the very word 'grace' is an indelible stain on their honour. Intermingled with the letters are pages from his diary describing the torment of a parched soul, the impotence of a spirit with wings worn ragged by the cares of the everyday world: he is on a road that leads down, from abyss to abyss, into darkness and madness, a road on which there is no turning back.

A thread running through everything is the repeated indication that the whole family has been driven for centuries from one crime to the next. It is a grim legacy, passed on from father to son, that a woman, be it wife, mother or daughter, will always appear, as victim or perpetrator of bloody murder, to frustrate their search for spiritual peace. And yet even in the deepest despair hope ever shines anew, like an inextinguishable star, that one day a scion of their line will come who will not bow before the curse, but will end it and win the crown of 'Master'.

Pulse racing, Leonhard devours episodes blazing with his father's passion for his own sister, episodes which reveal that he is the fruit of this union, and not only he, but Sabina as well. Now it is clear why Sabina does not know who her parents are, why there is nothing to reveal her origin. The past comes alive, and he sees his father trying to protect him by having Sabina brought up as a peasant girl, a serf of the lowest rank, so that both of them, son and daughter, will remain unaware of the stigma of incest, even if the curse on their parents should return and bring them together as man and wife.

This desire informs every terror-haunted word in one letter from his father, ill in a foreign city, to their mother. He implores her to do everything possible to prevent the children discovering the dark secret, including burning his letter immediately.

Leonhard is devastated. He tears his eyes away from the letters, but they are like a magnet, drawing him back to read on. He knows they will contain things that are exact parallels to what happened in the chapel, things that will drive him to the outer edge of horror if he reads them. With sudden insight, like lightning rending the darkness, he sees the cunning strategy of a gigantic demonic power which, concealed behind the mask of blind, impassive fate, is systematically trying to crush the life out of him. One poisoned arrow after another is being aimed at his soul so that he will waste away until the last threads of confidence wither and he falls prey to the same destiny as his forefathers in a helpless, impotent collapse.

Suddenly, like a tiger, resistance asserts itself and he holds the letter in the flame of the candle until the last glowing fragments scorch his fingers. A wild, implacable fury at the satanic monster that has the weal and woe of mankind in its grasp burns him to the very marrow. His ears ring with the cry for vengeance from a thousand throats, from all the past generations that fell into the clutches of fate and came to a wretched end. His every nerve is a clenched fist, his soul a bristling arsenal of weapons.

He feels he must perform some unheard-of deed, something to shake heaven and earth to their foundations. Behind him is the numberless army of the dead, their myriad eyes fixed on him, just waiting for a sign to follow him, the living man, the only one who can lead them into battle and fall upon their common enemy.

Staggering under the impact of a wave of power that pours over him, he looks round. What should he do first? Set the house on fire, tear himself limb from limb, or charge down, knife in hand, and slay everyone he comes across?

Each 'deed' seems more petty than the other. His sense of his own puniness threatens to crush him, he fights against it in an upsurge of youthful defiance and feels a mocking grin suffuse the space around which only serves to goad him to further action.

He tries a calm approach, forcing himself into the attitude of a general weighing every factor. He goes to the chest outside his bedroom, fills his pockets with gold and jewels, takes his coat and hat and strides out proudly, without any farewells, into the misty night, his mind awash with confused, childish plans of wandering aimlessly round the world and confronting the lord of destiny.

The castle disappears behind him in the milky haze. He would like to avoid the chapel, but has to go past it. He can feel the generations of the bloodline trying to stop him escaping their influence and forces himself to walk straight ahead, hour after hour. But the spectres of memory keep step with him. There! And there! Dark thickets yawn like the murderous trapdoor.

He is tormented by concern for Sabina. He knows this is the earthward pull of his mother's curse-laden blood in his veins trying to curb his soaring flight, trying to smother the youthful fire of his enthusiasm with the grey ashes of mundane reality. He resists with all his might, feeling his way forward from tree to tree until he sees a light in the distance, hovering above the ground at head-height. He hurries towards it, loses sight of it, sees it flashing in the mist, nearer and nearer, flitting to and fro, now here, now there. A path guides his feet, twisting and turning.

Soft, mysterious cries, barely audible, quiver in the darkness. Then the massive bulk of high, black walls with an open door rise up. Leonhard recognises his own home.

He has walked through the night in a circle.

Defeated and resigned to his fate, he goes in. As his hand touches the latch of the door to Sabina's room he feels an icy shock, an inexplicable, deadly certainty that his mother, flesh and bone, a corpse come back to life, is in there waiting for him.

He tries to turn away and flee back into the darkness. He cannot. An irresistible force is compelling him to open the door.

Sabina is lying on the bed, eyes closed, white as the sheets, a bloodless corpse. Beside her, naked, lies a newborn child, a girl with a crumpled face, a vacant, restless stare and a red mark on her forehead: in every feature the grisly image of the murdered countess in the chapel.

Leonhard sees a figure rushing across the face of the earth, its clothes ripped to shreds by thorns. It is himself, driven from house and home by a horror past bearing, the mailed fist of fate, no longer deluding himself with the vision of great deeds.

The hand of time builds up city after city in his mind – bright, gloomy, large, small, brazen, timid cities at random – only to crush them; it paints rivers like shining, silvery snakes, grey wastes, a merry patchwork of fields and pasture in brown, purple and green, dusty country roads, sharp-pointed poplars, hazy meadows, cattle grazing, dogs wagging their tails, roadside crucifixes, people young and old, showers of rain, the glitter of drops, the gold gleam of frog's eyes in ditches, horseshoes with rusty nails, storks on one leg, fence posts with splintering bark, yellow flowers, graveyards and cotton-wool clouds, misty peaks and blazing smithies. They come and go like night and day, sink into oblivion then reappear like children playing hide and seek when a scent, a sound, a quiet word calls them back.

A procession of countries, castles and mansions passes Leonhard and takes him in. His name is known, he meets with friendship and with hostility. He talks to the people in the villages, to tramps, scholars, shopkeepers, soldiers, priests, and inside him the blood of his mother is in constant struggle with the blood of his father. What one day fills him with awestruck musings, gleaming in vivid colour, like a peacock's tail made of a thousand shards of glass, the next seems dull and grey. It all depends whether his mother or father is dominant.

Then come the dreaded long hours when the two streams mingle and he is back in his old self, giving birth to remembered horrors, and he plods on blindly, step by step, in mute silence, the space between eye and lid filled with images: the baby with an old woman's face, the ominous, lifeless candle flames, the two stars close together in the sky, the letter, the sullen castle and its life-sapping torments, Sabina's corpse with its snow-white hands. In his ear he hears the babble of his dying father, the rustle of the silk dress, the crack of a skull bursting open.

Now and then he feels a sudden spasm of fear that he is going round in a circle again. Every wood appearing in the distance threatens to turn into the familiar park, every wall into the castle, the faces of people coming towards him look more and more like the maids and servants of his youth. He takes refuge in churches, sleeps out in the open, joins wailing processions, gets drunk in taverns with rogues and whores in order to hide from the sharp eye of fate, lest it to catch him again. He decides to become a monk. The abbot of the monastery is horrified when he hears his confession and learns he bears the name of a family still under the anathema pronounced on the old Knights Templar. He plunges into the maelstrom of life; it spews him back out. He goes in search of the devil. Evil is everywhere, yet its author nowhere to be found. He looks for him within his own self, and that self has disappeared. He knows it must be there, he can feel it with every second, and yet the moment he looks for it, it is gone, every day it is different, a rainbow that touches the earth but constantly recedes, dissolves, when you try to grasp it.

Wherever he looks, he sees the Cross of Satan formed from four running legs hidden behind everything, everywhere the same pointless procreation, the same pointless growing and dying, a wheel, eternally spinning in the wind, which he equates with the womb from which suffering springs, only the axis on which it turns remains, as intangible as a mathematical point.

He meets a monk from a mendicant order, travels with him, prays, fasts, castigates himself as he does. The years slip by like

59

the beads of a rosary, nothing changes, not inwardly, not out-
wardly, only the sun grows dimmer. As always, every last thing
is taken from the poor while the rich are rewarded twice over.
The more fervently he begs for 'bread', the harder the stones
the world gives him. The heavens remain as hard as steel. His
old boundless hatred of the secret enemy of mankind that
decrees our destinies breaks out again.

He listens to the monk preaching about justice and the
torments of the damned in hell. To Leonhard it sounds like
the crowing of the devil. He hears him rail against the wick-
edness of the Order of Templars which, though burnt at the
stake a thousand times, keeps on raising its head, refuses to die,
and lives on, ineradicable, secretly spread over the whole
world. It is the first time he has learnt anything precise about
the beliefs of the Templars: that they have two gods, one up
above, far from mankind, and one down below, Satan, who
hourly creates the world anew and fills it with abominations
that grow more loathsome every day until it suffocates in its
own blood; and that there is a third god above these two, the
Baphomet, an idol with a golden head and three faces.

The words burn into his soul, as if they had been spoken by
tongues of fire. He cannot penetrate the depths they cover like
a quivering carpet of swamp-moss, but there is not the slightest doubt in his mind that this is the only path by which he
can escape from himself. The Order of Knights Templar is
reaching out for him, the legacy of his forefathers which no
man can deny.

He leaves the monk.

Once more the dead are thronging round, calling out a
name until his lips repeat it and he, gradually, syllable by syllable, as if it were a tree growing, branch by branch, up from
his heart, comes to understand it as his mouth speaks it, a
name, completely unknown to him and yet inextricably
bound up with his whole existence, a name bearing the
purple and a crown, a name he feels compelled to whisper to himself and cannot clear from his mind as it is beaten
out by the rhythm of his feet hitting the ground: Ja–cob–de–
Vi–tri–a–co.

Little by little the name becomes a spectral guide leading him onward, now as a legendary Grand Master of the Knights of the Temple, now as a disembodied inner voice.

Just as a stone thrown into the air changes its trajectory and plummets to the earth with increasing speed, so the name is associated for Leonhard with a change in the direction of his desires as his whole being is gradually consumed with an inexplicable, overpowering urge to find the man who bears it.

Sometimes he could swear the name was new to him, at others he has a clear memory of having seen it mentioned on a specific page of one of his father's books as the head of an order of knighthood. He tries to tell himself there is no point in looking for this Grand Master Jacob de Vitriaco, that he lived in another century, that his bones have long since turned to dust, but in vain. Reason no longer has the power to control his thirst for the search, the cross with the four running legs is rolling in front of him, invisible, pulling him along behind.

He searches through the registers of nobility in town archives, asks experts in heraldry, but can find no one who has heard the name. Finally, in a monastery library, he comes across the same book as his father had. He reads it page by page, line by line; the name Vitriaco is not there. He begins to doubt his memory, his whole past seems uncertain, but the name Vitriaco remains the one fixed point, immovable as a massive boulder.

He resolves to erase the name from his mind and decides to head for a particular town. By the very next day it is nothing but a faint cry from afar that sounds like Vi-tri-a-co, and another road is leading him in a quite different direction. A spire on the horizon, the shadow of a tree, the hand on a milestone: however hard he tries to force himself to doubt them, they all become fingerposts telling him he is approaching the place where the mysterious Grand Master Vitriaco lives and is guiding his footsteps.

In an inn he meets a travelling quack and for a moment deludes himself with the vague hope that he might be the one he is looking for. But the quack is called Doctor Bleedwite.

He is a dark-complexioned man with small, shiny, pine-marten's teeth and shifty eyes, and there is nothing in this world that he does not know, no place he has not been, no thought he cannot read, no heart whose depths he cannot plumb, no illness he cannot heal, no tongue he cannot loosen and no coin that is safe from him. The girls crowd round for him to read their fortunes from their palms or in the cards. People fall silent and quietly slink away when he whispers details from their past to them.

Leonhard drinks the whole night through with him. At times in his drunken stupor he is overcome with dread at the idea that it is not a human being sitting opposite him. The doctor's features keep on blurring and all he can see is the white teeth, from which words emerge which are half an echo of what he has said himself, half answers to scarcely formulated questions. As if the man could read his innermost desires, he brings even trivial conversations round to the Templars. Leonhard keeps wanting to find out if he has heard of a certain Vitriaco but each time, when it is almost too late, he feels deep misgivings and bites back the name.

They travel on together, wherever chance takes them, from one fair to the next. Doctor Bleedwite eats fire, swallows swords, changes water into wine, pushes daggers through his cheeks and tongue without bleeding, heals people possessed by evil spirits, summons up ghosts, puts spells on man and beast. Leonhard has daily proof that the man is a swindler, can neither read nor write and yet performs miracles. The lame cast their crutches aside and dance, women in labour give birth the moment he lays hands on them, epileptics are cured of their fits, rats leave the houses in hordes and plunge into the river. He finds it impossible to break away from him; he is under his spell, yet thinks himself free.

Again and again his hopes that the quack will lead him to Vitriaco die, only to blaze up brighter than ever the next minute, fanned by some ambiguous remark. Everything the mountebank says and does is double-edged: he dupes people and at the same time helps them; he lies and what he says conceals profound truths; he tells the truth and the mocking face of falsehood appears behind it; he gabbles away at random and his words become prophecy; he makes predictions from the stars and they come true, even though he knows nothing about astrology; he brews potions from common weeds and they work like magic; he laughs at people's credulity and is himself as superstitious as any old crone; he scoffs at the crucifix and makes the sign of the cross when a black cat crosses his path; asked for advice, he brazenly flings the questioner's own words back in his face, yet from his lips they turn into answers that hit the nail on the head.

It is with astonishment that Leonhard sees a miraculous power revealed in this most unworthy of earthly instruments. Gradually he comes to grasp the key to the mystery. If he sees in him the swindler alone, then everything he learns from him dissolves into mere gibberish, but if he looks for the invisible power that is reflected in the quack doctor, like the sun in a muddy puddle, the mountebank immediately becomes its mouthpiece and a source of living truth.

He decides to take the risk, puts his misgivings to one side and, without looking at him, as if he were addressing the violet and purple clouds in the evening sky, asks the man if he knows the name Jacob de –

'Vitriaco.' The other swiftly completes the name, then stands still, as if in a trance, bows deeply towards the west and, with a solemn expression and a voice quivering with excitement, tells Leonhard that the hour of awakening has finally arrived. He himself, he goes on, is a Templar of subordinate rank whose task it is to lead searchers along the mysteriously winding paths of life to the Master. In a torrent of words he describes the glory that awaits the select, the splendour that surrounds the countenance of each Brother, releasing him from all remorse, from blood guilt, sin and torment, turning him into a Janus with two faces looking at two different worlds from eternity to eternity, an undying witness to the world below and the world above, a mighty human fish in the ocean of existence, freed for ever from the meshes of time, immortal both here and there.

Then he points ecstatically at the dark-blue edge of a range of hills on the horizon. There, he tells him, deep in the earth, surrounded by tall pillars is the Order's shrine, a towering temple made from druid stones, where once a year, in the dark of night, the disciples of the Cross of the Baphomet meet, the Chosen Ones of the God of the Lower World who rules over mankind, crushing the weak and raising the strong to be His sons. Only one who is a true knight, a blasphemer through and through, baptised in the fire of spiritual revolt, and not one of those grovelling whiners forever cringing before the bogey of mortal sin and castrating themselves on the holy ghost, which is nothing but their own innermost self – only such a one can enjoy the blessing of reconciliation with Satan, the sole sword-bearer among the gods, without which the gulf between expectation and event can never be closed.

The quack's bombast leaves a flat taste in Leonhard's mouth, his extravagant fabrications make him sick. A secret temple here in the middle of a wood in Germany! But, like the roar of a mighty organ, the fanatical tone drowns out his thoughts and he does as Doctor Bleedwite commands and takes his shoes off. They light a fire, the sparks swirling up into the darkness of the summer night, and he drinks the foul-tasting concoction his companion brews up out of herbs so that he will be purified.

'Lucifer, by the wrongs you suffer, I greet you,' is the watchword he must remember. He hears the words, but the syllables are strangely disjointed, like a group of stone columns, some a long way away from, some close to his ear. He no longer hears them as sounds, but sees them rise up as pillars forming aisles. It seems as natural as a dream where things change into others, large ones vanish into small.

The quack doctor takes him by the hand and they walk for a long, long time, or so it seems. Leonhard's naked feet are on fire; he can feel feel ploughed furrows beneath his soles. In the darkness hummocks swell up into vaguely recognised shapes.

Short spells of sober doubt alternate with unshakable certainty, but the firm belief that, as always so far, there is some truth behind his guide's promises gradually gains the upper hand. Then come strangely exciting moments when, stumbling over a stone, he is roused with a start to the awareness that his body has been walking in deep sleep, only to forget it immediately. Endless deserts of time stretch between these moments of startled wakefulness, diverting his suspicions from the present to epochs apparently long past.

The path begins to descend.

Broad, echoing steps hurry down.

Then Leonhard is feeling his way along cold, smooth marble walls. He is alone. As he turns round to look for his companion he is stunned by resounding trumpet blasts, like the call to awaken the dead. He almost loses consciousness, the bones in his body vibrate, then the night is torn apart before his very eyes as the deafening fanfares transmute into dazzling light.

He is standing in a vast, vaulted space. Hovering in the middle is a golden head with three faces. He glances up at the one facing him: it seems to be his own, only young again. The mark of death is on it, yet the brightness of the metal, which half obscures its features, glows with indestructible life. It is not the mask of his youth that Leonhard is seeking, he wants to see the two other faces which look out into the darkness, wants to penetrate the secret of their expression, but they turn away from him. Every time he tries to walk round the golden head it revolves, keeping the same face towards him.

Leonhard peers round, trying to discover what it is that makes the head move. Suddenly he sees that the wall at the back is transparent, like oily glass. Behind it is a figure, arms outstretched, dressed in tattered clothes, hunchbacked, a wide-brimmed hat pulled down over his eyes, standing motionless as death on a mound of bones from which sparse blades of grass grow: the Prince of this World.

The trumpets fall silent.

The light dies away.

The golden head disappears.

All that is left is the pale luminescence of decay surrounding the figure. Leonhard feels a numbness slowly creep over his body, paralysing him limb by limb, curbing the flow of blood so that his heartbeat grows slower and slower until if finally stops.

The only part with which he can still say 'I' is a tiny spark somewhere in his breast.

With the reluctant fall of moisture from a leaf, the hours drip into a spreading pool of endless years.

Almost imperceptibly the figure takes on the outline of reality. In the grey light of dawn the hands on its outstretched arms slowly shrink to stumps of rotten wood, the skulls reluctantly give way to dusty round stones. Wearily Leonhard pulls himself to his feet. Looming menacingly over him, wrapped in rags, features made of pieces of glass, is a hunch-backed scarecrow.

His lips are burning feverishly, his tongue feels parched; beside him the embers of the fire are still glowing under the pan with what is left of the drugged potion. The quack has gone and with him what little money he had left. The fact hardly registers on Leonhard's consciousness, the experience of the night is still gnawing at the depths of his soul. The scarecrow is no longer the Prince of this World, true, but the Prince of this World himself is now no more than a paltry scarecrow: frightening to the timid alone, adamant to those who beseech his aid, dressed in tyrant's robes for those who want to be slaves and array it with the panoply of power and a puny phantasm to all those who are proud and free.

Doctor Bleedwite's secret is suddenly made plain: the mysterious force that works through him is not his own, nor is it some invisible force behind him. It is the magic power of the believers who cannot believe in themselves, cannot use it themselves, but have to transfer it to some fetish, be it man, god, plant, animal or devil so that it will shine back on them, its potency magnified as if by a burning-mirror; it is the magic wand of the *true* Prince of this World, the innermost, all-present, all-consuming 'I', the source which can only give, never take, without becoming an impotent 'you', the self at whose command space must shatter and time freeze into the golden face of eternal present; it is the imperial sceptre of the spirit, the sin against which is the only one that can never be forgiven; it is the power made manifest through the blazing nimbus of a magic, indestructible present sucking everything down to its primal depths.

In it gods and humans, past and future, shades and demons all give up that illusion they call their life. It is the power which knows no bounds, the power which is strongest in those who are greatest, the power which is always within and never without, and immediately turns everything that remains without into a scarecrow.

The quack doctor's promise of the forgiveness of sins is fulfilled in Leonhard, there is not a single word that does not come true. The Master has been found: it is Leonhard himself. Just as a large fish will tear a hole in the net and escape, so he has freed himself from the legacy of the curse: a redeemer for those ready to follow him.

Everything is sin, or nothing is sin, all selves are one common self, of that he is clearly aware. Where is the woman who is not at the same time his sister, what earthly love is not at the same time incest, what female creature, and be it the tiniest animal, can he kill without at the same time killing his mother and his own self? Is his body anything other than an inheritance from myriads of animals?

There is no one who decrees our destinies except the one, great self that mirrors itself in countless reflected selves – great and small, clear and murky, good and evil, happy and sad – and yet is untouched by joy or sorrow, remains a perpetual present in past and future, just as the sun does not become dirty or wrinkled when its reflection floats in puddles or rippling waves, does not descend into the past, nor return from the future whenever the waters dry up or rain brings new ones: there is no one who decrees our destinies except the great, common self, the fountainhead from which all waters flow.

What space does that leave for sin? The malevolent, invisible enemy shooting poisoned arrows from out of the darkness has gone; demons and false gods are dead, having succumbed like bats to the brightness of light.

Leonhard sees his mother with her restless look arise from the dead, sees his father, his sister-wife Sabina. They are

67

merely images, like his own many bodies as a child, a youth, a man. Their true life is incorruptible and without form, like his own self.

He drags himself to a pond he sees nearby to cool his burning skin. His entrails are racked with a pain he does not feel as his, but as if it were another's. All spectres, including physical pain, disappear in the face of the dawn of an eternal present which seems as natural to each mortal as their own face and is yet as wholly alien as their own face.

Contemplating the gently curving bank and the small, rush-grown islands, he is suddenly overcome with memory.

He sees that he is back in the park of his childhood.

He has walked round in a great circle through the fog of life!

A profound content fills his heart, fear and dread have been swept away, he is reconciled with the dead and the living and with himself. From now on fate will hold no terrors for him, neither in the past nor in the future.

Now the golden head of time has only a single face for him: the eternally young countenance of the present as a feeling of never-ending, blissful peace; the two others are permanently turned away, like the dark side of the moon from the earth.

He finds comfort in the thought that everything that moves must go round in a circle and that he too is part of the great force that makes and keeps the celestial bodies as spheres. The difference between the sign of Satan with the ceaselessly running four human legs and the unmoving, upright cross is clear to him.

Is his daughter still alive? She must be an old woman, hardly twenty years younger than himself.

Calmly he walks up to the castle. The gravel path is a brightly coloured carpet of fallen fruit and wild flowers, the young birch trees gnarled giants in bright cloaks. The summit of the hill is topped with a black pile of rubble threaded with the silvery stems of weeds.

Strangely moved, he wanders round the sun-scorched ruins and an old, familiar world rises again from the past in trans-figured splendour. Fragments he finds here and there under charred beams fuse into a whole; like a magic wand, a twisted bronze pendulum brings the brown clock of his childhood into a newborn present, the blood sweated in old torments turns into a thousand red speckles glistening on life's phoenix plumage.

A flock of sheep, herded by silent dogs into a broad rectangle of grey, is crossing the meadow and he asks the shepherd who lives in the castle. The man mutters something about a curse on the place and an old woman, the last person to live there before it burnt down, an evil witch with a blood-mark on her forehead like Cain, who lives down at the kiln, then hurries off on his sullen way.

Leonhard goes into the chapel, which is hidden in a jungle of trees. The door is hanging from its hinges and all that is left inside is the gilded prie-dieu, covered in mould; the windows are black with grime and the altar and pictures decayed. The cross on the iron trapdoor has been eaten away by verdigris, brown moss is growing up through the gaps round the edge. He wipes it with his foot and a half-eroded inscription appears in a polished strip of the metal, a date and the words:

Built by
Jacob de Vitriaco

The fine gossamer threads that bind together the things of this world gradually disentangle in Leonhard's mind. The name of some foreign architect, barely scratched on the surface of his memory, so often seen during the days of his youth and just as often forgotten, that is the invisible figure who accompanied him on his circular journey in the guise of a Grand Master calling him. Now he lies here, at his feet, changed back into an empty word at the very moment in which his mission is completed and the secret longing of his soul to return home to its point of departure has been fulfilled.

Leonhard, the Master, sees the rest of his life as a hermit in the wilderness of existence. He wears a hair-shirt made of rough blankets he finds among the ruins of the burnt-out castle and builds a fireplace of bricks. The occasional figures that chance to pass close to the chapel seem as insubstantial as shadows, only taking on life when he draws their image inside the magic circle of his self and makes them immortal there. To him the forms of existence are like the changing shapes of the clouds: manifold and yet basically nothing but water vapour.

He lifts up his eyes above the tops of the snow-covered trees. Once more, as in the night of his daughter's birth, there are two stars close together in the southern sky, looking down on him.

Torches swarm through the forest.

Scythes clash.

Faces contorted with anger appear among the trees, a grumble of low voices. The old, hunchbacked woman from the kiln is once more outside the chapel, waving her skinny arms, pointing out the devil's silhouette on the snow to the superstitious peasants, staring all the time at the window-panes with wild eyes like two green stars.

On her forehead is a red birthmark.

Leonhard does not move. He knows that the people out-side have come to kill him, knows that it is the shadow with devil's horns he casts on the snow, an empty nothing he can dispel with a movement of his hand, that has aroused the wrath of the superstitious crowd. But he knows too that the body they will kill is only a shadow, just as they are shadows, mere phantasms in the sham world of ever-rolling time, and that shadows are also subject to the law of the circle.

He knows that the old woman with the blood-mark and his mother's features is his daughter and that she brings the end, closing the circle: the soul's roundabout journey through the mists of birth and rebirth back to death.

Extracts from: *The Great Bestiary of Modern Literature*

Franz Blei

THE KAFKA: The Kafka is a magnificent and very rarely seen moon-blue mouse, which eats no flesh, but feeds on bitter herbs. It is a bewitching sight, for it has human eyes.

THE MEYRINK: The Meyrink is the only mooncalf which dropped to earth and which is now in captivity. It is occasionally put on show by its captor. For a while pregnant women were banned from viewing it, because of the occurrence of a few premature births caused by shock, but the ban has been lifted, since women with child are by now so accustomed to the sight that it raises no more than a gentle smile. Officers of the Imperial Austro-Hungarian Army and German Deputies wanted to ban the public exhibition of the Meyrink because, so they said, it gave a distorted reflection of them in its one big eye. The owner succeeded in proving, however, that the reflection was not distorted, but that it was the object which distorted the eye of the Meyrink. The numbers visiting the Meyrink have declined considerably since the appearance of so many other mooncalves running around free; whether they all dropped from the moon is impossible to say, but they have certainly been dropped on the head.

THE SCHNITZLER: Schnitzler is the name of a racehorse which runs at Freudenau out of the Fischer stable and which, in its day, was a favourite with all the ladies and girls-about-town of Vienna because of the melancholy mettle it used to show. People would bet on Schnitzler because they liked it, even though they knew it would not even be placed. Because Schnitzler was such a favourite, and to encourage the grand-daughters of the girls-about-town to come to Freudenau, the

Jockey Club has agreed to let Schnitzler, whenever and as long as it runs, always come third, even if it pulls up after the first lap. Long may it run.

Folter's Gems

Paul Busson

With a violent jolt the cab stopped outside a large house in a
fashionable part of town. The young doctor jumped down
and rushed past the porter up the broad staircase. The servant
who had just telephoned him from the coffee house was waiting by the half-open door on the first floor. On the small brass
plate stood the name: Jerome Kerdac.

Once the doctor had entered, the servant immediately
closed the door behind him, took his coat and hat and, with
trembling hands, ushered him into a large room that was in
semi-darkness; a flick of the switch and it was flooded with
bright light from a chandelier of Venetian glass.

Dr. Klaar went up to the wide bed in which the sick man
lay. A thin wisp of bluish gunsmoke was still twirling round in
the light. There was a smell of scorched linen. The doctor's
foot knocked against a hard object: it was the revolver with
which Kerdac had shot himself.

The man in the bed had his eyes closed. His gaunt white
face was motionless and his breathing weak. The doctor bent
down over him and lifted the bedcover, which had been
drawn up. He had placed the barrel of the gun below his left
breast. There was a small, round hole with dark edges, a few
spidery splashes of blood on his shirt next to the burnt
patches round the bullet hole in his shirt, and that was all.
Carefully, the doctor ran his hand over the man's back as he
lay there unconscious. The bullet was still in the body. There
seemed to be some damage to the heart; whether that was
the case or not, there was not much that could be done for
him.

Dr. Klaar got the servant to repeat his story, which he did
with much sobbing and stammering, he had obviously not

yet recovered from the shock. For some time now, he said, the Master had been melancholy and highly irritable; there had often been weeks when, without actually being ill, he had refused to leave his bed and he had eaten nothing for days on end. Sometimes he had seemed to be feverish, had rambled and seen horrible threatening visions. At night especially, he had often groaned and cried out loud, and several times he, the servant, had woken with a fright and hurried into the bedroom to stand by the Master. He, however, had always reprimanded him harshly for this and finally forbidden him once and for all from entering the bedroom at night unless he rang for him. Today the Master had had a particularly bad day, had moaned and groaned a great deal and had not had a bite to eat. At half past five in the evening he had rung for him and sent him out to do some shopping, which should have taken him about an hour. However, he had not quite finished his work and had still been in the house some twenty minutes later when the sound of a muffled report came from the bedroom. And when he had seen that the Master had shot himself he had immediately run to the telephone and had rung up the Café Central where, as he happened to know, the gentlemen from the hospital used to go to read the papers. That had been a quarter of an hour ago.

'Good,' said the doctor. 'Bring me paper and ink and then take what I write down to the police station at once. It is my duty to report this immediately.'

At that moment the doctor noticed that Kerdac had opened his eyes wide and that his lips were moving. He hurried across to where his patient was breathing heavily.

'Send my servant back to his room,' whispered Kerdac. 'I would like to talk to you.'

Dr. Klaar told him to stay calm, he was just going to write something to send to the chemist's.

'The chemist's, oh really?' groaned the injured man. 'I heard everything that was said. Why the police? It will soon all be over. I have something important I would like to tell you.'

He broke off and began to fidget with the blanket. His

74

face was becoming visibly more emaciated and his nose stood out.

The Hippocratic face, thought the doctor, and he realised that in that case it really did not matter if the police should receive his report ten minutes later.

He decided to allow the dying man to have his way, told the servant to stay at the ready in his own room and sat down close to his patient, who raised his top lip in a grateful smile. He felt unwilling to subject the poor man to the torture of a further examination. It was his opinion that the bullet was lodged in the lower part of the pericardium. It was a miracle that the organ could still function. It would continue to pump the blood laboriously round his body for a while, the heart-beat becoming more and more sluggish.

'Feel under my pillow,' murmured Kerdac. The doctor did as he asked and pulled out a slim casket of reddish-brown morocco leather. There was a coat of arms stamped on the lid, which gleamed dully with the patina of age. It showed a winged snake with a woman's head. Beneath it was written in Gothic script: A Folter.

'Have a good look at it,' said Kerdac. 'I'm not going to die just yet. I feel fine.' His eyelids slid down so that the doctor started forward. Kerdac was lying motionless and his breathing was regular, even if very weak.

Dr. Klaar opened the casket. It was lined with velvet that had once been white, but had long since yellowed. In twelve semicircular compartments lay twelve thin, polished stones, smooth and transparent, with a crumbling black silk mask over them, like a protective covering. The mask had only one round opening, over the right eye, with a kind of raised lip, as if it were made for a small eye-glass to fit in. There was a narrow strip of parchment in the mask on which words in similar Gothic lettering were printed, or written by a skilful hand.

The doctor gave his patient a questioning glance and then, when he kept his eyes tight shut, looked back at the strip. He found it completely incomprehensible, both the heading and the rest:

Januarius. – Hyacinth. – Eve.
Februarius. – Amethyst. – Poppaea.
Martius. – Heliotrope. – Salome.
Aprilis. – Sapphire. – Selina.
Maius. – Emerald. – Diana.
+Junius. – Chalcedony. – Nahema.+
Julius. – Cornelian. – Astarte.
Augustus. – Onyx. – Semiramis.
September. – Chrysolite. – Lilith.
October. – Aquamarine. – Undine.
November. – Topaz. – Roxana.
December. – Chrysoprase. – Helen.

Call them all, except only Nahema.

Dr. Klaar read it aloud. Like a fading echo, there came from
the lips of the wounded man, ' . . . but not Nahema.'

And then Kerdac gave both the stranger by his bedside and
the familiar objects in his room an astonished look, as if he had
just woken from a deep sleep.

'I was unconscious?' he asked in a weak voice. 'I could feel
myself sinking . . . deeper and deeper into the blackness . . .'

A violent tremor ran through his body. His hand felt for the
doctor's.

'Tell me . . . doctor . . . there is . . . no hope, then? If you
were to operate . . . ?'

Dr. Klaar instinctively looked away and tried to comfort the
man with the usual meaningless phrases, to give him new
heart. It was not the first time he had sat by a suicide's bed and
witnessed the terrible awakening, the sudden recognition
of a senseless, pathetic act which could not be undone. He
thought of the poor seamstress who had died of phosphorus
poisoning in his hospital three weeks ago; right until the very
end all her thoughts, all her hopes had been concentrated on
recovery, in spite of her wretched life, which she had tried to
bring to a messy and excruciating end. Had she managed to

recover, it would have meant nothing other than a continuation of her *via dolorosa*, doubly hard to bear because of the tiny, deformed and nameless creature that she, abandoned like a beast in the wild, had brought into the world in her icy attic. Happy were those who managed to kill themselves quickly, who slipped over into death during sleep, or whose end struck them like lightning in their prime, so quickly that they had no time for thought.

Kerdac had tears in his eyes when he saw the doctor's expression. But he was brave enough to come to terms with it.

'Then I will tell you everything,' he said softly. 'You will be the only one to know.'

'You shouldn't talk too much,' replied Dr. Klaar, with an uncertain glance at the clock. He was surprised to find himself still sitting here, instead of making the mandatory report.

'Please . . . do stay . . .'

A deep moan followed by a sobbing gasp indicated a painful convulsive fit. Kerdac clutched the doctor's hand as firmly as he could with his helplessly weak fingers, as if he was afraid he would be left to die alone and wanted to hold him there. When he had recovered somewhat, he began to gabble; gradually his voice calmed down and became clearer, although it was so soft that the doctor had to hold his ear close to the injured man's lips to keep him from overexerting himself. During the whole of his story, Dr. Klaar kept the strange casket in his hand.

'No one will mourn for me,' said Kerdac, 'there is no one who loves me. I have been alone since I was ten years old, completely alone. Do you know how sad that is? Do you know how a poor, timid lad like that can suffer in his cheerless existence? Huh! No one can know! . . . It was a long time ago . . . Later, when I left the institution where I spent the whole of my bleak childhood, they sent me to university. At the age of twenty-four I received a letter from the Chancery Court; my fortune, which until then had been administered by a grumpy old lawyer who otherwise did not concern himself at all with his ward, was paid out to me. I registered the fact with the dull indifference, the lethargy, which had become second nature to me. My circumstances were better than before. I had a large apartment decorated by a talented designer and buried myself in my books. Buying books, by the way, was the sole luxury I had allowed myself so far.

Presumably as a result of my lonely life, which had turned me in upon myself, I became interested in rare and occult works. With time I collected a great number of such books, from Agrippa of Nettesheim to modern, spiritualist works. I devoted my energies passionately to deciphering unknown oriental manuscripts. At the same time I tried to practise magic. But apart from fleeting experiences and unusual dream-visions, which were probably the result of the obligatory incense burnt, some of which doubtless contained hallucinogenic substances, there was nothing that brought me closer to the mysteries I was seeking to fathom. Over the years I became acquainted with a few people who secretly concerned themselves with such matters and claimed to have seen more than I did. Perhaps they did really believe it. Once I came across a man who was said to be possessed of unheard-of magic powers and who pretended to be an Oriental. His disciples listened to his fantasies with imperturbable patience; in reality he was just a petty swindler who used his talent to pay for some of the minor comforts of life. His "magnetic healing" was the thing that caused the authorities to have him deported back to his native Bavaria. So that led to nothing, either. Would you dry my forehead please, doctor?'

Kerdac's forehead was covered with large beads of sweat, and Klaar gently patted it with a towel. Perhaps it might be possible to lengthen this wretched life a little; the needle with the injection which he had kept at the ready easily penetrated the loose skin of his lower arm. The injection seemed to do Kerdac some good, he took a deep breath and continued in a somewhat more lively tone,

'I told you that as an example of the many disappointments I suffered. It was always the same. For ten rupees, a fakir in India, in Dharwangar, showed me the famous miracle of the mango tree. As he repeated his incantations, a young, light-green shoot appeared from the seed he had planted and grew

78

higher and higher each time after he had covered it with a cloth. Finally I grabbed the pot with the seed from the fellow, in spite of his screams: the seed had been carefully split and a mango seedling very cleverly concealed within it. In the cloth were four other seedlings, each larger than the other.

Why am I telling you this? To show you that I am no novice in these matters and quite capable of distinguishing sham from reality; to make you understand that what drove me to fire that wretched bullet into my chest was more than the dreams of a fevered mind. It was real, of a reality that was so beautiful and yet so awful, that no living person can imagine the degree of horror I have lived through.

After the experiences I have described, I banished my magic books to the depths of a huge, locked cupboard and set off to travel, unencumbered by mental baggage. It was no good. The rapid change of scene did not cheer up my melancholy temperament. If the Mediterranean sun shone more brightly on others, if the roses in Fiesole had a nasty odour which I found oppressive, if the blue sea smelled of fish and seaweed, then the fault lay within me. There must be something wrong with my eye, my hearing must have a string with an ugly note. How else could I explain why all I saw of a beautiful woman was the smut that the wind had blown onto her cheek and her veil had smudged? Why all I heard in a Beethoven concerto were the opening bars of a vulgar song repeated over and over again? Why, at a play that moved other people to the depths of their souls, could I only see the grubby scenery and the wrinkles of the actor who played the young lover? It was me! I was the cause of my own suffering!

Once I was in love, madly, unreasonably; I could not live without her. It may sound like an empty cliché, yet it still expressed the truth. This time I saw no physical defects. But I was tormented by a fiendish jealousy. I knew she was deceiving me and at the same time I knew that was not the case. Can you understand? I could not help it. There was something compelling me to think the worst of the woman I loved, and I tormented the only woman there was for me in the world with my insulting suspicions and my sarcastic words of rejection until, hurt and deeply wounded in her most tender feelings, she left me, her face bathed in tears. And with that my life was really over, that is what has destroyed me. Of that I am sure.'

Kerdac gave a deep sigh. A great weakness accompanied by a quivering of the muscles suddenly came over him, appearing to presage his rapid demise. But this time it passed, and he continued:

'I cannot remember anything that has given me real joy. I have tried everything and been disappointed by everything. It was my own shortcoming, I was incapable of joy. Eventually I gave up all attempt to enrich my life as pointless and fell back into my old state of complete apathy. I got up when I had had enough sleep, ate, drank and made my bored and futile way round the city.

One evening – I was living in Paris at the time – I was sitting in a boulevard café drinking a glass of beer. It was a warm, rainy day in spring. The lights were reflected in the wet cobblestones. The people streamed past; occasionally one would split off from the throng and come into the café; others who left it were immediately swallowed up by the living stream. I almost found it amusing to observe all these little scenes, which were like a symbol of life.

Suddenly I realised that a man had sat down at my table, something which made me very uneasy. I gave him a hostile look. It was a miserable, poorly dressed Jew with a reddish, unkempt beard and restless, anxious eyes. He drank his sweet liqueur with tiny sips and tried to take up as little space as possible. When he saw that I had noticed him he started and sketched a bow. After a while he addressed me in bad French, with the characteristic singing intonation of the Jews. He spoke very hesitantly, as if he was very embarrassed and I soon realised what he wanted. He had, he said, arrived in Paris only that day, with his wife and three small children, one of whom was very ill. He wanted to settle down here, but he had spent the whole day running round without success and he was starving and dog-tired. His wife was waiting for him, somewhere far out in the suburbs, and he hadn't a sou in his pocket to buy bread for his children. I gave him an irritated look, my first thought was that he was one of those countless importunate beggars who make a better living from some paltry speech they have got off by heart than many an honest working man. But his eyes looked at me with such passionate, desperate pleading in them and were fixed in such anxious expectation on my face that, contrary to my intention, I pushed a five-franc piece across the table to him. He erupted in such a flood of thanks and loud blessings that he was becoming a perfect pest. And when he went on to ask me whether I would not be willing to buy something from him I told him rather sharply it was time he disappeared. But he stayed calmly in his seat and took the casket that you have in your hand, doctor, out of his pocket and handed it to me. It had belonged, he said, to a fine gentleman in Vienna who had shot himself; he had bought it from the sale of his effects. It must be very rare and very old. He had asked his rabbi what it was, but he had commanded him to burn it and under no circumstances to sell it. But that would be a waste, and he was poor. Would I give him twenty francs for it?

Against my will, I opened the thing and bought it at once. It was a long time since anything had excited or surprised me; the effect on me of this casket, with the mask and strip of parchment, was like a glass of cool water to a man dying of thirst. I immediately put it in my pocket.

The Jew was still nodding to me gratefully and muttering blessings. He disappeared as he had come: I looked away for a moment, and when I turned back to the table, he was gone; in the end he had not dared to take the money; the gold coin lay beside my arm. I was sorry about that. I would have been happy to give the poor fellow the money. I never saw him again.

I made my way home as quickly as possible. I had a very pleasant apartment close to the Madeleine. I sent my servant out to bring some cold supper. After I had eaten I gave the casket and its contents a thorough examination. In vain I searched my books to see if anything was known of a magician called Folter, whose "true gems" lay before me.'

A further fit interrupted Kerdac. The doctor, constantly expecting the end, was in an inexplicable state of excitement, and the minutes seemed to drag before the pale lips opened to continue their story.

'I must hurry,' he stammered. 'I shall go downhill fairly rapidly from now. I was talking about that first evening? Well, it took me weeks of thinking and searching, weeks of torment, before I found the secret. It was one evening in September when I put the mask on once again and inserted the month's stone, the chrysolite, into the round hole. It was something I had tried a hundred times. And as I had done a hundred times before, I stared through the thin disc towards the light. In contrast to former attempts, this time I decided to wait until something – anything at all – appeared, and I was prepared to wait the whole night if necessary. How long it took I cannot say. A very long time, certainly. Later on it happened more quickly. Well, there I sat for hours, spellbound, looking through the yellow stone. Then suddenly, involuntarily I would say, I started calling out the name Lilith countless times.

All at once it seemed as if something like a small cloud was forming in the centre of the transparent disc. But no . . . now it seemed to be outside, in the corner of the room. My critical faculties began to fall asleep; all I could do was to stare fixedly at the yellow cloud, watching it grow and grow, watching the movement within it. It was as if I were paralysed. The figure of a woman became clearer and clearer . . . a naked woman with long hair. Then I must have lost consciousness, for when I moved my hands again I felt as if I was waking from sleep, and the apparition had disappeared.

My first idea was that it was a vivid hallucination, which could only be explained by self-hypnosis, by the systematic overstimulation of the optic nerves. Then I went out. The whole evening, even in the theatre – a mindless vaudeville – the name Lilith kept appearing inside me. I remember that I had read various things about it: a she-devil, Adam's first wife, the succubus of the Middle Ages.

I was dreadfully tired, and went home early. Once I was in

bed I fell asleep almost immediately. And I awoke almost as quickly, from contact with a body close to me. There was a woman in my room, beautiful as a vision, veiled in long, golden hair which crackled as it flowed over her shoulders. The web of gold gave off blue sparks.

And the strange thing was that I felt neither surprise nor terror. It seemed quite natural that she had come. I knew that this slim, supple body was that of my lover, the she-devil Lilith. Oh . . . I had known her before. It was surely not the first time I saw her. I knew those sweet lips, those bright, blue eyes with the tiny pupils which were mere slits, like those of a cat. And I looked for the little drop of blood she bore like a ruby on her lower lip. I knew that it was always there, trembling, on her pale-red mouth. The yellowish, dusky light too, in which I saw my room, seemed something long familiar.

But those were not thoughts going through my mind . . . there was only feeling . . . I felt everything . . . it was all inexpressibly clear and yet impossible to put into words. Just like the thoughts you might have of music . . . or colours . . . I don't know how to put it. On this and other nights, thoughts that took the form of words, ideas, were something alien, crudely physical, that would have torn me from her arms.

Imagine you could perceive sounds, harmonies with all your senses . . . feel, smell, see them . . . No! I can't tell you what it was like . . . It was bliss. I dissolved into a dark, purple flame . . . I fainted from joys that no one can even guess at. I swirled up in bewitching eddies of light . . . bodiless and yet feeling with all my senses . . . I was one with the woman, one single, godlike being . . .

When I was woken by the gentle shaking of my servant it was past midday. I got out of bed and staggered across the floor; I was dazed, tired, drained. There was a livid mark on my neck, and on the crumpled pillow a shining spot. It was blood, Lilith's farewell kiss!

That day I avoided people. I did not want to see anyone. The light faded, evening came. I was in my bed once more, awaiting my lover, as my burning eyelids closed. But I slept the whole night through, a deep, dreamless sleep. She did not come, because I had not called her.

From that time on I lived for the night, and the day, with its noise and all its brightly lit ugliness, was a nightmare for me. At night I was a king, there was nothing on earth to compare with my glory, and I gave little heed to my wretched body, which paid for the flights of my spirit with fevers and anaemia. I regarded my body as a worthless machine, which was just to be kept going as long as possible. I could scarcely be bothered to have enough to eat.

But oh my friend, those nights! They all came when I called them in their months: Eve, the mother of mankind, in the beauty of her youth, with silky down on her arms and legs and a child's smile playing round her innocent lips; Astarte, the dark-brown goddess with the sultry eyes, dressed in gold, with cool, heavy jewellery; Selina, pale and sweet in her silver-blue tunic; Roxana with the scent of amber and yellow roses. With the blonde Poppaea I wandered through shimmering colonnades, her violet cloak rustling softly as I kissed her white face. Diana, supple and sunburnt, awaited me under the cork-oaks of the Pyrenees, and with Semiramis in her silver helmet I stood surrounded by the intoxicating glory of the blooms that filled her garden. Undine twined her thin girl's arms around me and, with a laugh, shook glittering drops from her green hair. To the dull thump of the hand drum, the piercing note of the whistle and the cascading harp Salome danced the dance that had once charmed Herod; her dark-green veils were spattered with the blood of John the Baptist. Oh, I can still hear Helen's soft, enchanting laughter and see the broad, bronze belt which jingled as it slipped from her slim waist . . .

Ah, my lost bliss! Finally I did what was forbidden. The idea lodged within me and tormented me: Nahema! I struggled and suffered. And I was defeated. On the first day of June . . .

I called her. She was the most beautiful of all and wore a wide cloak, grey and fine as the wings of a bat. Beside her everything seemed lifeless, pain and joy knew no bounds, every nerve seemed to respond individually, every sensation to grow to an extreme of intensity. I wept tears of joy and waited for the night, I only started to live when twilight fell, the twilight that was the colour of her cloak. And she came, night after night. The other stones had lost their power for me.

Then came the horror. It came wrapped in her cloak. Her divine body began to change . . . every night she seemed older . . . wrinkles appeared on her forehead . . . ugly shadows ringed her eyes. Years seemed to separate one night from the next.

In the end she was a lemur with loose, parchment skin and a toothless mouth. She tortured me with disgusting caresses. She came every night . . . and . . . she told me I must die . . . so that she might be rejuvenated. I must kill myself. She said it all the time, even by day she whispered it in my ear. The man in Vienna had been compelled to obey. In German *Folter* means . . . torture . . .'

Kerdac suddenly let out a shrill cry and opened his eyes wide. His jaw fell to his chest.

Dr. Klaar started violently and bent down to him: Jerome Kerdac was dead. A little black blood trickled out of the bullet-wound. The doctor called the servant and went down the staircase with unsteady steps. He took the casket with him.

He had already been sitting for more than four hours looking through the mask. The thin, polished aquamarine glowed a greenish-blue before his throbbing eye. There was a deathly hush in the room. He had spoken the name and seen a little cloud form, but his reason kept watch and woke him from his trance again and again. My God! It was nonsense! Angrily he tore off the mask and rubbed his inflamed eye.

It was one of those evenings when the heart of the lonely is seized with a wild melancholy, a leaden sense of lost time; one of those days when withered hopes and desires we thought dead assert their power over us. Then we are visited by a dismal procession of thoughts and ideas, which we imagined we had long since overcome.

Dr. Klaar made his glum way home from the third-class inn

where the young doctors used to take their meals. He almost burst into tears at the sight of his room with the smoking lamp, the furniture upholstered in cheap cotton rep and the ugly, cold stove. But then he managed to pull himself together and put his mood down to the nervous strain of the events of the afternoon. After that he calmed down a little.

It was the second time he had woken with a start. Something wet or cold had touched his face and he had the impression that a faint shadow had moved away from his bed and evaporated in the darkness of one of the corners of the room. He rubbed his eyes and blinked at the steady flame of the nightlight. Then he went back to sleep.

A few minutes later he gave such a violent start that he was out of bed before he was completely awake. Something was scurrying away from him . . . the figure of a girl, almost transparent . . . now it was gone. On the bedside rug were two elongated damp patches, on the floor the damp marks of tiny, slim feet . . .

Dr. Klaar gave a scream like a startled animal. The dampness quickly evaporated and the floor took on its old appearance again. The doctor was still standing by his bed, babbling to himself.

And then he gave another scream. 'Undine! That is madness! I'm going mad . . .'

Quivering all over, he tore open the window. Icy autumnal air flowed over his face. He collapsed in a trembling fit and clasped his head in both hands as he crouched on the floor. Then he jumped up, grabbed the casket like one possessed and tipped the stones out; one after the other he flung them into the darkness, and down below the brittle discs splintered on the cobblestones. The parchment and mask he held over the flickering candle; he did not feel the flame as it blazed up round his fingers.

Shivering, he sat on a hard wooden chair in the middle of the room, waiting in mortal fear for the clear, grey light of dawn which was slowly, slowly creeping across the roofs.

Sergeant Anton Lerch

Hugo von Hofmannsthal

On the 22nd of July, 1848, before six o'clock in the morning, a reconnaissance party, the second squadron of Wallmoden's Cuirassiers, one hundred and seven cavalrymen under the command of their captain, Baron Rofrano, set off from the mess in San Alessandro and rode towards Milan. The whole of the open, shining landscape was immersed in an indescribable calm; from the peaks of the distant mountains morning cloud rose into the gleaming sky like silent smoke-clouds; the maize stood motionless, and villas and churches shone out from among groves of trees that looked as if they had been washed. Scarcely had the troop advanced a mile beyond the last out-posts of their own army than they saw the glint of arms among the maize fields and their advance party announced enemy infantry. The squadron formed up by the road for the attack. The bullets hissing over their heads with a strangely loud noise, almost a miaow, they charged across the fields, driving a company of men with a variety of weapons in front of them like quails. They were men from Manara's Legion with strange headgear. The prisoners were put in the charge of a corporal and eight men and sent to the rear. The advance party reported suspicious figures outside a beautiful villa with a drive flanked by ancient cypresses leading up to it. Sergeant Anton Lerch dismounted, took twelve men armed with rifles, surrounded the windows and captured eighteen students from the Pisa Legion, all handsome, well-mannered young men with white hands and long hair. Half an hour later the squadron captured a man in the dress of a peasant from Bergamo who aroused suspicion by his exaggeratedly harmless and inconspicuous behaviour. Sewn into his coat lining were extremely important and detailed plans regarding the setting-up

87

of a volunteer corps in the Giudicaria and its cooperation with the Piedmontese army. Around ten o'clock in the morning a herd of cattle fell into their hands. Immediately afterwards they were opposed by a strong enemy detachment, from which they came under fire from behind a graveyard wall. The front line under their lieutenant, Count Trautsohn, jumped the low wall and cut down the enemy as they rushed between the graves in confusion before the greater part of them escaped into the church and then out through the sacristy door into a dense thicket. The twenty-seven new prisoners stated that they were Neapolitan volunteers under papal officers. The squadron had one dead. A detail, consisting of Corporal Wotrubek and dragoons Holl and Haindl, rode round the thicket and came upon a light howitzer drawn by two horses which they took by slashing with their swords at the guards, grabbing the horses by the bridle and forcing them round. As he had sustained a slight wound, Corporal Wotrubek was sent back to headquarters to report the successful skirmishes and other pieces of good fortune. The prisoners were again sent back, but the howitzer was retained by the squadron which, after the escort had left, still numbered seventy-eight men.

Since, according to their statements, the various prisoners were unanimous that Milan had been completely abandoned by enemy troops, both regular and irregular, and had been denuded of guns and other military equipment, the captain could not resist giving both himself and the dragoons the opportunity of riding into this large and beautiful city, lying there defenceless. Amid the peal of the midday bells, the four trumpets sounding a thunderous advance to the steely glitter of the sky, jingling against a thousand window-panes and sparkling in reflection on seventy-eight cuirasses: seventy-eight upraised naked blades; the streets left and right like a disturbed ant-hill, filling with astonished faces; figures disappearing, blanching and cursing, in house doorways, drowsy windows thrust open by the bare arms of unknown beauties; past Santa Babila, San Felde, San Carlo, the famous marble cathedral, San Satiro, San Giorgio, San Lorenzo, San Eustorgio;

their ancient bronze doors all opening and the hands of silver saints and bright-eyed women in brocade waving from the candlelight and clouds of incense; ever on the alert for shots from a thousand attics, dark entrances, low shops, seeing nothing but adolescent girls and boys with their white teeth and dark hair; looking out on all this from a trotting horse with gleaming eyes from behind a mask of blood-spattered dust; in by the Porta Venezia, out by the Porta Ticinese: thus the fine squadron rode through Milan.

Not far from the latter gate, where there was an esplanade planted with handsome plane trees, Sergeant Lerch thought he saw a female face that he recognised at the ground-floor window of a newly built, bright yellow house. Curiosity made him turn round in the saddle and, since at the same time his horse started stepping rather awkwardly, so that he suspected it had picked up a stone in one of its front shoes, since also he was at the rear of the squadron and could fall out without fuss, all this made him decide to dismount, which he did after he had guided his horse so its front half was in the entrance of the house in question. Hardly had he lifted the second white-socked forefoot of his bay, to check the hoof, than the door of a room in the house which gave directly onto the entrance actually opened to reveal a buxom, almost young woman in somewhat dishevelled dishabille, and a bright room with window-boxes, in which were a few pots of basil and some red geraniums plus a mahogany cabinet and a group of mythological figures in biscuit ware, became visible behind her to the sergeant, whilst at the same time in a pier glass his sharp eye spotted the opposite wall, which was taken up by a large white bed and a concealed door, through which a corpulent, clean-shaven, oldish man was just retreating.

Meanwhile, however, the sergeant had remembered the woman's name and many other things besides: that she was the widow or divorced wife of a Croatian corporal in the pay corps, that nine or ten years ago in Vienna he had spent a number of evenings, often late into the night, with her, in company with another man, her actual lover at that time, and now his eyes sought her former slim but voluptuous form beneath her present plumpness. She, however, stood there and smiled at him in a slightly flattered Slav manner, which sent the blood pulsing through his strong neck and behind his eyes, whilst a certain affectation in the way she spoke to him, as well as her dishabille and the room furnishings, somewhat intimidated him. At that moment however, as he watched a large fly crawl over the comb stuck in her hair and concentrated solely on raising his hand to drive the fly away and then letting it fall onto the back of her white, warm yet cool neck, he was filled from head to toe with the sense of the victorious skirmishes and other good fortune of the day, so that his heavy hand drew her head toward him, and said, 'Vuic' – her surname had certainly not crossed his lips for ten years and her first name he had forgotten – 'in a week we are going to move into the city and these will be my quarters,' nodding in the direction of the half-opened door to the room. As he was speaking, he heard several doors slam in the house and felt his horse pulling him away, first of all by a mute tug at the bridle, then by a neigh to the other horses. He mounted and rode off after the squadron without any other answer from Frau Vuic than an embarrassed laugh as she threw her head back. But the words he had spoken asserted their power. Slightly aside from the main column and no longer riding at such a smart trot under the heavy, metallic glow of the sky, his vision trapped in the cloud of dust accompanying them, the sergeant became more and more immersed in the room with the mahogany furniture and pots of basil and at the same time in a civilian atmosphere, which still had a martial tinge, an atmosphere of comfort and agreeable violence with no officer to give him orders, a life in slippers, the hilt of his sabre sticking through the left-hand pocket of his dressing gown. The corpulent, clean-shaven man, who had disappeared through the concealed door, something half way between a priest and a retired valet, played an important role in his daydreams, almost more than the beautiful, wide bed and Frau Vuic's delicate white skin. At times the clean-shaven man played the role of a deferential friend on familiar terms with him who recounted court gossip, brought tobacco and capons, at others he had his arm twisted, was forced to pay for Lerch's silence, was associated with all kinds of subversive activities, was in collusion with the Piedmontese, a papal cook, a procurer, the owner of suspicious properties with dark summer-houses for political meetings, and he grew into a huge, bloated figure in whose body you could drill twenty bung-holes and draw off gold instead of blood.

There were no new incidents for the patrol during the afternoon, and no restraint on the sergeant's daydreaming. But a thirst for unexpected rewards, for bounties, for ducats suddenly dropping into his pockets had been aroused within him. It was the thought of his first entry into the room with the mahogany furniture that was the splinter in his flesh around which his desires and lusts festered.

When towards evening, then, as the squadron, with the horses fed and reasonably rested, was attempting to advance by a roundabout route towards Lodi and the bridge over the Adda, where they could expect to come into contact with the enemy, the sergeant saw a village with a partly ruined bell-tower that lay aside from the main road in a darkening hollow, so heated was his imagination that he found it temptingly suspicious and, signalling dragoons Holl and Scarmolin to accompany him, left the main body of the squadron to ride off into the village, hoping to surprise a general with a modest escort and attack him or somehow or other earn a quite exceptional bonus. When they reached the squalid place, which appeared deserted, he ordered Scarmolin and Holl to ride round outside the houses, the one on the left, the other on the right, whilst he, his pistol in his hand, prepared to gallop down the street. But soon, finding himself on hard flagstones, over which, moreover, some slippery, greasy substance had been poured, he was forced to rein in his horse and continue at a walk. There was a deathly hush in the village; not a child, not a bird, not a breath of air. On either side were small grubby houses from which the plaster had all flaked off; here and there something obscene had been drawn in charcoal on the bare bricks; looking in through doorposts that were devoid of paint, the sergeant saw, here and there, a lazy, half-naked figure lounging on a pallet or dragging itself about the room, as with dislocated hips. His horse seemed heavy-legged and put down its back feet as if they were made of lead. As he was turning round to check its rear shoes, shuffling footsteps emerged from a house, and when he straightened up there was a female, whose face he could not see, crossing right in front of his horse. She was only half dressed; her torn and dirty skirt was dragging in the gutter and she wore dirty slippers on her bare feet; she crossed so close in front of the horse that the breath from its nostrils ruffled the shining, greasy chignon hanging down below an old straw hat over her bare neck, but she did not hurry at all or try to avoid the rider. Two bleeding rats with their teeth sunk into each other rolled out from under a doorway on the left into the middle of the street and the one that was coming off worse gave such a pitiful squeal that the Sergeant's horse pulled up and stared at the ground, its head to one side and breathing audibly. Slight pressure from the Sergeant's knees set it moving again, but by that time the woman had disappeared into a house without him having been able to have a look at her face. From the next house a dog rushed out, head raised, dropped a bone in the middle of the street and tried to bury it in a gap between the flagstones. It was a grubby white bitch with drooping dugs; it scraped away with fiendish determination, then grabbed the bone in its teeth and carried it off a little way. By the time it began scraping again, three dogs had already joined it: two were very young, with soft bones and loose skin; without barking or being able bite, they pulled at each other's chaps with their blunt teeth. The dog that had come at the same time was a light yellow greyhound whose body was so swollen its four thin legs could only carry it along very slowly. At the end of the fat body that was as taut as a drum, the head appeared much too small; its tiny, restless eyes held a horrible expression of pain and apprehension. Immediately two more dogs came running along: a skinny, white one of an exceptionally voracious ugliness, with black furrows running down from its inflamed eyes, and a half-bred dachshund with too-long legs. The latter raised its head and looked at the sergeant. It must have been very old. Its eyes were infinitely tired and sad. But the bitch scurried mindlessly back and forth in front of the rider; the two puppies snapped silently with their soft muzzles at the horse's fetlocks, while the greyhound dragged its grotesque body close to its hooves. The bay was unable to move. The sergeant drew his pistol to shoot one of the animals, but when it did not go off, he dug in both his spurs and clattered off over the flagstones. After a few steps, however, he had to rein in sharply. His way was barred by a cow that a boy was dragging by a taut rope to the slaughter. But the cow, shrinking back at the reek of blood and the sight of the fresh skin of a black calf nailed to the doorpost, braced its feet, sucked in the sun-kissed evening air though its flared nostrils and, before the boy had time to use the rope or his stick, grabbed with a pitiful look a mouthful of the straw the sergeant had fixed to the front of his saddle. Then he had the last house of the village behind him and, riding between two low, tumbledown walls, could see the road continuing over an old, single-span stone bridge across an apparently dry ditch, but he sensed such an indescribable heaviness in his horse's gait, such a lack of progress, that each single foot of the walls to his right and left, even each centipede and woodlouse sitting on it, crept past laboriously out of his vision, and he felt as if he had spent an immeasurable time riding through this foul village. His horse now started to breathe with a heavy, rasping sound, but he did not immediately recognise the unaccustomed noise and, as he was looking for the cause of it, at first above or beside him and then in the distance, he noticed on the other side of the stone bridge and, as it happened, at the same distance from it as himself, a soldier from his own regiment approaching, a sergeant on a bay with white socks on its front legs. As he was well aware that there was no such horse in the squadron, apart from the one on which he was himself mounted at that moment, and as he still could not recognise the face of the other rider, he impatiently spurred on his horse to a lively trot, at which the other increased his speed by the same amount, so that now they were only a stone's throw away from each other; and then, as the two horses, each from its own side, each at the same moment, stepped onto the bridge with the same white-socked forefoot, and the sergeant, with a fixed stare recognising himself in the rider, pulled up his horse and stretched out his right hand with the fingers spread against the apparition, at which the figure, similarly reining in and raising its right hand, was suddenly no longer there, Holl and Scarmolin, looking completely unconcerned, suddenly appeared from the right and the left out of the dry ditch and at the same time, from across the pasture-land, loud and not very far off, came the squadron's trumpets sounding the attack. Taking a rise in the ground at a full gallop, the sergeant saw the squadron already galloping towards a copse, from which enemy cavalry armed with lances was rapidly pouring out. Then, as he gathered the four loose reins in his left hand, he saw the fourth troop separate from the squadron and slow down, and now he was already galloping across the reverberating ground, already in the choking dust, already in the middle of the enemy, struck at a blue arm holding a lance, saw close beside him the Captain's face with eyes wide open and teeth bared fiercely, then suddenly he was hemmed in all round by hostile faces and foreign uniforms, plunged into a sea of brandished swords, stabbed the nearest in the neck and off his horse, saw next to him Scarmolin, with a laugh on his face, slash the fingers off a soldier's rein-hand and cut deep into the horse's neck, felt the mêlée slacken, and suddenly found himself alone, on the edge of a small stream, chasing an enemy officer on a grey stallion. The officer tried to take the stream, the grey refused. The officer pulled it round, turning his young, very pale face and the mouth of a revolver towards the sergeant at the moment the point of his sabre entered his mouth, the whole force of a galloping horse concentrated in its tiny point. The sergeant pulled out his sword and grabbed, in the place where the officer's fingers had released it as he fell, the snaffle of the grey, which lifted its hooves, lightly and delicately as a deer, over its dying master.

As sergeant Anton Lerch rode back with his handsome prize the sun, setting into a thick haze, cast an intense red glow over the pasture-land. Even places with no hoof-marks seemed covered in pools of blood. The red glow was reflected back onto the white uniforms and laughing faces, their cuirasses and saddle-cloths glistened and gleamed, and reddest of all were three small fig trees on which the laughing cavalrymen had wiped the grooves of their sabres clean. To the side of the red-stained trees stood the captain, and beside him the squadron trumpeter; his trumpet looked as if it had been dipped in red juice as he raised it to his lips and sounded the roll call. The sergeant rode past each platoon and saw that the squadron had not lost one single man and captured nine extra mounts. He rode up to the captain to report, the grey still by his side, its head raised, stepping lightly and sniffing the air like the handsome, vain young horse it was. The captain had only half an ear for his report. He beckoned over Lieutenant Count Trautsohn, who immediately dismounted and, with six dragoons who had similarly dismounted, went behind the line of the squadron to unhitch the light howitzer they had captured, and had the six men drag it to one side and drop it into a marshy place formed by the stream, after which he remounted and, first driving off the now superfluous two draught-horses by hitting them with the flat of his sword, silently resumed his place at the front of the first platoon. Whilst this was being done, the squadron, which had formed up in two sections, was not actually restless, but there was a somewhat unusual atmosphere, that might be explained by four victorious skirmishes in one day, and that surfaced in soft outbreaks of repressed laughter as well as muttered calls to each other. The horses were not standing still either, especially those which had the captured mounts inserted between them. After such good fortune all felt the space to line up in was too restricted, such victorious cavalry should be charging in open formation against new opponents, slashing at them and seizing new prize horses. At that moment the captain, Baron Rofrano, rode close up to the front of the squadron and, opening wide the large lids of his rather sleepy blue eyes, ordered clearly, though without raising his voice, 'Release the extra mounts.' There was a deathly hush throughout the squadron. Only the grey beside the sergeant stretched its neck and almost touched the forehead of the horse on which the captain was sitting with its nostrils. The captain put away his sabre, drew one of his pistols from its holster and, wiping away a speck of dust from the shining barrel with the hand holding the reins, repeated his order in a slightly louder voice and immediately afterwards counted 'One' and 'Two.' After he had counted 'Two' he fastened his clouded gaze on the sergeant, who was sitting motionless in the saddle in front of him, staring fixedly at his face. Whilst Anton Lerch's fixed, unflinching gaze, in which there was just an occasional flicker of dog-like anguish which immediately died away, seemed to express a kind of fawning trust, which was the result of many years under the Captain's command, it was not the immense tension of this moment which filled his consciousness, but a diverse flood of images of an alien comfort, and from depths of his being of which he himself was completely unaware there rose a bestial rage directed at the man before him who was going to take away his horse, such a terrible rage at the face, voice, posture and whole being of the man, as can only be created in some mysterious way by years of living in close proximity. Whether something similar was going on inside the captain, or whether he felt the whole silently infectious peril of critical situations was concentrated in this moment of mute insubordination is uncertain: with a casual, almost affected movement, he raised his arm and, curling his lip contemptuously, counted 'Three.' The shot rang out and the sergeant, hit through the forehead, slumped forward onto the neck of his horse and then fell to the ground between the bay and the grey stallion. But his body had not struck the ground before all the NCOs and men had got rid of their captured horses with a kick or a tug of the reins, and the captain, calmly putting his pistol away, was once more able to lead the squadron, still quivering as if from a bolt of lightning, against the enemy, which appeared to be rallying in the blurred, twilit distance. But the enemy declined the renewed attack, and shortly afterwards the patrol reached the southern outpost of their own army without further incident.

The Death of Christoph Detlev Brigge of Ulsgard

Rainer Maria Rilke

From: *The Papers of Malte Laurids Brigge*

Whenever I think of home, where there is no one left any more, then I imagine it must have been different in former times. In those days people knew (or at least they sensed) that they had death *inside* them, as the fruit has its seed. Children had a small death inside them, adults a large one. The women had it in their womb and the men in their chest. They *had* it there, and that gave them a peculiar dignity and quiet pride.

With my grandfather, the old chamberlain, you could still tell just by looking at him that he bore his death within him. And what a death it was: it lasted for two months, and was so loud that it could be heard on the outlying parts of the estate.

The long, narrow manor house was too small for this death, it looked as if we would have to add wings, for the chamberlain's body grew bigger and bigger and he was constantly demanding to be carried from one room to another and would fall into a dreadful rage if the day was not yet over and there was no room left in which he had not already lain. Then off up the stairs went the whole procession – servants, maids and dogs, which he always had about him – led by the steward, into the room in which his mother had died, which had been kept exactly in the state in which she had left it, twenty-three years ago, and which no one had been allowed to enter since. The curtains were opened, and the sturdy light of a summer afternoon examined all the shy, startled objects and pirouetted clumsily in the gaping mirrors. And the people were just the same. There were lady's maids whose curiosity was so aroused that they had no idea where their hands were, young servants who stared at everything, and old servants who went round trying to remember all the things they had been told about this locked room, where they now had the good fortune to find themselves.

But it was the dogs above all, who seemed to be uncommonly excited at being in a room in which all the things smelt. The tall, slender Russian greyhounds ran busily to and fro behind the armchairs, traversed the chamber with their long, rocking dance-steps, stood up like dogs on a coat of arms and, resting their slim paws on the white and gold window-sill, looked with pointed, expectant faces and receding foreheads to the right and to the left down into the courtyard. Little dachshunds, the colour of new gloves, sat in the broad, silk-covered chair by the window, an expression on their faces as if everything was as usual, and a bristle-haired, grumpy-looking pointer rubbed its back against the edge of a gold-legged table whilst on the painted top the Sèvres cups trembled.

It was a terrible time for those absent-minded, sleepy objects. It sometimes happened that books would be opened clumsily by some hasty hand and rose petals would tumble out, to be trampled underfoot; tiny, delicate things were grasped and, when they immediately broke, were quickly put back down again, some objects that had been bent were put behind curtains, or even thrown behind the golden trellis of the fireguard. And from time to time something fell, fell with a dull thud onto the carpet, with a ringing crack onto the parquet, but it broke on the spot, it shattered with a sharp crash or split almost noiselessly, for these things, pampered as they were, could not stand the least fall.

And had it occurred to anyone to ask what was the cause of all this, what had called down this wealth of destruction on that room, that had been so anxiously guarded, then there would have been one answer alone: death.

The death of the chamberlain, Christoph Detlev Brigge of Ulsgard. For he, bulging hugely out of his dark blue uniform, was lying in the middle of the floor and not moving. The eyes in his large, alien, unrecognisable face were closed; he did not see what was happening. At first they had tried to lay him on the bed, but he had resisted, for he had come to hate beds since those first nights in which his illness had grown. Also, the bed up in that room had turned out to be too small, and there had been nothing left for it but to put him down on the carpet; he had refused to go downstairs again.

There he lay, and one might have thought he had died already. As it was slowly beginning to get dark, the dogs, one after the other, had left through the half-open door, only the wire-haired pointer with the grumpy expression was sitting beside his master, and one of his broad, shaggy paws lay on Christoph Detlev's large grey hand. Now, too, most of the servants were outside in the white corridor, where it was lighter than in the room; those, however, who had stayed in the room, darted occasional, covert glances at the huge, darkening heap in the middle, wishing that it were nothing more than a large suit of clothes over some broken thing.

But there was still something. There was a voice, the voice that no one had known seven weeks ago. It was not Christoph Detlev, to whom this voice belonged, it was Christoph Detlev's death.

For many, many days now, Christoph Detlev's death had been living at Ulsgard, and talking to everyone, and demanding. It demanded to be carried, demanded the Blue Room, demanded the small salon, demanded the dining hall. Demanded the dogs, demanded that they laugh, talk, play and be quiet and all at the same time. Demanded to see friends, women and men who had died, and demanded to die itself: demanded. Demanded and screamed.

For, when the night had come and those of the exhausted servants who were not sitting at his bedside were trying to get to sleep, Christoph Detlev's death would scream, scream and groan and roar so long and so incessantly that the dogs, which at first joined in with their howls, fell silent and did not dare lie down and, standing on their long, slim, quivering legs, were afraid. And when, across the wide, silver, Danish summer night, those in the village heard his roaring, they got out of bed, as they did during a storm, dressed and stayed sitting round a lamp without saying a word until it was past. And pregnant women who were close to their time were put into the farthest rooms and into the cupboard beds behind the most solid doors; but they heard it, they heard it as if it were in their own bodies, and they begged to be allowed to get up, and came, white and wide-eyed, and sat down with the others with their blurred faces. And the cows that were calving at that time were helpless and withdrawn, and one foetus that refused to come was torn, dead, with all the entrails from the cow's body. And all did their daily tasks badly and forgot to bring in the hay, because during the day they feared the night and because they were so weary from being startled into wakefulness and staying up so long that they could not concentrate on anything. And when they went to the white, peaceful church on Sunday they prayed there might be no more Lord of Ulsgard, for this lord was a terrible lord. And from the pulpit the minister proclaimed aloud what they were all thinking and praying, for he too had lost his nights and could not understand God. And it was proclaimed by the bell, which had found a fearful rival which sounded the whole night through and against which it was powerless, even if it set all its metal ringing. Everyone proclaimed it, and there was one of the young men who had dreamt he went to the castle and murdered the master with his dung-fork, and they were all so incensed, so overwrought, that they all listened as he told his dream, and, without at all realising it, looked at him to see if he were up to such a deed. That was what people felt and said in the whole area where a few weeks before everyone had loved the chamberlain and felt sorry for him. But although that was what people said, nothing was changed. Christoph Detlev's death, that was residing at Ulsgard, refused to be rushed. It had come for ten weeks, and ten weeks it stayed. And during those weeks it was more of a lord than Christoph Detlev Brigge had ever been, it was like a king people call 'the Terrible', later on and for ever.

It was not the death of some ordinary man with the dropsy, this was the evil, princely death that the chamberlain had borne within him throughout his life and nourished with his own substance. All the excess of pride, will power and lordly strength, which he had been unable to use up, even in his calm days, had entered into his death, into the death that now sat at Ulsgard, squandering.

What a look would the chamberlain have given any man who had demanded he should die a different death than this one. He died a hard death.

Signor Scurri
or
Herr von Yb's Strange Voyage to the Seaside

Fritz von Herzmanovsky-Orlando

The story that follows will perhaps appear a little absurd to some readers, and at one particular point it even exudes an unpleasant and mysteriously compelling potency. In spite of that, it will be found to be infinitely instructive, especially for the younger generation, since the foundations of their out-look rest on the shifting sands of logical principles which are hopelessly out-of-date and no longer sufficient for the age of cosmic tension in which we live. In my opinion, a story such as this should be included in school anthologies for the sixth form: displayed among the classical columns of worthy native prose and the plaster torsos of officially sanctioned poetry, it can only be all the more effective. As to its truth, there can be no doubt at all. My friend, Achatius von Yb, was already of mature years at the time of the experiences I am about to relate, which he confided to me in a quiet moment; moreover he was a man who was most honourable, truthful and – as this story will show – punctilious to the point of excess.

Destiny had laid him in a magnificent cradle of gold, or rather, as precision is our aim, in a cradle of ebony inlaid with the most fantastic and confusing patterns of imitation ivory, as the tyrannical fashion of the *Deuxième Empire* demanded. In spite of all this ivory splendour and in spite of the stylish matching musical chamber pot, our hero's path through life was overgrown with – and this is no exaggeration – thistles the height of houses. The devil only knows in what conjunc-tion the great constellations stood, which thundered out the hour of his birth! At that time no one thought of casting horoscopes. The people who do that now were in those days making their living partly by dealing in insect powders and patent remedies for corns, and partly through advertisements with graphic illustrations which promised, depending on sex, an ample bosom or luxuriant moustache. It was an age of liberalism, an age of enlightenment; rubber galoshes were the latest thing, and everyone who was anyone at all was proud to trace their ancestry back to the ape, as was demonstrated daily and with crystal clarity by Science triumphant. Respectable families almost came to blows in the course of impassioned debates on the feasibility and advantages of horse-drawn trams, and on such occasions many an idealistic son was told never to darken the paternal door again, so that he left to seek his fortune in America or some other primitive country.

But even these luminous times still had their fortune-telling gypsies. One such forced her way to the bed, where von Yb's mother lay in the throes of childbirth, and proclaimed in prophetic tones that the child should beware of water . . . of great quantities of water . . . and of dung . . . yes, of dung too . . . in fact, of anything connected with waste products, she added, staring fixedly into the distance.

It gave Frau von Yb a terrible shock; moreover, she was furious that such common things as water and dung should be mentioned in a refined household such as hers, and refused the witch payment. At that, the rather grubby spawn of the land of the Pharaohs made her departure amid a splutter of curses.

It soon became apparent that the seed of her prophecy had fallen on fruitful ground. Age of Science or no, a family council was called, chaired by Uncle Doublear (a man known throughout the city for his caution: he even had a tiny lightning-conductor on his top-hat complete with silver chain dragging along the ground behind). Everyone was in complete agreement that, as far as little Achaz's future career was concerned, there were two things that must be avoided at all costs: he should never become an admiral, nor a member of the landed gentry. Instead, Uncle Doublear recommended a dry profession, guaranteed free from all contact with waste products: the boy should suck at the breasts of Science. The ladies leapt up in indignation and a flush of modesty ... but they were mollified somewhat when they realised that that was Uncle Doublear's flowery way of saying that Achatius von Yb should become a scholar of note, which was agreed upon.

I had the pleasure of making his acquaintance at the Congress of the Academy of Science, an occasion, by the way, on which more violent passions were aroused than at any other meeting of that august body. Someone stirred up a veritable hornet's nest with his question as to whether it was Archimedes or Ramon Lull who should be regarded as the inventor of the game of solitaire. It set off a furious squawking; bald-headed luminaries dashed heavy tomes to the ground in clouds of dust, or, trembling with passion, grabbed each other by the buttons of their frock coats; some even spat at each other's feet. Only the sudden appearance of a scholarly profile with an icy glint in his spectacles brought some light into the dark confusion. It was the great physicist, Ernst Mach, and my admiration for him dates from that first meeting. There was a gentleman beside me who was literally crowing with enthusiasm. We shook hands, and that was how I made the acquaintance of Achatius von Yb, whom I was to meet again so many years later and under such melancholy circumstances.

At the time of our first meeting he must have been in his early thirties, though his age was impossible to determine. His sparse, silky-thin hair was colourless, his posture somewhat hunched, his dress slovenly and, although of the very best quality, always looked crumpled and faded, even when it had just come from the tailor. His parents, who had died early, while he was still at university, had occupied a genteelly sombre apartment in a district of monumental architecture of which they had assigned to him a suite of rooms looking out onto the courtyard. Even after the death of his parents, von Yb continued to inhabit his gloomy bachelor's chambers, absorbed in abstruse studies and bizarre reflections. For all that, he was no misanthrope. Twice a year he gave great soirées, when his house would blaze with the light of count-less candles and the salons, empty for the rest of the year, would glitter with the illusion of life. When they were over, the deathly silence would gather round him again, and for months he would not leave his quarters. It would never have occurred to anyone to prophesy that one day he would have to scurry shyly from one to another of fifty cheap lodging houses, and all because of a minor lapse that was the result of an unguarded moment.

It began one morning when Herr von Yb left his dark-panelled study, to which in the early summer only an occasional stray beam of gold penetrated (when one did, it produced a bewitching display of melancholy brevity). He went to his library, a narrow room with a row of arched windows giving onto a small half-lit courtyard. Suddenly the unworldly scholar realised that the room, redolent with the smell of books, was brighter than usual. He went to one of the arched windows and saw up above, in the narrow opening of the courtyard, sunlight sparkling like jewels, saw a veritable orgy of glittering rays, saw a crystalline sky of that deep blue which usually only occurs over glaciers, and saw lustrous white clouds sailing across, like hosts of snowy angels in their swift flight. Deep down below, at the bottom of the courtyard, beside some mossy patches on the rough-hewn ashlar, a pitiful bird was twittering in its cage. Immediately opposite von Yb was a glassed-in corridor leading to the space where the trunks and cases were stored in the palatial house adjoining his own. In this room, with its jumble of luggage, an open gas flame burnt day and night in a frosted glass bowl; von Yb had often noticed it without paying any particular attention.

This time, however, the suggestive power of this combin-ation of circumstances was such that he was overcome with a longing he had never before experienced for the beauty of the world outside. With a joyful feeling such as only children feel on the eve of holidays, he set about realising this moment of inspiration. He resolved to go on a voyage, a long voyage in the course of which he would see the sea for the first time.

He decided on Genoa as the scene of the magnificent spectacle he was already looking forward to. This decision may well have been subconsciously motivated by the fact that his grandfather had fought with Radetzky in Northern Italy in 1849 and had laid down his life for his country there. Thus there was a blood tie with the region, and Herr von Yb, the grandson, set off, drawn by a some mysteriously compelling force to this Saxony beyond the Alps, a province that was mysterious and yet equally full of bourgeois enterprise.

After a pleasant journey in the half-empty midnight express he saw Carinthia through the morning mist. The train rushed along beside huge lakes, through gloriously dark-green forests then, finally, past gigantic peaks with a dusting of fresh snow piled one above the other, to reach the Italian frontier in the early afternoon. Here a new world began abruptly: dusty stone-built houses, a noticeable lack of trees, dirty washing fluttering in the breeze, donkey-carts in deserted streets and, permeating it all, a smell that was a mixture of oil, vinegary wine, smoke and the sickly-sweet stench of rooms where a corpse has been laid out. After an unnecessarily long delay for customs – it became obvious to von Yb that he was by now the only passenger – the journey continued. The train rattled at a truly frightening speed along the rocky precipices, was engulfed in the countless tunnels by a crescendo of inexplicable claps of thunder and scattered such a shower of sparks at every curve that the passenger had to duck.

With much clunking and clanking the train stopped at a small station. One excessively elegant lady got on, sat opposite von Yb and stared fixedly at him out of mysteriously large eyes. At the next station the apparition abandoned him and its place was taken by a man in black whose skinny frame was surmounted by a tiny, olive-yellow bird's head covered in deep furrows which were filled with a dark black patina such as is found on antique bronzes when they have just been dug up. After a while spent sunk in gloomy reflections, this man took a pinch of snuff from a little box, which then proceeded to emit the strains of a hymn to the long-lost General Palafox, the Hero of Saragossa. Then two large flies, which he must have brought with him, flew out. At this the man, clearly *au fait* with what was expected of a man of breeding, began to chase after them with a blue handkerchief, stepping, as he did so, rather heavily on von Yb's toes with his buckled shoes. This quite naturally led to a conversation. He was a Spaniard, explained the man in black, and this was the fourth time he had almost reached the frontier of Austria, the goal of a life-time's longing, and once more he had had to turn back because of a lack of money. Whilst von Yb was still wondering at the old man's disconcertingly high voice, the latter told him that he had been a priest and, in spite of his calling, had three times suffered knife-wounds, most recently and pain-fully whilst reading the lesson – from the *Lamentations of Jeremiah* – on the Maundy Thursday of the last Ordinary Jubilee.

Von Yb expressed his deepest sympathy and asked him why he had left the priesthood. At this the other muttered something about needing to be a whole man, shrugged his shoulders and stared silently out of the window; this he continued to do until the train drew into the station at Udine.

The station concourse echoed with noisy life. Everywhere there were bright lights, and the platform was overcrowded with people getting in the way of the porters and occasionally treading on sleeping children, who evidently regularly spent the night there. Our traveller was ushered into the restaurant, where bottles of icy sulphur water and pungently bitter liqueurs were ranged in rows of strident colour along a gilded sideboard which resembled a church altar. Generals in magnificent uniforms promenaded up and down with fat ladies with warts sprouting black hair who fanned themselves vigorously. The throng was enlivened by the twitter of strikingly pretty girls in gaudy dresses, some with combs in their hair and lace shawls.

As he was serving some southern dish, a waiter with an eerie, fixed glass eye extolled the charms of a girl who possessed an unusual physical defect. Von Yb rejected the suggestion with indignation. Deprived of his major source of income, the *garçon* tried to avenge himself by giving copper coins that were no longer legal tender in change: *soldi* from the last doge of Venice, one of the hastily minted coins of Theodor von Neuhof, the 'summer king' of Corsica praised by Voltaire; there was even an ornate admission token to a Neapolitan brothel from the time of Casanova. Von Yb was so delighted by them that he almost missed the shrill departure bell.

The train thundered off into the night. After only a short time, however, it started a mournful whistling, which rose and fell for several minutes, after which it stopped and then puffed its way back into the station.

Scarcely had it arrived than the station master and all available staff rushed to the engine, where a loud debate was carried on by everyone at once, gesticulating wildly with the lanterns. Von Yb joined the circle but, as the discussion was in the Friulian dialect, all he could make out was that 'It' had been seen, quite distinctly, and that now just the same would happen as had seventeen years ago. On no condition would they continue, neither he, Cesare, the driver, nor Pompeio, the stoker.

It did not matter whom von Yb asked, to him they were as silent as the grave. Eventually he found an old porter who, in return for an excessive tip, told him that it was the "funeral procession of the gnomes of Verona" which had never before been seen so close to Udine and which presaged disaster. And for the love of God his honour was not to tell on him, it would cost him his job, his livelihood; the ghostly apparition was an official railway secret that was kept carefully concealed from outsiders. There was no question of the journey continuing along this stretch of the railway. And indeed, the passengers were transferred to another train consisting of antiquated carriages from the earliest days of rail travel, which, only dimly lit and rocking gently, set off into the mild summer night.

Von Yb looked round the compartment. The atmosphere of the good old days of his grandparents struck a nostalgic chord that brought a tear to his eye. The ceiling was decorated with colourful tracery, the walls were neatly covered in waxcloth with a pattern of grey stars, the seats were deep and comfortable, the windows, rounded at the bottom as in old coaches, had bead-work loops to rest your arms in. He was about to lean back dreamily when he noticed a concealed door, which he would not have suspected in the confined space. His scholar's inquiring mind was immediately roused. He went into the neighbouring compartment.

To his not inconsiderable surprise he saw that it seemed to be a lady's dressing-room: it was littered with women's clothes and lingerie and filled with a delicate perfume. At the farther end there was another door. Von Yb, somewhat more tentatively this time, it must be admitted, opened it and could scarcely refrain from exclaiming out loud, so delightful was the picture that presented itself to his gaze:

In the middle of the room, bathed in a rosy glow from a hanging lamp, was a four-poster bed, on which a beautiful, raven-haired girl lay sleeping in an aesthetic pose.

After a few moments of ecstatic contemplation, von Yb returned, on tiptoe and totally confused, to his compartment.

Fortunately, it was not long before the ticket-collector appeared, making his acrobatic way along the footboard. In reply to his question, he was told that it was the youngest granddaughter of the celebrated dancer, Taglioni, who had died of cholera in 1854, that she owned the Port Said Opera House and that she had hired this carriage, formerly belonging to the Sardinian royal family, for her own personal use. Von Yb was in the chamberlain's quarters, added the shabbily dressed official, proffering a hand as hairy as a monkey's.

Scarcely had the guard – was that a satyr's smile playing round his lips? – disappeared, than von Yb was overcome with an unprecedented lust for adventure. To prise a large box of chocolates out of his case and slip over to the door to the shrine of the sleeping beauty was the work of a moment. His heart was beating in time to the muffled rhythm of the wheels. He was already on his knees beside her bed, brushing her half-open lips with a fleeting kiss, when he realised that he had no idea what to do next.

Just as he was about to stand up and slip out of the room,

the fair sleeper, still only half-awake, wrapped her arms around him and whispered, '*Oh . . . momognone mio . . .*'

Von Yb closed his eyes in rapture. He thought he was in paradise. But the very next moment his sleeping beauty was no longer half, but fully awake and shattered the spell with a scream of indignation after which he was drowned in a raging flood of Italian oaths. Von Yb was stunned; the only escape from his sheepish embarrassment that he could think of was to offer the box of chocolates wordlessly to the fury. And it did indeed produce an effect. Pouting, the fair maid devoured the delicious confection, calmed down and demanded to know, with an accent that had a delightful Levantine tinge, what von Yb thought he was doing in her compartment?

The latter maintained he had merely been looking for the way to the restaurant car for his usual bite of supper, but had strayed – it must have been the will of the gods – into her compartment and, whether consciously or unconsciously, he could not say, fallen down at her feet in adoration. Oh, if only he might hope! How gladly would he lay his life and his wealth at her feet! And, carried away by his unaccustomed ardour, he bent down towards her.

Once more it was his fate to be cruelly disappointed. The object of his fond desires placed a firm hand against his chest, gave him a brief, searching look then pushed him away with a toss of her fragrant locks. What on earth was he thinking! Never! She was a virginal priestess of art and wanted to have nothing to do with men. She knew all about them! Added to that, he wasn't even an artiste, one could see that at a glance; not a tenor, nor a lion-tamer, nor anything else.

Was there no hope at all? asked von Yb. Even if he could never take her hand in marriage, was there not a place, any place, that would keep him close to her, might they still not be good friends?

He was barking up the wrong tree there, was the angry reply. If that was his idea, then he would do better elsewhere, for example the Ziziani Theatre in Alexandria, Rue de la Porte, or the Palais de Danse in Damascus, or the *Friponnière* in Port Sudan! And so, goodbye!

It cut von Yb to the quick that he had never been trained for a real profession such as opera singing, mime, or at the very least fire-eating. Sadly he departed, casting a yearning glance back at the *belle dame sans merci*, who had already taken up a silver-framed mirror and was carrying out repairs to a portion of her gums that seemed to have aroused her displeasure. Sighing, he staggered back to his compartment, where he spent the night alone with his torment and many starving fleas, the latter presumably the property of the Italian State Railways.

A two-hour-long break for lunch in Mirandola gave von Yb the opportunity of admiring his unapproachable fellow-passenger as, in full dress and clouds of perfume, she took her meal, served by a snarling Arab in a white burnous and a pubescent Levantine girl with an amber complexion.

A timid attempt to make further advances got no farther than the connecting door, which was locked. Then the obliging guard offered to cause a slight derailment of the train, in the course of which von Yb would have the opportunity of rescuing the fair maiden; it would, however, cost at least five hundred lire. Von Yb rejected the offer with a shake of the head.

Shortly after sunset the guard's head reappeared against the lurid evening light with a reduced price of three hundred lire, but met with the same cold reception as before. He had no more success with his final offer of one hundred lire shortly before they entered the notorious Montegiove Tunnel, where smoky oil-lamps in front of decaying pictures of saints bore mute witness to countless accidents.

It was well on into the night when von Yb finally arrived in Genoa. Exhausted and alone in an exaggeratedly high-roofed, two-wheeled carriage with rattling windows, he drove through the narrow alleys that squeezed between the tall, dark houses. A ragamuffin with a coloured lantern on a long pole walked in front of his conveyance, which took von Yb to an old-fashioned hotel which, although respectable rather than luxurious, had been warmly recommended.

He immediately went to the restaurant, which was lit by a

few hissing gas-lamps. He could hardly keep his eyes open as he ate his dinner; hot waves of sleep washed over him, almost obliterating consciousness, and the few weary waiters took on almost ghostly form against a background that disappeared into darkness.

When he had finished his meal he called over the *maître d'hôtel* and asked, half asleep as he was, whether it would be possible to have a quick look at the sea. The head waiter replied with a nod and ordered one of his underlings to guide Herr von Yb. They passed through several gloomy corridors before reaching a door which the boy had difficulty opening. To von Yb's surprise – he had expected to step out into the street – they entered a fairly spacious storeroom where various herbs, empty wine bottles and all sorts of other junk were kept.

Where did they go now? von Yb asked the boy, who had lit the lamp.

The answer was odd: they were there. And the youth in his black tie and tails led him over to a small receptacle with a lid.

Von Yb immediately categorised it as a rubbish bin. His young cicerone took off the lid, and when von Yb gave him a questioning look he was told that the sea was in the bin.

It struck von Yb like an electric shock. He felt as if he were undergoing a dislocation of his personality, of his environment or of reality itself. What he saw beggared all description: within this mundane receptacle glowed the deepest, most luminant blue of an infinite abyss.

There was no doubt about it, that was the sea. His mind was thronged with words: Poseidon, Thetis, the sombre tones of Medusa. Just as he was about to exclaim, 'Thalatta, thalatta!' an inner voice thundered, 'Don't get carried away by your classical scholarship! It's crazy! That cannot possibly be the sea! Just think, infinity in a rubbish bin!?' – 'But why not, why not?' whispered Satan, whose telephone line has a connection to every human mind. 'Don't listen to the voice of so-called reason; it never learns anything new and will only allow you to accept the most banal facts as true, you poor soul . . .'

Unsure of himself, von Yb looked round in some confusion,

and saw the ancient *maître d'hôtel* with the Franz-Josef whiskers, who had followed them on silent, if somewhat flat feet and now, with much confidential clearing of the throat and an almost embarrassed wave of his serviette, began his tale, 'Yes, your honour, it is the sea. I know exactly what you feel, Your Honour, even though I am only a simple waiter. It is the sea, the genuine sea. Not the vulgar *kitsch* that is passed off as the sea to your common-or-garden tourist. I would never try to cheat your honour with anything like that, I, who had the honour of serving under your honour's grandfather in Radetzky's army in '49! I was company cook in Freydenplitz's Horse. Lively lads from Carinthia, all of them. We would have all gladly given our lives for the colonel. But fate decreed otherwise . . .'

The old waiter wiped a tear from his eye with his serviette before he continued, 'A Piedmontese bullet went right through your honour's late grandfather at the Battle of Mortara. It shattered my ankle whilst I was riding my steed through a hail of bullets, slicing up a Verona salami on my little portable chopping board to comfort the wounded. The bullet killed my packhorse, Schackerl, the dapple-grey who had twice been awarded the silver medal for bravery, the one that used to carry the so-called mounted coffee-urn on his broad back . . . And when I was discharged, as I was a war invalid, they gave me the sea as a kind of gratuity. Everyone was given something: one man a roundabout, another a licence for a barrel-organ, someone else the lease on a state tobacco shop, or a tame monkey in a French general's uniform. Yes. And I got the sea. The very same one the Holy Roman Emperor Rudolf is supposed to have had and that was afterwards kept in the treasury of the shrine at Mariazell. But they didn't like it there.'

Von Yb's head was spinning; he had difficulty in staying on his feet.

'Would your honour like to take a turn along the beach?' the waiter asked.

He took the unresisting von Yb by the arm and promenaded him round the garbage bin a few times. There was such a strong, fresh, tangy breeze blowing out of it that von Yb's hand went up involuntarily to hold onto his hat.

'Have a good look at it, your honour,' said the man with the Franz-Josef whiskers. 'Admiral Tegetthoff sailed his first ships on that as a boy.'

The strange dread, which all the time had kept von Yb fixed in a state between dreaming and waking, now seemed to grip him by the throat and take his breath away. He had to get away from here as quickly as possible, get away from the disturbing sound of that sea, from the mysteriously compelling sight of that blue abyss in the apparently harmless guise of a rubbish bin . . .

Like a man possessed, von Yb tore himself away and rushed out into the dark street. Tegetthoff . . . Mortara . . . Emperor Rudolf . . . the shrine at Mariazell . . . a blue abyss . . . the impressions of the last few minutes were rushing around inside his weary brain. Or was it merely himself, rushing along between the tall, dark houses of midnight Genoa?

He was brought to a halt by a shadowy, seething mass of bodies and, against his will, forced to look on as a massive, herculean silhouette disentangled itself from the silently grappling sailors, grabbed a Chinese stoker by one leg, swung him round in the air, in spite of all his wriggling, and smashed him against a door that glistened like bronze in the moonlight. It shattered with a splintering crack, and the wretched stoker was swallowed up by a black, yawning cavity. From a dimly-lit kitchen came the sound of sizzling fat and through another von Yb could see a hunchbacked writer dip his pen in the ink and scribble away. Farther along, a contralto of mature years struck the pose of a tragic mother as she practised an aria, whilst on the top floor grey, dripping washing was being hung out to dry, a task that had clearly been interrupted earlier. Suddenly a hysterical screaming rang out, a clattering and cursing, then a tangle of half-clothed figures erupted through the shattered door, and before von Yb had recovered from the shock, two pretty, full-bosomed girls with sparkling eyes had seized him and dragged him off.

Von Yb never could, or would, describe precisely what had

happened next. All he would say was that he had the feeling he was being quite well looked after. He could also remember a dream that kept recurring obstinately in which he was back in the Middle Ages as a palfrey being gently ridden by a lady round a flower-strewn meadow full of gushing streams.

He felt he had slept for several days and finally woken in a strange house. He was still somewhat the worse for wear but decided to set off straight away to see the sights of Genoa and . . . and . . . His head started to spin again and it was only with difficulty that he managed to remember what it was he had really wanted to see: the sea.

But he did not get that far. The two girls would not let him leave until he had paid a certain sum of money, which they counted out for him down to the last ha'penny on their nimble fingers. A sum which seemed rather high to him.

He looked for his well-filled wallet in his coat, he searched through every pocket and found nothing, nothing at all. The smiles gradually disappeared from the faces of the two girls, to be replaced by a businesslike seriousness.

When Herr von Yb, who was punctiliousness itself in money matters, tried to leave to fetch the money from his hotel, he found himself grabbed and detained by the two delicious creatures, who suddenly seemed to develop muscles of steel. They rolled up their sleeves and dragged the flabbergasted Herr von Yb down some dark steps and locked him in a musty cellar which smelt outrageously of sick poultry. The mildest of the insults they screamed through the bars sounded suspiciously like 'swindler.' He would not see the light of day, they shouted, until he had written a letter to his bank in Vienna that they would dictate to him! With that, they disappeared.

For a while von Yb tried to escape from his gloomy thoughts by declaiming to himself Goethe's immortal poem of 'the land where the lemon-trees grow, where through the foliage dark, golden oranges glow' in a variety of intonations. In the long run, however, even the most punctilious of scholars will be seized with despair when incarcerated in a disused chicken-run, and thus Achatius von Yb ended up staring wild-eyed at the sturdy if mildewed door that shut him off from the glories of Italy.

One day, after he had stared at it for a particularly long time, the miracle occurred. The door opened and, with the graceful step of the Goddess of Love herself, in walked his fair companion from the train journey, the dream-vision from the Pullman car. With a charming smile she approached, inspected the poor prisoner from head to toe through her lorgnon and maintained both her smile and her silence.

Bright red with shame, von Yb tried to think of an excuse to explain his presence here. Perhaps some reference to fascinating architectural features? But he was forestalled. The beautiful owner of the opera house in Port Said was looking for new singers for the chorus; she had heard, to her dismay, of the unfortunate situation that had befallen some distinguished visitor and recognised her former travelling-companion through the keyhole. She had come to bring him his freedom, more than that, even, to grant his deepest wish. No, not her hand in marriage, not that, but the place close to her that he had asked for so fervently. To put it in a nutshell, she was going to engage him. There was the contract, he only needed to sign. Then, however, he would be hers for the rest of his life.

'I am yours already!' cried von Yb in wild enthusiasm as he went down on one knee before her. 'But, my dearest, how can I serve you? I am a scholar, highly respected, it is true – I even have several honorary doctorates – but I am neither an actor nor a singer.'

'It is nothing like that that I have in mind,' was the amiable reply. 'It is something else. You know that in the south we like to fill the intervals of bloody tragedies with comic interludes. In my opera house, for example, we put the torture scene from *Tosca* on the open stage; every time it is greeted with thunderous applause and has to be encored. After that, of course, we need some comic relief . . . Let's not beat about the bush, any more. I want to use your undoubted talents as a buffoon to cheer up the audience during the intervals.'

Von Yb froze. He couldn't believe his ears. 'Buffoon?' he stammered. 'No. Impossible. Consider: a distinguished scholar . . . honorary doctorates . . .'

'Very well,' replied the vision, completely unmoved. 'Then you will stay here until the end of your days. Or rather, till the end of your money. They will squeeze every last penny out of you and then make sure you disappear, as has happened before to many an innocent traveller in this city with all its dark secrets. I would have bought your freedom and taken you with me, but as you don't want to come, adieu!' And she turned to leave.

What else could the unfortunate von Yb do but call back the pitiless mistress of the Port Said Opera and sign the paper which, with a smile on her lips, she held out for him.

As he put pen to paper, his brain seemed to be rent by an inner thunderclap. A buffoon! A buffoon for his whole life! And not even a chance of promotion, there was no career structure in buffoonery, no post of senior buffoon. If his grandfather had known, Arbogast Caspar Ferdinand von Yb, Lord of Upper and Lower Yb and member of the Upper House of the Estates of Carniola! Achatius gnawed at his bloodless lips.

Meanwhile the other signatory had inspected the document through the long lashes of her almond-shaped eyes. She gave a satisfied nod and handed her new recruit a banknote of a fairly high denomination: his signing-on fee. Then she indicated he should follow her. They were to go straight on board ship.

Von Yb went out into the street, with a sigh of relief, in spite of everything, keeping close behind his fair employer, who was leading him through dark alleyways towards the harbour.

Suddenly the thought flashed through his mind that now he would at least see the sea. For a few seconds he felt that fate had treated him kindly. But was it really the sea he was heading for? Was it the real sea? He felt dizzy, just as he had when the waiter with the Franz-Josef whiskers had taken him under his wing.

His companion was hurrying up. He could already hear the

screech of the sirens, the clank of the cranes. At most there could be one row of houses between him and the so-called sea.

'Flee!' It was like a flash of lightning in von Yb's tormented brain. 'Contract or no contract – flee!'

The screeching and clanking grew louder and louder, filling him with dread. He was still following his new mistress, who was striding along even faster. She was about to turn the final corner.

Then von Yb, that model of punctiliousness, turned on his heels and ran, still clutching, crumpled up in his hand, the large banknote, the earnest of his contractual obligation. As if the devil himself were after him, he tore up one street, down the next and came to a halt, before he realised where he was, outside the railway station. He rushed onto the platform, onto the Vienna coach of the waiting express, and into the lavatory and safety.

The signing-on fee was just enough to get him to Vienna. After an uncomfortable journey, he arrived there somewhat bent, having spent the whole journey crouched behind the lavatory-pan, and hurried home. It was days before he was anything approaching his usual self again.

But that was when the torment began. Poor von Yb started every time the doorbell rang. In his imagination he could hear the footsteps of the men sent to seek him out, von Yb the swindler who had misappropriated his signing-on fee. Breach of contract – this he knew from the experience handed down in the family by a long line of civil servants – breach of contract was no laughing matter. On the advice of the family lawyer, a gloomy gentleman with dark spectacles who told him in no uncertain terms how serious his situation was, von Yb left his splendid apartment and rented a number of cheap rooms in different parts of the town, scurrying from one to the other like a startled animal.

His social life was non-existent. Only the night-watchmen and members of the drinking classes staggering home in the early hours would see him flit timidly round the corner with a pensive shake of their heads.

Soon he was generally known as 'the scurrier' and then, when word got round that he had been to Italy, as 'Signor Scurri'.

The whole of Vienna, from the humblest purveyor of roast chestnuts to the emperor himself, knew of the dreadful predicament of this once highly respected gentleman. And it was not only the metropolis that bewailed his pitiful fate, in Brno, Graz and Olomouc as well he was the subject of sympathetic comments, even the occasional tear. As he still had a considerable income at his disposal, they could hardly organise a collection for him. Austria's keenest legal brains were systematically racked to try and find a solution to this special case of a buffoon in breach of contract. Experts in international law and reciprocal arrangements, specialists in extradition treaties and theatre contracts gathered together and, under pressure from public opinion, this assemblage of illustrious minds was allocated one of the empty rooms in the Imperial and Royal Academy of Sciences, where they could meet daily to discuss von Yb's wretched situation and, it was to be hoped, his deliverance.

It gradually became the done thing for anyone who wanted to make a name for himself in Vienna to slip into the magnificent baroque meeting chamber at around four o'clock in the afternoon, whisper a few discreet words to the attendant and then join one of the groups that were concerning themselves with von Yb's situation. Here and there a hoary-headed old greybeard would be leaning against a globe, deep in thought. In the middle of the room a number of scholarly profiles were sitting around a table, brooding over piles of black folders containing all the relevant files. In the corner an expert with furrowed brow shook his head to himself as he took a wad of cotton-wool out of his ear, placed it in an amber cigarette-holder and proceeded to light it. And almost every window had a complement of four frock-coats, standing with their backs to the room, staring out into the gloomy street whilst their fingers performed silent piano sonatas behind their backs. That alone made twenty-four first-class minds, but in total it was more than that who assembled there, day in, day out. Then, amid suppressed coughs and the soft chink of coins slipped into the attendants' open palms, they all left the ornate splendour of the stucco'd hall, where nothing was resolved, apart from the occasional dispute as to which umbrella was whose.

Thus it was Signor Scurri's dismal lot to eke out his days in obscure hideouts, sometimes even, when he felt the furies of fraudulence too close upon his heels, in rather dubious hotels. As he scurried in through the door, he would be allocated one of the rooms with a sympathetic nod.

He sank into a joyless decline, and on those few occasions when his mind was a little freer from worry and dread, they would be replaced by the torment of the great unresolved question of his life: had he actually seen the sea or not?

It was a question which von Yb, for whom there was no hope of improvement, never resolved. Given the knowledge of spatial relationships at that time, he could not know that one cosmic dimension can penetrate to within an arm's length of another.

On his death-bed Achatius von Yb, known as Signor Scurri, presented a curious sight: beneath his incredibly wrinkled forehead, his eyes were opened wide, and the yellowed index finger of his right hand, bearing the old family signet ring, was pointing fixedly up in the air, like someone who has just seen the light saying, 'Aha!'

The Head

Karl Hans Strobl

It was completely dark in the room . . . all the curtains closed
. . . not a glimmer of light from the street and quite still. My
friend, myself and the stranger were holding each other by the
hand in a quivering, convulsive clasp. A dreadful fear was
about us, within us . . .

And then . . . a gaunt, gleaming white hand came through
the darkness towards us and began to write with the pencil
that was lying ready on the table where we were seated. We
could not see what the hand was writing, but we could feel it
inside . . . as it was being written . . . as if it were there before
our eyes in letters of fire . . .

It was the story of the hand, and of the man it once
belonged to, that the gleaming white hand was writing on the
paper in the deepest midnight darkness:

'I am walking up the steps covered in red cloth . . . and . . . I
do after all have a strange feeling in my heart. Inside my breast
something is swinging back and forth . . . a huge pendulum.
But the rim of the pendulum disc is as sharp as a razor-blade
and each time the swing of the pendulum grazes my chest I
feel a keen pain . . . and it takes my breath away, and I want to
groan out loud. But I bite my teeth together, so that no sound
can pass, and clench my fists, tied behind my back, so that the
blood spurts out from under the nails.

Now I am at the top. Everything is prepared, all they are
waiting for is me. I am calm as they shave my neck, and when
it is done I ask for permission to speak to the people for one
last time. It is granted . . . I turn round and see the endless
mob, a sea of heads thronging round the guillotine, all those
dull, stupid, animal faces, some with expressions of vulgar

curiosity, others of obscene lust, human beings *en masse*, making a mockery of all that the word human stands for, and I find the whole business so ridiculous that I am forced to laugh out loud.

Disapproving lines appear in the officious expression of my executioners . . . how damned insolent of me not to take the matter seriously, tragically even . . . but I had better stop teasing these good souls and begin my speech:

'Citizens,' I say, 'citizens, it is for you that I die, for you and for Liberty. You have misunderstood me, you have condemned me . . . but I love you. And as proof of my love, hear my testament. Everything that I possess, shall be yours. For example . . .'

And I turn my back on them and make an unmistakable gesture . . .

From all around comes a roar of outrage . . . with a sigh of relief I quickly lay my head in the opening . . . a rushing, hissing noise . . . all I feel is an icy burning in my neck . . . my head falls into the basket.

Then I feel as if I have put my head under water and it has filled my ears. The noises from the outside world that reach me are dark and muddled, at my temples is a droning, buzzing sound. All across the area where my neck has been sliced through I feel as if large quantities of ether were vaporising.

I know that my head is in the wicker basket, my body up on the scaffold, but I have not yet the sense of complete separation; I feel my body fall onto its left side, the feet kicking feebly, my clenched fists, tied behind my back, twitch slightly, my fingers stretch out convulsively and then retract. I can also feel the blood flowing out of the stump of my neck, and as it empties I can sense my movements becoming weaker and weaker, and also my awareness of my body weakening, darkening, until below the cut in my neck all gradually becomes blackness.

I have lost my body.

In the complete darkness below my cut-off neck I suddenly sense red spots. The red spots are like fires on a dark, stormy night. They dissolve and spread like oil on still waters . . .

when the edges of two of the red spots touch I can feel a light electric shock in my eyelids and the hair stands up on my head. And now the red spots are beginning to rotate, faster, ever faster . . . a multitude of wheels of fire, blazing, molten sun-discs . . . they twist and swirl, drawing long tongues of fire behind them, and I have to close my eyes . . . but I can still feel the red wheels of fire within me . . . between my teeth I feel as if every gap is packed with dry, glassy grains of sand. Slowly the flaming wheels pale, the whirling slows down, one after the other is extinguished and everything below the cut through my neck goes black for a second time. This time it is for ever.

I am filled with a pleasant lethargy, an easy-going lack of responsibility, my eyes are heavy. I cannot open them any more and yet I can see everything around me. It is as if my eyelids were made of glass, transparent. I see everything as through a milky-white veil with a delicate tracery of pale pink veins over it, but everything I see is larger, clearer than when I still had my body. My tongue is paralysed; it lies in my mouth, heavy and sluggish as a lump of clay.

My sense of smell, on the other hand, is a thousand times sharper, I not only see things, I smell them, each one different, with its own characteristic odour.

In the wicker basket beneath the blade of the guillotine there are three other heads apart from my own, two male and one female. The woman's head has rouged cheeks with two beauty spots, powdered, coiffured hair with a golden arrow stuck through it, and two dainty diamond earrings in its tiny ears. The heads of the two men are lying face down in a pool of half-dried blood; across one runs the poorly healed scar of an old wound, the hair on the other is already sparse and grey.

The woman's head has its eyes screwed tight and is motionless. I know that it is watching me through its closed lids . . .

We lie like that for hours. I watch the sunlight edge its way higher up the scaffold of the guillotine. Evening comes and I begin to feel chilly. My nose is stiff and cold and the chill of evaporation I feel on my neck is becoming unpleasant.

Suddenly raucous shouting; it comes nearer, quite near, and

all at once I feel a powerful hand grab me by the hair and lift me out of the basket. Then I feel some pointed object pushed into my neck: a spearhead. A mob of drunken *sans-culottes* and harpies has fallen upon our heads. A giant of a fellow with a puffy red face is brandishing the spear with my head on it high above the frenzied, jeering, screaming throng.

A tangle of men and women is fighting over the jewels from the woman's head. They writhe and roll, kicking and punching, biting and scratching.

Now the fight is over. Shouting and cursing, they separate, each one who has secured a part of the spoils surrounded by a jealous crowd . . .

The head is lying on the ground, begrimed and mutilated, showing the marks of the grasping hands, its ears torn by the violence with which the rings were ripped off, its exquisite coiffure dishevelled, the powdered strands of deep blond hair trailing in the dust. One nostril has been slit open by a sharp blade, its forehead shows the mark of the heel of someone's shoe. Its eyelids are half open, the blank, glassy eyes staring straight ahead.

Finally the crowd sets off. There are four heads stuck on long poles. The fury of the crowd is directed mainly at the man with grey hair. That man must have been particularly unpopular. I do not know him. They spit and throw lumps of filth at him. There, a handful of mud from the street thumps into his ear . . . What is that? Did he not twitch? Slightly, imperceptibly, with one muscle only, visible to me alone?

Night comes. They have arranged us heads on the iron bars of a palace gate. I do not recognise the palace, either. Paris is big. In the courtyard armed citizens are camped round a huge fire . . . Scabrous songs, jokes, roars of laughter. The smell of roast mutton reaches me. The fire gives off a costly fragrance of rosewood. The wild mob has dragged all the furniture from the palace out into the courtyard and is now burning it, piece by piece. The next to go is an elegant sofa with delicate scrollwork . . . but they hesitate and do not throw the sofa on the fire yet. A young woman with coarse features and wearing a loose bodice which reveals her full, firm breasts, is insisting on something with the help of vigorous gestures.

Is she trying to persuade them to let her have the elegant sofa, has she suddenly felt the desire to see what it is like to be a duchess?

The men are still hesitating.

The woman points at the bars with our heads on the spikes and then back at the sofa.

The men hesitate, finally she pushes them aside, draws one of the armed men's sabres, kneels down and uses the blade to lever out the little enamelled nails with which the heavy silk covering is attached to the wooden frame. Now the men are helping her.

Again she points to our heads.

One of the men walks over rather hesitantly. He looks for the one she wants. Then he climbs up the iron bars and takes down the maltreated, violated woman's head.

The man shudders with horror, but he seems to be acting under some kind of compulsion. It is as if that young woman by the fire, the young woman in the red skirt and open bodice, has hypnotised all the men around with her savage, sensual stare, like some beast of prey. His arm held out stiffly, he carries the head by the hair back to the fire.

With a wild screech of delight the woman grabs the head. Twirling it round, she swings it three times over the blazing fire.

Then she squats down and takes the head in her lap. She strokes it caressingly over the cheeks a few times . . . all the men have gathered in a circle around her . . . now she is taking one of the little enamelled nails in one hand and hammer in the other, and with a light blow she drives the nail right into the skull.

Another tap of the hammer, and another nail disappears into the luxuriant hair.

As she hammers, she hums a song. One of those terrible, strange, sensual folk songs, full of ancient magic.

The bloody monsters around her are silent and pale with horror, their eyes staring aghast at her out of dark sockets. And she hammers and hammers, driving nail after nail into the head, all the while humming her strange, old charm to the rhythm of the hammer blows.

Suddenly one of the men gives a piercing cry and jumps up. His eyes are bulging, his mouth is covered in foam . . . he throws his arms backwards, twisting his body to either side as if in painful convulsions, and from his mouth come piercing, animal cries.

The young woman hammers on, singing her song.

Then another jumps up, howling and swinging his arms around. He grabs a brand from the fire and jabs it into his chest, again and again, until his clothes begin to glow and thick, stinking smoke spreads all round him.

The others sit there, pale and motionless, and do nothing to stop him.

A third jumps up, and now the same frenzy grips the rest. A deafening noise, a screaming and a wailing, a screeching and a howling and a roaring, a tangle of flailing limbs. Any that fall do not get up . . . the others continue their stamping over their bodies . . .

In the middle of this orgy of madness sits the young woman, hammering and singing . . .

Now she has finished; she sticks the head covered with tiny enamelled nails on the end of a bayonet and holds it high above the howling, leaping mass. Then someone scatters the fire, the burning wood is pulled out and thrown in a shower of sparks into the blackest corners of the courtyard . . . it grows dark . . . grunts of lust and a wild scuffling, as if from some furious struggle. I know that all these crazed men, these wild beasts, have thrown themselves on the one woman, biting and clawing at her . . .

Everything goes dark before my eyes.

Did consciousness remain just long enough for me to witness all these horrors? Dawn comes, dark and indistinct, like the fading light on a dull winter's afternoon. Rain falls on my head. Cold winds tousle my hair. My flesh becomes loose and weak. Is it the beginning of decomposition?

Then there is a change. My head is taken to a different

place, to a dark pit; there it is warm and quiet. Light and clarity return to me. There are many other heads with me in the dark pit. Heads and bodies. And I notice that the heads and bodies are joining up again, as well, or as badly, as they can manage. And with the contact they rediscover their language, a soft, inaudible language in which they think to each other.

I long for a body, I long to be finally rid of the unbearable coldness where my neck is cut, such a coldness that it almost seems to burn hot. But I look round in vain. All the heads and bodies are joined together. There is no body left for me. But eventually, after a long, laborious search, I find one . . . right at the bottom, hiding in a corner . . . a body that is still without a head, a woman's body.

Something inside me rebels against uniting with this body, but my desire, my longing overcomes it and, impelled by will power alone, I approach the headless body and see that it too is striving to reach my head; and now the two cuts touch with a mild shock and a feeling of gentle heat. One thing stands out above all: I have a body once more.

But strange . . . after the initial feeling of comfort is over, I sense the enormous difference between my two components . . . I feel as if completely different fluids are meeting and mingling, fluids that have no similarities with each other. The woman's body, which my head now crowns, is slim and white, and its skin has the marble coolness of an aristocrat who bathes in wine and milk and uses costly oils and lotions. But on its right-hand side, covering the hip and part of the stomach, is a strange drawing, a tattoo. Composed of fine, extremely fine, blue dots is a pattern of hearts, anchors and arabesques with the elaborate initials I and B intertwined and repeated. Who can the woman have been?

I know I will learn that some time, and soon! The vague corporeal darkness below my neck is developing an outline. I already have a picture of my body, though an unclear, blurred one, and this picture is becoming more definite, more precise, by the minute. At the same time there is the painful mingling of the fluids from my two component parts. And suddenly I feel as if I had two heads . . . and this second head, a woman's

127

head, bloody, disfigured, distorted, I can see before me, completely covered with small enamelled nails. That is the head that belongs to this body, and at the same time it is my head, for in my skull and my brain I can clearly feel the hundreds of little points. I want to roar with pain. Everything around me merges into a red veil, which ripples as if it were torn back and forth by violent gusts of wind.

I can feel now that I am a woman, only my mind is masculine. And now an image is emerging from the red veil . . . before me I can see myself in a room decorated with sumptuous extravagance. I am lying down, buried in soft white furs and . . . naked. Before me, bending over me, is a man with the harsh, coarse features of one from the common mass of the people, with the work-calloused hands and weather-beaten skin of a sailor. He is kneeling over me, pricking my soft flesh with a sharp needle to make his strange design. It hurts and yet causes me a strange, sensual pleasure at the same time . . . I know that the man is my lover.

Then a short, needle-sharp pain makes my whole body contract in a quiver of delight. I wreathe my white arms round the man's neck and pull him down to me . . . I kiss him and place his hard, calloused hands on my shoulders, on my breasts, and kiss him again in a wild frenzy and wrap myself round him and clutch him tight so that he gasps and groans.

Now I have my teeth round his brown throat, round the throat I love, the sight of which has often sent me into raptures, my tongue is licking his throat in a moist caress . . . and now . . . now I must press my teeth into the hard brown flesh . . . I cannot help it . . . I must bite into his throat . . . I bite and I bite . . . his groans become a death rattle . . . I feel the man twist and turn convulsively in my arms . . . but I do not let go . . . his body becomes heavy, heavy . . . a warm stream flows down my body. His head falls back . . . I let him slip from my arms . . . with a muffled thud he lands on his back on the soft carpet, a thick stream of blood pouring from the bite in his neck. Blood, blood everywhere, on the soft white polar-bear skins, on me, everywhere.

I start to scream, hoarse rough sounds come from my throat. The chambermaid rushes in, she cannot have been far away, perhaps by the door in the next room . . . was she eavesdropping? For a moment she stands rigid, as if unconscious, then, without a word, she throws herself over the body of the dead man . . . without saying a word, without shedding a tear, she buries her face in the blood streaming down his chest. But I see her clench her fist; now I know everything . . .

And then I see another scene . . .

Again I can see myself, and yet at the same time it is I myself who am sitting in the wooden tumbril which is taking me to the guillotine. Then I am standing up there on the scaffold, looking at the sun for the last time, and as I turn round I catch sight of a young woman who has pushed her way right to the front of the crowd . . . that woman . . . the lover of the man who was the instrument of my pleasure . . . in a red skirt, her bodice loose, her face pale and twitching, hair streaming . . . her eyes have a savage gleam, like a beast of prey, moist, as if from stifled grief, and with a lustful sparkle, as if in expectation of pleasure. She raises her clenched fists to her face, her lips move . . . she wants to speak, to mock me and curse me, but all that comes is a strangled, incomprehensible cry . . . I lay my head below the blade.

Now I know everything.

I know whose head it was that, in the night, by the blazing light of the bonfire, suffered a gruesome vengeance that reached beyond the grave. I know, too, who the young woman was, who, in the same night, in the darkened courtyard, was crushed and torn limb from limb by wild beasts . . . my head aches from the hundreds of sharp nails . . . I am tied to this body . . . to this body wracked with horrible memories and terrible pains, to this beautiful body steeped in sin that has tasted all the delights of hell.

I am being torn apart by my two conflicting halves . . . oh, but not for long . . . I feel a slackening in all my limbs, my flesh softens, falls away, my internal organs are becoming spongy, dissolving . . . decomposition is beginning . . .

Soon night will embrace me and my two conflicting selves
. . . the night of decay . . . the bodies will disintegrate and the
spirit will be free.'

The hand stopped writing and vanished.

The Ghost of the Jewish Ghetto

Paul Leppin

Only ten years ago, in the middle of Prague, where today tall, airy apartment blocks form wide boulevards, stood the Jewish quarter: a squint, gloomy jumble of nooks and crannies from which no storm was strong enough to blow away the smell of mould and damp masonry and where, in summer, the open doors exhaled a poisonous miasma. Filth and poverty each outstank the other, and the eyes of the children that grew up there had a dull, cruel glint of depravity. Alleys would sometimes pass under low, vaulted viaducts through the belly of a house, or they would suddenly twist to one side to come to an abrupt end at a blind wall. The sharp-faced junk dealers, who piled up their wares on the bumpy cobbles outside their shops, would accost passers-by. Girls with painted lips leant against the house entrances, full of coarse laughter, whispering in the men's ears and lifting up their skirts to show their yellow or lime-green stockings. Ancient, slack-jawed bawds, their hair streaked with white, shouted from the windows, hammered, waved and gurgled with gratified zeal when a man took the bait and came closer.

Fornication had made its home here, and in the evening its red lamps lured men in. There were streets where every building was a house of ill repute, low dives where vice shared its bed with hunger, where consumptive women carried on a meagre trade with their withered charms, secret chambers where villainy, with whispers and sly winks, violated school-age girls and sold their helpless, bewildered innocence for a few pieces of tarnished silver. There were smart, luxuriously furnished taverns where one's foot sank into the carpets and where well-fed, voluptuous whores strutted about in long silk gowns.

Not far from the synagogue, beside the squalid shacks of Gypsy Lane, was a two-storey building which housed the *Salon Aaron*. In this seedy environment it had an almost well-cared-for look, in spite of the fact that part of the plaster was crumbling from the walls and the dust and rain had smeared gaudy stripes across the blind windows. By day it was quiet; only rarely did a customer slip up the worn steps into the dark vestibule, to emerge an hour later, furtively, his coat-collar turned up around his ears. But at night here loud, bright, quivering life welled up from some secret spring. The windows glowed, and inside, the laughter fluttered round like a bird trapped in a cage.

Johanna's laughter was part of it. It was a hot, throaty purring, that rubbed itself up against you; it could be clearly distinguished from the voices of the other girls, and sometimes it would even echo through the morning silence like a happy, infatuated lark. Johanna was happy because the men came to her. They desired her more than her colleagues because she gave each and every one of them something of the fearful, tormenting, restless sweetness which filled her and which was absent from the lethargic bodies of the others. Their profession, which to the other women in the house seemed a boring, irksome chore, aroused within her an ecstatic yearning for love, was a spur she could feel goading her flesh and which brought a virginal lustre to her eyes. With lips that were cracked and sore from kissing, she would slake this thirst on the mouths of men, again and again imbued with the bridal ecstasy that had accompanied her first lovemaking. In the intervals afforded by her promiscuous activity – and unbearably long and lonely they seemed to her – she listened for the steps of the passers-by outside the house, and when the bell over the door jingled, she would flush and sigh. There were often days when she enjoyed the delights of love until she was sated with it; but as she lay in bed, with heavy head and aching limbs, her mind went back to this lover and then to that one, savouring the memory, luxuriating in it, and she would smile in the darkness. Sometimes, especially in the summer, when she finally made her way to her bed in the last hours before morning, her restlessness would turn into torment. Then she would go to the open window in her nightdress and look down onto the Jewish quarter. She would stretch out her bare arms, feeling the warm rain like drops of blood on her skin. The streets below were where she belonged: the ghetto where the sleepy lights of the brothels twinkled, where bulky shadows crouched in sordid alleyways, whilst in the distance the whine of a violin or the harsh tinkling of the pianolas were making one last effort to entice revellers. A rapturous melancholy bathed her face in tears. Tenderly, the night wind fondled her breasts, and she would let her head fall back and her lips would purse in a kiss.

In the evenings, beneath the festive lights of the *Salon Aaron*, as the wine-glasses chinked on the marble tables, she would dance to the music. The sensuality that she suffered from made her limbs soft and relaxed, goading her, skirts swirling, into an urgent abandon that suffused her rigid features with a strange beauty which was more provocative, more enticing, than all the wiles of the other women. She danced alone or with the customers. Her slim figure would bend back in the arms of her partners, press up against them insistently, tremble and shiver; and if one had danced with the blonde Johanna, he was sure to go up to her room with her as well. Her lips were greedy and feverish. The more men that found their way to her door, the more unbridled was the lust with which she fell upon them; her desire had the power to move men and leave them dazed; her passion was a willing instrument that could blaze up into sheer bliss.

Then came the day when disease demanded its penance from her body. It welled up from the decaying walls of the ghetto, from its debauched streets, and poisoned her kisses. It burnt up her blood and made her veins dry and cracked; it choked the laughter and the amorous murmurs in her throat; it disfigured her body with red blotches and dragged her through the gauntlet of the vituperation of the foul-mouthed whores to the fear and trembling of the hospital. There she lay in a hot bed, and the thoughts fell from the ceiling onto her forehead like heavy drops. She thought of the women who were sitting at that moment in the *Salon Aaron*, drinking the yellow wine from thin glasses. She thought of the music and of the scarlet petticoat she had worn when dancing. She opened her arms and threw back her head onto the pillows, but there was no one there to kiss her. A pining sadness roused the sobs in her throat and sent her into despair.

The cowardly weeks drew out time in a spiteful, lingering pretence. Johanna's disease had broken out with unexpected virulence. The antidote with which the doctors tormented her was powerless against it. It lodged in every tissue, it flickered under her skin, it scratched open festering sores in the pits and hollows of her flesh, it refused to move. It paralysed her thoughts and soiled her sleep with lustful dreams, from which she started up, groaning, to recognise the dreadful, hateful reality around her. Johanna missed men. Her febrile body twitched under the torture of deprivation. Every day of burning torment, every hour increased her agony. Until she could bear it no longer. One night she made her escape from the hospital. She jumped out of the window into the garden and barefoot, with just her coat over her nightdress, she climbed over the wall and into the street.

She ran through the city, burning with unearthly, sultry anticipation. Her hair, undone, fluttered round her face, and her eyes shone. One bright, marvellous thought drove her on, filling her with happiness: she was going to find the men! Her muscles strained and her feet flew over the cobbles. The shadows of belated night owls swayed across her path, and she started at the harsh light of sudden street-lamps; she was intoxicated with a delicious, heavy, tantalising sweetness. The twin spires of the Tyn Church appeared before her, standing pale among the stars. She was as good as home! There was the street where the raucous music blared behind curtained doors, and where the women's laughter beat with its wings against the red window-panes . . .

She stopped and stared, dazzled, at the squint-eyed moon stuck against the sky which was shining down on splintered beams and rubble. The *Salon Aaron* had disappeared. Pick and shovel had demolished the house piece by piece, and the stones were stacked beside the synagogue. One single, jagged crest of masonry rose up among the ruins, and Johanna recognised her bedroom wall. Numb with horror, her eye followed the line of the street. The gaudy lights of the houses of pleasure had been extinguished, and dust rose like smoke from the blasted roofs. Everywhere ruins emerged from the darkness. While she had been wrestling with the disease in her damp bed in the hospital, they had destroyed her home.

A scream detached itself from her throat and quivered its hideous way through the deserted quarter. Her hair spilled over her coat; the night breeze blew it open and fumbled her under her nightdress. A bunch of tipsy soldiers came along. Unable to control herself, she fell to her knees before them, moaning confused words of love. And among the ruins of the demolished brothel, she gave herself to the men that chance had thrown into her path. She gave herself to them, one after the other, and her wretched body, wasted with disease, did not tire but, shuddering in the ecstasy of love, dug itself ever deeper into the rubble.

Between one summer and the next, the ghetto was torn down. New houses pressed down on the dark, unhealthy crannies, which for centuries had been the haunt of misery and vice. Clattering along on its high-heeled shoes, debauchery fled to the farthest edges of the suburbs. A city for the rich and respectable grew up over the old squares. But never in the history of Prague were the ravages of syphilis so terrible, so devastating as in that year. It invaded family life and struck the young mothers with terror. It hung on the smile of love, turning it into a leaden grin. Young boys killed themselves and old men cursed life.

Pour avoir bien servi

Leo Perutz

I heard this strange story some time ago in the saloon of a French steamer, which was taking me from Marseilles to Alexandria. We were not able to go up on deck very much; we had constant bad weather and had to find some way or other of passing the time. Of all the discussions and conversations I heard during those days, what particularly stuck in my mind was the story from a Mr. J. Schwemmer, an engineer from Kiev, who told it after a long and heated debate in order to dispute the claim that the modern doctor has the right, nay, even the duty, forcibly to terminate the sufferings of a patient who has no hope of recovery.

I cannot say why this story in particular made such a deep impression on me; in fact, as soon became apparent, it was only marginally connected with the topic under discussion. Perhaps it was the sudden appearance, in the midst of all our banal and superficial discussions, of the dreadful reality of two pale, suffering human beings, their lips twisted and quivering with pain. Even today I sometimes see the young woman in my mind's eye, see her leaning back wearily in her wheelchair, her fearful, longing glance resting almost tenderly on the green vase on the mantelpiece. And in my dreams I still sometimes hear her husband's cry, it rings in my ears with a terrible sound that freezes me to the marrow, even though in reality I never heard the cry from the lips of the husband himself, but from a weak, croaking, old man's voice that belonged to the aforementioned Mr. Schwemmer from Kiev.

This is the story told by the old engineer, and I will recount it as he told it to us on board the *Héron*, a little more briefly, perhaps, but I am sure I have not omitted any essential details:

Years ago I lived in Paris. I shared an apartment in a small, one-storey building in a side-street in an out-of-the-way sub-urb with a former student friend whom I had not seen for several years and then, to my delight, come across in Paris. In the years in between he had completed a doctorate at a German university, published two books on art and obtained, shortly before his marriage, a position as librarian to some count. He was still young, thirty at the most, and it was only his wife's misfortune that could have made him so tired and prematurely aged.

His wife was ill. She was paralysed; she had been attacked by one of those nervous disorders whose victims, or so I believe, come mostly from people who overexert themselves intellectually: as a girl she had studied medicine in Zurich. By day she sat in her wheelchair, usually silent and without complaining much, but the nights! Those nights! One night her screams were so dreadful that the concierge's two children dashed out into the street in sheer terror and refused to come back for the rest of the night. During such nights the doctor and her husband did everything they could to comfort her, promised that the pain was bound to lessen soon and that in a short time she would be well again; but she, as a former medical student, knew better than any of us that there was no cure for her suffering, that the resistance her young body put up to the disease was in vain, that one day the end would come but, and that was the worst thing about it, not all that soon.

And her husband loved her. His work only occupied him for a few hours each day, but he soon came to hate it, to feel it irksome. As a young student, he had found his subject fulfilling, satisfying, almost intoxicating even – to the rest of us his passion for old books and rare manuscripts had seemed almost morbid – now he had lost all interest in it. In his study, in the street, in the omnibus, wherever he was there was but one thought in his mind: to return home as quickly as possible! Basically, his whole day was a detour on the way to his wife. Several times he told me what the reason for his unease was: his wife possessed a revolver. She had had it since she was a girl and it was concealed somewhere in the flat, of that he was quite certain. But he had never been able to discover the hiding-place, however often he had searched through the rooms. Of course, she was paralysed and could not reach the revolver herself. 'But once, just imagine, she tried to bribe the maid!'

Every time he told me about this he went quite pale with fear at the thought that she might have managed to get the gun while he was out. I responded to his story with the feeling, faint and tentative at first, then stronger and stronger, that that would almost be the best thing for the couple, and that fate had chosen me to help these two wretched people. Now, of course, I know that it was a crime not to stifle that thought at birth. How can a foolish young man presume to take into his own clumsy hands the destiny of two people whose past he was not part of and whose secret thoughts and hidden desires he cannot know.

But in those days I was young and inexperienced and full of misunderstood catchwords and immature ideas, and I felt so sorry for my poor friend, scarcely thirty years old and already grey-haired.

These are the two people in my story. Russians, both of them, I think I said that already, didn't I? They had very little contact with Parisian society, nor did I ever meet any of our countrymen in their house. Sometimes I had the feeling people were avoiding them. Once someone told me the husband had betrayed a Russian student, who was wanted by the police, and was, anyway, a Russian government agent. But I gave little weight to that kind of claim; such stories are told about many of my countrymen who, for whatever reason, live abroad, and it's always more or less the same story.

And now I will tell you of the day when I committed a crime – for it was a crime – and of the green vase with the Chinese dragons covered in red scales which was the constant focus, day and night, of the invalid wife's tender, longing glances. And if I recount the events of that day, in which my part, as I am well aware, was not one to be proud of, then I do it without shame and without regret, for it all happened a long time ago and I know now that it was not I who was to blame,

138

but that unfortunate delusion, the silly idea that I had been chosen by fate to put an end, with a surgeon's steady hand, to the wife's torment and the husband's misery. It was on that very day that the feeling within me was stronger than ever before, for the young woman had had a very bad night and none of the three of us had had a wink of sleep. It was only as morning came that things improved slightly, the man had left the house, dog-tired, to go to his work, and she was in her wheelchair. I was sitting opposite her, but I have forgotten how the the conversation came round to her younger days and the time she spent in Zurich. 'Would you like to see an old picture of me?' she asked, and when I said yes, she thought for a while and then said, in a voice which sounded perfectly calm and nonchalant, 'Bring me the green vase, there on the mantelpiece.' She said it quite calmly, but I could feel the blood rushing to my head, my knees trembled and I suddenly knew that this was the long-sought hiding-place of the gun. I just managed to stand up, brought the vase and began to empty it out onto the table; I was acting as if in a dream. On top was a letter and one pink and one light green ribbon, then a fan and a withered posy and finally the photographs: two pictures of herself, then the portrait of a young man with intelligent, handsome features. 'That is my friend Sacha,' she said, and I knew that he was dead without her saying so. And I found a photo of her husband too. It was from his university days and showed him surrounded by his fellow students, and I was in the picture as well, looking rather comical because I had a long wooden student's pipe in my mouth. And then, right at the bottom, was the case with the revolver.

My hand was trembling as I took the case out of the vase, for this was the moment of action, that I knew, and I was in no doubt as to what I should do. I wanted, I *had* to hand the gun over to the sick woman, even though others in their stupidity might say it was murder and call me to account for it. If no one had the courage, then I did, and I was doing what was best for this man and this woman. And I remembered a few words that I had once read on an old French medal, 'pour avoir bien servi'. I went all soft inside at the thought of the service I was doing my friend, and then I heard her voice, a cool, calm voice, saying, 'Please, let me have the case,' and I pulled myself together and managed to say, 'I will open it myself.'

When I felt the revolver in my hands, I was suddenly struck with cowardice, all my decisions and plans collapsed and I was seized with horror at the service the invalid woman was demanding of me. The thought of the responsibility I was taking weighed down on me, what I really wanted to do was to throw the gun as far away from me as possible, instead of giving it to her, and the woman must have read all that in my eyes. 'See,' she said, 'the thought of this revolver was my one comfort during those terrible nights, the only thing I had to cling on to. My whole life over the last three years has been a constant movement towards and away from that green vase. Sometimes my wheelchair was so close that I could almost have touched it with my hand. Once my husband almost discovered the hiding-place. He was within a hair's-breadth of my secret. I felt my heart stand still with fear.' And then, abruptly and quite simply and without any drama in her voice, she said, 'Please give me the gun.'

I wouldn't have done it. I wouldn't have given her the gun, I would have thrown it away into a corner of the room; but at that moment I saw her husband coming through the garden. And the way he dragged his feet, slowly and wearily, over the gravel, back bowed, a broken man, and the way he nodded to me with such an old, earnest face, all gave me back my assurance. I was the surgeon once more who would make the healing incision with a cool eye and steady hand. I was no longer in any doubt as to what I should do and as I looked out of the window and returned the husband's greeting, I handed the revolver over the table to the woman.

What happened next is quickly told. I was suddenly filled with a terrible fear of what was bound to happen in the next few seconds. 'Don't watch!' a voice screamed within me. 'I can't bear to see her raise the gun, put it to her forehead, press the trigger. I can't bear to see that.' I turned my back on her and faced the door. I heard him coming up the stairs. Then he opened the door, said 'hello,' was stretching out his hand, coming towards me. Two steps and he stopped, turned as white as the walls and screamed, 'Jonas, Jonas, what have you done!' And, 'For God's sake, Jonas, take the gun away from her, quick!'

I still had time to do it. With one step I could have been beside her, torn the gun from her grasp. But I stayed with my back to her and clenched my teeth. Stand firm! Just for this one moment! The healing incision. I am his doctor. He'll thank me for it later. *Pour avoir bien servi!*

He behaved in an odd way. Instead of rushing up and taking the gun away from her, he had fallen to his knees. For a few seconds there was complete silence in the room, I could hear his teeth grinding. Then he suddenly screamed, a terrible, loud scream, 'Don't do it, Maria! Don't do it! I swear I didn't write the letter, Sacha wrote it himself.' He gave one more scream, which went right through me, suddenly turned to me and said, 'Jonas, what have I ever done to *you*?' and gave me a look which I could not understand. Then he buried his face in his hands. And that was when the shot rang out.

When the smoke had dispersed I must have given a scream like a madman. The woman was still sitting in her wheelchair, still unharmed, the smoking revolver in her hand. On the floor lay her husband, motionless, spattered with blood, a bullet through his forehead.

I just stood there, I didn't know what to do. I tried to work out exactly what had happened, but the whole room was spinning. I bent over the dead man. His face was twisted in fear. I tried to recall where I was and what it all meant, but my mind was empty apart from a few ridiculous words going round and round inside it, *pour avoir bien servi*; and then I heard the invalid woman's voice, cold and cutting and dripping with hatred as she said:

'He was the one who betrayed Sacha to the police, the swine. Thank you for helping me, I have waited three years for this moment.'

The story was over. The old man leant back in his chair and stared with his dull, weary eyes at the ceiling. The rest of us sat there in horrified silence, only the two lively girls from Vienna, who were playing with the Captain's bulldog in the corner, began to giggle and laugh, because at the end of the story it suddenly turned out that the old gentleman, who so far had been known as Mr. J. Schwemmer, was called Jonas – Jonas!

Outside the Law

Franz Kafka

Outside the Law stood a doorkeeper. A man from the country came to this doorkeeper and asked to go into the Law. But the doorkeeper said he could not let him go in just then. The man thought this over and then asked whether that meant he might be allowed to enter the Law later. 'It is possible,' said the doorkeeper, 'but not now.' As the door of the Law was open as always and the doorkeeper stepped to one side, the man bent down to see into the interior. When the doorkeeper noticed that, he laughed and said, 'If you are so tempted, why don't you try to go in, even though I have forbidden it? But remember, I am powerful. And I am only the lowest door-keeper. But outside each room you pass through there is a doorkeeper, each one more powerful than the last. The sight of just the third is too much even for me.' The man from the country had not expected such difficulty; the Law is supposed to be available to everyone and at all times, he thought, but as he took a closer look at the doorkeeper in his fur coat, with his large, pointed nose, his long, thin, black Tartar moustache, he decided it would be better to wait until he was given permission to enter. The doorkeeper gave him a stool and let him sit down at the side of the door. There he sat for days and years. He made many attempts to be allowed in and tired the doorkeeper with his requests. Quite often the doorkeeper would briefly interrogate him, asking him questions about the place he came from and many other things, but they were uninterested questions, such as important people ask, and at the end he always said he could not let him in yet. The man, who had equipped himself well for the journey, used every-thing, no matter how valuable, to bribe the doorkeeper. The latter accepted everything, but said, as he did so, 'I am only accepting this so that you will not think there was something you omitted to do.' Over the many years the man observed the doorkeeper almost uninterruptedly. He came to forget the other doorkeepers and this first one seemed to him to be the only obstacle to his entry into the Law. He cursed his misfortune, loud and recklessly in the first years, later, as he grew old, he just muttered to himself. He grew childish and since, as a result of his years of studying the doorkeeper he had come to recognise even the fleas on his fur collar, he asked the fleas to help him and persuade the doorkeeper to change his mind. Finally his vision grew weak and he did not know whether it was really becoming dark round him, or whether his eyes were deceiving him. But now, in the dark, he could distinguish a radiance, which streams, inextinguishable, from the door of the Law. Now he had not much longer to live. Before his death all the things he had experienced during the whole time merged in his mind into a question he had not yet put to the doorkeeper. He gestured to him, since he could no longer raise his stiffening body. The doorkeeper had to bend down low to him, for the difference in height had changed considerably, to the man's disadvantage. 'What is it you want to know now?' asked the doorkeeper, 'you are insatiable.' 'Everyone seeks the Law,' said the man, 'so how is it that in all these years no one but I has asked to be let in?' The doorkeeper realised that the man was nearing his end and so, in order to be audible to his fading hearing, he bellowed at him, 'No one else could be granted entry here, since this entrance was intended for you alone. I am going to go and shut it now.'

A Country Doctor

Franz Kafka

I was in a very awkward predicament: an urgent journey lay
ahead of me; a seriously ill boy was expecting me in a village
ten miles distant; heavy snowstorms covered the wide open
spaces between myself and him; I had a carriage, a light one
with large wheels, just the type of thing for our country roads;
wrapped up in my fur, the bag with my instruments in my
hand, I was in the courtyard, all ready to go; but there was no
horse – no horse. My own horse had died the previous evening as a result of overexertion during this icy winter; the maid
was running round the village to find a horse to borrow; but it
was pointless, I knew, and I stood there, useless, more and
more covered in snow, becoming more and more immobile.
The girl appeared at the gate, alone, waving the lantern. Of
course, who is going to lend out their horse now, and for such
a journey? I strode across the yard once more; I could see no
way of getting there. Distracted, tormented, I kicked out at the
broken door of the pigsty, which had not been used for years.
It opened, flapping back and forward on its hinges. Warmth,
and a smell like that of horses came out. There was a dim
stable lamp swinging from a cord inside. A man, crouching
down in the low shed, turned his open, blue-eyed face to me.

'Shall I harness the horse?' he asked, crawling out on all
fours. I did not know what to say, and just bent down to see
what else there was in the sty. The maid was standing beside
me.

'You never know what there is in your own house,' she
said, and we both laughed.

'Gee-up, brother! Gee-up sister!' shouted the groom, and
two horses, powerful, strong-flanked beasts, appeared one after
the other in the doorway, which they filled completely, and

pushed their way out, their legs tucked into their bodies, lowering their well-formed heads like camels, propelled by the force of their twisting rumps alone. But immediately they stood up straight, long-legged, the steam rising thickly from their bodies.

'Help him,' I said, and the willing girl hurried to get the groom the harness for the carriage. But scarcely was she beside him, than the groom puts his arms round her and rams his face against hers. She gives a scream and flees back to me; the marks of two rows of teeth are stamped in red on the girl's cheek.

'You animal!' I scream in fury, 'do you want the whip?' But immediately I remember that he is a stranger; that I do not know where he came from, and that he is helping me of his own free will when everyone else has failed me. As if he guesses my thoughts, he does not take my threat amiss, just turns round once to look at me, harnessing the horses all the while.

'Get in,' he says then, and indeed, everything is ready. I realise that I have never ridden behind such a fine pair of horses and climb in with a sense of pleasure.

'But I will drive,' I say. 'You don't know the way.'

'Certainly.' he says, 'I'm not going, anyway, I'm staying with Rosa.'

'No!' Rosa shouts, and runs into the house with an accurate presentiment of her fate. I hear the clatter of the chain as she fastens it; I hear the lock engage; I also see her put out all the lights, first in the hall and then rushing right through the house, so that she cannot be found.

'You are coming with me,' I say to the groom, 'or the drive is off, however urgent it is. I wouldn't dream of giving you the girl as the price for the use of the horses.'

'Off you go!' he says, clapping his hands and the carriage is swept away, like logs in the current. The last thing I hear is the door of the house breaking and splintering under the groom's attack, then my eyes and ears are filled with a booming which penetrates all my senses equally. But only for a moment for, as if the patient's courtyard opened directly onto my gate, I am there already; the horses are standing quietly; the snowstorm has stopped; moonlight all around; the parents of the sick lad rush out of the house; his sister behind them; they almost lift me out of the carriage; I can understand nothing of their confused chatter; in the sickroom the air is scarcely breathable; the stove has not been tended and is smoking; I am going to open the window; but first I want to see the sick boy. Skinny, not feverish, not cold, not hot, with empty eyes and no night-shirt, the boy pushes himself up under the eiderdown, winds his arms around my neck, whispers in my ear, 'Doctor, let me die.'

I look round. No one has heard; his parents are standing silent, bent forward, awaiting my verdict; his sister has brought a chair to put my bag on. I open the bag and rummage around among my instruments; the boy keeps on reaching out towards me from the bed to remind me of his request. I pick up a pair of tweezers, examine them in the candlelight and put them back. 'Well,' comes the blasphemous thought, 'the gods do really help in cases like this, send the missing horse, add a second to speed things up and, to cap it all, throw in a groom . . .' Only now do I remember Rosa. What can I do, how can I save her, how can I pull her away from under that groom, ten miles distant, uncontrollable horses hitched to my carriage? Those horses which have somehow managed to loosen their harnesses, and now, I don't know how, push open the windows from outside. Each one puts its head in through one window and, unruffled by the screams of the family, look at the sick boy.

'I'm going to drive back right away,' I think, as if the horses were asking me to leave, but I let the boy's sister, who thinks I am overcome by the heat, take my fur coat. A glass of rum is put out for me, the old man pats me on the shoulder, the sacrifice of his treasure justifies the familiarity. I shake my head; I would feel sick trapped in the old man's narrow circle of thoughts; that is the only reason I refuse the drink. The mother is standing by the bed, luring me over there. I follow and, as my horse neighs out loud to the ceiling, place my head on the boy's chest, my wet beard making him quiver. It confirms what I already know: the boy is well, his circulation could be better, his doting mother could give him less coffee, but he's well, the best thing would be to kick him out of bed. But it's not my place to set the world to rights, so I leave him be. I am appointed by the district and do my duty to the utmost, to the point where it is almost too much. Badly paid, I'm still generous and obliging to the poor. On top of all that I have to provide for Rosa; the lad may well be right and I want to die as well. What am I doing here, in this endless winter! My horse has died and there's no one in the village who will lend me his. I have to get my horses from the pigsty; if they didn't just happen to be horses I would have to drive a pair of sows. That's the way things are. And I nod to the family. They have no idea about all this, and if they did, they wouldn't believe it. Writing prescriptions is easy, but to communicate with people beyond that is difficult. Well, that's my visit here over, I've been called out unnecessarily once again, I'm used to that, the whole district uses the night bell to torment me, but that I had to sacrifice Rosa this time into the bargain, that beautiful girl who's been living in my house for years without my hardly ever noticing her – the sacrifice is too great, and I have to think up all kinds of far-fetched explanations for myself, to stop me laying into this family which, with the best will in the world, cannot give Rosa back to me. But then, as I'm closing my bag and waving to them to bring my fur, and the family are all standing together, the father sniffing at the glass of rum in his hand, the mother, probably disappointed with me – what on earth do these people expect? – biting her lips with tears in her eyes, the sister waving a blood-soaked handkerchief, I somehow find that I am, all things considered, prepared to admit that the lad is perhaps ill. I go over to him, he smiles at me, as if I were bringing him the most strengthening of soups – aha, now both horses are neighing, I presume the noise is prescribed by higher authority, to facilitate the examination – and I discover that, yes, the lad is ill. A wound the size of the palm of the hand has opened up in his right side, in the hip region. Pink, in many shades, dark at the centre, getting lighter towards the edges, delicately grained, the blood seeping through unevenly, spread out like an open-cast mine. That was from a distance. From close to a further complication appears. Who could see it without giving a soft whistle? Maggots, as thick and as long as my little finger, pink from their own blood and bespattered with the boy's, are twisting up, with tiny heads and lots of legs, towards the light, anchored to the inside of the wound. Poor lad, there's nothing I can do for you. I have found your great wound; this flower in your side will destroy you. His family is happy to see me busy; his sister's telling his mother, his mother his father, his father a few visitors who are coming in through the moonlight of the open door, on tiptoe, balancing with arms outstretched.

'Will you save me?' whispers the boy with a sob, dazzled by the life in his wound. That's just typical of people round here. Always demanding the impossible of their doctor. They've lost their old faith; the priest is sitting at home, plucking the vestments to pieces, one after another; but the doctor is expected to be able to do everything with his delicate, surgeon's hands. Well, it's up to you: it wasn't my idea; if you insist on making a holy man of me, I'm happy to let you have your way. What else could I expect, an old country doctor who has been robbed of his servant girl! And they come, the family and the village elders, and undress me; the school choir led by the teacher is outside the house and sings, to an extremely simple melody:

> Undress him so that he can cure us.
> And if he can't, then strike him dead!
> It's only a doctor, only a doctor.

Undressed, my fingers in my beard, my head bowed, I calmly look at the people. I am quite composed and superior to all of them, and I remain so, despite the fact that it is of no help to me, for now they have taken me by the head and by the feet and are carrying me to the bed. They lay me down along the wall, against the side with the wound. Then they all go out of the room; the door is closed; the singing falls silent; clouds cover the moon. The bedding is warm around me; the shadowy horses' heads sway in the windows.

'Do you know,' I hear a voice in my ear, 'I have very little faith in you. You didn't come on your own two feet, someone just got rid of you. Instead of helping, you are taking up space on my deathbed. Most of all, I'd like to scratch your eyes out.'

'Quite right,' I say, 'It's a disgrace. But I am a doctor. What should I do? Believe me, it's not easy for me either.'

'You think I should content myself with that excuse? I suppose I'll have to. I have to be content with everything. I came into the world with a handsome wound; that was all I was endowed with.'

'My dear young friend,' I say, 'your fault is that you don't see things from a wider perspective. I tell you — and I have visited every sickroom, far and wide — your wound is not that bad at all. Created with two blows of the axe at a sharp angle. There are many who offer their sides, but they hardly even hear the axe in the forest, let alone it coming nearer.'

'Is that really so, or are you deceiving me in my fever?'

'It is really so, take the word of honour of a medical officer of health with you to the other side.' And he took it and fell silent. But now it was time to think of my escape. The horses were still faithfully at their posts. My fur and bag were quickly gathered up; I didn't want to waste time dressing; if the horses made as good speed as on the way here I would jump straight from this bed into my own, so to speak. Obediently, one horse stepped back from the window; I threw the load into the carriage; the fur flew too far, just one sleeve caught on a hook. That would do. I jumped onto the horse. The reins trailing loose, one horse hardly hitched to the other, the carriage swaying to and fro, the fur coat at the rear dragging through the snow. 'Gee up!' I said, but they did not gee up; as slowly as old men we went through the snowy wastes; for a long time we could hear behind us the children's new, but erroneous, song:

Rejoice, ye patients all
The doctor is laid in your bed!

I'll never get home like this; my flourishing practice is lost; a successor will steal everything, but to no avail, for he can never replace me; my house is tyrannised by the loathsome groom; Rosa is his victim; I refuse to visualise it. Here I am, an old man driving round and round, naked, exposed to the frost of this miserable epoch, with an earthly carriage, unearthly horses. My fur is hanging over the back of the carriage, but I cannot reach it and none of my nimble patients will lift a finger, the scum. Cheated! Cheated! Respond to a faulty night-bell just once and it can never be remedied.

Gracchus the Huntsman

Franz Kafka

Two boys were sitting on the harbour wall playing dice. A man was reading a newspaper on the steps of a monument in the shadow of its sabre-wielding hero. A girl at the fountain was filling a tub with water. A fruit vendor was lying down beside his wares and looking out to sea. Through the empty openings of the window and door one could see two men at the back of the inn drinking wine. The innkeeper was sitting by a table at the front, dozing. Gently, as if it was being carried over the waves, a boat floated into the little harbour. A man in a blue smock came on land and pulled the ropes through the rings. Two other men in dark coats with silver buttons followed the seaman, carrying a bier on which there was obviously someone lying underneath the large silk cloth with a floral pattern and fringes.

No one on the quay took any notice of the new arrivals. Even when they put down the bier to wait for the boatman, who was still occupied with the ropes, no one came up to them, no one asked any questions, no one had a good look at them.

The boatman was held up a little longer by a woman who, a child at her breast and her hair all tousled, now appeared on deck. Then he came and pointed to the straight lines of a two-storeyed, yellowish house that stood on the left, close to the sea; the bearers picked up their load and carried it through the door that was low, but flanked with slim pillars. A small boy opened a window, just caught sight of the group disappearing into the house, and hastily shut the window again. Then the door was closed as well, it was made of neatly mitred planks of black oak. A flock of pigeons, that until that point had been flying round the bell-tower, landed in front of the house. As if their food was kept in the house, the pigeons gathered outside the door. One flew up to the first floor and pecked at the window-pane. They were brightly coloured, well-fed, lively birds. The woman on the boat threw them some seeds in a great arc; they picked them up and flew across to the woman.

A man in a top hat with a black ribbon round it came down one of the steep, narrow alleyways leading to the harbour. He looked round attentively, everything worried him, the sight of rubbish in a corner made him frown. There was some peel on the steps of the monument, he flicked it off with his stick as he passed. When he reached the door, he knocked, at the same time taking his top hat in his black-gloved right hand. It was opened immediately; the long hallway was lined with at least fifty small boys, who bowed.

The boatman came down the stairs, greeted the man, led him upstairs; on the first floor he walked with him round the delicate, flimsily built loggia encircling the courtyard and then both of them, the boys crowding along behind at a respectful distance, entered a large, cool room at the rear of the house which looked out not onto another house but a bare, grey-black rock-face. The bearers were setting up some long candles on either side of the bier and lighting them, but that did not create any light, the only effect was literally to rouse the sleeping shadows and send them flickering round the walls. The cloth was drawn back from the bier. On it lay a man with a tangle of hair and beard and a bronzed skin, more or less resembling a huntsman. He lay there motionless, apparently not breathing and with his eyes closed, yet it was only the surroundings that suggested he might be dead.

The new arrival went to the bier, laid his hand on the forehead of the man stretched out on it, then knelt down and prayed. The boatman made a sign to the bearers to leave the room; they went out, clearing away the boys who had gathered outside, and closed the door. Even then the silence did not seem sufficient for the man at prayer, he glanced at the boatman, who understood and went out by a side door into the adjoining room. Immediately the man on the bier opened his eyes, turned, with a smile of pain, to face the man in black and said, 'Who are you?' He, not showing any surprise at all, got up from the floor and replied, 'The Mayor of Riva.'

The man on the bier nodded, indicated a chair with a weak gesture of his outstretched arm and said, after the mayor had accepted his invitation to sit down, 'I knew, of course, but in the first few moments I always find I have forgotten everything, everything goes round and round, and it is better that I should ask, even if I know. And you probably also know that I am Gracchus, the huntsman?'

'Certainly,' said the mayor. The announcement came during the night. We had been asleep for some time. It was towards midnight that my wife called out, "Salvatore," – that is my name – "look at the pigeon at the window." It really was a pigeon, but the size of a cock. It flew over and said into my ear, "Gracchus, the dead huntsman, will come tomorrow, welcome him in the name of the town."'

The huntsman nodded and passed the tip of his tongue through his lips, 'Yes, the pigeons fly on ahead. But, mayor, do you think I should stay in Riva?'

'I cannot say yet,' replied the mayor. 'Are you dead?'

'Yes,' said the huntsman, 'as you can see. Many years ago – many, many years it must have been – I fell off a cliff whilst I was chasing a chamois in the Black Forest, in Germany. Since then I have been dead.'

'But you are alive, as well,' said the mayor.

'In a way,' said the huntsman, 'In a way I am still alive. My funeral barge went the wrong way. A false movement of the tiller, a momentary lack of attention on the part of the boatman, the distraction of the beauty of the Black Forest, I don't know what it was, all I know is that I remained on earth, and that since then my barge has been travelling the waters of this earth. During my life I wanted no other home than my mountains and now, after my death, I am travelling through all the countries of the world.'

'And you have no part in the world beyond?' asked the mayor, wrinkling his brow.

'I am still,' replied the huntsman, 'on the great staircase leading up. I roam the infinite space of this flight of steps, sometimes at the top, sometimes down below, sometimes to the right, sometimes to the left, always in motion. The huntsman has become a butterfly. Don't laugh.'

'I'm not laughing,' protested the mayor.

'Very understanding of you,' said the huntsman. 'I am forever in motion. But if I pull myself up as far as possible until I can see the gate shining at the top, I always wake up in my old barge to find it drearily stuck in some earthly waterway. The basic mistake in my erstwhile death is grinning down at me from the walls of my cabin. Julia, the boatman's wife, knocks and brings to my bier the morning drink of the country we happen to be travelling along. I lie on a bare wooden bed, wearing – I am not a particularly pleasant sight – a grubby shroud, my hair and beard, grey and black, are inseparably entangled, my legs are covered by a large, silk cloth with a floral pattern and long fringes, intended for a woman. At my head is a church candle which gives me light. On the wall opposite is a small painting, obviously representing a bushman, who is pointing his spear at me and concealing as much of himself as possible behind a magnificently decorated shield. You see all kinds of silly pictures on ships, but this is one of the silliest. Otherwise my wooden cage is quite empty. The warm air of the southern night comes in through a porthole in the side, and I can hear the water slapping against the old barge.

I have been lying here ever since the time when I was still alive, was still Gracchus the huntsman and fell off a cliff while I was chasing a chamois in the Black Forest where I lived. Everything took its proper course. I chased, fell, bled to death in a ravine, and this barge was supposed to bear me to the afterlife. I can still remember how happy I was the first time I stretched out on these planks. The mountains never heard me sing as these four walls did, murky as they were even then.

I had lived happily, and I was happy to die. Before I came on board I gladly threw away all the junk – shotgun, game bag, hunting rifle – that I had always been so proud to carry, and put on my shroud like a girl her wedding dress. I lay here and waited. Then the misfortune occurred.'

155

'A dreadful fate,' said the mayor, raising his hand as if to ward off a like evil. 'And you are not at all to blame for it?'

'Not at all,' said the huntsman. 'I was a huntsman – what is the blame in that? I was employed as a huntsman in the Black Forest where there were still wolves. I would lie in wait, shoot, kill, skin – what is the blame in that? My work was blessed with success. "The great huntsman of the Black Forest," I was called. Where is the blame in that?'

'It is not my place to decide on that,' said the mayor, 'but I don't find anything to blame in it, either. But who is to blame, then?'

'The boatman,' said the huntsman. 'Nobody will read what I am writing here, nobody will come to help me. If helping me were a set task, all the doors of all the houses would stay shut, all the windows would stay shut, everyone would lie in bed, the blankets pulled over their heads, the whole earth would be an inn at night. There is some point to that, for no one knows of me, and if they knew of me, they would not know where I was, and if they knew where I was, they would not know how to keep me there, they would not know how to help me. The idea of helping me is an illness and the cure is to stay in bed.

I know that, so I don't shout out for help, even if there are moments when I lose control, as just now for example, and think about it intently. But all I need to do to drive away such thoughts is to look around me and recall where I am and where, as I think I am justified in saying, I have been living for centuries.'

'Extraordinary,' said the mayor, 'extraordinary. And now you propose to stay with us in Riva?'

'I do not propose,' said the huntsman, laying his hand, to excuse his irony, on the mayor's knee. 'I am here, that is all I know, that is all I can do. My barge has no tiller, it sails with the wind that blows in the lowest regions of death.'

The First Hour after Death

Max Brod

The odd little incident occurred as the minister, Baron von Klumm, was leaving the Palace of the House of Representatives at the head of a largish group of leading diplomats.

A frail man pushed his way through the ring of policemen and, in full view of everybody, ran very quickly, or rather tumbled, up the steps and fell to his knees at the top, crying, 'Minister, grant justice to our enemies and we will have peace!'

Baron von Klumm, not in the least put out, smiled his courteous smile and asked, 'You are – ?'

'Arthur Bruchfeß.'

'And your profession?'

The man flicked a lock of blond hair, that had fallen into his face as he ran, back from his forehead, 'Chimney sweep.'

'My dear Herr Bruchfeß, if you were to grant justice to your chimneys, do you think they would blacken you any the less?'

By this time five, eight, fifteen policeman had run up panting and laid hold of the petitioner, who was looking bewildered.

Von Klumm had already moved on, surrounded by the throng of dignitaries, who sighed with relief as they giggled belatedly at the minister's witticism.

A gaunt, bronzed old man went up to him, followed by a crowd of eager faces. 'A statement for the press?'

The minister looked up and glanced round uncertainly for a moment.

The Head of the Secret Police had guessed what he was thinking. 'Oh yes, minister, everyone saw what happened and took note of it.'

The minister immediately began to dictate to the thin air: 'Attacked by a mental defective; police on the spot; took necessary steps; would-be assassin taken to lunatic asylum; being examined by doctors; minister carried out his duties as usual – omit my little joke, of course. And now, if you'll excuse me, commissioner – '

'I don't know what I admire most about you,' said Herr von Crudenius, the military attaché of an allied power, as they sped towards the embassy shortly afterwards in von Klumm's car, whilst the assembled populace broke into cheers. 'You do make the choice difficult for your admirers. Is it the masterly rhetoric of your speech before the House of Representatives today, the ready wit of your riposte to the chimney sweep, or the remarkable tact with which you immediately suppressed the publication of your riposte.'

'A matter of routine, my dear Crudenius, nothing more. Of course, not routine in the pejorative sense, with its connotations of a heartless lack of scruple. There is no point in my running myself down unnecessarily, not that I'm the most modest person in the country, anyway. What I mean is that it's something one learns, one becomes accustomed to, just as one becomes accustomed to everything. Nineteen-twentieths of our life consists of blind, unthinking habit.'

'That is precisely what you said just now in parliament, Baron Klumm. Your courage took my breath away. At the very beginning you forfeited the approval of the conservative-nationalist group by speaking out against any policy of national prestige, and at the end you threw down the gauntlet to the so-called progressive parties by your praise of the main-tenance of traditional values.'

'Not praise,' interrupted von Klumm, whose intelligent features bore not the slightest trace of mental exhaustion, such as might have been expected after a strenuous five-hour ses-sion. 'I praised nothing, I merely stated the facts; stated them, if you insist, with a certain regret. I have, as you are well aware, a fanatical love for objective facts and established truths. I feel responsible for the well-being of the empire, responsible, in the fullest sense of the word, before my own conscience. As a responsible person, I must pursue a path of the most down-to-earth political realism, and I am a declared enemy of all ideologies, whether they come from the right or from the left, whether they rattle a jingoistic sword or wave an idealistic olive branch. To tell you the truth, my dear Crudenius, in my view it is people who hawk ideologies, utopias, irresponsible visions who are the worst, indeed, the only enemies of mankind,'

The attaché laughed. 'And when you think of it, that is the kind of people you are dealing with all the time, my poor chap. That man on the steps, and all those "men of the people" inside to whom you had to explain the true moral dignity of warfare: is it not, at bottom, always one and the same enemy you have to deal with? Woolly-headed idealism, getting everything the wrong way round, against sound common sense?'

'You are just the kind of person I could happily trust to write my biography,' said the minister, not without a hint of irony. 'You know the way my mind works, so to speak. With one reservation, perhaps: I have no liking for your trade,' and he pointed to the betasselled hilt of Crudenius' sabre. 'Although today I said some things that might suggest I have, I said them because they had to be said. Nor do I have any liking for this war, that has lasted for twenty years already.'

'But you said that people had become accustomed to it, provoking a storm of indignation from the Social Democrats.'

'I said it because it is true, an undeniable fact. You have the proof: every year those very same socialists approve our war-credits without quibbling. But there's still a difference between being accustomed to something and liking it, isn't there? There are bad habits as well, and I have no compunction in describing this state of permanent warfare as Europe's bad habit. But who can seriously dispute the fact that we have managed to make war one of our so-called "instinctive functions"? It is no surprise; most of the generation at present in positions of responsibility were mere schoolboys when the war began. We have grown up with war and will doubtless come to our ends before it does. Young people today have no idea what "peace" means; they have never experienced it, it is a myth to them. Of course, strictly speaking, peace has never existed, and it is my firm conviction that it never will. All that we had was an absence of war, a state of mutual hostility and deep antipathy between the states, papered over by commercial hypocrisy and cleverly drawn-up treaties. This was very well portrayed at the time by a writer who was already mature when the war broke out and was therefore able to compare conditions both before and after from personal experience; I am referring, of course, to Max Scheler, whom I have had put on the school curriculum. According to him, the difference between covert and open warfare, which merely discloses the hatred already existing, is not all that significant. On that point I am in complete agreement with him. Otherwise it would be impossible to explain why we endure it so well and how we have managed to integrate it so completely into the social fabric. It is just that war has always existed, since the world began. War is the natural condition of mankind, only its outward form changes. Just look around you, my dear Crudenius. Does this busy street, the crush outside the theatre, the throng all round and inside the department stores look abnormal? After having overcome some initial disruption, which appears child's play to us today, the economic machinery is in perfect working order. Exports have vanished but the internal market has developed. And with what success you can tell by the unheard-of dividends our companies are yielding. The material destruction is more than compensated for by the spur to our native inventiveness and the exploitation of new raw materials. We are approaching the ideal of a closed economy as proclaimed by Fichte. The transformation of professional life was as radical as it was smooth. Man is the warrior, woman is trained for all kinds of civilian work, along with the old and those unfit for service. Of course, there is no one who regrets more than I do the fact that each year thousands of young men must die defending our frontiers, but did no one ever die in the so-called peace? We have put into effect many sensible measures which people before the war considered a pipe-dream: dynamic initiatives to encourage population growth, an expanding network of state child-care, the abolition of monogamy, programmed leave for soldiers for the purposes of reproduction, land reform, detached houses, hostels for war veterans, garden towns, et cetera, et cetera. And the result of all this is that the population is showing an even higher annual rate of increase than ever before, and that the general level of health is constantly rising. As a consequence of the drop in infant mortality the number of deaths per year, including all military losses, has even shown a decline, albeit a very small decline, in absolute terms compared to the pre-war period. Those are statistical facts. Nowadays we are raising people, so to speak, whereas in earlier times the state, one cannot understand why, supported measures which were downright anti-people, such as the preservation of large estates and tax concessions to unhygienic production methods.'

'But then how do you explain the general dissatisfaction? There is a rumble of discontent going round the world, dull but unmistakable, that finds expression in embarrassing scenes like that this afternoon."

'Being accustomed to something is not the same as being happy with it. Didn't I say that before? People have become used to the most dreadful conditions because they have no choice, but that does not mean they are happy with them. We have even become accustomed to death. Don't laugh; I'm serious. As a race, as the *genus humanum*, we have become indifferent to death. And yet when you think of it by yourself, as an individual, the thought of dying is terrible, unthinkable even, the notion that from a particular moment onward you will not feel, not think, not exist any more, not temporarily, but simply for all eternity. What will it be like inside our heads an hour after death? And five hundred thousand years after? What you must remember is that this horrifically long state of non-being is certain for each one of us, inescapable, not merely a nasty misfortune which we might avoid if we are lucky. It is this absolute, unconditional certitude of death which is the most horrible thing about the whole affair.'

The young officer flushed with emotion. 'I thank you, Herr von Klumm. Oh, what a debt of gratitude I owe you, since you have befriended me in this alien city! You have made a human being of me. Without you I could not go on living.'

'You have just become accustomed to me, my friend. Everything is a matter of habit.'

'No. I love you. You are my only support,' replied Crudenius passionately. 'It was hard for me, harder than you can imagine, to be torn from my home, torn from my parents, whom I respect, from the company of my friends, and brought here to a court that is, let us be open about it, stiff and ceremonial and whose language I can hardly understand. You have often laughed at me for my sentimentality . . .'

'Yes; and I still do today. The world is the same all over, the modern world, at least. Everywhere you will find sleeping-cars, bathrooms, underground railways, concrete, asphalt, jazz, the same elegant ladies' dresses, even the same perfumes. Modern man can find things he is used to everywhere. Apart from latitude and longitude, I can see no difference at all between the great cities of today.'

'But there must be between peoples, otherwise there wouldn't be this war.'

The minister twisted in his seat in mock horror. 'Oh dear me! Is that the result of all the lectures on realism I have been giving you for the last few months? Have even you fallen for clichés such as the different character of the nations, the different genius of the races? If I have made any significant contribution, however modest, to history, it is in my protest against such suggestions. You must come to understand that the inevitability of war is based not on the differences between nations – which I do allow, though in microscopic degrees that are of no account – but on the ineluctable similarity of all nations. Because their needs for survival are identical, it is in their nature to compete for space, for the opportunity to develop. The simple truth is that like needs come into conflict, and will do so until the earth evolves several surfaces, one above the other like organ keyboards, until there are as many earths as there are nations. In the distant future every nation will require the whole of the earth's surface for itself. And that distant future will come all the more quickly, the better and stronger the nation is, the more powerful its development, the greater its sense of moral responsibility. And along comes some poor devil demanding vehemently that I should "grant justice to our enemies." I do, I do, and I always have done. Do you imagine I approve of the dreadful, jingoistic, obscene language the popular press uses against our enemies? Of course, as a means of making sure the nation does not slacken in its efforts, it is indispensable, just as mines and flame-throwers are indispensable, and one wouldn't describe those as particularly nice. But it really is naive to assume that we in the government actually think what we get the papers to write about "barbarians" and "hypocrites". No, we are fair; we fully recognise the enemy's qualities, and the justice of their claims. But our fairness also leads us, without hatred or rancour, to a clear recognition of the fact that we have good qualities and justice on our side as well, that, as ill luck would have it, there is not one justice in the world, but two, several indeed; that our real, material inter-ests (and they are what count, not some figments of the imagination) collide with the equally real material interests of the enemy, that the nations must fight because, and for as long as, they must breathe. It is just the same as a chimney: however fair and good-natured it is, it has no choice but to pour out soot. Are there really people so short-sighted that they cannot see that, cannot see the whole, real, irrefutable *tragedy of human existence*? I must also say that anyone who does not accept that is not a good Christian. As Luther says, the very clay from which we are formed is sinful. The essence of humanity is lust, original sin, and it seems very superficial to me to blame the wretched condition of mankind on transitory errors by the government, or on individuals' dishonesty, narrow-mindedness or megalomania, instead of on this darkness underlying all human life, even the most benevolent and best-intentioned. Let us look reality squarely in the face! The man of the church can renounce the whole world at one fell swoop, but that is not possible for the statesman, whose task it is to direct the worldly affairs of this world. He may desire to be just as good a Christian as the unworldly ascetic, but there is one thing he must be clear about: his policies can never be directed towards abolishing war, nor human suffering and misery in general, but only towards – what shall I call it? – improving the organisation of our misery. That is the most he can hope to achieve.'

They had reached the ambassadorial palace. His companion took his leave. 'I must say,' was the minister's final comment, 'that it was precisely the war which taught me this true, this deadly earnest Christianity, this sublime religion of suffering. By the way, you're coming round after ten for bridge, aren't you? The fair Gabrielle will be there, and I've invited your Nannette as well.'

In the ministry there was a long queue of officials waiting to make their reports. After sessions in parliament, Baron von Klumm, whose industry and meticulous attention to detail were proverbial, used to make up for wasted time, as he put it, and at such times he would often work without rest until late into the night. So on that evening as well there was a constant stream of advisers and clerks, telephone calls and dictation. A delegation from the annexed territories was admitted and presented their petitions and requests. The minister made a note of a number of books and pamphlets which were mentioned in the course of the audience. Even though it was nine o'clock, he sent the messenger to the ministry library and then, in the car on his way home, immersed himself in one of the recommended books, that dealt with the most abstruse financial and currency questions.

Gabrielle, a ballet-dancer with the Court Opera, was already waiting with the other guests in the baron's private residence; the whole company was charmed at her lack of inhibition in assuming the role of lady of the house. The company was decidedly mixed: actors who needed no encouragement to play their part in the entertainment by recounting more or less spicy anecdotes, a few provincial governors, wrapped up in their eternal hunting stories, two or three ironic conversationalists from the diplomatic corps and a Jewish writer, who was the first to get drunk, at which he indulged in revolutionary speeches, to the great amusement of the rest. Nannette, a cabaret singer who obviously came from the lower classes and had not yet been "discovered", delighted the military attaché with her lively dialect, which he found bewitchingly natural, although each expression had to be transposed into the standard language, which he then, just for himself and ignored by the rest, translated into his own mother tongue and indulged in reminiscences of the fields and peasant girls of home. His diffidence, the result of this dawdle through the byways of sentimentality, was dispersed by a brisk observation from the minister, and the cards soothed all passions. Gabrielle, for whom there was always a suite of rooms ready in the villa, had long since retired to bed when the last guests, supported by sleepy lackeys, crunched their way over smashed champagne glasses to the door.

Baron von Klumm had his valet make a cold compress for his forehead. He intended to do a little more work before going to Gabrielle. Throughout the dinner his mind had been occupied with ideas suggested by the book on economics; it was one of his major characteristics anyway, always to be brim-full of important matters, even in the midst of shallow entertainment. He sat down at his desk. As was appropriate for a genuine bachelor residence, his study was spacious and centrally positioned. It was more of a hall than a room and with its four windows took up most of the first floor façade. Its three high walls, covered from floor to ceiling with books and files, disappeared into the darkness, and from the windows, through which came the howl of the night wind, the snow-covered, moonlit range of nearby mountains could be seen.

'You've let some snow in, Peter.' The baron pointed to a lumpy, shining white patch on the parquet floor.

His servant gave an uncomprehending shrug of the shoulders, tugged at the window handles to show that they were all shut, then quickly produced a rag and gave the floor a wipe at the place the baron was still indicating with his finger, though with the hurt expression of one who has been given an eccentrically elaborate task and is only doing it out of good will.

Then he left.

The minister began to read, but was soon disturbed by a soft, crunching noise. Was he still treading on broken glass? He looked up. To his great astonishment the white patch in the room, which, moreover, lay beyond the strip of moonlight in the shadow of a cupboard, had grown into a regular mound, indeed, it was still rising visibly, like a mushroom sprouting at unnatural speed. No, that wasn't a patch of snow, it was moving. Suddenly he recognised it. It was a human head.

It took a mere second for the baron to recover his composure, seize the revolver he always carried with him and fire a shot at the head. 'I didn't realise there were trapdoors in the house.' He fired again. Six shots, then the revolver was empty.

The shots obviously missed the head, but produced a different, quite unexpected effect.

'Ah, that's it,' cried an ungainly voice, thick with phlegm and half asleep, and with one jerk the whole, very long form of the apparition, like a tautly inflated gas balloon, floated up into the room all at once but without, remarkably, causing any further damage to the floor. It was an imposing, white-haired old gentleman who rose before the minister, his eyes closed and his arms pressed against his sides. The liberating force suddenly seemed to weaken, so that the feet and calves of the strange being remained below floor level, without this fact particularly disconcerting either the apparition itself or its audience.

Beneath his cold compress the baron's hair was trying to stand on end. He fell back into his armchair; all strength, indeed all sensation, had drained from his legs so that he felt as if he had an iron hoop round his hips, pinning him in a sitting, or half-lying position, incapable of moving a muscle. However, he was not the man to take a ghostly apparition, or, more likely, some silly practical joke, lying down. He automatically sought for a conversational opening, but the only thing to cross his lips was a small amount of spittle followed by a gurgling and babbling, not unlike a baby's first attempts at

166

articulation. Finally he managed to produce some recognisable sounds, 'You are – ?'

The apparition had opened its eyes by now, beautiful big brown eyes, not at all eerie, and was looking down with a quiet, friendly expression in the approximate direction of the minister's struggles. As was his habit, the minister returned its look with a firm, severe gaze, in spite of his helpless position, stretched out in the chair, his upper body lying between the arms, rumpled and disjointed, as if it had been thrown out on the dung-heap. 'You are – ?' he repeated, his voice steadier now, and tried to regain control over his limbs by blinking vigorously. Eventually he realised the pointlessness of the exercise and lay there quite still, since he was afraid of looking silly in front of the ghost. All the time his brain had been working furiously and had come to the conclusion that he was dealing with a genuine ghost, and not just a hoax. The size of the apparition alone suggested that. It was more that twice the height of a normal human and thus much taller even than the usual giants one sees exhibited; for all that it was perfectly proportioned, thus lacking the coarse, freakish quality which makes the fairground monstrosities seem so sinister. The only sinister thing here was that this bizarre figure, as if to compensate for its size, appeared to be made of some strangely loose material, through which the windows behind it could be seen and even the dull gleam of the moonlight reflected on the distant mountain ridge. A remarkable sight which, as von Klumm observed with scientific precision, could not have been produced by any kind of trickery. However, the most inexplicable fact about it was that the figure slowly and gradually began to shrink, to condense, so that its texture became firmer and firmer, without, however, distorting its outline or features in the least. Everything about it simply became more delicate, more familiar, more human, so to speak. It was now plain to see that the phantom was not at all interested in frightening anybody. On the contrary, it gave the impression (perhaps a delusion, perhaps an accurate observation of the baron's returning senses) that it wanted to gain the minister's confidence; indeed, it was not long before he was confronted with the incredible sight of a ghost that was most afraid of itself, that would have preferred to have cowered timidly in a corner so as not to cause any fuss, but was unfortunately fixed to the spot, to its great embarrassment and confusion.

The minister pulled himself together and forced himself to sit upright. The first thing he did was to remove the cold compress, which he felt somewhat spoilt the tone of a private audience. Then he said, quite coolheaded once more, 'But you must tell me your name, *your name.*'

'Name,' repeated the ghost, as if it were making a great effort to work something out. 'Name . . . name . . . what is that now: name?' Its voice was not sleepy any more, but clear and high, only with a little too much vibrato to come from human vocal chords. It had an unmistakable note of great shyness and humility.

The baron looked up at the figure again, scrutinising it from head to toe, or rather, to knee, since parts of its lower extremities were still below floor level. Again there was a pause, which the baron used to settle himself more comfortably in his chair, whilst the apparition seemed to realise for the first time that it had arms; at least it now looked down at them in astonishment and detached them, hesitantly, incredulously, from its sides, lifted them a little and then let them fall back down again. As it did so, the movement of its head, which was the first it had made, seemed to fill it with amazement, even terror, for the expression on its face became more anxious by the second, and after these experiments in movement the rigidity of its contours became even firmer for the next few minutes.

When occasion demanded, the baron could be 'quite tart' as his close colleagues called it. An occasion for his tartness had arrived. As if to compensate himself for the fright, which he had only just managed to overcome, he barked at his visitor, 'Damn it all, man, you must know who you are, what you're called, why you're here and how you managed to get in here!'

At the sound of these harsh words the apparition summoned up all its energy. An old man knitting his white eyebrows as he desperately tries to remember something, that was more or less what the apparition looked like. But all he managed to do was to twitter, 'I think I must have just died into here.'

' "Died into here?" What on earth is that?'

Another pause.

'Come on, man, I asked you a question. What is that?'

'If only I knew, sir,' replied the old man. 'Do have pity on me. I have only just died, a little while ago, and I committed so many sins. How should I know where I am? I'm all of a daze. It's not easy, believe me.' And after these few sentences, the first coherent things he had said, he closed his eyes again, as if exhausted from so much exertion.

'Remarkable,' said the baron, 'strange. Hmmm . . . Never heard anything like it.' As if seeking help, he felt around with his hand and grasped the shade of his desk-lamp. The contact seemed to give him an idea. Holding on to the lampshade for support, he twisted round in his chair until he was in the bright light of the standard lamp, thus for the first time removing the ghost from his sight. Suddenly he began to rummage desperately among the piles of papers and books. They contained his normal, everyday work, his usual thoughts and ideas. He tried to cling to the individual words and figures he read, to fasten onto them, but they went blurred before his feverish eyes, he could not decipher anything at all. However, after a while he thought he had come sufficiently back to his senses to risk a glance into the room behind him. He took it slowly as he returned to his former position. There was the room, melting into endless darkness, of which the electric lamp only illuminated his immediate surroundings, not much farther than his feet. And right in front of him was that bean-pole again who – it was grotesque – had not used the interval to arrange himself in a comfortable position, but was still standing there, stiff and in deadly earnest, apparently waiting, in complete oblivion of everything else, for the minister's reply.

'Now, you tell me . . . You say you have died . . . And yet you're alive . . . What is that supposed to mean? Can't you express yourself a little more rationally? Have you really died or are you here?'

'I died into here . . . because of my sins.'

The baron shook his head. 'Because of your sins? You've said that already. What kind of sins? You're a murderer, aren't you?'

A violent shudder of loathing passed through the ghost's body. It shook itself thoroughly then, still somewhat clumsily but with emphatic vigour, raised its arms and even clasped its hands above its head, as it cried out piteously, 'A murderer!? Me, a murderer!? No, the Lord be praised, I kept well away from that all my life. However painstakingly I examine my heart, as it was and as it now is, I cannot find the slightest trace of murderous thoughts.'

'So you must have been a thief, an embezzler, a black-marketeer, a swindler, or at least dishonest in some way, mustn't you?'

'Dishonest, yes, that might be it. I did not always bear the eternal truth of things in mind wherever I went and whatever I was doing, although I kept on making a firm resolution to do so.'

'And that was the sum total of your dishonesty?' The baron burst out laughing.

'Oh, it was a sin, the very worst sin of all! That is why my punishment is this dreadful transfer to another world, that is why my death did not lead to promotion to a higher sphere, but to this terrible exile in a parallel, if not lower stage of development.'

'Incredible. So you still insist that you are dead?'

'Of course. What I am going through at this moment is the thing men should stand most in fear of, or rather, since it is a sign of divine justice, most in awe of: I am going through the first hour after my death.'

'That must be terribly interesting.' The words had passed the baron's lips before he had time to think about them. 'That is . . . I mean . . . Wouldn't you like to sit down? You must tell me more about it. What is it like, this first hour after death? You must realise that I have often spent an idle moment thinking about it, or rather, trying to visualise what it must be like. Unfortunately I am always very busy. But sometimes, you know, between important matters of state, such abstruse ideas do occur to one. I feel I must call them abstruse, for how can a living person know or imagine with any degree of accuracy what will happen inside him after his death. It's a downright impossibility, an absurdity. Now, I feel I must preface my remarks by saying how close this matter has always been to my heart, I have kept it constantly under review . . .' As he warmed to his subject he automatically began to use the elegant phrases with which he had been fobbing off petitioners and deputations for years, showing just how much this conversation had lost its bizarre and phantom character for him, how much he was beginning to regard it as a normal conversation and not at all eerie. 'To put it in a nutshell, I imagine that in that first hour everything, if that is the right word, around one will be quite dark and empty and desolate. Nothingness, do you understand, nothingness in the most precise meaning of the word. That's how I imagine it. Of course, I wouldn't dream of putting my experience on a par with yours, or even of comparing it. You must forgive me for going on like this. I would much rather listen to what you have to say than to go blethering on myself. There, I'm all ears. But please, do sit down, over here . . .'

The ghost had let its eyes wander round the room with a rather bewildered air, but now they focused on the leather armchair the minister was drawing up. It seemed to have understood the words, for it sat down obediently, and as quickly as the fact that its feet were still stuck in the floor would allow; it did, however, reveal a certain lack of familiarity in the use of seating as it flopped down across both armrests at once. But it would anyway have had difficulty in squeezing itself into the wide seat of the chair, since it was still of gigantic proportions.

'Off you go then, tell me something about this paradise that the preachers claim to be so well acquainted with.'

'Paradise!' replied the ghost with a sigh. 'How should a miserable wretch like myself be able to tell you anything about paradise. I might enter it after a billion years, perhaps never.'

'Tell me about hell then, if you like,' countered the minister with a casual wave of the hand, as if he were making conversation.

'Well, unless I am very much mistaken, I do seem to have escaped hell,' replied the apparition, with a not very confident glance round the room; but it seemed to feel that even that glance was presumptuous and immediately corrected itself with quiet modesty. 'Anyway, you must not think it is something special. The extremes, that is complete redemption and complete damnation, are probably, at least that is my assumption, just as exceptional in eternity as in our mortal existence. The middle ground, with its thousand shades of grey, is much the commoner. Although I am not entirely sure about it, a plot of that middle ground seems to be my lot as well.'

'To my mind nothingness, the absolute nothingness that follows death, would be hell enough.'

'Nothingness?'

'Yes, the nothingness I spoke about before, the disappearance of all sensation, of all desire and joy and sorrow.'

'I'm very sorry, but I can't have understood you properly before. You must be patient with me. I'm doing my best, but I've been so confused, so dazed by all the new things around me, that I find it difficult to follow you, in spite of all your kindness. Nothingness after death, you said? I should have contradicted you straight away there. It's the precise opposite, in fact. After death one is assailed by a wealth of fresh and unsuspected impressions. It takes a great effort to fend them off . . .'

'New impressions . . . at the moment of death?'

'Not precisely at the moment of death. That is accompanied by a brief instant of diminished consciousness, during which you feel nothing apart from a violent tearing, the previously unknown, quite strong but brief sensation of the soul detaching itself from the body, a tug, of which it is impossible for me to say whether it is closer to pain or pleasure. However, as I said, it only lasts for a fraction of a second, then the soul is

172

free of physical matter, completely pure and unhampered. But that is just what is the most strenuous thing about it. How can I describe it? We spend all our days trying to saturate our physical being – which, let's be honest about it, is the main focus of our existence – with mental, emotional and spiritual life, which we extract for our own use from the streams of life flowing all around us. Suddenly our soul is free, is what you might call a non-material cavity, a vacuum, a bubble surrounded by matter. But matter, which is accustomed to feeding on spiritual life, to drinking its fill, so to speak, naturally falls on the cavity from all sides, wild with desire, and tries to penetrate it. All types of substantiality, even those of the lowest forms of life, would like to take possession of the liberated soul, to feed on it and fatten themselves up. Those first minutes are terrible. I must say that I came through it quite well, I kept a tight hold on my tiny bundle of soul. But there are many souls that are ripped apart in those first moments of their new life, simply torn to shreds. It gives me the shivers to imagine the suffering a soul that has been reduced to atoms like that must go through. In spite of everything, they retain their awareness of the self as a unity, whilst at the same time having to continue a physical existence as an earthworm, a leaf, and perhaps a few bacteria on it that are devouring each other. I assume it is this condition which people call hell.'

'Could be, could well be,' interrupted the baron with the smile he reserved for opponents he had caught out. 'The only thing that puzzles me, however, is where you get all this precise information not only about your own destiny but about that of other souls into the bargain? Without wanting to offend you, you are aware, aren't you, that with all this you are treading on ground which is wide open to all kinds of fantasies and delusions, especially self-delusions? Have you searched your heart enough in this regard? Are you completely sure that a little .. I won't say lie . . . that a little exaggeration or distortion of the truth is quite out of the question?'

The old man was not offended. On the contrary, he seemed grateful for any admonition and, after having achieved a relatively calm tone in his last speech, now reverted to his initial abject contrition. 'Oh, you are right, you are so right. Obviously you are ordained to be the judge before whom I have to justify myself, no, not justify, before whom I am to confess my sins. Yes, it is true, I certainly have not truly searched my soul, nor have I guarded against vain self-delusion sufficiently, although that was my firm intention. My insight, if I might be allowed to use that word for the wretched sum of my life, was just sufficient for me to survive the first test after my death, the attack of physical matter. At that moment I was endowed with a truly remarkable clarity of vision which allowed me to see not only what was happening to me, but to all the other newly dead around me. I saw terrible things in only a few minutes and had a clear premonition of some even more terrible. Moreover, in spite of my desperate defence, I did not succeed in remaining completely pure myself. I see I have all kinds of alien matter stuck to me that should have nothing in common with immortal substances.' As he spoke these words, he fingered his coat buttons sadly and pulled the jacket he was wearing tight across his stomach with a gesture that showed that he found the article of clothing incomprehensible, that he thought it was perhaps a part of the body.

'Don't worry, there's something grotesque about all clothing,' the minister graciously comforted him.

'Clothing you call it . . . Ah, now I understand. Though our clothing was quite different. In the Sylphian sphere, where I come from, clothing consists of a certain very high velocity at which individuals spin round their own axes like tops.'

'So you are a Sylph, a Sylphide.' A vague memory of the fair Gabrielle and her Dance of the Sylphides in the last ballet floated through the baron's mind. 'Though our image of Syplhs does not quite correspond to your figure, I'm afraid.'

'They are quite different, that is true, and their mode of life is quite different from mine at this moment. At the moment I am in the middle of a transfer to your world; I'm in a halfway house, so to speak, and doing my best to behave as a human being. That is the second trial I have to go through. You suddenly find yourself in a completely different world with completely new standards. You shed all your habits, all the things you did as a matter of routine, and that is the acid test which shows how much real reality, reality that is valid for any possible world, you have managed to acquire in the course of your life . . .'

'So you're not a dead human being at all, but from another world?' asked the baron, leaning back in his chair, somewhat bewildered again.

'I have died into this world from another one,' repeated the ghost patiently.

'From the moon, maybe, or from Sirius?'

'No. As I said before, I come from a completely different world system.'

'From the Milky Way or the Orion Nebula?'

'However far you go in your physical world, you will not find my home. My home is a realm of different senses, or rather, it was so until today, and I still belong there a little. We Sylphs do not see, we do not hear or smell, nor are we heard or seen. We have different organs, are subject to a different gravity and different natural laws. As far as space is concerned, we live amongst you humans. There just happens to be an infinite number of worlds, but they are interlocking rather than running parallel, and despite their contiguity they know nothing of each other. Until this moment your world, with its starry sky and Milky Way and everything your senses perceive, was completely hidden from me as well. I am absolutely amazed to find myself in such an unsuspected, novel environment without moving from the spot, merely by means of an inner conversion of my organs.'

'Wait a moment, not so fast! I need to digest that first,' cried von Klumm, pressing his hand against his forehead, which was once more throbbing painfully. 'Everything here is quite new to you? . . . Well, I must say . . . assuming all these things you have been telling me are correct . . . I must say you show commendable good manners and self-assurance. Many people have sat there, where you are sitting now, and been so embarrassed they didn't know what to do with themselves. Perhaps I should tell you that I am – I can say this without being presumptuous – a man of some influence, and strangely enough people say of me – I have really no idea how I have acquired this reputation – that there is something imposing about my personality, so that even the boldest or most impudent citizens find it difficult to preserve their sangfroid when face to face with me.'

At this the ghost, who up to that point had been following the conversation just as intently as the minister, gave the first sign of boredom, a rather clear sign in fact, as it fixed its eyes on the window and began to look at the landscape outside with visible enjoyment, craning its neck and even half rising from its chair.

The minister was too polite to notice it.

'What beautiful mountains,' said the ghost, and its breast heaved with a sigh of longing.

'So you recognise our earthly mountains as well,' said the minister in a tone of coolly polite commendation. 'I must compliment you on your capacity for rapid orientation. Are there things like mountains in your world too?'

'No. At home everything manifests itself, or rather, everything manifested itself, in electric waves, spinning funnels of air and whirlpools.'

'And yet . . .'

'In our kind of matter there is also natural beauty, sublime expressions of eternal forces, of growth and decay. It is probably because during my whole life, whenever I managed to get out and enjoy nature, which was rarely enough with my awful job – indeed, it was probably precisely the fact that it was so unusual that gave me a thirst for the glories of nature and a true delight in them – but whenever I did commune with nature, it automatically aroused in me the feeling that the joy I felt brought me into contact with eternal, general truths, with the bedrock of reality; and that is probably what enables me to respond so quickly to any kind of natural beauty, even in this new world, and to sense immediately whenever I am in the presence of anything significant in that respect here as well."

'Most strange. To tell the truth, I couldn't match you in

that. If I came from a place where the Alps consisted of nothing but whirling air-pools . . . that's what you said, wasn't it? . . . of nothing but soap bubbles, with no rocks, no snow, no plants, no colours . . . of course, without colours . . . well, I must say, if I were confronted with real mountains I would be totally baffled, totally . . .' The baron fell into a brown study from which he eventually came to with a start. 'In a word, I would be baffled.'

'I think you are mocking me,' moaned the ghost. 'Am I not sufficiently baffled or confused? It is only with nature that I feel I know where I am.'

'Not at all, there are other areas where you seem surprisingly sure of yourself. Even, it seems to me, the most important ones. You have a precise idea – let me be honest: an unnaturally precise idea – of where you come from and where you are going.'

'But sir, I don't know, I don't know at all.'

Then baron refused to be distracted, 'You are even aware of the fact that you are at a transitional stage. You have some idea of the trials that await you, of a court of judgment that you must face and of the good works you can cite in evidence before the court. Added to that, you have, remarkably, no difficulty at all with our language or our concepts in this rather complex field. You talk like a book, you talk of eternal justice as if you were related, you talk of God, and death, and hell, and the devil knows what else . . .' The baron had worked himself up into a rage and was pacing up and down the room.

'Yes . . . well . . . fortunately I took something of an interest in that kind of thing during my lifetime,' said the spectre, very timidly, 'even if it was nowhere like enough. Not that I really understood them, but I felt a certain yearning that kept drawing me back to them; and there, too, I had the feeling that I was dealing with the foundation of reality that was valid for all places and all times . . . Unfortunately it meant that I neglected other things, and I'm paying dearly for that now . . .'

'Come on then,' said the baron impatiently, as the ghost

paused. 'That is just what I would like to hear about. What is it that you are paying for now? What was your sin?'

'I was . . . I was . . .' he stuttered with the shame of it. 'How shall I put it, I was very clumsy about minor details. That is, I *thought* they were minor details, but now I see that they have their own significance and even, if you take proper care over them, contain a grain of reality which one should respect. Now is the time I need them. That is the special rule that governs us in this first hour after our death. Action and reaction are completely reversed. All the things which during our mortal lives we regarded with respect, awe and wonder are now familiar to us. But the things we treated casually, that we debased to matters of soulless routine, appear alien and incomprehensible to us here. That is why I am having such problems with . . .' again he broke off, 'with my clothes. To be honest, I neglected them badly. Matters of polite behaviour I never understood at all. I looked down on them with a certain arrogance and, because of my interest in higher things, I even believed my arrogance was justified. Now I'm being punished for it. I'm sure even etiquette – civilised behaviour between creatures, moderation, keeping your distance – contains something of universal value, is part of God's design. It could be that keeping your distance is exaggerated, that it contains a grain of truth amid a large amount of deception. But it was my duty to find that grain of truth. However crude the deception that concealed it, it was not a sufficient excuse for letting myself be put off by the wrapping. My punishment is that now I am totally at a loss as to how to behave. Just imagine how embarrassing it is for me that that I still can't work out what form you take. I can't see you at all. I think that your voice comes from that beautiful, radiant body,' he pointed to the desk-lamp behind the baron, who at these words, perhaps for the first time in his life, felt small and insignificant, though the only effect it had was to intensify his rage, 'and I take the light for the centre of the personality I am conversing with. But unfortunately, beyond that I can find no shape distinguishable from the surroundings. And I can't work out what to do with my own body, however hard I try to adapt to

178

my new world. One moment I seem to wrinkle up, the next I feel as if I'm spreading in all directions. I feel uncomfortable in every pore. Believe me I have no spatial orientation at all, everything is reeling through my head in a most dizzying manner. I can't find the right level for my movements. I see everything lop-sided.'

'Yes, I realise that now,' said von Klumm with a mocking laugh.

'Only now do I realise how right a friend of mine was who kept telling me about his homesickness. He had only come from another city, not from another world, but he kept on complaining how alien he felt, as if it were a punishment even. An aspect of his life which at home had been concealed beneath a blanket of agreeable habits in the close-knit, almost bodily warmth of the family circle was stripped bare there: a certain inner emptiness and meaninglessness.'

'That is just what the military attaché was saying today,' murmured the baron, and his suspicion intensified.

'If,' the apparition continued unperturbed, 'you spend your life under the delusion of constant activity, if you are always industrious and ambitious, concentrate on the so-called "serious" things, which mostly concern just the bare, and banal, essentials, and waste your leisure on "unserious" things, which are just as unreal as the "serious" ones . . . in brief, if all you can see is dreary routine and necessity, never the liberating, absolute truth . . .'

'That's going too far,' the baron shouted, striding over to the spectre with clenched fists. 'Now you're talking about me!'

'No, about my friend,' screamed the apparition, pulling its upper body back as far as it could.

'Hah! So he could not see absolute truth anywhere? Listen, I take my hat off to him; he is a grand fellow, your friend, he's just my man. That's the way I am too. The bare facts of life I recognise; some things are more expedient, more reasonable than others, relatively speaking! But all this drivel you talk about the foundations of reality that are valid for all places and all times . . . Damn it all, I see the whole purpose of my life – a modest purpose, but perhaps not without some significance – in combating such foolish ideas. Good grief, is there anyone so short-sighted that they cannot see that? There are no rights that are valid for all, no justice, because everyone is in the right, every single one of us. That is why there must be war without end, conflict between man and man, and warfare between the nations . . .'

Scarcely had the minister spoken these words than a transformation came over the ghost. If, up to this point, it had been one of the plaintive sort, almost entirely lacking in spirit, it now flew into a frenzy of rage equal to the baron's. 'What?! What?! That's rubbish,' it shouted, putting aside all its meekness at once. 'There is no such word as "must", things that are reasonable are not so merely "relatively speaking". With views like that you're just blinding yourself to the true nature of reality.'

'Me, blind! Me, whom everyone recognises as the most down-to-earth, most realistic of modern statesmen!? And who says so? A utopian daydreamer like you! Do you know that I consider people of your kind the worst, indeed the only enemies of mankind?' The baron was so overcome with indignation that he had grabbed the apparition by the arm and was dragging it backwards and forwards. But the apparition had lost its temper as well. In its fury it hit out in all directions, but so clumsily that it missed the baron. 'Such an enemy of mankind, in fact,' screamed the latter, jumping out of the way, 'that I have no hesitation in shooting you and your silly ideas down on the spot.' He rushed to the desk, opened a box and began to reload the revolver, his hands trembling. At the same time he kept on shouting and arguing, his voice getting hoarser and hoarser with excitement and rage, 'You and your stupid talk of eternal justice! Don't you realise you are blaspheming against mankind's most dearly held belief. If there were one right, one justice valid for all, then what about the intrinsic wrongness, pointlessness of all earthly existence which depends on the very fact that all those who are lashing out at each other, all of them, are in the right at the same time.

What about Christianity, the religion of suffering, what about the essentially tragic nature of earthly life?'

'You miserable wretch!' The ghost, for its part, now screamed with all its might, and in its voice there was a rumble of something like underground thunder, even the windows seemed to echo it darkly, and the wind outside blew with even greater force, bringing from the mountains a strange, soft, whistling, rustling sound, as if somewhere in the distance the age-old rock was cracking and preparing to trickle down in streams of fine sand. 'You miserable wretch!' In its fury, the whole of visible nature seemed to be joining in the scream. 'Is it any business of yours to meddle in God's affairs, to take the tragic nature of His creation under your gracious patronage, when enough, probably more than enough, is done to make it tragic if, in His infinite goodness, He allows harmful pests such as you to go on living, instead of exterminating them!' At these words the ghost bent right back, as if it was preparing to run at the mannikin, knock him down with the mere force of its body and crush him. By this violent movement, however, it unexpectedly freed itself completely from the floor, in which it had still been stuck as far as its knees. It shot up, as if through a trap door, and amazingly did not stop when the soles of its feet reached floor level but, as if with the force of its own violence, continued to rise in the air, not, however, straight up, but at an angle, as if it were floating up an invisible staircase. In the course of this it passed close by the baron like an icy draught; that is, it missed him. 'Woe is me!' it cried now, with a searing, plaintive sound, as it suddenly stopped in mid-air, almost fixed to the spot apart from a gentle pendulum motion. 'My sins! My sins!'

The baron had tumbled trembling to his knees, the gun flying in a wide arc from his hand and clattering to the floor. It was not so much what the ghost said that demolished his painstakingly erected composure, as the awful sight of its body hanging in the air, as if from an imaginary gallows, far surpassing in its eeriness all the strange things he had seen on this memorable evening. And now the trembling words from above him, that sounded as if they came straight from a tormented heart, plucked at a nerve in his soul which had not resonated for years, perhaps not since his earliest childhood. 'My sins! My sins!' he started to whimper as well, and rolled his eyes, for the tears would not come; over the long years he had forgotten how to cry.

For a while their piteous moans filled the whole room, arousing an eerie echo in the gentle creaking of the furniture. The moon had set, and outside the circle of lamplight there was complete darkness. Only now did the soft glimmer of bluish-white light around the apparition become visible, like the crackle of a comb as it is drawn through the hair. It really gave the impression that every tiny fibre in the ghost's clothes was standing painfully on end and shivering in the alien, refractory medium of the earth's atmosphere, which made itself felt at the slightest movement in an unpleasant soreness.

'What is the matter with you? Lord above, what's the matter?' cried the minister, whose fury had completely dissipated, and who now felt only pity, pity for the poor, lost, spectral apparition, and even greater pity for himself, for he was beginning to suspect that his fate in that inevitable first hour after death would turn out to be similar to that of the ghost, only much, much more horrible.

'Can't you see?' came the pitiful wail from above. 'I have no sense of space, that is what is the matter. I can see that there are rooms and stories, a certain regularity in the arrangement of above and below, of right and left. But I can't integrate this peculiar arrangement into my senses, I can't feel it from within . . . And now I've realised for what particular event in my life this punishment has been visited upon me.'

'Oh, how terrible,' lamented the minister. 'What crime did you commit? Perhaps I can help you. If it lies within my power, you can rest assured that I will leave no stone unturned . . .' The usual diplomatic clichés came tumbling over his pale lips, only completely tonelessly.

The ghost did not respond to his offer at all, it seemed sunk in recollection and to be talking to itself. 'Once a real gentleman, some kind of minister I think, came to visit me in my attic. He probably came with the best of intentions, full of

182

goodwill. He wanted to learn from me, he said, wanted to examine with his own senses my original way of life, my home-grown philosophy. Those were his very words. Then I became puffed up with proletarian pride and threw him downstairs single-handed, crying out in exultation, "Let that be a lesson to you that for me there is no difference between high and low, superiors and inferiors." '

'No difference between high and low? And that's why you're hanging in mid-air, you poor man? Well, it wasn't a very nice thing to do though, was it?'

'Yes, that's what I shouted after him. My voice rang with conviction, I believed I had done something fine. Unfortunately I'm very quick-tempered, as you have just had an opportunity to see. It seemed the right thing to do, the obvious thing even, to grab him by the collar and throw him down the stairs. For a long time afterwards I was really pleased with myself for having had such a brilliant idea, it seemed to come from my innermost soul, I could not imagine it could have happened any other way. Now, however, I feel that it is precisely that apparently obvious and self-enclosed nature of things, their lack of love, their blatant palpability and certainty which is the worst danger, the worst temptation for mortals. It's just the way things are, we think, or rather don't think. We salve our consciences with the idea that although misery and hypocrisy and mass murder and wastage exist, that's it and we can do nothing about it. We think we can't change or improve anything, quite forgetting that we could make a start with ourselves . . .'

The baron interrupted him, his teeth chattering in an outburst of abject fear, 'But my dear fellow, just think what will happen to me, if you have to suffer so much just because of one single, insignificant transgression, merely a piece of robust behaviour? I'll be well up in matters of etiquette and keeping one's distance, it's true, but what about all the other and, so it appears, more important things, which I just treated as routine and which will consequently all rise up against me? I was in the habit of saying that we had even become accustomed to death. I'm going to find everything, simply everything in this upside-down world, in the afterlife, I mean, startlingly new and inexplicable, aren't I?'

'Ah, now I can feel it,' exclaimed the ghost joyfully at that moment, completely ignoring the horror-struck minister. 'Now, now the chastisement is slackening. I can feel that I am being forgiven. I can feel a sense of unparalleled harmony flowing through my every limb . . .' The ancient apparition was silent, its eyes glistening with tears of joy as, with a gentle smile on its lips, it slowly floated down to the floor. It was now not much more than the normal shape and size of a human, and the prickly sparkle had disappeared from round its body. Now its feet were on the floor. Immediately they were freed from their puppet-like restraint, and it walked easily towards the baron, whom it now seemed to have no difficulty in distinguishing from his surroundings. It noticed that the later was kneeling on the floor. 'Get up,' it said in a friendly voice, and gave the groaning minister a helping arm. 'No one is entirely lost . . . But I am being drawn powerfully to some other place. What other trials await me? Or are they already at an end and I have been purified, ready for the highest level? I do not know. All I feel is that my time in this terrestrial world is over and that I am about to plunge into another sphere, perhaps – oh, the mere idea is bliss! – into a purer one than this and my own are. Fare thee well!'

'No, stay!' cried the baron in despair. 'Stay with me. Speak to me still. It makes me so happy. And you mustn't think that simply means I have become accustomed to you. Your staying will be something quintessentially real.'

The apparition shook its head earnestly. 'I may not.'

'Not even if I go down on my knees to you? Not even if I tell you that your words could be of infinite, decisive significance for my soul's salvation, that my eternal redemption is in your hands?'

'It is a higher law that compels me to go.'

In a gesture of humility such as he had never before known, the minister bowed his head. Gently, the apparition held out its hand to him.

'Then tell me one thing at least. What shattering experiences and lofty studies, what scholarship and distinguished instruction did you go through in your Sylph world to achieve such a sublime level of understanding that after death your whole punishment was a mild embarrassment? You must have studied with philosophers and been a philosopher yourself, or were you a great, misunderstood artist, even an apostle, prophet, founder of a religion?"

'No,' replied the apparition with a curiously restrained smile, 'my life was nothing out of the ordinary. I could not stand injustice, it is true, but I had little time for study. My profession, however, was what might be called a philosophical one. You see, I was often alone, in a dark, narrow chamber, far from other people, all on my own. That kind of thing invites reflection. In your earthly world you would call me something like a chimney sweep.'

The minister started. 'Chimney sweep . . . chimney sweep,' he repeated, gibbering.

When he looked up the apparition had disappeared without trace.

Suddenly he gave a shout and rushed over to the telephone. 'Hello, is that the lunatic asylum?

It was the nurse on night duty.

'Is Arthur Bruchfeß there? The chimney sweep who attempted to assassinate me this afternoon? Did he not die just half an hour ago?' The minister was convinced the apparition he had just been speaking to must have been the ghost of that man.

'I will check immediately, Your Excellency.'

After a while, during which the tension stretched almost to breaking point, he returned. 'No, the patient is alive, even remarkably calm and cheerful. He has not gone to sleep, but is walking up and down in his cell, warbling away to himself. The doctors have not been able to find the least trace of mental disturbance, not even of any abnormal stimulation of the nervous system.'

'Release the man. Immediately,' panted the minister. 'The whole case against him must be abandoned. We must change everything, the law, the whole world, everything . . . Have you understood? He is to be released immediately.'

'Yes, Your Excellency.'

Breathing heavily, the minister collapsed into his chair. All the time he was gently slapping himself on the head, as if to rouse himself to comprehension of the unutterable.

Then there was a rustling from the doorway.

It was the beautiful Gabrielle. The loud conversation had not woken her, but the ringing of the telephone had. 'When are you coming?' she said, pursing her lips in a pout. She stood there, shivering slightly since she was wearing nothing but her thin, semi-transparent nightdress with just two light-blue silk ribbons over her gleaming shoulders. Her unsophisticated, young face, her delicate, rounded arms and the slight, apple-smooth curve of her small breasts: the most natural things in the world, and promising the oblivion of intimacy and the accustomed sweetness of unconscious repose. A stronger man than the baron would have been unable to resist the gentle power of this ravishing sight. In a moment he was beside her. 'How long do I have to go on waiting, all by myself?' she breathed tenderly, as he clasped her to him with a wild joy and a deep sigh of relief. He shook himself free of the horror, which with his accustomed wisdom he had already filed under the heading of 'dream', or 'temporary nervous disorder', and abandoned himself to the sweet, motherly warmth of sleep her body exuded, and the gentle touch of a loose lock of hair like a willowy wand on his cheek.

The Kiss of the Stone Woman

Franz Theodor Csokor

It was about two o'clock in the morning and the disc of the
moon was dissolving beneath a bank of mist in the western
sky as the lieutenant and his platoon reached the enemy town.

Often enough in the course of the dreary march they had
been asleep on their feet, and now more than one of them
blundered into the wrought-iron gates of the suburb they
were passing through, and yet they stumbled doggedly on.
Here they felt even more deserted and forlorn than outside
the town on the track bordered by the wall of dark trees. In
the semi-dark the bare trees of the avenue looked charred.
Small villas squatted palely behind the sparse foliage of clumps
of bushes which raised their twigs like hackles in front of
them. They all seemed to have been abandoned, and the lieutenant did not even bother to stop, since none of them seemed
to offer a billet large enough for the whole unit for the rest of
this autumn night, already quivering with the approach of
morning. So the column wound its way through a gateway in
a massive tower into the old town. There was a soft clinking as
the ranks broke step. Here marching was much more difficult
than on the broad highway. Alleys suddenly shot off, confus-
ingly haphazard. The cobbles were a hindrance, too, buckling
the feet: they were bumpy, as if they were being squeezed up
by the ancient houses flanking the street which cowered there
beside the road, low and chalk-white, in an attitude of senile
malevolence. And not a sound nor light in any of them; only
here and there, outside gaping doors dripping with blackness,
stood abandoned household effects. Wailing from behind
broken window-panes suggested abandoned infants; when
torches slashed through the darkness, it was cats that scurried
out of bare rooms. The men would have liked to clamp a rest

187

onto such incidents; mercilessly the lieutenant drove them on. The houses looked ready to pounce, their exits yawning black like tunnel openings, and, although there seemed no reason to fear an enemy attack, in view of the many reports of partisan activity he felt it was not advisable to halt outside them, let alone camp out in one. The main contingent could do that when they arrived the next day; the advance guard needed open space around their quarters, in an emergency they would also have to serve as a fortress.

But such a place was not that easy to find, and so they marched on in growing irritation through this dead waste of stone, where the echo of their steps created an ambush at every corner. The skein of alleys became more and more warped and cramped, as if twisted by a gigantic pair of pliers, impossible to disentangle. Then, after twenty minutes of weary tramping, around a tight bend the cathedral square abruptly opened out before the exhausted men, broad, sprinkled with nooks and crannies, paraffin lamps on its stone arcades glowing like bloody nails. And opposite them something needle-sharp steeled up from a huge dark mass, slitting the midnight-blue sky, whilst its unfinished twin tower peered at them dispiritedly over the high-pitched minster roof, as if it had made a similar attempt and then slumped back down.

The men straightened up, broke the silence; one sang. They were the first peaceful lights their eyes had seen in weeks of blazing forests and burning farmsteads. Soon the window of one of the dark houses round the square must surely pierce the night with its friendly yellow glow, full of the promise of rest! Their hope was not deceived. One building, detached from the others, had a red lamp burning over the lintel; as they approached they saw the bright spot of a lamp on the first floor and the glitter of light flashing through a gap in the shutters of a ground-floor window. The lieutenant sent men to reconnoitre the house, and it turned out to be precisely what he was looking for, even though the exterior seemed so strangely derelict and eerie to him, as if it were the product of depravity and decay, that he made a cautious circuit of it himself. On all sides it was separated from its neighbours, with the additional protection against attack from the rear of a broad, dark canal. The façade was set against the cathedral, which returned its look defiantly. The single entrance was on this side too, high, well-preserved double doors. He ordered weapons at the ready as the bell was rung. After a while there was a shuffling of footsteps and the rasp of a key in the lock, then the doors creaked open.

An old woman appeared, wrapped up in a few clothes she had thrown on. 'What do you want?' she murmured. 'The girls have left.'

'What do you think?' growled the sergeant. 'Warm beds and no bugs.' The man next to him switched on his torch. 'What do we need girls for? We've got you!' In the bright beam the old woman screwed up her face to such ugliness that the raucous laughter came tumbling out of the platoon and she joined in with a toothless giggle.

'Stop messing around, men,' said the lieutenant urgently, then, turning to the old woman, 'Have you room for us?'

'And how long for?' added the comedian with the torch.

She grinned. 'Until Judgment Day, sonny, if you like.'

'Sergeant,' ordered the lieutenant, 'take three men, comb the building and report back here.'

'And you can be our guide, my pretty maiden,' said the sergeant, pulling the old woman along by the shoulder.

When they had gone, the rest unbuckled their knapsacks and squatted down, their knees drawn up with their rifles across them. It was drowsily warm in the hallway; added to that was a strange, overpowering smell, which struck every one of them the moment they entered, a sickly, rotten smell that might come from the mouldy walls. 'Make-up on old apples,' someone said. The sergeant and his men reappeared from the stairs, grinning and winking, and solved the puzzle. He had not noticed anything suspicious, but he had figured out the previous use of the building and revealed it to his superior officer, only with difficulty maintaining the serious-ness appropriate to an official report. His announcement was

189

greeted with stifled laughter until the lieutenant's command to find somewhere to sleep put a stop to it.

The old woman lit a lamp and hobbled along in front of them. On the first floor she unlocked a door which had the extra protection of an iron grille and the soldiers, apart from one whom the lieutenant left on the landing, stamped into a spacious room with the light they had seen from the market square outside hanging from the ceiling under a red vellum shade. It was overheated and the smell etched itself even more strongly on the stale air than in the corridor, but the soldiers paid that as little attention as the garish prints of Rubensesque deities on the walls and all the tawdry splendour of the room. All they had eyes for were the six-foot-long plush armchairs grouped around circular stone tables. Hardly had the officer given permission than they were stretched out on them, almost dead to the world. The old woman seemed disappointed. 'Why all the hurry? Each of the fine gentlemen could have had a room to himself. The little doves have all flown.' But none of them felt like getting up again and the lieutenant thought it better to keep them all together. 'But it's no place for you here, captain,' she went on.

He hesitated. 'Only if there's a room nearby.'

'Along the corridor, captain, it's just along a short corridor,' she assured him. 'Make up your mind. I'll get the bed ready anyway, just in case.'

With that she limped off without waiting for his answer. The lieutenant still felt uneasy about the whole arrangement. 'A second guard downstairs!' he ordered. 'Outside the old woman's door. Any volunteers?' The young soldier who had teased her in the hall stood up. 'Here, sir! I'm wide awake enough to catch any of you who fancies slipping into her bedroom,' he joked, turning to his comrades, who grunted sleepy denials of any such intentions. The old woman appeared again, 'Ready, captain.'

They went out into the corridor, followed by the young soldier. Through the window, that the lieutenant ordered her to shut fast, they could see the mass of the cathedral looming over the roofs, dark and heavy, as if it were made of bronze.

The lieutenant indicated it to the old woman, 'What do you call the church?'

'It is the cathedral of Jehan the Warrior; he had it built seven hundred years ago in memory of his dead wife.'

'She was a martyr?'

The old woman nodded. 'They say her corpse had no head and in its place on the skeleton lay a swan's skull. The inhabitants believe she protects the town; they prayed at her tomb yesterday, before they fled.'

'And you, why did you stay?' She shrugged her shoulders. 'I know your language; I've done nothing, you wouldn't harm me. This is the room, captain.' Turning round, she noticed the other soldier. 'What does he want?'

'He will be on watch in the corridor.'

'At your boudoir door,' crooned the soldier.

'God, such a young thing,' said the old woman, touched with compassion. 'Wait, I'll put a glass of wine outside the door.' The old woman held the lantern over the stair-well and let him go on ahead. Mechanically, the lieutenant registered her shadow; curving round the snail-shell wall of the stairs, it seemed to pounce on the guard's shadow. 'Such a young thing!' he heard her giggle through her cough; then, all at once, it was dark and still.

The lieutenant opened the door to his room. A paralysing warmth clutched at him. A match replaced the weak light of his torch, but he almost jumped with fright when it flared up. It blazed back at him a hundredfold from all sides, and when the two candles on the oak tables cast their flickering light, he was astonished to see that the walls and ceiling of the room were covered with square mirrors. Looking up, he felt as if he were standing at the heart of a crystal, for above him were fantastically crinkled rooms ranged one over the other, with disjointed reflections of himself and the candles upside down inside them. In spite of this proliferation, the light from the candles did not bring brightness; it somehow seemed to contain darkness, as if seen through sooty window-panes. With a shake of the head, the lieutenant began to inspect the room. Beside the door roared a well-stoked iron stove, its angled pipe

191

eating a black hole in the wall. A wardrobe with a mirror front and a glass-topped wash-stand gave the room a touch of opulence, which was underlined by the blood-red velvet armchair by the window. The most bewildering item, however, was the massive four-poster bed, whose black drapes made it look as if some noble were lying in state there. In order to avoid the temptation to stretch out on it, the lieutenant, overcoming his curiosity, did not touch the curtains, but first of all searched through the rest of the furniture to see if he could find a needle and thread, of which he was in urgent need. The wardrobe contained nothing but a pair of stiletto-heeled slippers and fragments of twigs; all the more numerous were the things the occupant had left behind on the wash-stand when she fled: make-up, soaps, bottles of perfume. But what he was looking for was not there, no more than in the drawer, which revealed a tube of lip-salve and the photograph of a jockey punctured with pins, documenting a wretched existence eked out among blows, exploitation and hysteria. These thoughts sent a rush of scorching blood to the lieutenant's face as they awoke the picture of the little actress he had left behind, unprotected; he tore open his uniform and went to the window, where he had to break the glass with his bayonet because the bolt had jammed in the heat. He breathed in deeply as he leant out. Below him the canal rippled darkly; occasionally something even blacker glided across it, but that could have been a delusion from his overheated brain. The only thing left to be done before going to sleep was to take the map and make a quick sketch of tomorrow's march. He pulled the armchair up to the table and started by plotting in the route they had taken since leaving the regiment yesterday. But he could not find the name of the town. Or were his shimmering eyes already failing him entirely? He was dully aware of a swarm of memories, plans, desires buzzing round his head: was he hearing them, thinking them, seeing them . . . ? He could not distinguish between them any more; the one thing he did know was that he had to get up out of the soft upholstery of the armchair if he did not want his eyelids to fuse together, and he felt himself stand up ponderously and set off towards the swirl of fresh air at the window. But the way there led past the bed, surely a soft bed with fresh linen such as he had not slept in for months. His hands refused to obey; they parted the curtains . . .

He started back. There was already someone lying on the pillows.

The lieutenant rubbed his eyes and forehead, but the apparition remained: a woman, a sleeping woman. All his tiredness left him, such was the spell her face cast over him. And yet it was hardly what he would have called beautiful. It had an ageless expression, and only the dishevelled dark blond hair gave it a suggestion of youth, though there was also something virginally austere and capricious about its shape. The forehead was large for the rest of the features. The hard, thin nose that sprang from the slender, arched brows held a hint of crookedness, and deep furrows stretched down from the tight nostrils to clasp the lips. They, too, had something odd about the way they were set: compared with the full, rounded curve of the upper lip, the lower one looked as if it had been ground down and was pale, almost bloodless, giving the mouth a constant, almost frozen smile. The closed lids were bluish, as if stretched taut over brass spheres, suggesting deep sleep, but abruptly, as though they felt the brush of other eyes, a movement appeared in them which quivered through the whole body, dislodging the blanket for a round shoulder to take shape over the black silk of the nightdress. At the same time the eyes opened; neither fright nor surprise clouded the greenish-grey pupils. The girl simply said, as if he was expected, 'I'm sorry, I've been waiting too long.'

The lieutenant looked at her in surprise then, remembering the recent history of the house, could not suppress a smile at the clever way the old dame had presented her last remaining protégée to him. So he sat down on the edge of the bed and fell in with her intimate tone. 'A good job you woke up, otherwise I would have taken you for a ghost.'

'You would have regretted it,' she said calmly, 'the people they appear to here never talk about it afterwards.'

'Why ever not?' he joked. 'Do they die from it?'

193

'You said it,' she smiled. This took him aback, but then he told himself he was a fool to be chatting to a whore about ghosts instead of making the most of the opportunity.

'So what?' he cried, 'I'll risk it and more, my pretty little ghost!' and he drew her to him as she reared up with a snake-like thrust. But then he felt himself pulled down, as if he were clasping a block of marble, and he yielded to her, overcome by the self-absorbed, icy sensuality of the way she took him. As he entered her, he sensed her lack of response; giving nothing herself, she received him coolly, eyes half-closed. Her coldness whipped him up to a furious compulsion to squeeze one groan, one sob of passion from her, but he spent himself in vain. She bestowed her favours with a sovereign disdain that made the slightest twitch of her high, taut shoulders an act of the utmost condescension. He sought her lips, but she with-held them with a sharp, 'Not yet,' and however much he twisted and turned, he could not manage to kiss them. He was about to plant his mouth on them when, with a shrill laugh, she slipped from under him and pushed him away. 'Enough!' Her voice was so firm that he gave up any idea of a further assault. She lay back in the pillows and stretched, staring absently at the ceiling, as if she were alone.

The lieutenant felt he looked a fool. He racked his brains for a topic of conversation that would offer a bridge between them, for with this creature violence would just mean further humiliation. 'Do you live here?'

'No, across the market place.' She pointed towards the corridor.

'But that must be where the cathedral is?'

'Perhaps,' she said in a flat voice. 'It varies. Once I did live here, and every evening I used to feed the black swans with the purple beaks. Did you see my swans?'

He recalled the dark shadows gliding over the water below the window. 'Yes. But why do you call them your swans?'

'My husband gave them me as a present. Oh, he was a wild lord and his swans protected me when he put out to sea. One of his brothers once thought he would swim down the canal till he reached my house, but my favourite swan sailed out to meet him, and beat him with its wings and pecked him with its beak until he sank. When my husband heard of it on his return, he killed the swan and me – and – '

The lieutenant felt everything around him dissolving into confusion until he was no longer sure who he was and whether it was not his own fate he had just been listening to.

'Stop!' he croaked and clenched his fists at her as she went on speaking in a monotone, as stony as her embrace had been, ' – since then I have belonged to anyone whose fate it is to meet his end in my lord's town; but first of all – '

He had been about to throw himself at her, but some inexplicable fear grabbed him by the throat and thrust him into the armchair, where he collapsed as if his spine had been broken.

'Stop!' he panted once more, but she finished what she had to say in the same soft, level tones, ' – but first of all I kiss them. Wait!'

As if she were a viper, he dashed her from his lips as she suddenly struck upwards at them. 'No!' Then she began to laugh; softly at first; but then it swelled, becoming loud, shrill, and the lieutenant could not stop her; kneeling on the floor, he stared at the woman and she laughed and laughed, her mouth unmoving. Or was it still the woman laughing? That was more like a stone statue, the head and overslender body with its small, imperious breasts held rigidly erect! A spasm of hatred jolted his body. She must be silenced! She must! He thrust himself up and grasped at her throat – something dark seemed to crash down on him; blindly he clawed about him as he plunged into a bottomless abyss.

Finally he found a hold and shovelled his way up through invisible, glutinous mud towards the half-light – reached it – was sitting – at the table in his room – with a guttering candle – opposite a huge cross – no, it was the wood of the window set off against a pale-red sky; but the laughter still continued. He stumbled over to the bed and tore back the drape – it had not been slept in. A dream then, apart from the laughter, that horrible laughter, now it was coming in hoarse gusts, from below by the sound of it. From the earth? No, the old woman's bedroom was down there! An icy hand laid itself on his heart. He turned the door-handle: locked. He kicked it in. From the corridor he could see something dimly flitting to and fro across the market square, which was veiled in clouds of crimson smoke; at the same time there was the crackle of a distant rifle skirmish. 'Partisans!' was the lieutenant's immediate reaction; they had presumably lit damp wood and were waiting until the smoke would force the trapped soldiers out. He shouted for the sergeant, tripping, as he did so, over something soft in the smoky corridor; when he touched it, it felt sticky and warm. The light of the match revealed the guard from the hall who, with his throat cut through, had dragged himself to his doorway to report the attack. Now clouds of smoke were billowing up the stairs, and still the laughing continued, although weak and ailing now. He threw himself into the fumes of the stair-well, heard voices pleading his name; shadows whisked down to the hall, hung in the air, sank to the ground; and there was the door to the old woman's room, wide open – but where was the young soldier? He raised his light. She had gone, and a whimpering bundle was writhing about on her bed like a worm on a pin; it was tied hand and foot to the bedstead, its clothes hanging in tatters, dripping blood down to the knees. A scream of horror rose to the lieutenant's lips, but before he could help the mutilated soldier, he was torn away by cries from his men as the infernal uproar outside seethed ever closer. In the hall he met up with what was left of the platoon. They had managed to drive the insurgents out of the house, but only with difficulty, and they would be no match for them when they returned with reinforcements. Quickly, he glanced around to assess the situation. 'Men!' he ordered, 'we must get across the square. We can only hold out in the church tower. Save your ammunition! Fix bayonets!' A metallic click, and they set off.

In a few seconds they had stamped out the rampart of glimmering brushwood and were facing the enemy, who scattered in surprise, without waiting for the onset. Lips clenched, blackened with soot, fingers on the trigger, they set off for the cathedral, led by the lieutenant. But now the partisans, after the initial shock of the platoon's sudden sally, had recovered their nerve. The one out in front was hurling screams from a mouth set like a foaming abscess in his face, and from around him black waves surged towards them. They approached in swaying clusters amid a cacophony of raucous shouts, jeers of abuse from the women and adolescent squeals; fists punched the air, here and there the gleam of firearms. The outnumbered unit seemed lost in the maelstrom of attackers, but finally the cathedral steps came down to meet them and they shoved their way up, hobbling, half naked, brushing the tangle of pursuers back with a few well-aimed shots. Then they were inside, hastily shutting the bronze doors, barricading them with pews and heaving a sigh of relief in the cool of this high nave which had probably not witnessed any fighting since the days of religious conflict. Now axes were smashing against the portal; it would surely hold until they were in the tower. Safe for a while, the soldiers swept their torches up and down the church. Along the side walls stone knights surveyed them from memorial slabs, hands on swords, small lions beneath their spurred feet. Impossibly emaciated saints gazed at them ecstatically from the niches in the massive clustered columns. Looking for the door to the tower, they came to the chancel and one of them lit the candelabra by the choir-screen. The high altar rose in terraces behind it, square grey blocks and faded gold, with a drop of blood floating in the air in front: the eternal flame of the sanctuary lamp. At the north side they turned back and found the confusion of figures on a baroque pulpit surging towards them: on the base Lucifer was being cast down into hell with a force that seemed to burst through the stone flags, whilst Saint Michael and all the angels thrust with their spears from the canopy; in the quivering candle-light it almost came to life. They opened the door next to it, but it was not the stairs they were hoping to find. It gave onto the curving, filigree stonework of a courtyard surrounded by cloisters and two figures running across into the adjoining convent; quickly they barricaded this door as well. But now the hammering on the west portal had stopped, a crescendo of noise surged in from the cloisters, the marble floor blazed in a swirl of colour from the flames shining in through the great rose window. Shots ripped through the side-door and clattered against the walls. Finally their assailants grouped together to batter the door down with brief thrusts, accompanied by the screech of metal and the groan of splitting wood. Then the lieutenant found the stair and called to his men. But at that moment the barred door yielded under the impact of the cheering blow, cutting them off and sweeping them back against the pulpit, which they quickly climbed to pour shot after shot into the howling mob. At this the attackers divided into two groups: the cautious mass squeezed along the rear wall farthest from the soldiers towards the spiral stairs leading up to the pulpit, and in so doing shut the door to the tower, behind which the lieutenant was hiding; the rest furiously stormed the pulpit head on. That brought the unequal struggle to a rapid conclusion, and the lieutenant could do nothing but watch from the organ, where he stood panting. Amongst the tangle of plaster figures, which seemed to join in like demons, the struggle foamed its way up to the platform of the pulpit, swallowing up the defenders one by one. They were all engulfed in the storm of triumph echoing back a hundredfold from the groined vaults. It pierced the lieutenant to the heart, and without thinking he raised his revolver and emptied the whole magazine into the snarl of bodies. The shock of the attack stunned the mob for a second, then their howling fury erupted against the tower steps. The lieutenant threw away his empty revolver and set off at a run. There was only one thought left in his mind: to stay alive until the reinforcements arrived! But then this hell-hole would explode in fire and blood! Now he was inside the first of the gigantic twins, the mutilated tower. He flew up the winding wooden steps, past the thudding from the housing of the huge clock; rats squeaked below, bats swept up past him, kestrels shot mewing out through the narrow slits in the masonry, whilst nearer and nearer came the raging thunder of the pursuit. That did not worry him, he knew they could only climb the narrow spiral in the tower one by one. Moreover, where he turned into the open gallery along the facade that led to

the completed tower, he managed to use his bayonet to dis-
lodge the ladder giving access, thus putting a temporary gap
between himself and the enemy. He was bathed in warm air as
he stepped out into the open. He was standing in the full,
strong light of the morning sun, which glowed through the
dissolving mist like a sharply incised disc, whilst in the town
laid out below him only the spikes on the gables were caught
in its rays and blazed up, as if in a presentiment of the revenge
to come. For grains and threads of grey were trickling down
the hillside opposite. The lieutenant realised what it was and
gave a scream of wild delight. Fifteen − no − ten minutes
hidden in the stone forest of the pinnacles of the second
tower, and then the battle-cry of his liberators would freeze
his pursuers to the marrow and drive them back into their
hiding-holes; but this time they would find them, all of them!
They only needed to ask him, him! He rushed on, panting.
Gargoyles jutted out in his way; he crawled underneath them.
The royal forebears of the stem of Jesse stuck their sandstone
arms into his chest; he broke them off with a blow from the
bayonet handle and threw the crumbling rock to the ground
below. Nothing could stop him now, not even if the whole
façade should come to life against him and swarm with men,
as at the time when it was being built. Now he held the fate of
this town in his hand, a remorseless, merciless fate! He had to
steady himself for a moment. His lust for revenge was almost
making him drunk, and his eye was already fixed on the
square below, choosing the sites for the gallows.

But abruptly the enormous statue of a woman barred his
path along the gallery, as if it had stepped out from the wall.
Her profile seemed familiar, as did the imperious posture of
her thin body, which pushed visibly against the thin folds of
the drapery. He could only get past by climbing behind her,
over the iron bar attaching her to the masonry. He quickly
twisted himself into the gap; there was a crackling and crumbling of sandstone, but here was no place to pause for thought.
For a mere heartbeat he had to step on the iron, but even that
was too much. The bar bent and he was clinging to the
woman in desperation. He swung round onto her front, the

abyss below him: one more swing would take him to the safety of the gallery on the farther side! To get a good push off, he pulled himself up until he was close to the stone face, that regarded him with a fixed smile. It was the face of the unknown woman he had spent the night with! He was about to scream out loud, but at that moment the overthin neck broke, and, as he plummeted in a breathstopping fall, his last sensation was of those lips, which she had withheld from him, now harshly sucking at his own.

Shadowtown

Franz Theodor Csokor

Sixty-five!

Set your face firm! Steel your muscles till the skin stretches tight, fit to burst!

Seventy-five!

The red car is turning into a raging animal trying to buck sky-high, but we stay in the saddle, clamping it between iron-hard thighs, furiously spurring it on!

Ninety!

'Faster!' hisses the woman. It's folly, intoxication, drunken madness – and we feel like whooping with exhilaration. The road pours into us; the air whishes past our ears with the sound of scythes through cornstalks; behind us the dust is swept up, heaves and billows, swirls and tussles with the storm we raise; fields flit past; bushes bristle at us with a menace of twigs, gnarled willows grin. Something scurries into in our path. Animal? Human? Over it we go!!

I noticed how grey and wretched we looked, all of us. The director at the wheel, his thin lips frozen in his courteous smile; his wife beside me, just as when I found her with gaping lips: the dose of veronal was not quite enough. And me, reflected in the rear-view mirror, hollow-cheeked, bedaubed with dust, a poor harlequin.

A hundred and ten!

The horn squeals as if the car were in unbearable pain.

Was that not the bulge of a town on the horizon? It disappears in a smudge of dust; another glimpse, and it's gone again. Barns resembling monstrous coffins spin past with the ploughed fields, gliding like silent ships through the swell of the earth all around. Spires scribble all over the blue of the sky. Poplars bubble up along the road, standing on parade: straight as arrows, atten-shun! As if we were driving into a churchyard, I think; I can see the town gate glooming up ahead, distant but growing, blocking our path; masonry, lath and plaster is piled up around it, pushes up against it as if the stones felt the cold.

A jolt: the director at the wheel is roused from his inertia to give a genuine laugh such as I have never heard from him before. It disconcerts me. Then a red net wraps itself round my skull and my pulse starts to ripple and slither, but that doesn't frighten me any longer: praecordial trauma my doctor calls it. A lasso tightens round my heart, dragging it through all my arteries, then slackens off, again and again.

As it does now! I come up for air, up from the depths of my body, my blood is released, its thunder drowns the engine. Hurrah! In front: the town we shall take by storm, the gate girt with walls, a slim belfry, crumpled gables; it rushes towards us, expands, devours us. And inside we ease up, we glide along softly, as if everything were submerged beneath water. We are tamed by the narrow street; it runs on ahead of us, silent and empty of people, although the air is warm and inviting, redolent with the rich, balmy sun of a spring twilight. It is May.

May. The actress beside me cannot see my caressing glance, she is watching her husband. They have been tormenting each other for nine years now, nine years to equal a thousand. They inhabit adjoining territories, the words between them are weary and silent; she has lovers, he always has a new mistress, the only thing that attracts him is the act of seduction. But at heart she loves only him, he only her, with a clear, merciless, inescapable love, as if it were predetermined from the beginning of time. Occasionally they come together, and then they do not know whether to kill each other or to die for each other.

The director looks up from the steering wheel and turns to his wife, he turns to me as well, but at the same time his gaze, dispassionate as ever, is toying with the distance beyond us. 'Shadowtown,' he says, but I do not know whether that is the name of the place or whether it is something he has just thought up. And why does he throw a challenging look at his wife as he says it? She must be the loser, I suddenly realise, he is a hundred times more of a woman than she, and with a man's mind and will power into the bargain!

These alleys squeeze us, lead us round in a circle or shrink to a stump. A wall keeps returning; over it we can see a lake shimmering. An old woman comes out of one of the very low houses – there is nothing but low houses here, with their roofs pulled down tight over their ears! She hardly gives us a glance. 'Which is the way out?' I ask. She shakes her head, as if it were impossible and disappears into one of the cellars.

We can't get lost in a little town like this? Or are we never going to get back out into the open again? A ridiculous idea! The tall, red church I saw as we entered is our marker now. We were heading straight for it. It stood like a huge animal, guarding the tangle of alleyways at its feet; round curves and corners it drew us towards it. But then the road forked, mocked us whenever we thought we were almost there. A close of canon's houses, ancient masonry, presumably the presbytery, all of them devoid of life, blocked our path; finally the square embraced us. There the cathedral towered up, gothic brick, twin-towered, an adamant monk with his arms stretched up to heaven. On the sills a profusion of grass and saplings: structure returning home, to nature.

We were turned away by the locked gate. A strange relief on the tympanum puzzled us. We went up close to look at it: with his bare hands a Saint George was strangling a snake, which had wrapped itself round his armoured legs and was trying to pull itself up him. His charger, a unicorn, stood by, its halter round the tree from the Garden of Eden. This symbol of chastity was his only companion; unlike every other portrayal, this one lacked the lady he set free. His triumph was overlaid with sorrow; his features radiated the aching purity of those who have suffered long torture.

I was overcome with a leaden sadness, which clearly oppressed the others as well. The actress abruptly bent over her husband's hand and kissed it; she was sitting beside him now, her shoulders sagged forlornly against him, seeming to bear the sorrow of the whole world. His hands did not leave the wheel; only his smile was clouded, a calm severity made his features almost like those of the knight above the cathedral door. 'Let's go!' was the vehement desire within me, for my heart was already rushing to my head as well; it needed the rhythm of the machine imposed on it, that would put everything to rights. And it happened; my silent wish was fulfilled.

In front of us cowered a row of almshouses; their monastic structure resembled the church and they were probably from the same period. And there was someone standing there, the old woman again. She must have made incredible speed, or did all the old people in this strange town look the same? Had they come to be akin over the long years, just as earth, when trodden down, is indistinguishable, earth, which they would soon become themselves? 'Force her to speak,' I commanded myself. But for that I would need some banal question that belonged to the coarse material world – the whereabouts of an inn, for example – which would break the spell cast by the old woman, who seemed to come straight from the brush of a Rembrandt. I received my answer even before I had spoken; 'The Traveller's Rest,' it came like a voice from the crypt, and the old woman waved her hands around at the same time. Was she making the sign of the cross over us, or was she indicating the direction? My friend seemed to assume the latter; he drove on.

From the cathedral square six echoing blows thudded to the ground; it was the Angelus, the hour when the mind opens to receive divine thoughts, but also the soft hour of seduction, of betrayal. There was a strange brightness revealing everything; in spite of the fading sun, we and all the things around us appeared with precise and painful clarity; we could almost see into each other's minds. I wanted to point this out to the woman, but her eyes were embracing her husband. 'That is the way people look at little children when they haven't any of their own!' I thought.

The car floated through an arched gateway – yes, 'floated' was the word, we moved so smoothly we could hardly feel the ground. In a niche an ecstatic saint was stretched upon the rack; his stone arms, broken off, were excruciating to see. Above him was a sundial with a strange motto curving round the circle of the hours, *Quaelibet vulnerat, ultima necat*: 'Each one wounds, the last one kills.' But that was, I assumed, the end of all the strangeness, for beyond the gate was a welcoming inn, a broad, grey, ancient farmhouse; on the threshold stood the innkeeper, a tall man with a quiet face that seemed not unfamiliar to me.

There was nothing that might be called special about it when we went in. The room, its ceiling festooned with withered wreaths, was obviously used for local dances and country celebrations, and here we came across signs of life. That is, there were many people sitting there in the half-light; they were drinking or smoking, only no one was talking. They looked as if they had long since said everything there was to say, and were afraid of irritating each other with the mere sound of their voices.

Without a word, the innkeeper moved softly behind the bar. 'Like a dead man,' I thought to myself, for his features revealed a weary sagacity, such as befits only God's ripe harvest, the dead who have truly rounded off their lives. I did not attempt to pass this thought on to my friends. Since we had entered the town I had the feeling, which was becoming stronger all the time, that we suddenly knew so much about each other that speech was unnecessary between us.

A twitching melody came from another room. It was a Javanese dance tune; it consisted of a despairing repetition of the same sequence of notes which sounded as if it was derived from one of their dirges; the playing was clumsy, with the same mistakes being repeated.

'We must go through your role,' the director reminded the actress, as we sat down at a table where another man was sitting, his face turned towards the shadows. I was surprised. She had no engagements for the near future, and yet my friend was behaving as if there were nothing more urgent. Besides, they were the very first words he had addressed to her since we had driven through the town gate.

The gentle innkeeper brings some wine. He doesn't talk to us, just looks at us as if he wanted to express something, but he definitely says very little, only 'Some wine' – or 'Amen;' yes,

'Amen,' that was probably it. And the man at the table turns to face me, and it is my brother. 'Julian,' I murmur, without surprise. He nods.

Behind me the director starts muttering something to the actress; it is presumably her role. I feel I know the work it is from, but can't remember the name of the writer. One single sentence keeps being repeated, 'Our Father, who art in Heaven . . .'

And then I suddenly realise my brother Julian fell in the War, on the Stry; he is buried somewhere in Russia. And yet he is sitting here. And now a lithe woman, a puma in clothes, is waving to me from the door; it's Evelyne, Evelyne who died last year, who laughed as she toyed with all kinds of male beasts until she tumbled into love and drowned; and there is Heinrich, the theatre manager, with his sardonic grin; it was at the same time that I heard he had chosen death; and there are lots of others here from the other side, I gradually recognise them. And the Javanaise trickles on. And a couple stand up and dance to it, slowly. And the innkeeper's soft, sad glance embraces them all. And the red wine has a bittersweet taste. And the actress behind me keeps repeating after her husband, 'Our Father, who art in Heaven . . .'

No, I must be dreaming, so I try to close my eyes in my dream – that makes you wake up. It's an old remedy that our nursemaid taught us to drive away a nightmare. But the vision I have behind my closed lids, surely that must be the dream? There is a crashed car and blood running over the ground, a lot of blood, and bodies screaming with gaping flesh. And as I look on, my neck and arms are racked by terrible pain. I must open my eyes! I want to wake up, damn it! 'Our Father, who art in Heaven . . .' I can hear it beside me, so they must all still be here, they are all round me, why won't they help me, then? Poor advice, nanny! I am crying, I can't hear myself, but I know that I am crying. All I can see is a lot of stupid faces staring at me in horror; what can they want? I'm asleep, of course, dreaming . . .

Then at last a human countenance appears above me; my old nursemaid is looking down at me. 'Nanny,' I feel myself say, 'take me home.' And she is stroking me, and now it's the old woman from the town, of course, that's who it is, and now I can open my eyes, carefully, and everything reappears out of a mist, the inn and the people around me, but now there is colour in their cheeks, as if the blood had come back in their veins; they are alive like me. And the Javanaise plays on, and a couple are dancing . . . And the actress is repeating, louder and louder, 'Our Father, who art in Heaven . . .' And my brother is smiling, and I want to embrace him, but someone is holding my hands down. Or have I no hands any more?

What does it matter? I am awake again. Back in life once more, in the life of this little town, which isn't so odd as it at first seemed to us. In fact, everything seems perfectly straight-forward here, it is what must have come before that now seems like a pointless diversion. And my brother must be of the same opinion, he's nodding to me warmly, and the actress is smiling a smile of relief at her husband, who for the first time is giving her a clear-eyed look, full of love, and the words she is saying speak to me of home, and my old nanny is bend-ing over me again, and all around me she is like a safe, dark cave which will protect me as I fall asleep . . . like a dead man . . .

No . . . like a child . . .

The Playground: *A Fantasy*

Franz Werfel

> *Heart longing alone hears aright.*
> *(Wagner: Siegfried – The Woodbird.)*

During the night before his thirtieth birthday Lucas had had a dream which he could not remember in the morning. What a strange awakening it had been! His body had lost all feeling. He felt just as your foot feels when you sleep with it in an awkward position; you can grab it and hit it, but it has become alien, it does not belong to you any more than a table or a book that you might hold. Only your own hand touching it can feel itself. That was what Lucas felt about his body when he woke up. It was as if his soul were hovering over the bed with a strange corpse in it, cool and without memory.

Slowly, he coalesced with himself again, but ever since that moment of awakening there had been a slight dislocation within him and in the way he saw the world.

Whenever he went to the window and looked out onto the central square of the little town, he would suddenly put his hands to his eyes as if his vision had to be corrected, for it was set at too great a distance and did not register the two ungainly carriages outside the 'Red Crab', nor the women with their baskets of fruit, the onion-shaped dome on the Town Hall or the young waiter dusting down the tables in the garden outside the beer hall.

Whenever he arrived home from the ministry in the evening and sat down on the broad chair by his table, he had to jump up again straight away, for his heartbeat would suddenly start to race so that he felt dizzy and near to collapsing. Then he would lie down on the old, waxcloth-covered sofa, whose white, enamelled pins shone with a patriarchal glow through the half-light of the paraffin lamp.

But there was no rest there, either.

He sprang back onto his feet, stretching his head forward into the darkness like a hunter. Massive silence was all around him. The high, muted violins of the sphere, which fills all space, shimmered. And in his ear the jets of ancient fountains began to sound as they splashed down into eroded stone basins in hidden courtyards. He listened with bated breath. But the word did not emerge from the rippling of the mysterious water.

He would go to bed exhausted.

A great and alien sorrow stopped him from falling asleep.

He felt as if he had been in an unknown world for an hour, where he had buried the being dearest to him, a woman, a friend, a child. Then he had woken up with the pain, but no memory of what the pain was about.

During the day he would sit in his office, staring at the clock above his desk. There was a scratching of pens. Malicious, dusty steps shuffled across the floor. Sometimes a silly remark was heard. A cackle of laughter came from one corner in reply.

But all he could hear was the seconds dripping into the bowl of time. On the hour it was full and would overflow, the superfluous drops ringing out. He could not hold himself back either, and had to repress a sob in his throat.

Once the office supervisor came up behind him.

'Mr. Lucas, how often must I say this? There is something wrong with the files again. Case Number 2080 is not closed. I keep on telling you! You can believe me with my experience!! People who are born with a silver spoon in their mouths and can pull strings are usually slipshod dreamers! If daddy was one of the bigwigs, well then, of course . . .'

'I am a dreamer, only I forget the dream.'

Lucas said it quite clearly and was surprised to hear his voice.

The clerks, spiteful as schoolboys, creased up with laughter. The most spiteful of all kept a solemn face and was always the last to double up.

'You can't concentrate, can't concentrate,' said the supervisor as he turned once more in the doorway, wiping his spectacles with a studied air.

One morning when Lucas woke up after a nasty, uneasy sleep, he heard himself say aloud, 'Forgetting is a sin. Forgetting is the worst sin there is.'

He propped himself up on his elbows, but he could not control his mouth, which was talking without him willing it.

'I must get up and search, search.' He dressed slowly. There was a cloud round his neck, like a warm, misty lace ruff.

He took his rucksack out of the cupboard and stuffed some bread and spare clothing into it.

Then he took his walking stick and left.

'Where on earth am I going?' he asked himself, as if he was in a daze, when he stepped out into the empty square, blazing red in the sunrise.

'To search for the dream,' answered the voice.

Lucas stepped out and had soon left the little town behind him. Some strange power drove his legs on so that his heart, exhausted from all the sleepless nights, could hardly keep pace. The many conical hills of the uplands faced him, strange and unfamiliar. The fog had long since dissipated. Only around the summit of Thundertop was one cloud gathered, as if it were the last breath of the extinct volcano.

A nuthatch with blue wings flitted past. High in the air hovered a bird of prey.

Lucas walked beneath a thin roof of birdsong. None was like another. The trees, both deciduous and coniferous, which surged in waves over the tops and tors, still had the somewhat ragged look of a belated April. But the fields and meadows were already full of dandelions.

Lucas left the road, left the footpath and turned off into a narrow green valley between two wooded hills. The grassy pasture was yielding to the foot, and that lightened his heart as he made his way. His desperate restlessness eased a little, and suddenly he threw himself to the ground and bit passionately into the earth. It was a lover's kiss. 'O star that I kiss, you smell of woman.'

He felt as if with this kiss he had come closer to the mystery he had been commanded to seek.

Without consciousness of a goal he continued on his way.

It must have been about midday when he left his airy valley for a narrower, rockier one. He had to clamber along the side of the mountain, for there was a stream roaring in the bottom. However, he soon found a cart-track. This path had many little wooden bridges with pointed roofs which it flung across the gorges. In the roof-space over each bridge hung a Madonna with an oil-lamp.

Suddenly Lucas stopped.

He should proceed no farther, he felt.

Something within him was quivering, like the tiny deflection of the needle of a compass.

He closed his eyes and scrambled up the steep slope. At the top a calm, dense wood stretched out. The trunks stood rigid. Only the tops waved to and fro to a lumbering melody that came booming out of an immense distance, hovered massively for a moment and then boomed back into the immense distance.

Thus far Lucas had had no thought for food and drink. Nor had he needed it. Something was driving him ever onwards.

There was a memory that would not leave him. As a child he had gone with his father through a forest, his bearded father in front, he behind. Often his father would bend down for some herb or mushroom, often he would part the bushes when he suspected they might conceal a good find. They did not speak a word to each other. Suddenly his father was no longer there; he had disappeared amongst some saplings and left the boy alone. But he, mad with anxiety, ran on down the path, looking for his father. He did not dare to shout. Some bashfulness, some qualm always stopped him from addressing his father as 'father'. He was consumed with a double fear, for himself and for the man who had disappeared and who had perhaps collapsed somewhere off the path and was lying amongst the bracken.

Later his father had appeared from a thicket and the child showed no sign of what he had felt.

Lucas could not get this memory of his childhood fear out of his mind.

He kept hurrying onwards. A wordless message called, 'Keep going, keep going.'

Already the evening was draping its yellow and red flags across the branches.

The mountain leant down. He ran down to the bottom. Now he was out of the trees.

He hurried through grass that grew higher and higher until it reached his hips. Like a new-created being, he sensed a different air and a swaying wind. Suddenly he was standing on the bank of a wide river. The current drew long, vigorous lines and wrinkles in the stream. The water bore off the dying evening like the still smoking beams and debris of a conflagration.

The river banks were narrow. A strip of sand and grass on either side; but to the right and left the measureless forest rose up again.

Not a soul was to be seen.

Without wetting their wings, waterfowl shot in unerring arcs over the curvature of the water; above a marshy place near the water's edge a host of dragonflies trembled in glaring and delicate colours.

Dancing round in the eddies, peeled tree-trunks floated down on the current, and sometimes things of more mysterious form which disappeared in the twilight gloom. From the other bank now arose the great evening noise of the frogs and toads. Banks of mist gathered there too, billowing up and dispersing like dust clouds on a road. Wandering back and forth, they were like belated passengers on a rainy evening waiting for the bell of the approaching steamer somewhere along the Rhine, the Don or the bank of a great lake.

Lucas walked along the bank in the direction of the setting sun, where the last light was still floating on the surface of the water.

The twilight was almost gone now. From behind his back came the hum of darknesses edging forward like magic bees.

And now it was night.

Still he felt no hunger, nor a need to rest. He was all soul following a scent, a track, like a ghost at the moment of apparition. His joints strewed his steps lightly on the ground before him, as if there were no resistance to overcome. He bounded along, carefree and secure, like a child led by the hand.

Suddenly he saw a light in the darkness, not far away and on this bank.

It came nearer.

Half still on the bank and half already in the water lay a mighty ferry, broad and flat. In it stood a huge man with a lamp buckled to his belt and thrusting a long oar into the sand, as if he were about to push off. His face was illuminated from below. On his head the man had an enormous straw hat, but it only covered half his hair, which was long and fell down onto his neck and over his ears. He had a snow-white walrus moustache and the ends were twisted and twirled and hung down well out from his face. Eyebrows, nose, cheekbones, they all resembled the portrait of the Hussite general, Zizka von Trocnow. Only the ferryman was no longer grey but yellowy white and seemed to be as old as the hills.

As Lucas approached the ferry he looked up. 'What do you want?' he asked in an unfriendly tone and with the voice of a soldier from the days when you could still buy your way out of the army.

'I want to cross over.'

'Why do you? Now? In the dark?'

'I must search.'

The old boatsman began to laugh. 'And where will you spend the night, my good sir?'

'Nowhere . . . or in the wood . . . what do I know?'

'In you get, quickly.'

That was a lot friendlier already. With a mighty heave the old man pushed the boat off. A chain screeched in the water. Now the ferryman tucked his chin into his chest and the top of the oar against his shoulder. And thus he went, panting, snorting, pressing his whole life against the water, from the higher bows along the whole length of the boat, that was working its way forward at an angle to the current. Every time the old man had completed one length, one attack, he returned to the bows, dragging his oar behind him through the water.

The lamp at his breast twinkled and swayed. Lucas started. The old boatsman's eyes gave off a brighter light than the lamp! They stood above the blurred shapes of the water and the night like two unpredictable blue flames. After each thrust of the oar they seemed to grow wilder, to shine out farther. When they had reached the middle of the stream the old man paused from his work and spoke to his passenger.

'You might find what you are looking for at my house.'

'What am I looking for, then?' said Lucas absently, trailing his fingers through the black water.

'You don't need to think I am stupid, young man! You are searching for a dream.'

'Yes. I am searching for a dream I cannot remember. But how it is that you know that?'

'Don't let that worry you. It's nothing to do with the matter,' said the ferryman in a deep, loud voice, turning his staring blue flames towards him.

Lucas closed his eyes.

'You could find your dream in my sloop, should the night be graciously inclined towards you. That's why I say you should spend the night with me.'

Lucas was silent.

'Now then, there's no need to give yourself airs and make a fuss. Or do you find the idea of spending the night in my sloop so unpleasant, does it go against the grain? What? You silly boy! Other gentlemen have spent the night here and found their dream. Quite different gentlemen, fine gentlemen, the very finest! What do you say to my invitation?' The old man had thrown his straw hat away. His thick, long white locks bobbed up and down round his head. He held his oar high in the air. The reflection of the pale light behind the clouds lay on him and on the water.

Not at all apprehensive, with a feeling of reverence Lucas said, 'Yes, I will spend the night in your house.'

'House? House? It's a sloop! You can see it now. Right by the water, my dear young man.'

The ferry landed. The old man immediately tied it up then waited for Lucas to jump down from the side.

'The toll,' he said earnestly.

Lucas paid the ten pennies.

Then they both headed for the boat that served as a shack, the old man leading the way, this time carrying the lamp in his hand.

The ferryman led Lucas into a low room and hung the lamp on a nail. It was high enough for the room to be quite well lit and Lucas could see everything in it.

At first sight it did not look much different from the crib of an untidy and alcoholic worker. The inside window was open. On the shelf were empty and broken bottles, half a flowerpot, a bag of nails scattered everywhere and all sorts of other things. The things on the rough deal table in the middle of the room were in a mess as well: two beer glasses, greasy paper with left-over scraps of food, a small paraffin lamp and a few torn-up newspapers. But one wall was taken up with a wide bed with fresh, snow-white sheets. It was turned down, and seemed to be waiting for a guest, for a gentlemanly occupant. On a table of its own by the wall opposite was an ancient model of a galley such as came into use at the time of Columbus. But what most captured his eye were the countless pictures, large and small, which papered the wall, and of which some, like the last dwarf pines in the mountains, even crept up as far as the ceiling. Above the bed hung a very large oleograph. It represented God the Father, a huge figure seated in the clouds; at His feet, His hand outstretched in a gesture of authority, Christ the Son, and flying down to earth in a halo of light, the dove of the Holy Ghost. That would not have been anything special, for it is a print that can be found in many peasant houses. But right next to it was a picture of a different trinity: Uranus at the top with his arms round

215

Cronus, on whose knees a youthful Zeus was sitting. A third picture showed a mighty idol in the form of a phallus with two arms outstretched and each hand holding a further idol. A fourth picture seemed to represent an Egyptian trinity, a fifth the Trimurti, a sixth the Nordic group of three gods, a seventh the Indian. And when Lucas looked closely he could see on all the pictures the same motif of the the genealogy of the gods and the trinity.

His sight grew dim. Truly, a strange chapel, this boatsman's hut. While Lucas' soul was held in thrall by the countless gruesomely mysterious pictures, the ancient ferryman had sat down in an armchair, pulled off first one heavy boot then the other with a groan, and thrown them clattering to the floor. Now he stood up; barefoot and with swaying steps he came to Lucas' side. He seemed to be taller than before. His head touched the ceiling!

'Well may you stare, my lad,' he said. 'Comes to look for his dream and finds the most unusual collection!'

He pointed to the picture of God the Father, Christ and the Holy Ghost. 'Father, son and holy ghost, and the same, again and again.' His finger described a circle.

'Always the same. Father and son, father and son. Excellent. The third weak and watery, a hypocrite beside them, begets not and is the vindication of all kinds of wind-bags. Father and son. Father and son everywhere. Excellent!'

Suddenly his expression darkened.

'Always father and son. But who has heard of the *grandfather?* Just as he is a father, so he must have a father. And as he begets, so he must have been begotten. Who has heard of the grandfather?'

The eyes of the old giant were clear, fiery and fearful. His whole body trembled. In the curve of his back there was something of the proud humility of one who has been dethroned. At that moment Lucas could understand the pain he felt. He gave him a profound look. The old man noticed it and suddenly changed the subject.

'My son, this bed is waiting for you. Lay yourself to rest. May you find here the dream you have lost.'

216

Lucas obeyed. All his wakefulness and strength seemed suddenly to have left him.

The ferryman waited until he was finished. Then he took the lamp and turned to the door. Lucas sat up.

'What do they call you?'

The old man's voice suddenly took on a squeaky, toothless tone as he replied, 'Well . . . grandfather, that's what people call me.'

This was the dream vision that appeared to Lucas in that night.

He was lying, dead and rigid, on a massive catafalque swathed in black; however, he was not in a coffin, but in a hollow in the catafalque which fitted the dimensions of a human body. His head alone was raised, resting on a pillow. To his right and left were two similarly sized depressions in the black trestle. He could not move, he was not breathing, and the unbeating inertia of his heart, the immense feeling of repose in his body, which was stretched out loosely, as if after terrible exertions, all said to him, 'It is over. You are dead'.

His eyes were open. He could see everything. And he saw that he was lying in the middle of a huge cathedral. The height of the vaulted roof was enormous, impossible to gauge. Immediately above his head, however, it had been pierced by a circular opening through which burnt a sky of deep gold, pouring its molten ore over his face without injuring or blinding him. His heart was not beating. His mind was not thinking. And yet: *he existed*. But this existence was a bliss which could be compared with nothing else. Whether hours, years or seconds passed, he knew not. The golden fire in the opening of the pantheon remained the same. Now and then gigantic storks flew over the cupola. Lucas could clearly see their legs hanging down gracefully like red threads below their wingspan.

All at once the three doors of the cathedral flew open: the massive middle door and the two somewhat smaller side-doors. At first there was nothing to be seen apart from the exuberance of a day such as the earth, such as no planet has ever known. A divine conflagration of all the colours streamed into the church, but all the dead man felt was, 'This is the true day'. And behold, in the middle door stood the old ferryman. With his height he reached to the point of the arch over the doorway. In his hand he held his oar, but now it was made of gold. From his shoulders to his feet a blue cloak hung round him.

Through the side-doors two processions entered, keeping pace with one another. In each, six masked figures bore a bier and placed it by the catafalque. Every step, every movement on the right and left was in time. From each bier they lifted a corpse and laid it in one of the hollows beside Lucas. It was all done very quickly. Hardly was the task finished than the cathedral doors closed; the ferryman and the masked figures had vanished and Lucas was alone with the two dead bodies.

Was it that his dream was interrupted, or was it that he became confused? Whichever it was, it seemed to Lucas that a long night had fallen and he kept his eyes shut.

And he woke once more in the cathedral, dead and stretched out on his catafalque. But the light in the dome had changed. It was hard, milky, dawning, and it did not stream but dripped. Before him, however, stood the old man. This time his oar was of ivory, his cloak black and embroidered with tiny silver magic stars. Each of the points at the end of his moustache had a bell hanging from it which jingled at every movement. And Lucas heard the old man's voice,

'Up you get, sleepy-head. Perhaps you will find what you are looking for here.'

He touched him with his oar. Lucas felt life return to him and stood up on the top of the catafalque. He wanted to address the old man. But he had disappeared.

Lucas looked behind. The two other corpses, who had been laid out next to him, were also standing. The harsh light flowed softly round the apparitions.

They were both men, the one in the prime of life, the other young, still almost a boy. Both were the same height and had the same figure as Lucas.

Although he had woken from the dead, his vision was still

veiled. He still could not recognise the faces of his companions. A breeze passed through the church.

The lights swayed.

And now Lucas recognised the older man. It was his father. How happy, beaming and red-cheeked was his face! The hair of his head and beard was thick and black, his posture defiant and swelled with the breath of health. That was not how his son remembered him. His memory was of a tired, sick man who dragged himself from one chair to another, a grey head at the table who groaned and fell asleep early. And yet perhaps, in the drawer of some forgotten desk, there was a photograph in which his father looked as he did now, so handsome, so manly, so *brotherly*.

Lucas felt himself crying. His bashfulness was gone, his bashfulness towards the man, the severe judge who sat in the bay window and demanded to see the maths test with red ink scrawled all over it. Without apprehension now, without fear or hatred, he went up to the man who had come through the trial of death at his side in this cathedral. He grasped his father's hand: the warm, soft, heartfelt clasp of a man who knew how to live. And his father drew his hand to him and pressed it fervently to his heart. For the first time in his life the son felt his father's heart, his living heart, beating, and his own heart beat with awe at this mystical experience.

The catafalque had disappeared and the men were standing under the open dome on the stone flags of the church, father and son close to each other, the youth a little way off.

Then his father said to Lucas, 'Come,' and led him by the hand to the youth.

Lucas looked at him and thought, 'My father has black hair, mine is brown and his is blond.'

Everything became brighter and brighter.

The young man gave the two a joyful laugh. His long hair waved, as if blowing in the wind. He was as sharp and strong as a blast from a trumpet, and the laugh of acceptance of the world never left his countenance.

His father leant over to Lucas and whispered, 'We know

each other, but he is our perfection.' And Lucas saw that his father was crying, and tears of some unknown joy were running down his face too. He could not stop them. He fell to his knees and kissed the feet of the handsome, laughing boy. But the kiss was a magic spell.

A great thunder arose, the cathedral broke like a delicate castle of glass and was gone.

But the three held each other by the hand; Lucas in the middle, his father on the left, the youth on the right. All around them raged vast festivities. The golden light and the unearthly conflagration of colours had returned. A thousand columns of people with fiery banners and huge, gleaming musical instruments were mingling in a dance of profound but incomprehensible design. The three, however, were taller than all the rest. Lucas could feel the waves of the throng breaking against his hips. He was aware that what he was feeling was the highest joy of creation. A thousand hymns sounded around him, but all had these words,

> See them marching, see them marching,
> Generations without end.

Now he was floating up a hill of a tender green colour, his father holding his left hand, the youth his right. Women, whose dresses had slipped down from their breasts, threw themselves to their knees before them and begged them to touch them in blessing. But Lucas and his companions strode through the adoration of the thousand women. His gaze was fixed on the summit of the mountain. There stood the old ferryman. Now his cloak was of gold, his oar of some radiant, transparent metal. The little bells on his moustache were jingling wildly. In his free hand he held his lamp. The flame in it was invisible. Nearer and nearer Lucas came to the old man. Nearer and nearer! Then the flame in the lamp seemed to come to life, became brighter and brighter. But everything else grew pale.

And now the lamp was very bright and passing over his eyes.

He had woken up. The old man was leaning over his bed, shining the light on him.

'Up we get, young man, time you were out of the sheets. I have to go to my work.'

Lucas sat up in bed. It was early dawn.

'Well, did you find your dream in my room?'

'There was a dream. It was a magnificent dream, but a different one from the one I lost.'

'So you will have to continue your journey,' said grandfather with a furious expression. 'There, have your breakfast.' He handed Lucas a large bowl of coffee and a slice of bread.

Lucas ate and drank.

Then they both went out into the open. Lucas had not cast one more glance at the pictures of the deities. He was afraid of them. In his soul rang out the words, 'Search, search.'

They came to the ferry. The old man untied it. On the other bank Lucas could see figures in the half-light. They looked like shades in Hades, waiting to be carried across the Styx.

'Where should I go now?' asked Lucas.

The old man pointed his hand straight in the general direction of the forest. 'Keep walking until it is evening. In different lodgings you will have more luck. Farewell.'

The unrest in Lucas was reawakened. He did not look round again and walked into the forest.

Again he spent the whole day wandering through the vast forest. His eyes were turned inwards, but the dream of the night was unable to tie them down. They looked deeper and did not see what they were looking for. The youth was the first of the dream figures to fade. Lucas did not know who he was or what his significance was. His heart no longer recognised him. His father, too, soon changed back, in his consciousness, into the person he had been when he had sat at table, or in the bay window with the rug over his feet, making remarks about the passers-by.

A mysterious shyness stopped Lucas from thinking about the ferryman who called himself grandfather. He never again wanted to think back to the horrible sorcery of the pictures of the gods in the boatsman's parlour.

The forest and the mountain meadows, the torrent and the mossy rocks, which had accompanied him on his way yesterday, had been the right answer to the flutterings of his imprisoned soul. For on that day it had been filled with longing, homesick for a far-distant childhood. The rustle of the leaves, the bustle of the water, how soothing had been their serenade. Whenever he had passed a pit in the woods, he had shivered and an awesome, long-forgotten word from boyhood rose within him: cavernous.

But today it was a different longing that would not let him rest. He was no longer homesick for the past. He was homesick for the future, he felt a yearning, incomprehensible and strange.

He left the forest and for hours walked through the countryside, across freshly sprouting fields and heaths, past many orchards.

Everything was in bloom. And he knew, as he went, eyes screwed up, through the scent and sweet, clear mist, that all this today was a descant of blessings above the dull vibrations of the puzzle within him.

But he was as restless as the day before. The most he could manage was to rest for a quarter of an hour on some bank or other. Then he was dragged straight back to his feet again: 'Keep going, keep going.'

Towards evening he reached some hills that were unknown to him. Misty blue conical hills that grew all of a jumble together. They looked like the hills in Chinese pictures. He came across people as well: an old man in a soldier's uniform carrying a mess tin, a beggar-woman squatting by the roadside, someone tottering down the mountain track with a pole carrying two tubs balanced across his shoulders. He had to go through a village. Tousled girls passed him driving geese. In the village square, beside the pond where ducks were quacking and boys splashing about in the shallow water, a beautiful tall lime tree already had its first leaves. Next to it was the shrine with a statue of the Madonna. From the knob at the top hung a bell on an iron ring. An idiot was pulling the rope and ringing down the evening. Lucas continued along the village street. When the village was a long way behind him he had to pass an inn. It was called 'The Seven Devils'. Whenever the door opened a brief wave of noise, music from an orchestrion, the stamping of dancers and the stench of beer poured out from the bar.

'Don't stop,' he said aloud. The road kept climbing higher and higher towards the east. Above a mountain half the disc of the sun was still to be seen. Violet, pink and yellow glaciers surged above the wooded slopes and melted in the valleys. Lucas suddenly turned off the road and climbed up a hill. Then he went along the edge of the wood and came to a small farmhouse which, however, did not look quite like a farmhouse.

He stopped; his heart was beating wildly.

A woman appeared in the doorway. She was very tall. She wore no scarf on her head and her blond hair blazed in the evening light. But Lucas saw that at the side, at her temples, two thick grey strands were twisted into her massive crown of hair. She was not dressed as a peasant but was wearing a wide black dress of plain cloth, that, however, did not look particularly out of place in the doorway of the farmhouse. Her feet were bare and, in spite of the toil along stony tracks, the early rising and all the housework, white and without crooked toes. She was no longer young, but not old either.

'Welcome,' she said in a deep voice. 'I was expecting you.'

'You knew that I would come?'

'You were announced.' She raised her strong, right arm, letting the sleeve fall back.

'Do you know . . .'

The woman interrupted Lucas. 'I do know. You will find a bed for the night here. Come.'

She stepped back into the door. Lucas followed her. Her walk! It was calm, sublime. In spite of her beauty, Lucas felt no surge of desire. He sensed, 'That is no mortal woman!' They entered the parlour.

On the threshold Lucas could not restrain himself and asked, 'Who are you?'

'The wife of the miner.'

The room was low and filled with a colourful dusk. Lucas saw a mattress, furs and blankets, but no white linen. There was nothing white to be seen at all. In one corner was a gigantic globe. It was covered all over with sharp nails made from a wide variety of metals. Christ was standing on it on one foot, like a dancer piercing his old wounds with new nails at every step. Two huge cupboards stood close by each other, like neighbouring mountains. From one a very large amethyst druse with marvellous crystals shone down, from the other the bronze interlacings of a massive block of aragonite.

Lucas went over to the globe.

'What is that?' he asked.

'That is the Saviour ever pierced with nails.'

'Did his sufferings not end on the cross?'

'No. Now he suffers more, since he dances over the sharp pins.'

'Why are the nails made from different metals?'

'The hard heart of the earth takes many forms.'

'But what is his sorrow?'

'The greatest.'

'And what is the greatest sorrow?'

'Fulfilment destroyed,' said the woman.

Lucas did not grasp the contradiction of these last two words; but he knew that only a woman could have spoken them.

The woman left him alone for a while.

Then she came back and set a meal before him, and put a glass of dark-red wine on the table as well and last of all a candle, for it was already quite dark.

Lucas thanked her. A feeling of great awe stopped him from eating in the presence of this dark, mysterious woman, to whom he had been announced and who knew about his seeking heart.

In the meantime she was going about some puzzling business.

There was a small, low table standing in a corner. On it were three little vases with dried flowers. In them the woman put fresh posies of spurge laurel. Then she dusted the table and laid a cloth over it. She placed the vases in a row and in front of each one a tiny, flat lamp with a little flame. In front of each of the lamps she placed one small bowl with milk and one with wheat grains. Lucas watched her, spellbound. She straightened up and stood there, tall in her black dress, tucking her arms into the wide sleeves as if she felt cold.

'It is for the children . . .' And then, after a silence, 'Good night. I hope that you find your dream.' And with that the miner's wife had disappeared through the door.

This was the dream that Lucas dreamt in the second night.

He is walking through a marvellous, overgrown park full of blossom, keeping to the soft gravel path in the glittering sunshine. His heart is filled with a solemn strength. A brook is whispering at his side. Whole clouds of white butterflies lurch past overhead. Sometimes there is a bench, with no one sitting on it; wagtails bob up and down on willow branches which dip into the water; warmth and song is in the air. He walks quickly, tapping with his stick in rhythm on the gravel. Suddenly he notices that there is a figure far in front of him taking the same path. As he comes nearer he sees that it is a woman. She is wearing a flowing dress of gold brocade, but has thrown a shawl of grey crepe over it. He knows who this woman is, whom he has never seen, and his body tenses with joy. He reaches her, goes trembling up to her side and says, 'Beloved woman.'

'My man.' And his eyes and hers mingle.

'Why did you go on ahead?'

She, 'Well, now you have caught me up.'

He kisses her! Then he dreams of himself speaking.

'How is it possible! How is it possible! I know I had the heart of a dreamer, but it was fleeting and transient, as the hearts of dreamers are. From the gallery of the great opera houses I saw the beauties in their boxes. Tears poured from my eyes when an ethereal foot jumped down from the carriage step. Once I spent many hours every day for a whole year standing at a tramway stop, because I once saw a woman board the brightly coloured carriage there. Two years later I found her. But my dream had become more powerful than the woman herself. Even the meekness of her hair could no longer help her. But now! Now you are here before I dreamt you and that is your great power. How was it possible?'

'Yes!' she said. 'The things I had all to go through! To be kissed in my sleep and not to know it! That sleep, all the time! And that after a childhood full of fear, after great ambition and girlhood radiance. I with the children in the last room. They are not allowed to scream, to cry. But he, the good master, ponders and ponders. And his high countenance reaches perfection. He is tired. In the night I have to stand outside chemists' shops. He becomes more and more tired. His thin lips will hardly close any more and his powerful teeth lie open in the effort of will. Then comes that day. I pass my hand over his forehead damp with the sweat of fear, and trembling he kisses this hand for the last time. But where was I then? Where was I? I must have everything around me. Everything! Everything!'

Lucas feels as if a wild, demented urge to destroy suddenly shoots out from her eyes. But then she says, gently and almost with a tiny fear, 'But you, my only one, you belong to me!'

And Lucas feels an almost malicious pride within him. 'Yes. I am enough for you.'

'Oh my beloved! I have lived. The beasts both wild and gentle gather round me. But you have woken me from the death that was that life.'

They sit down on a bench. Somewhere an orchestra is playing. Above the orchestra floats the pure voice of a singer. She is singing an Italian cavatina.

Lucas feels himself speak. 'Is this melody not like a sweet mountain goat that a divine bearded huntsman chases from mountain to mountain? Now it is tumbling down the rocks of its cadenza and lies at our feet. Dead – Blest!'

'How you touch the heart of my heart.'

'I spoke of music.'

'We alone know what it is.'

'It is our acceptance of God,' he says.

'It is our acceptance of God's world,' she says

They stand up, they walk through endless meadows in silence.

Suddenly they find themselves by a huge Indian temple. Grotesque dancing idols stare down at them.

'We must enter.' She strides on ahead. Lucas follows her.

Now they are in a large courtyard. In the middle a basin spreads its massive circle. But instead of mud and patches of water all that is to be seen is ashes, cinders with, here and there, a little flame still spurting up. In the middle of the basin rises a fountain-pipe, to which a long string is attached. 'Your metal is full of dead stone, my love. You must step into the bath to purify yourself' Lucas jumps into the basin. She pulls the string. A wild rain of fire pours over him, without burning him. He steps out of his bath. 'Am I pure now?' he asks. 'Somewhat purer,' she laughs. 'But that was not fire, just fireworks, beautiful to look at.' They leave the temple by the other side. Now it is summer. The corn stands high, ready for harvest, and the ears burst, just like a violin string breaking. Cornflowers and poppies everywhere, wayberries too, and the beautiful corncockle. The sun is burning hot.

'Oh, how warm is this ripening within me,' says the woman. 'I am nature. I.'

The wind blows a lock over her forehead. She strokes it back with her hand.

'How beautiful that is', thinks Lucas. And he says, 'How beautiful you are. I love you.'

She does not look at him. But a soft, blissful groan passes her lips. 'This whole seething star is within me.'

With a movement of her hand she swells the air, as if she were caressing the invisible pregnancy of a spirit.

Then she kisses him passionately.

I never knew there was such a thing.

'I never knew it either.'

'I thought there could be no such thing as happiness and that people lied because they did not dare to admit it to themselves.'

'I thought it was the ugliest thing and brought nothing but disgust and exhaustion, which we men concealed in order not to be cruel.'

'And now we have felt it.' She takes his hand.

'Oh, hand, hand, hand,' he says.

And she, 'Now the evening is coming.'

Lucas is standing with the woman by an open window. Outside it is dark and the garden is humming.

'Tonight I shall kiss you.'

'I feel blissful,' she says.

'Do you feel blissful because you have me?'

'Yes, but there is something else as well that makes me feel blissful, my love.'

'Will I be permitted to kiss you tonight?'

'You will be forbidden to do anything else!'

Outside an angry bird begins its ugly, rasping call.

'Is that an evil sign?' he asks.

And she answers, 'I do not know.'

'Is what we are doing sinful?'

But she laughs.

And they embrace each other.

A terrace. How warm this night is. She is sitting, golden dark, in an armchair. Lucas, his hands behind his head, is lying on the ground staring into the stars.

'If we were crossing the equator those stars could be the Southern Cross.'

A fixed star begins to sparkle coldly and in a hundred colours, like an evil splinter of ice. Lucas sees the secret star grow and grow. He senses, 'Now, in this very moment, the pitiless eye of the hunter has seen us.'

'Don't speak', the voice within him calls out anxiously. But he is already saying it. 'I feel an evil star above us.'

He feels as if a whip should lash him across the back immediately: the punishment.

But she says, and fear is in her voice, 'Don't look up and don't speak of those things.'

The bird starts up again. Its croaking is powerful. It rasps as if it had a long, jagged beak and were sawing down the trees in the garden, the trees of life, the forest of life. Lucas thinks, 'I will not mention it.' He looks at her and feels, 'She behaves as if she could hear nothing.'

Then, 'Is there not a fatal trap laid for love?'

'Which one?'

'Desire.'

There are tears in her eyes.

He goes on, 'I feel now what the curse of dissipation is. It digresses. It distances itself from the loved one and that is how it kills.' He throws himself down before her and whispers,

'We must become more and more like brother and sister to each other.'

Now they are in a room. She is wearing a gown of white gauze and holding a candle in her hand.

The bird continues to saw through the night.

She shivers and says, 'Close the window.'

Lucas is sleeping. He is enveloped in a sweet smell of thyme. Suddenly he seems to hear a dreadful knocking at the door. He wakes up, jumps out of bed. And now he is on the staircase of a big house. Many people are running up and down in haste and terror. Women with their hair loose and in night attire. Some are carrying bowls and towels, some burning candles. They are all whimpering and moaning. He can hear words, 'The woman!' 'She is dying!' 'Before it's too late!' 'Send for help!' 'The woman!'

Raving, he dashes out of the house, screaming, bellowing. He runs through the garden and clears the fence in one bound.

It is already morning. Giant clouds float past. He races down a slope for many thousand yards; undergrowth throws itself in his path; he becomes entangled. And still he cries,

'God, God, God!'

Now he runs into a swamp, sinking in farther and farther. The mire reaches up to his chest. He is at the end of his tether.

But he manages to work his way out. Now he is on the road. He cannot grasp anything any more.

On tiptoe he enters a room. She is dying in her bed. A cloth is across her forehead. She is so beautiful, her physical matter is floating. He curses the evil body in his clothes. He drags himself to her bed and falls to his knees.

'I am to blame!'

'There is no blame.' She smiles, and in that second she is the triumph of the heathen world.

'I have killed you.'

'We have killed,' she comforts him softly.

He wails, 'You must not die! You cannot die!'

But she says, and her features become glorious, 'If I die, then I am sacrificing myself for your destiny. Oh dreamer without pain! Harsh must be the reality that is to become reality for you. You must have reality, or you will never live or die. Oh my lover, perhaps you are in hell.'

She raises herself up a little, 'Write your name on a piece of paper. They must put it under my tongue. That is how much I have loved you.'

'Live . . . live . . . live,' babbles Lucas.

She says, 'What could have been the most sacred part, our perfection, has gone.' She places her hand on Lucas' head as he kneels before her. 'Now go.'

'Where?' he asks.

'Search, search,' is the last he hears.

And then he awoke. Beside his bed stood the miner's wife. Now she wore a scarf over her head and a shawl round her shoulders.

'The hour has come, I must go to join my husband in the pit.'

He looked round, confused. Outside dawn was just beginning to break.

'Did you find your lost dream?'

'No. It was not that one. It was another one. A sweet and terrible one.'

The woman set milk and bread before him. He ate and drank.

230

She watched him eating, and said,

'What was commanded us both has taken place. You found lodgings in my room.'

'I have come closer to what I am searching for,' he replied, 'but I have not yet met it.'

'You will certainly meet with it at the third time.'

Now both were standing outside the door.

She bore two vessels in her hands. In one was milk, in the other red wine.

'That is the offering that is put for the dead at the entrance of the underworld', thought Lucas. And then he addressed himself, 'Where to now?'

In kindness, the woman took his hand. 'Keep on going straight through the forest. Let yourself be led. If you have not found your dream by midday, it is lost for ever. Climb Oak Hill when it appears before you. I have been there myself. There my dearest comes to meet me in the midday light. Women are not barred from reaching that place, but men always are, unless they are sent.'

He felt that the miner's wife was no longer holding his hand. When he looked up, she was gone.

Once more Lucas entered the forest and walked for hour after hour. But this day there were no clearings, no valleys interrupting the forest and nothing jerked the wanderer out of his self-absorption. All the time his thoughts were with the woman in the dream, how she had lain there dying, and once more he felt himself sinking into the swamp, screaming for God; his fear had been reawakened, and all the dreamwords were like a cool air across the back of his neck.

His first day's journey had been homesickness, his second day's journey yearning, and that of the third day, love. It was midday, and every breath and odour was silent. And there was the hill covered with old oak trees that the miner's wife had spoken of. Did this hill live somewhere in his memory? Had he been at this place in his childhood? Lucas suppressed these notions. Then he followed a little footpath up the hill. On the top, in the middle of the oak wood was a clearing, and in this clearing was a large, low, round half-timbered building, old-fashioned, with gleaming windows. The whole was inexpressibly clean. The double doors stood wide open and a glistening gravel path ran through it.

Lucas went through the door into the yard. He was compelled to close his eyes, for he felt, 'I have dreamt all this.'

The sky above this yard was immeasurably blue. A lark was plunging up and down in the blue, beside itself with song. There was a raised pavement round the shrill white walls. And on this pavement a hundred strange things stood next to each other, blinding the eye.

They were all mechanical toys, a delight for children and simple minds. Lucas saw a puppet theatre. A conductor cut out of cardboard was raising his baton, but the curtain was down. Next to it was a little ebony Savoyard, holding the handle of his hurdy-gurdy. Here was a mechanical pierrot in white baggy trousers, over there a group of statues representing a scene from the life of Napoleon, and then a barrel organ and other mechanical instruments; all these and many others too.

For a moment Lucas forgot everything. A wild surge of childhood seized him again. He ran over to the mechanical toys and stared at them, engrossed.

Suddenly he felt that his right side was leaning down and that he was holding something warm and delicately small in his hand. It was a child's hand. A small child was looking at him.

Lucas felt a shock that spread to the last recesses of his being, a shock such as only people can know who have passed close to death, close to the abyss of extreme knowledge, or who have met themselves. It was his lost dream. Who was this beautiful, lively child with the soft blond hair and the most profound wisdom in his face, full of observant otherness? On his childish features lay the wisdom of those creatures who have never become estranged from themselves by birth or become one with themselves in the moment of death. But what was that? Were those not his features, right down to the last detail? Was that his childhood? Was that the design which he had been, to which he had inevitably failed to match up? Was it he himself? Was it his . . .

He was overcome by an unknown, infinitely warm feeling, and yet the mysterious shock did not leave him.

Then the child said, 'Go on, put a penny in.'

They were standing in front of the puppet theatre. He put the coin in the slot. The curtain flew up. A thin, ragged, chirruping polka started. On the stage a few little puppets in pink and sky-blue tutus revolved jerkily and without rhythm. One kept halting, another whirled round like mad on its axle. Then it was finished, and the curtain fell even more quickly than it had risen.

The boy gave Lucas' hand a squeeze.

'That was lovely, let's see some more.'

They went over to the Savoyard. Again Lucas put a coin in the slot. The motor rattled. The brown hand on the crank moved in short jerks and, with much whistling and jingling, an ancient, almost mythical tune from an operetta rang out and then suddenly broke off.

'Good.' The boy nodded his head. 'Let's go on.'

Lucas made the clown dance and contort its limbs.

The child laughed wildly with joy.

Lucas lifted him up and looked him in the face. 'Yes, it is you. Come with me. Come with me. Away from the beautiful playground. I will buy you other toys, much more beautiful ones.'

The boy had an earnest expression.

'You can't take me with you.'

'Why not?'

'Because only my mummy can take me.'

'Where is your mummy?'

'Not here,' said the child.

But Lucas kissed him passionately. 'I know where your mother is. She has not died. She is alive. I spoke to her last night. I'll carry you to her, my child. We'll find her, we shall find her.'

The child shook his head. 'We must to talk to grandmother.'

'Where is your grandmother?'

'In there.'

'In the house?'

'Come, I'll show you.'

The child leads Lucas into the parlour of a farmhouse. There is a smell of decay. Spider's webs stick a thousandfold to the ceiling and to the arch over the low window. There is a wooden partition dividing the room in two. The old woman is sitting at the spinning wheel, right at the back in the half-light, in an ancient peasant costume, with a headdress from years gone by: no, it is a model, a doll. The grandmother is filled with straw and she does not move.

'Grandmother,' calls the child.

The figure moves, creaks and stands up. It takes a few steps and becomes quite human. Now it comes to the barrier. It seems not to see Lucas properly at all. 'There you are, sonny,' says the grandmother in a strange dialect.

The child stammers, 'Just think, grandmother, he wants to take me with him. He's seen mummy as well.'

'First they send you to foster parents and then . . .'

She lifts the child over the barrier and he holds up the palms of his hands.

Lucas sees the lines of his own hands. He feels, 'Never will I forget these little hands.' Already without hope he says, 'Grandmother, give me the child.'

The grandmother does not listen to him. She takes the boy in her arms. He suddenly seems much smaller and is crying softly.

He too is like a wax doll.

'We're closing now,' the grandmother barks at Lucas.

He leaves the room, he leaves the playground, he leaves the gate. Only when he is back in the clearing does he turn round.

But by then the playground has disappeared and the *dream he had found again*.

He goes to the other side of the hill and sees before him the small town, which he had left three days ago.

How tired he is, infinitely tired.

'Now I have to go down there,' he says out loud.

The Dream

Georg Saiko

The sudden outward thrust of a curve sent the whole carriage lurching sideways and for a few moments he was conscious of being in the compartment of this train, which had not come to a halt for twenty-four hours now, then he was silently borne off to sleep once more, back onto the spinning disc of a different state of being. Paris, it was still Paris but, in some way he could not quite conceive, he had the whole city inside him, as if he had swallowed it down into his body, a body which, lying there motionless, felt as if it had swollen to gigantically capacious proportions. Somewhere far away he was aware of the curvature, vast beyond human vision, of a tyre inflated to bursting point which yet, with a certainty he could not explain, signified himself. His skin was burning with a sharp transparence and his mouth was particularly sore. Although he was keeping it clenched shut, it felt as if his jaws were wide apart, dislocated, his mouth and the concourse of the Gare du Nord were one and the same, glass and iron and yet his muscles, his nerves, sooty iron and black glass seething with frenzied tumult, stifling miasmas from scrunched-up tatters of light and the clamour of many voices, many desires. More and more trains kept pouring into the vast twitching cavern that was his mouth, an infinite chaos of swaying lines of carriages overflowing with people. They gushed out in blue-grey waves shot through with rivulets of colour, uniforms, nothing but uniforms, gathered into heaving pools at the exits then surged on, eating their way into his body, into the city rumbling in his veins. He knew that the avenue des Champs Élysées cut him in two, right down the middle, cars were whizzing along his spine, his tortured marrow squirmed, flattened and torn away from many threads that were bouncing to and fro, perhaps his nerves, but definitely connected to the ridiculous old-fashioned harp, to which the old woman of St. Julien le Pauvre kept whining the same monotonous melody. She was standing by the side entrance, outside the decaying garden, her stony grey face, eroded and devoid of movement like the gargoyles over the arches, grew in a completely impersonal manner until he could feel it as his left hip-bone, pressing fitfully against the cushioning of the back wall and somehow, passing through an oppressive stretch of darkness in his body, clearly ending up on the quai d'Orléans. He sank down into the toxic gelatinous block of the river, into the middle of the luxuriant row of very green treetops, from beneath which the deep bowl of all finitude shone up with its redemptive light; he was pushed on by a yearning sensation towards a boundless ecstasy of dissolution; already he was teetering on the cusp of his ultimate second, when the magic reality of the embankment above held him tight with its trees, which were nothing more than bulging sacks of paralysing fear. It lasted a long time and was yet very brief when he lost himself in the tangled skeins of apartment blocks rank with nauseating odours until, up behind the iron bars of the Tuileries, he felt his lungs, a jellied mass with round humps, a branched complex of clipped foliage over low trunks with the drowsy scent of many lurid flowers in the rich arabesques of the flowerbeds, their muted up-and-down calming, like the touching caress of a large, slightly hard hand; perhaps it belonged to his first nurse and at the same time to the whimpering old woman of St. Julien le Pauvre and both had the same cloud of security about them. But beyond it the cars on the avenue des Champs Élysées were tearing along with the drawn-out rasp of tyres on the thin layer of gravel, many of his nerves were aching and the old woman was whining to her harp, which was stretched, cruelly taut, across his body. Then, suddenly, he sensed a thick, reddish-blue aorta turning off to the left where white light was pulsating towards him from behind huge globes of frosted glass and a negro in a garish uniform was ceaselessly pushing at the shiny brass of the revolving door. He was hesitating, but what could he do anyway when even the faintest flicker of intent was absorbed into the inevitability of what had to be, just as he was being absorbed into this too bright, overheated room filled with a sound like knuckles beating on wooden drums and his heart, obedient to the jazz band, was rising and falling in a rhythm that would never end, constantly washed over by the husky song of two bars of music, which kept on breaking out of the endlessness, only to reestablish it again immediately. A slight shiver made him contract, stretching a fine, brittle layer of resistance and impermeability over his skin. But in a trice the room, surging to the roar of distant breakers, engulfed him. A warm wave, sharp and sucking, swept him away, the little tables along the round walls floated past as patches of glossy white. The heavy-draped immobility of curtains, the long serrations of fans, the fleshy spikes of shrubs from which the intensive violet light in which everything was simmering had removed all appearance of organic life. He made a determined effort to distinguish between them and the women, white and coloured, too white and too dark from a thick layer of make-up, bobbing clusters of feathers round blond or black wigs, round twitching, thrusting hips with their glittering hint of brightly coloured veils between them. He sank to his knees in thick jelly, but that was the carpet, and stood up again in the middle of the dancers. The men remained expressionless faces, tailor's dummies on black sticks, but the women were entirely pumas from the cage in the Parc Montsouris, smoothly coiling their brown and white bodies to dart forward with sudden menace, no longer behind bars but between the plate-glass windows of the rue de la Paix, among ladies' hats, old lace, exotic plumes and jewellery. Some were bounding along on hands and feet, their thighs pumping up and down as they spiralled round him in narrower and narrower circles, towards him alone; the others, too, were basically seeking him out, only him. They were interlocked in the dance in a way that was difficult to make out, incomprehensible crosses between chorus girls, negro idols or birds of paradise. Their arms and legs, multiplied by movement, mixed a ponderous amalgam of rigidity and crisp drumbeat with a blend of bronze devotional image and mindless vaudeville. Immediately before his eyes a skinny, too-white hand with red-painted nails scraped across a back that looked like cigar-brown, overgreased leather. He turned his head, but it was still there, now with this thick smell of many kinds of strangeness whisked up together which bore him panting into a state of hysterical obliteration, aah . . . like the incense that set his chest coughing as a child, St. Germain des Prés was the village church at home and he curled up tiny in the lap of his gigantic nanna in the pew at the front and knew what God was like. God was like nanna's lap and nanna's great hand, tenderly placed on the top of his head with coarse hairs on its strong wrist sticking out from the blue knitted glove, God was like nanna's shawl and nanna's lap and nanna's nice warm chest and had a bitter smell of black bread like nanna . . . And then it began, the horror, making him almost suffocate with shame. It started with the disappearance of the sense that he was dreaming. Nanna's rough hand or the other white hand with red nails had wiped it away. As if, with puzzling clarity, a skin painted with the wildest delusions had been stripped away from people and things so that they were revealed in all their wretched ordinariness. An expensive brothel for international philistines, European provincials, Argentinian cattle breeders. All at once he recognised most of the frozen expressions over the low-cut necklines, but he could not have put a name to any of them. There was a gossamer film of strangeness peeping out from beneath them which signified something else that lurked within him as a petrifying fear and strove with violent convulsions to get away from the women. Had he made a gesture of invitation? The black woman right in front of him was jerking back and forward with movements more like a large shaggy dog snapping up a morsel someone had thrown it. But there was his old nanna, that white hand had fallen off her back, it smelt a little yellowed now and – he hesitated at what was to come – belonged to grandmother's arm. Beyond the broad negro mouth, behind the familiar features of his nurse, was the pale quiver of an infinitely delicate bubble, his grandmother's face. With a certainty beyond hope, he sensed that she too knew what all accepted without surprise: his heart, immense and floating free, was in the middle of them, rising and falling, giving the beat for which the negroes with their instruments were merely a façade. They were all staring at this huge heart, which was swelling up, larger and larger, setting the tempo for the women so that they lived by it, through it, and slackened when it pumped more slowly. But then there was this black woman, pushing right up against him.

The Reason for It

Hermann Ungar

Leopold stood by the door of the house he had just left and thought. He had the feeling he had forgotten something up there. He slowly turned round and went back up the three steep flights to the musician.

'Excuse me,' he said, going into the room.

He saw the picture straight away. Before, he had only caught a glimpse of it. Now he knew that the memory of this picture was what he had forgotten.

'A remarkable picture,' he said, looking at it in consternation. 'Truly, a remarkable picture.'

'Yes,' said the musician. He was astonished that was all Leopold had to say.

At the door Leopold turned round.

'I'm going to Wilhelm Rau's inn in Brunnenstraße now,' he said. 'You know the place. I'll be there until ten. Then I'll go home.'

The musician didn't ask, why are you telling me this?

He was young and shy.

The thought of this picture weighed heavy on Leopold. It was in a simple frame. You saw a table. A man with bony hands together, palm upward on top of the table, was counting silver coins. Upfolded hands. They were slender and had long fingers. Beside him sat a woman whose loose dress revealed her sagging breasts more than it concealed them. She had her hands upfolded too. Some liquid had been spilt on the table, a sticky liquid, he guessed. Their faces were angular, white and severe. They were bony faces, slender, sorrowful and folded like their hands.

Leopold thought that this picture could be called 'The Supper' or 'The Consecrated Host'. It reminded you of things it definitely had nothing to do with, no more than it had with the Last Supper. Basically it was a non-religious picture. It was the hands that made it sacred, the hands and the eyes.

Their hands were upfolded. That was the remarkable thing. Leopold had never heard the word used in that way before. But he knew it was a well-known sacred word. Perhaps it came from some forgotten hymn.

The musician began to play. Leopold could hear him because the musician's window was wide open. The street was deserted.

He remembered he had promised the musician he would go to Brunnenstraße. The musician might come and look for him. It was nine o'clock.

Leopold started to walk quickly.

The thought of the picture weighed heavy on his mind. Now it seemed to Leopold that the liquid that had been spilt on the table was not wine or schnapps, as he had originally assumed, but blood. Although the picture had given the impression black and white were the only colours, the damp patch on the table seemed red, sticky, not yet dry. He could tell with his fingers that it did not have the feel of wine or spirits, that the stickiness did not come from sugar, that it was the stickiness of blood. It seemed to have flowed out of those bloodless fingers. But perhaps it had already been sticking there. The innkeeper came over to wipe it away but withdrew when Leopold didn't take his fingers out of it, left his beer untouched and gave him a forbidding look.

There was no doubt everything would soon be cleared up, as soon as the musician who owned the picture came. He could say what it was.

Leopold straightened up, moving his elbows out from his body. But he kept his fingers upfolded. He was horrified that the blood was on the table and looked towards the door that ought to open. There was no one apart from the innkeeper in the room.

Leopold rubbed his forehead, for the thought of the picture lay heavy on his mind. It was a thought he was trying to forget.

But the money, he thought. What about the money? There's a reason for everything. 'A reason.' He said it out loud and the word seemed incomprehensible, alien, scarcely bearable.

He left without having drunk his beer. It cost a lot, he thought, and his wife was starving. But he had promised the musician. And now he hadn't come.

The clocks were striking ten when he went out into the street. He began to run.

His wife was sitting in her dress in the room. He saw her sagging breasts which the dress revealed more than concealed. It was less than a month since the baby had died.

Leopold took the money out of his pocket and put it on the table in front of his wife. It was the six silver coins he had received from the musician for copying out the score. There was a smell of fresh meat. The meat was in a bowl by the window.

'Moritz?' Leopold asked.

Moritz had been the name of the black cat.

He took the meat out of the bowl, brought it over and put it on the table.

'Let's eat,' he said.

They ate and threw the bones into the corner. All that was left of Moritz was a damp patch on the table. They were sitting beside each other.

'We'll have visitors soon,' he said.

They waited for the musician to come.

Towards morning her dress slipped down and the breasts he knew so well hung over the table. Poor, empty breasts. Severe and upfolded.

When she had been nursing the baby blood had come out of her breasts instead of milk. He looked at her breasts. There was a terrible patch on the table.

The blood killed the baby, he thought.

Beautiful breasts, he thought, empty, upfolded breasts. Is blood still coming from them? Onto her dress? Might there not be a crust of blood sticking to her dress? The thoughts you think lie heavy on your mind, heavy on your mind.

Perhaps if the musician comes, Leopold thought, and sees this, her breasts, the patch, the money and her dress, her empty, bleeding, darling breasts, perhaps he will be able to say what the reason for it all is. It is there. But incomprehensible, alien, scarcely bearable, Leopold, oh Leopold.

The Moving Frontier

Jeannie Ebner

When the drum began to sound with that soft, insistent beat, audible for miles, which tells the peoples that a tribe is on the warpath, all the warriors were seized with a frenzy of expectation. Later on the dull throbbing which, rapid and monotonous, lashed at our nerves for days on end, gradually stirred the blood of even our peaceable shepherds and patient labourers out in the wheat-fields. They left their villages, taking up the arms which for years had hung, mute and glinting softly in the firelight, on the walls of their huts.

At first we advanced rapidly in the direction of the sun for several days before making camp and resting, without being able to relax, until a new drumbeat joined in with the deep boom, boom of our own war-drum and eventually a large army of light-skinned warriors met up with us. Together we marched on, then rested again until, strengthened by several hundred yellow warriors, we moved forward once more, when red and black armies joined with us. This time a campaign with warriors from all over the world seemed to have been planned, all the races being expected to seek out a common enemy.

When we finally heard that our objective was to storm the moving frontier and take possession of the splendid land beyond it, a wave of wild, ecstatic excitement swept though the camp and did not subside for days and days. We moved on, advancing faster and faster, marching in close formation until the order came to deploy, maintaining absolute silence. Thus, in a line extending over many miles, we started to move into the thick scrub and creep up on the enemy.

With our machetes we cut a way through the forest and stopped at the farther end, concealed in the lower bushes, waiting for the other warriors to come up. Before us the plain stretched out endlessly to the horizon. Roughly two-thirds of the way across it a white line, no more than a hair's width, could be seen: the frontier. It was very strange that this frontier, which, after all, is only an imaginary line, was visible to the eye, and even stranger that every eye saw it in the same place, even though everyone has the potential to imagine it wherever he likes.

When all the troops had finally gathered and been provided with new and better weapons (while we were pushing forward they had been working tirelessly on the home front to improve our equipment; now we had armour made of metal rings, swords and iron shields) we continued our march and advanced on the frontier. But as quickly as we went forward, it drew back, so that after several days' march we found ourselves on the other side of the river but still just as far away from the frontier as before.

From the hinterland came shipments of magnificent horses. We exchanged our chain-mail and swords for lighter equipment and took to the saddle. Mules dragged along our new artillery, fat-barrelled mortars with supplies of stone balls. But the moment we spurred on our chargers, the frontier retreated effortlessly at the same speed. We rode for what must have been a millennium through reddish darknesses, and the cavalry songs we sang out of a strange kind of metaphysical fear, which spread quickly, had a melancholy sound and a bitter taste of futility.

We had long been motorised, leaving swirling clouds of dust in our wake, and still the frontier retreated from us, moving with the ease of a ballet-dancer while our strength had diminished. We could no longer stand frost or heat and needed large quantities of different things, such as clothes, tents, tinned food, medicines and vaccines to protect us and keep us alive. Tiredness had seeped into our bones, the vague fears and the horror of earlier times had given way to an inner emptiness, to a sense of our own insignificance and the pointlessness of this wild pursuit. But all that merely intensified the wish of every one of us to reach the frontier at last and rest secure in the peace of the longed-for country beyond it.

Finally it was decided to employ a different tactic, which would exhaust our technical rather than human resources. We made a final halt, in a long, densely massed front, and established our camp. A few kilometres beyond our position we set up a line of heavy artillery, flame-throwers and rocket-launchers, which we operated day and night in alternating shifts. For weeks on end we bombarded the moving frontier, which remained the same distance away, at rest, light and clear, like the friendly irony of a divine smile. But we could not injure it. Although our instruments recorded direct hits, at the point of entry the shells vanished into thin air and the frontier remained unbreached.

By this time we had a full range of amenities and could drown our lack of success and the emptiness of what we were doing in drink and music. We put on plays, read, debated, swore or prayed to forget the dreariness of a warrior's existence without an enemy to attack. We were probably too well off. The only thing missing was the fighting we had been trained for and had counted on, the only thing that could give meaning to our lives as soldiers. Eventually, for lack of an adversary to engage with outside our ranks, war began to rage in our camps. Rebellions broke out, we murdered a few dozen officers, any, just those we happened to get our hands on, and set fire to tents and supplies. More and more joined in and groups began to form which attacked each other furiously. The long-range guns stood abandoned and silent, their empty barrels yawning in the direction of the frontier.

We were suddenly gripped with a great fear of the emptiness between the guns and the thin-lipped grin of the frontier line and we retired a few kilometres. But as if that was just what it had been waiting for, the frontier, like a sly animal that pounces the moment it sees a flicker of fear and uncertainty in its enemy's eyes, took a bound towards us. With its fearful, silent swiftness it was suddenly back in our field of vision.

Seized with terror, we stopped fighting each other, turned

our backs on the frontier and fled. Every time we looked round we could see it at our backs, always the same distance away, apparently motionless. We threw down our weapons and all our equipment so we could run without encumbrance, but still it moved up behind us, unimpressed by our haste, unsurpassable in its inevitability, a constant presence we felt at our backs, like a ghostly breath.

Our headlong flight lasted a further millennium. Finally we were completely dispersed and fled on in terrible isolation, each returning to the place he had come from. We would have continued to flee, but our wives received us with furious contempt because we had left them alone for so long. All the while they had stayed where they had been since time immemorial. They had spent their precious young lives working to send us new weapons and now we came back without having achieved what we set out to do and dragging along with us the nightmare of a frontier, beyond which lay the promised land, still unravaged and unoccupied.

The women threw themselves at us and brought the wave of those flooding back to a halt. They dragged us forcibly into our houses, made us go back to work, fettered us to the work benches, to the machines, desks, tractors and fields, kept us on leads, like dogs, while we tilled the soil, and they allowed no one to break away, neither towards the frontier nor fleeing from it. Our life was cramped, bitter and cheerless.

Now I have grown old. I am foreman in a towel factory. With unmerciful gentleness, my wife comes to collect me every day after work, puts on my lead and takes me home. There she locks me in my room and here I finally find the time to write up the history of the campaign against the moving frontier

I have spent a lot of time thinking about it and sometimes I believe that if only my wife would let me go I could turn my back on the frontier and keep walking straight on. And if I stick to it one day I ought, the world being round, to come to the land I have left behind me, the land beyond the frontier.

Unfortunately my wife will have nothing to do with it. It's

all nonsense, she says, at best I'll go right round the world and end up back home, so why should I leave in the first place? I should forget these fancy ideas and stay here, where I belong, and do my bit for my work, for my wife, for the children.

Perhaps she's even right?

The Singing in the Swamp

Jeannie Ebner

I used to live with the corn-rich people, close to the pyramid-shaped stores and silos that are built on pillars over all the rivers. I found life clear and beautiful at the edges and on the surfaces, and sang to myself, loudly, blithely, not a thought in the world.

But then I somehow got into the swamp. At first I was dismayed that the swamp sucked me in. I had always thought it would spew me out, I thought I would be either too good or too bad for it, but it did not let go. It sucked me in very slowly.

The men who live in the swamp are sunk up to their arm-pits, the women to just below their breasts – essential if they are to suckle their babies. But all of them have to keep tread-ing all the time so as not to sink any deeper. They tread, tread, with phenomenal gentleness, steadily, tirelessly, without paus-ing at all. In this way there is almost no one who sinks deeper than their armpits or breast before they die. Of course, it is not the ideal place for weaklings or cripples. It does occasionally happen that one of these suddenly disappears, but it hardly causes any stir, just a short, gurgling noise and all those in the vicinity silently look away in embarrassment. They cannot save anyone, no one would save them if they were in danger of sinking, they need all their strength to keep their heads above water.

Like others before me, I managed to get onto one of the round, grassy islets, which are just big enough for a person to squat, kneel or stand on. But if you stay on these islets for any length of time, you are bound to starve, even though the air over the swamp is supposed to be quite nutritious. Sometimes, too, it is possible to catch one of the swamp birds with their beautiful plumage and, if you are lucky, get them to lay a warm, brown-speckled egg in your hand.

Every morning a dignified gentleman in black drives up in an old-fashioned carriage. He always gets out backwards, struggling with the folds of his shoulder cape, for he is very old and rather clumsy. He stays for half an hour, murmuring words we do not understand and blessing us, hands raised, from time to time. But that is of no help to us. And if we were not worried about spoiling our beautiful white hands, which we always take care to keep out of the swamp, placed on our shoulders or clasped behind our heads, we would perhaps throw slime at the old man. But in the swamp such urges are not violent and never lasting.

In the morning rich people drive over in their cars and make drawings or photographs of the faces and hands of the swamp women, who are famed for their beauty. Or reporters, journalists, politicians, sociologists and film-makers flood the area with spectacles, briefcases, pencils and film cameras, and make a great fuss of us. It seems everybody wants to write articles, or make speeches or programmes about the swamp. But no one can do that who has not been in the swamp himself and none of them ever has been in the swamp, because anyone who gets in never gets out, and anyone who's in doesn't have the opportunity to make a film or a speech or write about it, he's fully occupied treading and keeping his hands clean. And anyway, here you very quickly lose interest in anything written.

Once or twice, though, there were conscientious journalists who were determined to try at all costs. They came with cranes and pulleys and had themselves let down into the swamp, hanging in slings. They talked to us very loudly in the swamp dialect about horses that always run in pairs, such as justice and injustice, wealth and poverty. We didn't reply. How could someone who is in goal for fourteen days and knows exactly when he will get out communicate with people who are condemned to life imprisonment?

In the afternoon the school-children come, delightful little things with jolly ribbons in their hair and boys with red cheeks and coloured balls. They appear to confuse us with their uncles and aunts who usually buy them chocolate, and although they are almost starving on the grass islets, the women sometimes give them a speckled bird's egg, if they happen to have one.

Apart from that there are lots of sightseers and passers-by, messenger-boys, day-trippers and tramps who come past. Individual swamp-dwellers keep trying to clutch onto the clothes of people going past and pull themselves out, but they never succeed, though occasionally the passers-by are dragged in. It appears to be easier to get in than out.

In the evening, especially in spring, the poets come. They are less cautious and come close; a lot of them have already been dragged into the swamp. They stand by the edge of the swamp, put their heads on one side in a pensive pose, look at a flower, which they solemnly hold in front of them, form an oval with their mouths and let out a song. They say they are singing for us, because they want to do us good. But I think that's nonsense. We don't hear them because the air here is very dense and doesn't let the sound waves through. Most of them have a very weak voice as well, too little breath, and so they sing in a circle round their heads and their song has no effect on us.

It seems that the swamp water makes people fertile. When two swamp inhabitants fall in love – and here we fall in love swiftly and violently – they light up like an electric bulb screwed into the socket while the lamp's switched on. And the women who are loved immediately have children, even though the lovers cannot come together and their faces just shine on each other longingly from a distance. And the women who have once been loved keep on getting children long after they have stopped being loved.

The mothers place their babies on grass islets within reach, and their nourishing milk makes them strong and healthy, although their mothers have to keep treading and cannot give them much attention. The children grow up all by themselves. As soon as they are a bit bigger, their mothers push them into the swamp so they will learn to tread at an early age. Many jump into the swamp of their own accord, even when they are quite young, since once they reach a certain age they need more than milk and air.

There is always something to eat in the swamp, not too much and not too little. Never enough to give someone else some, since you need to keep up your strength for treading, but just enough to keep you going from one day to the next.

The incessant treading releases seeds from the stalks far below the feet of the swamp people. In olden times a rich cornfield must have been buried there. It has an inexhaustible wealth of corn which the constant movement of our feet brings up to the couple of inches of shallow, brackish water which lies on top of the mire and is clear. We peck at the grains with our lips, since we want to keep our hands clean and naturally we don't get that many, just as much as is essential to stay alive. The other grains are quickly carried off. They float away, out of the swampland into the little watercourses which flow into a few great canals the corn-rich people have dug. There the grains are gathered together and sent on, to be distributed to the countries and cities of the world. Thus it is essential that we keep on treading, not only because it stops us sinking and starving, but also in order to feed the world.

The corn people who live outside the swamp collect the corn in stores and silos, and when one of us gets so old and sick he can't keep treading enough, thus creating an area around him that is low in corn, they throw him grains from their supplies, one at a time, the way you feed hens. But most of them float away and return to the stores. A person who is old or sick cannot peck so quickly, nor with precise aim. They could throw such people more than is absolutely necessary. But, some say, then lots would pretend to be old and sick before their time and tread less, in order to get more without effort. And if too many stop treading, too few grains will come to the surface and too many will be thrown in, and the stocks will grow smaller and eventually everyone will starve.

Or, and this is what I used to think, then everyone would have to tread.

It was a thought that fascinated me for a brief while, but

then I realised that there would be no one to dig canals, build storehouses, collect the grains and distribute them in emergencies. Everyone would get just the amount they needed to stay alive themselves. One of the horses that always run in pairs (such as justice and injustice) would have to run alone. But what would we get out of it? We would still have to keep on treading, as we have always done, only everyone would be in the swamp then, perhaps so many that they would tread on each other.

But perhaps – this was another thought that occurred to me – we could come to an agreement to take turns. From time to time all the swamp people would be pulled out of the swamp, perhaps with the aforementioned pulleys, and the corn people would take their places. Would it not be more just if the people with whom we share the corn shared the swamp with us?

I told this idea to an old man who had renounced corn and settled on a grass islet. He was a sage, one of those whose wisdom had reached the stage which makes it possible for him to live on the air, which is supposed to be very nourishing here.

The sage told me, however, that it was not a new idea. It had even been tried before, the last time less than thirty years ago, and many corn people had died, for only those who are born here, or have a particularly strong constitution or great will power can tolerate the swamp air. Some managed to survive the change, but never learnt to tread properly and only brought up a few grains. On the other hand the swamp people, when they first reached the corn country, had gone wild in the storehouses, the sage told me, and destroyed, scattered or eaten much of the stocks. It had taken a great effort for them to learn how to store the corn properly, so that it didn't go musty, and how to manage large supplies economically and efficiently. The consequence was that during the next twenty-five years there was more hunger and suffering than ever, and many people had died before the relocation was carried out. That was some time ago and now things were back to normal. And now here I was on my grass islet, trying start the same trouble again. With that he threw something at me that a swamp bird had laid in his hand and was definitely not an egg because he had caught a swamp-cock by mistake. He was very old, and wisdom is no substitute for keen eyesight.

I assumed he meant well, even with the thing he threw at me, so I thanked him for his explanation. Perhaps he was right, perhaps wrong. The horses always run in pairs.

Not surprisingly, at the beginning, when I was sucked into the swamp, I was angry, then bitter, then sad, until I eventually accepted my fate and calmed down. I stopped thinking about it, but then I felt the hunger even more, and to take my mind off it I started singing. To avoid opening my mouth in a wide oval like the poets, I kept my lips closed and hummed softly to myself. I remember that first time I sang as clearly as if it had been yesterday:

Darkness was spreading slowly over the swamp. The moon set its pointed shoe lightly on the treetops. The swamp people were silently treading, their hands clasped behind their heads, their eyelids lowered. They trod gently, steadily and tirelessly, even though they were sleeping. Not only did they not stop treading, their treading was even more intensive while they were asleep because all their strength had withdrawn from their senses and brains into their legs. Masses of bright grains welled up and swirled around on the surface, like reflections of the stars. Seen by no one, pursued by no starving lips, they floated more slowly into the canals than by day and, carried along on the waves into the silos, they piled up inside those pyramids of stored fruitfulness against the fine-meshed nets that stopped them continuing on their way with the water.

And so every morning the corn people find a huge shining sun over their land and a rich harvest piled up in their dark storehouses, effortless as a draught of fish in the trout mating season.

The swamp people know nothing of that. Exhausted, they sleep soundly at nights. But I know about these things because I have lived in both places. I know both worlds. Two worlds which for me combine in a familiar and varied picture of

254

great beauty and great sadness, like the two interweaving voices of a song. It was these harmonies that enticed me to start humming.

Later I slipped from my grass islet back into the swamp, held up my hands, trod very slowly and hummed. My humming could not penetrate the dense air. It circled round my head and slowly rose to my hands. Its vibrations imparted slight, rapid movements to my fingertips and bore my hands up so that they did not tire. Instead, they hovered in the air above my head, fluttering and warbling like larks. Attracted by the buzzing of my fingertips, swamp birds circled round my hands. Perhaps the delicate oscillation makes them think they are insects.

It was quite still.

The feet of the people treading as they slept made no sound. They were deep down and mute as the silent activity of roots.

And since I know about both worlds and have felt much within me, root-quiet and corn-joy both flow into my song. I sing, for myself alone, absorbed in my song, mute and breathless. And there is no end to my hymn of praise.

Something to Say for the Rain

Rudolf Bayr

They got the police to force an entrance to my apartment and just because I'm lying in bed – I think and think after the scene was all over.

It's raining, it's been raining for days and nights, lines can be seen against the darker windows opposite, the lighter ones absorb them, and the lead goes black in the rain, and the water turns some of the skylights into mirrors, and individual roof tiles stand out as more reddish while the others remain an inconspicuous dull grey, and the wind peppers the roof with rain, throws pellets of rain on tin and tiles, I can hear everything quite clearly, the attic roof is immediately above the ceiling, you can hear the water gurgling in the gutters and the drops spattering on the flashing, in ones, twos, a lot at once, and the wood in the room is moving, the dampness, for days and nights on end . . .

The policemen took a statement and apologised. But I had to understand, they said, that it was happening more and more often that people shut themselves in and laid themselves down to die, being sick and without hope.

Yes, I understand, you don't need to apologise.

Mostly, one of them said with a laugh, because I understood and apologised, mostly people don't realise someone's gone until you can smell them from the stairs – you, he said to me, as if to distinguish me from someone you can already smell, you had simply gone missing, they didn't know where you were at the office either.

They'll soon know. The company doctor will note that I am lying in bed, although not confined to bed for medical reasons. Company doctors are the medical arm of the employer, they balance the usefulness of a person against the content of the Hippocratic oath. The company doctor will say he cannot give me a sick note because I am well . . .

I went to bed when the storm finally came, and I stayed there after it had left the rain behind, pushing the house, the street, the town into the dull lighting which wipes up the shadows, the lighting in which no light can be made out and the wet blocks out the colours.

Rain, says the radio announcer, continual, abundant rain, and the wind peppers lead and tiles with pellets of rain, they make the silence lined up behind the wind crumbly, porous, I lie there and sometimes I get up to see the lines against the dark windows and I tell myself that it's raining and the differences are shrinking, and it is as if earth were clawing its way upwards, and darkness.

No, I'm not mad, I'm just doing loosening exercises, I'm trying to loosen my connections with the room where I'm lying, the ownership connections with things I like to have, with my table, my chest, the drawings on my walls, my books, to practise separation by imaginative anticipation.

One night when I was eight I lost a lot of blood after a not entirely successful operation, the pain I had been suffering disappeared with the blood, I felt light, weightless. With a thin sleep cooling my eyes, I asked my mother if I was going to die, I couldn't see my toys because of all the tubes I was hooked up to, and my mother said, no, I wasn't going to, and I remember it was a disappointment.

I have seen people take that one long, last look, turn round one last time, look back at the room, at the house they are being carried out of, driven away from, and then I have seen them look forward, in the direction they are being carried, driven, and I have heard the people carrying or driving them say that's right, loosen up and leave it all behind, and I have heard them describe the decor for the final scene, they talked of peace, lots of peace and greenery and gravel paths and benches, years of it, years in which the sun will never set and the nights will carry no fears in the folds of their mantles.

I have to practise that, I tell myself, take myself away before they carry me away, I would like to spare myself that one last look, not have any reason to turn round one last time, not cling on, not to anyone, not to anything, practise, practise and keep the door closed.

This morning the windows were opaque, condensation had gathered on the glass, it has turned colder and the wind is still peppering the roof above me and spattering the flashing, and the lighting has no light and I stay lying in bed and think that I will stay there and practise, and that that is how it will turn out, how it will be one day, more or less . . .

Ebb and Flow

Anton Fuchs

For generations our family has lived in a spacious house formed of stone and dark beams. It stands halfway up the hill in that funnel-shaped valley with a fortress at the bottom. Seen from the dormer windows of our bedrooms, the two-storey building, with its massive projections, six towers, battlements, parapets and permanently closed shutters, gives the impression of being uninhabited.

A dangerous illusion to which anyone will fall victim who lacks the patience for prolonged observation. For at irregular intervals, mostly around midday, the two doors of the main entrance will suddenly fly open. Then you can see the military police march, in goose-step and close formation, to the parade ground, where they halt and stand to attention for a while in an open-sided square at the flagpole before – presumably at a command, from that distance we cannot hear anything – falling out. Scarcely have they dispersed into the country, however, than they can only be made out with difficulty in the brush on the surrounding slopes. Only with the aid of a telescope on its sharpest setting can you see one or other of them, earnestly searching the ground for clues. Then sometimes you can identify here and there a piece of braid, a star on a collar, a shoulder strap, a belt buckle, occasionally a rifle with fixed bayonet.

As our father sometimes tells us, when he was a child he was always afraid of these patrols combing the hills which could strike at any moment. But those times are past. Our generation has become used to seeing them. We know from experience that they will not detain us as long as we have not broken any law. Some of my brothers and sisters go so far as to feel comfortable under their protection. They even think of them as 'keepers of the peace', remembering how close behind all reality terror and anarchy lurk, just waiting for the opportunity to destroy the residence our kindred raised in days beyond recall. After all, they add, we have learnt to toughen ourselves up against many other, often far worse afflictions. We've survived a good fifteen thousand wars, massive earth- and seaquakes, whirlwinds, hurricanes, not to mention the ice ages, erupting volcanoes, avalanches. Once there was even persistently dense rain. It didn't stop raining. For forty days and forty nights. Until the fortress at the bottom of the valley was covered by the muddy waves with only the towers still above them, and the police on the battlements, packed together, with wet helmets, looking up at the skies to see if they were going to clear at last.

We've survived all these catastrophes, they continue. They went as quickly as they came. People would surely have soon forgotten them if some historians hadn't recorded them in their chronicles.

That's the way they talk today, and that's the way they've always talked when our large family's sitting together round the table, each with his pewter mug in front of him. I love watching their carefree faces, the serene, southern *grandezza* of their gestures. The fact that I prefer to listen rather than join in their conversations has nothing to do with either timidity or a sense of superiority. More with coolness, with observing from a distance and the enjoyment I get from drifting along on the sound waves from their voices. Above all, however, I must be careful not to mention the rumour that was reported to me recently, late in the night, when they were all asleep.

Entangled in chaotic dreams after the usual evening spent drinking and roused with a sudden start, I at first stubbornly insisted on confusing the man, who was bending over me holding his hurricane lamp, with someone else, until I began to comprehend who he was and what he was saying.

He was, he repeated in a whisper, a messenger from below and he had a message for me, the implications of which none of us would probably grasp. A tap had started to leak, he went on, bringing his lips even closer to my right ear, in one of the extensive, pitch-black dungeons of the fortress where no one had set foot for decades, and had been dripping ever since without stopping for a single moment.

'But . . .' I said, turning towards the shadow-filled face illuminated from below, 'how can you . . .' But before I could finish my question, he had switched off his lamp and silently disappeared.

I could not get back to sleep that night. It was no use trying to take my mind off the message by working out mathematical formulae in my head or trying to remember as far back into my childhood as possible to see if I could get to the moment of my birth . . . My concentration only had to slacken slightly and the news I had just heard was back. Sometimes it seemed more frightening than anything I had ever heard, at others a harmless, even ridiculous exaggeration. Indeed, there were times when I felt my encounter with the messenger from below had been nothing but a dream.

In the morning, however, I set out earlier than usual. I climbed between rocks and withered juniper bushes up the steep slope, debating with myself all the time whether it was not my duty to bring the impending danger to the attention of my relatives, even at the risk of my news meeting with nothing but disbelief or laughter.

When I had finally reached the ridge, I spent a long time looking down on the gigantic basin in the form of a crater which has exerted a strange pull on many of us. The fortress still lay in semi-darkness, but the outlines of its courtyards could already be clearly distinguished. And once more the two-storey building with its massive projections, six towers, battlements, parapets and permanently closed shutters gave the impression of being uninhabited.

After a while I turned round and looked through my prismatic telescope out into the desert. In the first rays of the morning sun, the hills of wavy sand seemed to recede even farther into the distance than usual.

If the nocturnal messenger is right, was the thought that came into my head as I set off down again, then at some time in the future these uninhabited dunes, completely uncontaminated by vegetation, will be all that our planet will leave behind.

Now I'm sitting among my people again. Again I let them do the talking. So as not to arouse suspicion, I nod from time to time, or order my hands to make a vague gesture. Inside, however, I am ceaselessly picturing the water rising in the fortress. Picturing it filling all the cellars, then all the rooms, halls and stair-wells, finally rising higher and higher, from one landmark to the next, up the surrounding slopes of the basin.

It will probably be several centuries before the flood can reach us. But one day its playful waves will flow over the threshold of our entrance hall. And after a few more centuries, or even just moments, our house, I say to myself as the others raise their goblets, assuring each other it will stand for ever, our house, far below the surface of a huge reservoir that has long since grown into an ocean, in darkness and temperatures close to freezing, under the weight and pressure of a huge mass of water, will disintegrate until it is beyond recognition.

★

Flow and Ebb

On the bottom of the ocean, in darkness and temperatures close to freezing, under the weight and pressure of a huge mass of water, disintegrated and beyond recognition.

There are drowned cities of the ancient world, their streets, courts and backyards under three fathoms of mud and mire, and floating high above them, as brightly transparent as glass, the billowing skirts of the jellyfish with their reddish-brown, stinging tentacles.

And there are shipwrecks from all ages, in the landlocked seas and on the continental shelf close to the shore and in the unexplored depths of the three oceans. Sunken galleys and triremes, Hanseatic cogs, junks, carvels and countless warships and peace-ships from our epochs. Ships, whose sinking almost no one has ever heard of, and others which still arouse our imagination, like the Titanic.

I saw, to the east of Labrador, icebergs slowly drifting southwards. Once by sunlight and once by the light of the stars.

And I saw on the fourteenth of April in the year nineteen hundred and twelve – it was approaching midnight – a ship immensely long, immensely wide and seven stories high, a ship such as had never been seen before. It was crossing the Atlantic, transporting from one continent to the other, at more than twenty-two knots per hour, dining-rooms with chandeliers and laid tables, smoking rooms, swimming pools, dance floors, winter gardens, carpeted stairs, long corridors, lift shafts and three thousand beds with many passengers already asleep in them; all the while below, in the extensive catacombs of the ship, full holds, coal bunkers, dynamos and pumps were making their way through the black waters; the crew's quarters as well, stables, garages and five dozen bulk-head hatches; between them, dark passageways, steep, narrow iron ladders and the echoing, dazzlingly lit rooms where eighteen giant boilers with one hundred and twenty-six burners ceaselessly produced fifty thousand horsepower, driving the three propellers, each nine metres in diameter, full speed ahead, to the west, through chilly darkness and banks of mist, towards the iceberg the current has left off Labrador . . .

Four hours later this gigantic ship, which was claimed to be unsinkable, had altered course for good. It was now, on 41 degrees 46 minutes north, 50 degrees 14 minutes west, rushing at increasing speed almost vertically towards the ocean bed. It finally hit the bottom, sending the mud and mire of millions of years swirling up in a huge cloud, which took months to calm down and settle.

I can no longer remember how many hundreds of miles it is south-south-eastwards to where another wreck is disintegrating in a depth of twenty-three thousand feet. And another one, ninety miles closer to the shore, with cephalopods living in it, the deep-sea octopus and the giant squid. Shipwrecks of all ages on the bottom of the three oceans, scattered far and wide, occasionally close together. Broken hulls, planks, overgrown with plant life. Figureheads, funnels and sirens, portholes, wire-mesh and wickerwork all eaten away by bristle worms and rust, by the salt of the sea. And many a wreck sunk so deep into the covering mire that no one could ever find it.

The ocean, the sea . . .

I spent nine thousand years travelling on the bottom of the Pacific, far below sharks and shoals of herring and sardines, in that black, almost unmoving zone where there is neither day nor night nor seasons. I made my way across the long deep-sea plains to the west of the Andes and the Rocky Mountains. Emerging from the Antarctic basin deep in the south, it was decades before I reached the equator, and further decades before I came to the Aleutian Trench in the north, and turned west.

It was as if I had been completely released from gravity, so effortlessly did I drift along among luminescent prawns, hatchet fish and the dark sea butterflies, sank down slowly and then rose up again, often with just a sketchy movement of my arms wings fins. Sometimes I climbed the steepest cliff-faces of mountains with ease, taking months to reach the summits, which rose to a height of up to three thousand feet below the surface. And sometimes I dived for a long time – it seemed unending – dived in oppressive silence, farther and farther down, to the bottom of the Mariana Trench, where I was closer, apart from the time when I still lived in a womb, to the centre of the earth than I had ever been.

Following the tropic of Cancer, I went to see the spawning grounds and graveyards of the eels in the Sargasso Sea in the western Atlantic, then felt my way along endless undersea cables encrusted with feathery corals and sessile crabs. I passed through forests of seaweed, eelgrass and algae, saw coral reefs, shoals of unbelievably colourful fish, saw – sometimes carried many miles off the course I had intended – the sea aglow with phosphorescence, individual lights, here and there the earnest eye of another solitary wanderer fixed on me. We always kept our distance, although I regarded him as a kind of brother, like every other angler fish, ray or giant pill bug who has crossed my path over the centuries.

I will never forget the Indian-Antarctic Basin, the shallow Bering Sea, the Tonga Trench, the Kuril Trench. And once, just once, I even entered the Arctic Sea, following with fascination the trail of Jules Verne's 'Nautilus' under the North Pole. When I turned over on my back I could see the lower hemispheres of icebergs, like menacing clouds above me.

But everywhere, wherever I was, wherever I am, the shells of dead plankton float down to the bottom, like snowflakes on dark December nights. Sand too, the ashes from erupting volcanoes, the dust of burnt-out meteors. In the same rhythm as one new life after another is born, one corpse after the other sinks, and gradually disintegrates as it sinks

When I started out on my expeditions, I was hurt by the distrust towards me and my claim that the undersea landscapes exceeded those of all the continents in extent, variety and beauty. But I have long since accustomed myself to the fact and calmly journey from one sea to another, obedient to the law of buoyancy eventually discovered by every scientist who once ran naked into the market place at night crying, 'Eureka! Eureka! I've found it!'

I often dream – and wonder, in my bewilderment, why I dream such dreams – of the immense wave from the bottom of the Mariana Trench to the summit of Mount Everest. It is an incontrovertible fact that the crest of a wave becomes the trough, the trough of a wave the crest. Thus it is possible that, as aeon succeeds aeon, the seabed will become a mountain, a mountain the seabed. Then the bottom of an ocean of water will become the bottom of an ocean of air. And just as now, thirty thousand feet above our darkness, the cabins, bridge and engine rooms of a sea-ship are crossing the ocean, in the future high above it, with a straight white trail, an airship will pass, carrying in its fuselage, stacked in four long rows, the beings who do not need gills.

I can already feel the bottom lifting slowly, as if the pressure, the darkness were decreasing. Scarcely noticeable as yet. But the time will come when we will swim among sharks, among the shoals of herring and sardines in lighter, brighter waters with the surface just above, a never-still mirror of quicksilver.

Until at last we will emerge, dripping wet, into the sunlight to build, in the bright, wind-blown dryness, a spacious house out of stones and dark beams that will house generations of our family.

Cannibals

Marlen Haushofer

She could have been fifteen, thirteen, or perhaps no more than twelve. Nowadays you can never tell how old a girl really is. He was sitting opposite her in the compartment of the train and had been observing her for about twenty minutes. Actually, he had intended to read the newspaper, to read it properly and enjoy it which, as a slow reader, he hardly ever did. But then he had noticed the girl opposite and had hoped to spend an hour or two enjoying the agreeable sight. Now he was becoming uneasy.

There were only the two of them in the compartment and it was much too warm for the time of year. The countryside was dipped in gold and slate-grey, and although it had not rained for a week there was a moist gleam over everything.

He had felt the headache as soon as he woke, just behind his left eye. A gnawing, nagging pain that he had suppressed with coffee and pills. Throughout the morning he could still feel the gnawing and nagging, but without the pain. He knew that he actually had a violent headache, but as if with a local anaesthetic. After lunch he had taken another pill and since then his head had felt light and clear and as if it were made of cotton wool, as if it might come away from his shoulders at any moment and float up to the ceiling. The idea was irritating, he was sure it was the result of the pills he had taken and the atmosphere caused by the warm, dry wind, the Föhn. It was not normally his habit to indulge in thoughts other than the the usual ones, that is, in thoughts he assumed were usual.

For twenty minutes, then, he had been observing the girl in the corner seat opposite. 'The little girl' was how he thought of her and she really was little, and in his opinion a pleasant contrast to the young girls you see everywhere nowadays.

Even his own fourteen-year-old daughter was already as tall as he was. He was only medium height, true, but still it was too much for a girl. And there was no end in sight. He put away the thought of his daughter, which he found somehow disturbing, and turned back to the little girl. She looked exactly the way people used to imagine a pretty teenager when he was young, that is, thirty years ago. A very feminine creature with narrow, sloping shoulders, small, round breasts and the hips slightly rounded already. To the modern eye she probably had a poor figure, too narrow at the top, hips too broad and legs too short. But she was enchanting, so refreshing after all the beanpoles you saw stomping around like young giants everywhere. And she had the daintiest hands and feet. It was pleasant once in a while not to be reminded at the sight of a young woman that she too had a skeleton inside her.

He felt a certain disquiet. It was surely not quite proper to observe this girl, still half a child, with the eyes of a man. On the other hand, there was nothing in that particular area that was proper, and he was doing nothing that might offend the little girl. He was only looking at her surreptitiously, and that only when she was not looking in his direction, which happened rarely enough, and then only as if he were a rather oddly shaped suitcase or umbrella stand. He was slightly hurt at this; on the other hand he was pleased, since he did not have the slightest desire to get into conversation with her.

In fact, she did nothing at all but regard her rosy fingernails with unconcealed delight. Now and then she glanced at her reflection in the window and gave it a loving smile. It was funny and rather touching to see, at the same time he admitted to himself that he would have found this kind of narcissism irritating in his daughter. He immediately put that thought out of his mind and watched, enthralled, as the little girl moved her toes up and down in her sandals until she finally seemed happy with them.

There was a book on the seat beside her. *Natural History for Classes 1–3 of High Schools*, that meant she was at most fourteen. At one point she made a worried frown, as if something very depressing had just occurred to her, picked up the book and started to leaf through it. Immediately she seemed over-come with a terrible tiredness, dropped the book back on the seat and gave a charming, if uninhibited yawn.

His daughter had that book at school as well. He was get-ting a bit more annoyed now at the way his mind kept insist-ing on making this connection. His daughter and this little girl, they were as different as chalk and cheese, and anyway, it would never occur to a man to stare at his daughter in this way. Or would it? There was something slightly disagreeable about the situation, and to his astonishment he realised he was observing not only the little girl, but himself as well and, what was disquieting, found himself pretty revolting. He told him-self it was due to the Föhn and all the pills he had taken, but the wind most of all. He had read an article in the newspaper about this wind only last week and felt he was an expert.

He would get down to reading the sports pages in peace and ignore this little miss from now on. What was all this anyway? He wasn't so old a slip of a girl like that could disturb him. And disturbed wasn't the right word at all. What he felt was just pleasure in a beautiful creature, it was quite natural, it was entirely platonic. He peeped over the top of his news-paper again and looked at her face, a face that seemed oblivi-ous of her perfect little figure. It was simply the face of a charming, superficial and not particularly intelligent child, and it glowed with health. The white of her eyes still had a bluish tinge, her lashes were childishly long and thick, and her hair, tumbling down in ringlets over her low forehead, was the soft, shining hair of a child. She really must be very young, her skin was still unblemished and healthy.

Then the unease he had been unable to shake off all the time intensified, turning into a feeling of emptiness and hun-ger such as he had never known before. He felt slightly sick and wiped his face with his handkerchief. The little girl had not noticed anything, thank God, she was just smiling, enraptured, at her own reflection.

His heartbeat was unnaturally loud and he was filled with fear. He tried to work out what was happening to him. One thing was certain: what he felt for this child was not sexual desire, it was something much deeper and more dangerous. And then he knew. This insane craving that was tormenting him was the desire to eat up the girl, to devour her entirely and fill the sad, empty hollowness inside him with her youth. It was an insane idea, especially for someone who only knew of such things from books. That must be what came over those despicable criminals before they carried out their incomprehensible, monstrous deeds. Now he understood and for a brief moment they were his brothers, and he hated the little girl for bringing him to this, and he hated her because nothing he could do with her could satisfy that terrible hunger.

The train stopped at a station and four other passengers got in the compartment. He was glad he was no longer alone with the girl and forced himself to think of other things and look at the new arrivals. He very quickly established that they were not worth looking at: an ugly, red-haired man with protruding teeth, horn-rimmed spectacles and a horribly gnawed thumbnail (presumably an intellectual); an agricultural-looking man in a traditional folk-style suit with a watch chain across his belly; a bony, middle-aged lady covered in valuable jewellery and countless freckles; a good-looking young man who didn't even so much as glance at him but sprawled in the corner seat by the door, stretched his long legs across half the compartment and immersed himself in a book about sailing boats.

At least the interruption had calmed him down to the extent that he hoped he would now be able to read the sports section. He didn't manage it this time either, of course, because his hands were trembling so much, a common Föhn phenomenon. Also he had probably drunk too much coffee with his lunch.

Suddenly he noticed that it had gone quiet in the compartment, unnaturally quiet. Even when there is no one talking, there are lots of other noises in a railway compartment, shuffling, rubbing, rustling, wheezing, nose-blowing noises. It's so quiet you could hear a pin drop, he thought, and the idea went through his mind that he was thinking almost entirely in expressions he had heard or read somewhere. He stole a look over the top of his newspaper at the scrawny lady sitting next to him and saw to his astonishment that she was staring, oblivious of all around her, at the little girl's knees.

The knees, with their little dimples at the sides, were certainly worth looking at, but he didn't like the way the lady was staring. There was envy there, admiration and desire. Suddenly he realised that she too was feeling that emptiness inside her, that terrible hunger that was forcing her to clench the handle of her bag so tightly that her knuckles stood out white. The expression in her eyes sent a hot flush over his face at the thought that he must have looked like that only a short while ago. He slid back down behind his newspaper again and carefully tore a little hole in it with his fingernail through which he could observe the girl opposite.

The unnatural warmth seemed to have made her tired and she yawned, displaying white teeth and a portion of pink flesh on the roof of her mouth. It was the yawn of a little kitten and set his heart beating. Then she stretched her narrow shoulders, placed one arm across her thighs and examined with interest the delicate skin in the crook of her arm while gently stroking it with the tips of her fingers. A smile of rapture spread across her face.

He forced himself to look away from her and saw that the whole of the compartment was holding its breath. Then the bony lady gave a painful, distressed sigh and he saw beads of sweat appear on her forehead. She had gone very pale, making her freckles look like a spattering of mud. A poor, spotted hyena. And the way she had drawn up her lower lip, as if she were crouching ready to pounce.

They were all now quite openly watching the girl. With the sole exception of the young man by the door engrossed in his book on sailing boats. Sometimes he kicked the man sitting opposite on the shin with the tip of his shoe but didn't notice, or refused to notice, he certainly did not say he was sorry. He seemed to be enclosed in an air bubble, in a world of the most marvellous sailing boats, the only desirable objects.

Lost to the world, the child was still stroking the delicate skin on the inside of her arm. Then her knee caught her attention and she scrutinised it with the hint of a furrow between her gleaming brows. Then she inspected her finger-nails once more, finally immersing herself in an earnest study of her pink palm with the delicate lines across it.

He looked round, not at all surreptitiously this time. No one was paying any attention to him. The lady, the presumed intellectual and the man with the watch chain were all staring at the girl like beasts of prey eyeing a piece of meat the keeper had thrown into the cage. The man with the watch chain was sliding his tongue restlessly over his lower lip, which made him look like an idiot, the intellectual had white bubbles at the corner of his mouth and the lady was sweating, very pale and spotted.

He felt ashamed, he felt wretched and humiliated. And yet he had not really done anything he need feel ashamed of. Anyway, what had actually happened? Nothing at all. None of them had even spoken to the little girl, let alone touched her. Still he felt thoroughly wretched. He knew now the inevitable conclusion of the affair. One day one of the beasts of prey would pounce and noisily devour the tasty piece of flesh. Later it would stop, a foolish look on its face, and realise that the hunger was still there, gnawing, tormenting and insatiable. He had to do something now.

He cleared his throat with a loud and threatening noise. It had the effect of a bomb. They all seemed to freeze for a second. The lady put her hand over her mouth, as if to repress a scream, then leapt up, muttering something incomprehensible, and pulled the window even farther down. The man with the watch chain laboriously heaved himself up from the seat, went out into the corridor, stumbling over the young man's feet, and lit a cigar. The intellectual remarked to the lady that he had never known an October when the Föhn was so bad. And so hot! Then he took a periodical out of his suitcase.

The young man, who, when the man with the watch chain had stumbled over his feet, had looked up with a blank, uncomprehending expression on his face, stretched out his legs again and returned to the world of sailing boats.

He and the girl were the only ones who had not noticed what had happened in the compartment. She was still inspecting her palm, entranced by the shallow cup with the mysterious lines across, then she yawned for the third time on the journey, leant her head against her summer coat hanging in the corner and immediately went to sleep. With her innocent child's profile facing the compartment, she suddenly smiled in her sleep, far away and beyond the reach of the spotted hyena and all other beasts of prey.

At last he could read the sports section, but he did not enjoy it as much as usual. And the gnawing and nagging had started behind his left eye again. He knew it would soon turn into pain. He stared out at the moist blue landscape, wishing he were at home in bed, in the pleasant quiet and darkness, able to forget this and all the other days of his life.

The Toad

Florian Kalbeck

I recently visited a friend of mine, an old doctor who had worked as a psychiatrist. We were discussing current affairs, and I confessed to my friend that there were certain recent events with which I could not come to terms. There was nothing in this world, the doctor replied, with which we could, or ought to come to terms, as I insisted on putting it. But then I was still young, of course. When I refused to accept this answer, he said, 'Let me tell you about a case I came across many years ago. No, you'd better read the story yourself.'

He took a slim volume bound in black cloth down from the shelf of medical books in his library and leafed through it. I noticed there was no title or author's name on the cover. The doctor handed it to me.

'What I am giving you here are the memoirs of a madman who was my patient many years ago. I was young myself at the time and working as a junior doctor in the psychiatric clinic in ✱✱✱.

My patient, the author of the book, was a high-school teacher, a very gifted man in his mid-thirties. He wrote his own case history in the clinic. Later on I had it printed; you will see how strangely modern it all sounds. Although suffering from an incurable mental illness, the man still writes well, is surprisingly coherent, both stylistically and syntactically. But read it for yourself.'

I took the book, curious as to what I would find in it. This is the point at which my friend opened it for me to start reading:

'I have to recount how I killed my brother. It was hard work and took three nights and three days. I lay in wait for him, at night, when he came home from my beloved's bed. She kept on insisting she was not having an affair with him, but I knew she was. I often caught the two of them exchanging secret glances when they thought I wasn't looking. She's a beautiful woman, though at heart she's a common whore.

That night, then, I lay in wait for my brother in the dark until he had slipped in by the front door, cautiously removed his shoes and placed his foot on the bottom step of the stairs. Then I hit him over the head from behind with the poker. I dragged him down into the cellar, where I had a bucket of cold water ready, and brought him round. That was when the work started which took me three nights and three days. It was not always easy to keep my brother awake when he was half dead from the tortures I inflicted on him, but I spared no effort. Once he almost died on me before I had had the chance to try out the most interesting ones, but with the help of an excellent fluid, which I injected into his arm, I managed to keep him alive and conscious until the evening of the third day, thus allowing me to add the final touches to my work. When he was finally dead, I threw him in the cesspit behind the house and went to bed, for I was truly tired.'

I stopped, horrified and nauseated. The doctor took the book out of my hand and opened it at the first page, saying, 'You are unlikely to find what follows that interesting: page after page of descriptions of all kinds of different tortures. I presume you're not one of those people who like that type of thing after lunch, as an aid to digestion. The passage you've read is just the outline, so to speak. Have a look at the opening of the memoir.'

However, when I gave him a questioning look, which at the same time expressed all my repugnance, he added, 'Be reassured. What I forgot to tell you is that the torture and murder of his brother never actually occurred. Or at least it only occurred in the mind of the madman. He did have a brother who died, but he died of a common-or-garden heart attack. It was just a few days after his brother's death that my

275

patient succumbed to the delusion that he had tortured and killed him. But read it for yourself.'

So I read:

'One day I was arrested, and that is where I shall start my story. So that woman betrayed me. I'd known for a long time that she would and I was ready for it. They drove me to the high court in an elegant vehicle then locked me up in a cell. During the night I was taken to the courtroom, a beautiful, spacious room with green wallpaper and many books. Standing in his white coat behind a large desk covered with files is the judge. He comes up to me and shakes my hand. He seems to be a tolerable person. I say, You have some lovely books. He smiles and nods, then asks me to sit down. So the people here are in it too! Trying to lure me into their trap. No thank you, I reply sharply, I prefer to stand. I know I'm lost if I sit down. The judge immediately apologises and says something I don't understand. I notice the large window for the newspaper people to look in through when there's a trial on. Outside there's a full moon, I could swear it's shining right down on the scaffold. So I say, Please switch off the electric light, the moonlight's sufficient and it's best to save energy. Of course, that was only a pretext, what I really wanted to do was to look down into the courtyard. At first the man behind me wouldn't go along with my request, but I insisted and the judge instructed him to put the light out. So I go to the window and look down into the courtyard, which is in bright moonlight. And, yes! I knew it! There's the infamous frame. They say they use it to beat carpets on. The judge asks me some trivial question. I say, you can put the light back on again, I've seen what I wanted to see. If you want to know, yes, I did torture my brother to death, it's there in your files, I'm quite happy to admit it, to accuse myself. And no, I don't need a lawyer, I know perfectly well that the court and the defence counsel work hand in glove and cast lots for the spoils, before their victim's body is even cold. I do not need anyone's help. On the contrary, I will defend myself. Scarcely had I raised my voice to speak those last words than I saw the judge, who until then had listened to me with a kindly expression on his face, give a sign to the two guards behind me. So that's the way things are, I thought, he's going to stop me making my speech in my own defence. He's afraid of my revelations and their effect on the public. I protest vehemently, but what's the use? The guards drag me out. I lose consciousness.

I've been waiting in my cell for days now for the trial to start. I spend most of the time standing up, of course, I only lie down when I'm tired. But I never sit down. Sometimes the judge, accompanied by his two guards, comes to my cell and I receive him standing up. I hate him. The moment I bring the conversation round to the murder and the trial, he changes the subject. So that's it. Delaying tactics, using the long, tormenting imprisonment to force me to sit down and make me obedient to their will. But he's making a big mistake, I'll thwart his cunning plan. I've had them give me a pencil and paper and I'm writing my memoirs standing at a high desk. I'm calling them 'The Confessions of a Fratricide'. The world will hear of my deed, even if I'm denied my right to a proper trial.'

Again the doctor took the book out of my hand and looked for a passage towards the end.

'Did you notice? The judge in the white coat, that's me. Now read his statement in his defence.'

I read:

'I am writing this in my defence, so that the world will know why I tortured my brother to death and that I am innocent. The court is afraid the truth might be revealed. That is why they won't allow the trial to take place. They intend to hang me from the gallows without trial. I know that because I have seen the infamous iron frame at the place of execution. But they have miscalculated. I will submit this statement to the government myself. The truth will out!

The presumption is that I killed him because of that woman. They have got their psychology all wrong, typical of my opponents' way of thinking. The real motive was not jealousy, it was sederophobia. It was all due to the fact that my dead brother preferred to sit, preferred that position to all others, since he thought he looked good sitting down. But I hate sitting down. I can't sit. When I sit down I'm helpless, all my strength and confidence goes. I'm lost if I spend just a minute in that hated position. My brother was well aware of this weakness, no, this disinclination of mine and took advantage of it whenever and wherever he could. Oh, with what fiendish perception he discovered it, even though we never spoke about it and he never let me see that he knew, and with what fiendish enjoyment he exploited it! How else could he calmly sit down in my presence, playing the innocent, as if nothing at all had happened? I hated him, the hypocritical bastard, and I still hate him today. No, I despise him. For there is nothing more loathsome beneath the yellow moon than sitting down. It is not merely the expression of a cowardly, devious nature, unworthy of a gentleman, of a free man, it is also the unmistakable sign of degeneracy. Only toads sit, but the proud heron stands upright, when not flying, and the supple snake crawls on its belly. 'The Toad' was my secret name for my brother, and the revulsion and disgust I felt for this person, with whom I was compelled to live in the same house, grew daily more intense. The situation was almost unbearable.

One day I fell in love with that woman. Naturally she knew of my dislike without my having said a single word about it. But when I went to visit her for the first time – oh horror! – what happened? With a casual air, she sat down on the sofa, smiled at me and invited me to sit beside her. The humiliation! The insult to my innermost feelings! I wished the ground would open up and swallow me. I realised the strumpet was in league with the Toad and the pair of them were deceiving me. No one but the Toad could have incited that woman to do that to me. The fiendish cunning drove me wild with fury, I dashed out of the room, out of the house. There was a secret conspiracy against me. Doubtless it would spread over the continent, over the whole world, if I didn't do something about it quickly. I decided to kill the monster that had risen up to plunge me in contempt and misery. I decided to avenge myself on it a hundredfold, to crush it, to extirpate it. Yes, it was my task, my colossal task, to free mankind from the conspiracy of *bufo sedens*, the sitting toad, to save it from certain disaster.

Recently the prosecutor was here, the scrawny man in black. He is my enemy. His words were smooth as oil, for he is two-faced and cowardly and seeks to destroy me. He pretends he does not believe in my deed and in my mighty will. Did I not feel shame and remorse, he asked, in the face of divine conscience? Shame and remorse? I, who have freed the world from the Toad, should be ashamed of my deed?! What kind of a God is it who allows the Toad to exist, who loves an abomination and demands shame and remorse from its conqueror? I do not acknowledge him. I have cut those two words out of my heart, I no longer understand what they mean. Only the sublimely voluptuous pleasure of my revenge, my liberation lives on in me. Oh, how good it was to torture the Toad, slowly to squeeze the abominable life out of it!

Is it dead? No, that cannot be true. The Toad lives on, there is no doubting it, the Toad still lives. I didn't torture it anywhere near enough. It has a thousand lives, it appears in a thousand shapes, in ever new mutations, here, there, everywhere, like a fatal disease. It stares through the bars on the door of my cell, at night, when I want to sleep, it stares at me from dark corners with its foul eyes. But I recognise it, wherever it is sitting, whatever shape it takes on. I recognise it, therefore it has no power over me. It cannot kill me. No, once I am free I will crush it beneath my heel, again and again, wherever I meet with it. It is no crime to crush the Toad.

The Toad is sitting inside the hated prosecutor too. I know. He is a sederomaniac, he feels a compulsion to sit down. With a strangely alien language, which I do not understand and which is an insidious poison, he is trying to undermine and weaken the power of my disgust and my gloriously voluptuous pleasure, to make them collapse and bury me under the ruins. They are soporific words, words of a sweet, empty tediousness, but I know the danger they hold. They are toad-words. I have armed my heart against them with the steel of my voluptuous pleasure, the divinely voluptuous pleasure and liberation I breathe when I crush the forces of darkness beneath my heel, when my ears are caressed by the cracking of their bones and their whimpering squeals. Oh the savage glory of it when I ripped the palpitating life from my brother's body and offered his entrails as a sacrifice to the sun!

The day will come when people like me will rule. But the powers of darkness will overwhelm even that day. Dark imbeciles will condemn the toad-destroyers because they cannot understand their voluptuous pleasure. Black-gowned prosecutors who have not killed the toad in their hearts they call conscience. Those who are beyond conscience however, the mighty killers, the purifiers of the earth, will be accused of having no conscience. As if that accusation made sense! Those who are beyond conscience are accountable to their law alone, only that can pronounce them guilty. They will be punished like naughty children. Like children who do not understand why they are being punished. Thus the punishment will be no punishment and the court no court. Yea, even the pity that softhearted fools bring to them will run off them like water off an oiled wall. And they will rise up anew, ever again, and crush the toads and delight in their voluptuous pleasure. And again and again they will torture their brother to death until there are no more brothers left in the world. Then, and only then, will they be victorious. Only when a bloody sun shines on the cold corpse of mankind will the world be free and purified of its fear of sitting!

> What do I hear in the yard
> Groaning in the wind?
> Is it the terrible frame?
> But that's only the children's
> Swing, from which I hang,
> Playing my merry game.

Is that you, dancing master, with your pot belly and white cotton gloves, are you waiting already? You executioner! See, you have a pale face and no teeth in your hollow mouth. You will wait in vain. For I am Cain with the mark on my brow, Cain whom no one may kill. I am Cain and the heavens tremble before me.

I am Cain ———'

The book sank onto my knees as I stared out into the thickening twilight.

'He actually hanged himself from that frame in the courtyard where they beat the carpets. He did it himself, no one else could kill Cain. How he managed to obtain a rope and get out of his cell and into the courtyard at night remains a mystery. He was found the next morning.'

'He was a prophet,' I said.

'Yes,' agreed the doctor. 'The future was in him, if I may put it like that. Also time immemorial. That was his madness. To be out of one's mind is to be out of one's time as well. There have been madmen, prophets like that in all ages. When, as a young doctor, I read the madman's memoirs, I was seized with such fear, such unease that I could not sleep for nights on end. Perhaps I had a premonition that his madness would become reality, history.'

'Is there anything one can do? Is there anything we can do today?'

'We can try to understand. But it must be done before the illness breaks out, before it keeps on breaking out, again and again. My unfortunate patient was never understood, you will have deduced that from the fragments about the pre-history of his madness. He must have suffered terribly. Afterwards it was too late. We must be vigilant, my young friend, everywhere and all the time.'

'Yes,' I said, 'we must be vigilant.'

An Up-and-coming Concern

Erich Fried

In our district the greengrocer's has gone from the large corner building on the high street, the little old stationer's as well.
The hardware store closed some time previously, and until a
few weeks ago all you could see on the empty ground floor
were the cement mixers, the labourers, the men who were
carefully installing the big new shop windows and, last of all,
the painters. But no one knew what the new business would
be. It had a car park as well, in the empty lot in the side-street,
as we could see from the signposts that were ready well before
the opening.

Since the day it was opened, however, it has not been a
secret any longer: in the new store you can buy women
who get younger instead of older, from three weeks up to
three months per year, depending on type and customer
requirements. The prices, apart from the occasional and rare
special offer, are pretty high, but there are two or three
different kinds of hire-purchase agreement allowing prospective buyers the advantage of paying by instalments.
Married men can part-finance their new wives by trading in
their used models, which are accepted up to a certain age
limit.

Since the moment it opened, the place has been a hive of
activity, not only in the new store, but on the corner outside
the window display as well and, of course, in the side-street
leading to the car park and in the car park itself. Lots of men
come with friends to help them persuade their used wives to
go along with them and make the short walk to the store on
their own two feet or, if all else fails, to help them carry their
used wives into the store. In cases where this leads to
unseemly behaviour, the police step in and a doctor, employed

for this purpose by the store, is very quickly on hand with a little sedative injection.

Sometimes, of course, the reason the friends accompany the prospective buyer is simply to assist him in making his choice. The new store employs all the latest marketing techniques to influence the customer and it is clearly not always that easy to think things over calmly in there. Apart from the fairly lively music, the lighting effects and the fragrance of joss sticks used in most departments, the self-rejuvenating girls and women are such that even the lightest of touches to check the goods exerts a noticeably reinvigorating effect on the customers themselves, not to mention actual caresses, which are permitted, on payment of a deposit, to help the buyer make a final decision between several different articles.

If you add to that the screaming children now surplus to requirements and left at the entrance because their mothers are being, or have already been traded in, the noise of the welfare vans screeching to a halt when they come, at regular intervals, to collect the children and transport them to homes where they will be well looked after, plus the loud cries of the flower-sellers, 'Lovely fresh flowers for your lovely fresh wife,' you can imagine the hubbub on our formerly quiet street corner. And if that wasn't enough, there is always loud music coming from the store, mostly pop songs such as 'New love, new life' or 'Off with the old love and on with the new'.

One compensation for this noisy disturbance is the feeling we have that with the new store genuinely new life, I might almost say a sense of new and unsuspected opportunities, has come to the whole district, which was in the past, if anything, a little too quiet. Unfortunately there has also been a certain amount of unpleasantness. There has been no lack of attempts to make political capital out of the affair. Extremist agitators have set up a so-called information stand on the corner opposite the new store. Day after day the same inflammatory speeches directed against everything we hold dear can be heard, speeches which, if for no other reason, run counter to our constitution in that they are aimed at restricting the universal freedom of trade.

The company behind the new store has defended itself against these troublemakers with impressive dignity and restraint. By means of posters in their own store windows and leaflets distributed throughout the neighbourhood, they have made it clear that: a) well before they opened their store with its innovative merchandise and customer service, they took the precaution of establishing through consultation with leading figures from the legal establishment that there was no constitutional objection within the framework of a free market economy, and: b) the rumour that used wives who are traded in are all processed into animal feed and fertiliser was nothing but a malicious slander. On the contrary, the company was proud to announce that a wide range of trade-ins, serviced and reconditioned to the highest standards, was available from the used-wife warehouse at greatly reduced prices, in many cases with up to a three-year guarantee.

Anyone who was interested, the statement went on, was welcome to inspect the company's records. These showed that in the short time the service had been in operation there had been several cases of customers returning their purchases within the legal period for exchange of goods and taking home with them their original wives from the used-wife warehouse. The firm was proud of this contribution to the restoration of marital harmony, though it had to be admitted that not one of the men who were thus reunited with their former partners had recognised their own used wives unaided. The workmanship of the company's renovation and reconditioning plant, which operated according to the strictest scientific principles, was simply too thorough and too good. It was true that a number of trade-ins, especially some of the older ones, had had to be written off, but that kind of thing was inevitable in any enterprise at the leading edge of technological development. The reintegration of these discards into the organic chain was evidence of the company's commitment to recycling and did not justify the malicious sweeping accusations made by an insignificant minority of subversives.

For all its dignified restraint, that was plain talking. But the radicals only withdrew a few days later, after the police had been forced to shoot two of them in self-defence. The troublemakers' arguments would really have been too childish to warrant such a serious confrontation with the forces of law and order had they not had the audacity to reduce the lively activity of the new company, as well as just about everything else in this country, to the lowest common economic denominator of profit-seeking, which is what they claimed was the decisive factor here. How even the most well-developed desire to make a profit – or obsession with profit, as they call it – on the part of an entrepreneur can explain the constant stream of customers, some together with their used wives, pouring into the new store, if the latter did not fulfil some deep-seated need, that is if, in the final analysis, the human soul were not driven by a profound longing for beauty and eternal or, to be more precise, recurrent youth, which can nullify the steady progress towards death – that is another thing to which those blinkered, long-haired rabble-rousers at their information stand have no answer.

It is still, of course, to be regretted that our police marks-men, who have been through the most scrupulous training to deal with this kind of situation, could apparently see no alter-native, given the danger to the public the behaviour of the radicals represented, than to resort to firearms – only with the greatest reluctance, I am sure. A few well-aimed gibes ought to be sufficient to get rid of immature youngsters like that.

Recently, however, a rumour has been going round our district which is beginning to arouse far greater unease than the, certainly tragic, but not all that unusual shootings. People are saying that the same firm that opened the store on the corner of the high street has plans for a second store, also in our area, beside the post office, near to the main entrance to the museum park. This time, however, if the rumours are to be believed, it is to be a store in which women can purchase men who get younger year by year.

In my local watering hole, where I often go for a drink of an evening, after the day's work is done, there is much unease, not to say indignation about this rumour, although of course no one takes it really seriously.

Quite apart from the fact that such tampering with the existing order of things represents an unwarrantable encroachment on the privacy of the individual, indeed an invasion of the most private sphere, and the fact that it is contrary to nature, which has decreed that man shall age more slowly than woman, thus exposing once and for all the superfluity of such anti-male innovations, any attempt to introduce this kind of wrong-headed notion is bound to run into practical difficulties which would condemn it to failure from the very outset. 'I'd just like to see,' a casual acquaintance remarked to me yesterday over a glass of beer, 'how these women think they're going to drag us, their used husbands – that's what they'll call us, you know, I read it in the paper! – into their newfangled bloody shops to trade us in – yes, trade us in! – in part exchange, like some animal or an old typewriter! No, squire, we'll put up a fight and then you'll see who's strongest. It'll be mayhem, I can tell you. Next thing you know, the authorities'll have to step in, on our side, of course. After all, that's what we pay 'em for.'

I can only endorse this statement. It is entirely unacceptable that in a community such as ours, which has always placed the greatest value on freedom, they should open this so-called man shop, that is, the male counterpart to the store on the corner of the high street. That, to put it bluntly, would amount to selling men into slavery and that must be, at least *ought* to be out of the question, though we cannot, unfortunately, be entirely confident about that. The authorities have turned a blind eye to things far too often in the last twenty or thirty years. But even if this plan should go into operation, we can confidently say that it will not last; such an attack on freedom would be in blatant contradiction to all that is best in our traditions. It would be to cross the boundary separating an acceptable pursuit of honest profit from unbridled profiteering. After all, such an arrangement would not be in the interest of the women themselves. It is not for nothing that the exhortation of our national poet, Schiller, is engraved over the portal of the woman shop:

> Hold women in honour, they weave and entwine
> Our earthbound existence with roses divine.

No customer can miss them, and Schiller's words have helped to ease the pain for many a used wife. 'The Dignity of Women' is the title of the poem from which they come. But where is the dignity of women, and how can we hold them in honour, if they can sell off their husbands, trade them in like some inanimate object? No, that cannot happen here.

Where I Live

Ilse Aichinger

Since yesterday the flat where I live has been one floor lower down. I don't want to say it out loud, but my flat's lower down. The reason I don't want to say it out loud is that I haven't moved. I came home from the concert yesterday evening, as usual on Saturdays, opened the house door, pressed the button for the light and went up the stairs. I went up the stairs unsuspecting – the lift hasn't worked since the war – and when I got to the third floor, I thought, 'I wish I was home already,' and leant against the wall by the lift for a moment. I'm usually overcome with exhaustion when I get to the third floor. Sometimes it's so bad I think I must already have gone up four flights. Not yesterday, though. I knew I there was another floor above me. So I opened my eyes to continue up the last flight, and right away I saw my nameplate on the door to the left of the lift. Had I made a mistake and already gone up four flights? I tried to see the sign with the floor on it, but at that moment the light went out.

Since the button for the light is on the other side of the landing, I went the two steps to my door in the dark and opened it. To my door? Well whose door would it be, if my nameplate was on it? I must have gone up four flights.

The door opened at once, without any problem, I found the light switch and there I was, in the hall, in my hall, and everything was the way it always is: the red wallpaper I've been meaning to change for ages, the bench up against the wall and on the left the corridor to the kitchen. In the kitchen the bread that I hadn't got round to eating for tea was still in the bread-bin. Everything was unchanged. I cut myself a slice of bread and started to eat it, when I suddenly remembered I hadn't shut the front door, and went back into the hall to shut it.

As I did so I saw, in the light from the hall, the sign with the floor on it. Third Floor, it said. I went out and pressed the button for the landing light and read it again. Then I read the nameplates on the other doors. They were the names of people who until then had lived on the floor below me. I was going to go up the stairs to see who was living on the same floor as the people who, until then, had lived on the same floor as me, to see whether the doctor, who until then had lived underneath me, was now living above me, but I suddenly felt so weak I had to go to bed.

Since then I've been lying here awake, wondering what to do in the morning. From time to time I still feel a temptation to get up and go upstairs to check. But I feel too weak, and then someone up there might be woken by the light on the landing and come out and ask me, 'What are you doing here?' I'm so afraid of that question, put to me by one of my former neighbours, that I prefer to stay here in bed, although I know it will be even harder to go up there during daylight.

From the next room I can hear the breathing of the student who lodges with me. He's studying marine engineering and his breathing is deep and regular. He has no idea what has happened. He has no idea I'm lying here awake. I wonder whether I'll ask him tomorrow. He doesn't go out much, so he was probably at home whilst I was at the concert. He ought to know. Perhaps I'll ask my cleaning woman too.

No. I won't. How can I ask someone if they don't ask me? How can I go up to someone and ask, 'Do you happen to know whether my flat was one floor higher up yesterday?' What could they say? My only hope is that someone will ask me, ask me tomorrow, 'Excuse me, but wasn't your flat one floor higher up yesterday?' But if I know my cleaning woman, she won't ask. Or one of my previous neighbours. 'Wasn't your flat next to ours yesterday?' But if I know them, none of them will ask. So there's nothing left for it but for me to behave as if I'd been living on the floor lower down all my life.

I keep wondering what would have happened if I hadn't

289

gone to that concert. But now that question's as academic as all the other questions. I must try and get some sleep.

My flat's in the cellar now. It does have the advantage that my cleaning woman doesn't have to go all that way down for the coal, it's right next door and she seems quite pleased with that. I suspect she doesn't ask because it's easier for her like this. She's never been that thorough with the dusting and polishing anyway, but it would be ridiculous to ask her to wipe the coal dust off the furniture every hour. She's happy with it, I can tell that from the way she looks. And the student goes whistling up the cellar steps every morning and comes back down in the evening. At night I can hear his deep, regular breathing. I keep wishing he'd bring a girl back to his room with him who would think it funny he's in a flat in the cellar, but he doesn't bring any girls back.

No one else asks, either. The coalmen, who empty their sacks with a loud crash in the bunkers on either side, raise their caps and say hello when I meet them on the stairs. They often put their sacks down and wait for me to get past. The caretaker, too, gives me a friendly hello as I'm going out. I thought for a moment he was friendlier than usual, but I was just imagining it. Many things seem friendlier when you come up from the cellar.

I stop when I get to the street, to clean the coal dust off my coat, but there's always some left on. It's my winter coat and it's dark. In the tram I'm always surprised the conductor treats me just the same as the other passengers and no one shifts along the seat away from me. I wonder what things will be like when my flat's in the sewer. I'm already getting myself used to the idea.

Since I've been living in the cellar, I've started going to the occasional concert in the evening again. Usually on a Saturday, but sometimes during the week. After all, by stopping going I didn't prevent myself from ending up in the cellar. Now I'm sometimes surprised at the way I used to reproach myself, at all the things I saw as connected with my descent at the beginning. At the beginning I kept on thinking, 'If only I hadn't gone to the concert. Or across the road for a glass of wine.' I don't think that any more. Since I've been in the cellar I don't worry and go out for a drink whenever I feel like it. It would be pointless to start worrying about the bad air in the sewer. If I did that I would have to start worrying about the fire at the centre of the earth, in fact there's too much I would have to worry about. Even if I stayed at home all the time and never stepped outside the house, I'd still end up in the sewer one day.

The only thing I wonder about is what my cleaning woman will say. It would certainly mean she wouldn't have to bother with airing the flat. And the student would whistle as he climbed out of the grating and back down again. I do wonder what would happen about the concerts and my glass of wine. And whether it would ever occur to the student to bring a girl back to his room. I wonder whether my rooms would still be the same in the sewer. So far they are, but the building stops before the sewer, and I can't imagine the arrangement of bedroom and kitchen and sitting room and the student's room will continue down into the bowels of the earth.

But so far everything is unchanged. The red wallpaper and the chest against it, the corridor to the kitchen, every picture on the wall, the old leather armchairs and the bookshelves, even every book on them, the bread-bin out in the kitchen and the curtains on the windows.

The windows, though, they have changed. But at this time of the day I'm mostly in the kitchen and the kitchen window's always looked out onto the landing. It's always had bars. That's no reason to go and see the caretaker, even less the change in the view. He could justifiably argue that a view is not part of a flat, the rent is calculated according to size, not the view. He could tell me my view was my own affair.

And I don't go and see him. I'm happy as long as he's still friendly. The one objection I might make is that the windows are now only half the size. But then he could say it's not possible any other way in the cellar. And I wouldn't have an answer to that. I could say I'm not used to it, because until recently I was living on the fourth floor. But then I should have complained when I was on the third floor. Now it's too late.

In the Gulf of Carpentaria

H. C. Artmann

The four of them – the shipwrecked millionaire and his platinum blonde companion, the helmsman and a Malay cook – the last survivors of the luxury yacht *Archipelagus*, the sensation of San Francisco, which had sunk in the storm, were sitting in the darkness round a camp-fire on the shore of Arnhem Land trying, as best they could, to dry their clothes.

The Southern Cross had already risen in all its splendour, but a drift of blue-and-blood-red cloud on the western horizon still indicated the point where the sun had just gone down. The sea was calm. The fatal hurricane that had destroyed the *Archipelagus* had swept away across these latitudes as quickly as it had come up. Eleven of the fifteen on board had fallen victim to the ravenous sharks, only Rufus O'Shea, Millicent Naish, George Farrar and Billy Tuwap had managed, with great difficulty and incredible good luck, to reach the temporary safety of dry land. But exactly where they were and how they would get to the nearest human (ie white, of course) settlement, none of the four could say, not even Farrar, the helmsman.

From the eerie bulk of the dense jungle looming up close behind them came the muffled roaring, grunting, screeching, hissing and cackling of the nocturnal animals and, attracted by the red flicker of the camp-fire, huge bats appeared, swirling round the sea-salt-encrusted human flotsam and jetsam.

'They're real vampire bats!' whispered Millicent Naish, the platinum blonde girlfriend of the Texan oil magnate O'Shea.

O'Shea, about forty years old and stocky rather than corpulent, put his khaki shirt, which was more or less dry, back on again and looked at the flying monsters.

'Damn', he said. 'My forty-five's probably out of action for the moment – taken in too much salt.'

He picked up his shoulder holster, which was lying by the fire and just about to start smouldering, took out his revolver and aimed at one of the shadowy monstrosities. All that came, instead of the report of a shot, which no one expected anyway, was just a click.

'Kaput,' he said, putting it back in its scorched holster. He turned to the helmsman, who was also putting his shirt back on. 'I guess we've no option but to spend the night here, Farrar . . .'

'Yeah, I guess so,' said Farrar, with a brief glance at Millicent Naish who, with her back to the men, was taking off her wet brassière and putting on her dried shirt.

Billy Tuwap was the first to wake up next morning. The sun had already risen some distance above the glassy blue sea. He could hear the sound of the breakers close by but at first could not find his bearings, still half asleep and thinking he was in his cabin. Then he looked over to the others: he saw Farrar, who was lying on his front with one leg drawn up and snoring loudly; he saw Rufus O'Shea, his boss, who had slept squatting, head bent forward – but no trace of Millicent Naish.

'Tuan O'Shea!' he shouted. 'Tuan Farrar! Quick! Wake up! Nonya Millicent has disappeared.'

Like a pair of marionettes, O'Shea and Farrar both woke with a start. The millionaire was first to his feet. He rubbed his eyes and looked round, searching. 'Millie,' he shouted. 'Millie, call out if you can hear me.'

But it was pointless and he soon gave up. Millicent Naish had disappeared. Baffled and emitting the occasional curse, the three men moved towards the huge belt of primeval rain forest, though none of them had any idea of what they were actually going to do.

At that point Millicent Naish with her blonde, film-star looks was already ten miles away in the jungle to the south, in Nkw, the stone-age village where the mammoth bats, domesticated by the Nkwyi, had carried her.

In the middle of this huge settlement, the existence of which no geographer even suspected, was a basalt hill about three hundred feet high. As much as anything, it resembled a Yucatan pyramid, except that it was round. Steps had been cut into it, and on a square plateau at the top was a barbaric-looking temple. This was the *ziggurat* – what else should one call it? – of the Nkwyi, an undiscovered antediluvian, if not older, tribe of the fifth continent.

The arrival of the platinum-blonde American triggered off immense excitement in the city. Everyone wanted to see the pale-skinned captive as she was borne through the streets towards the basalt ziggurat in a kind of cage woven from the pliant branches of an unknown tree. Millicent, realising how hopeless her situation was, screamed like a woman possessed to be let go, shaking the flexible bars and spitting at the crowd gaping open-mouthed at her.

The Nkwyi were all of a tall, athletic build; hardly any were less that seven foot. Both women and men had shaven heads. Their skin was light blue, their eyes a dark grey that one might have said recalled slate beginning to shimmer in bright sun-light. They had tails, about eighteen inches long and iri-descent like a Great Dane's, but there was nothing simian about them; their features were almost Caucasian. Their lan-guage, however, if one could call it that, seemed at first hearing animal. They wore no clothes apart from a kind of sash woven from raffia round their waists. For the women this was prob-ably just intended as an ornament, but it seemed to serve a practical purpose for the men as they kept their colossally long, upright sexual organs wedged under the tightly tied cummerbund.

The four men carrying the cage on a massive pole reached the foot of the ziggurat and put their burden down. There was a long-drawn-out note, like the mournful sound of a primeval conch horn. After it died away the crowd, including the four cage-bearers, sat down on the ground with their knees drawn up, maintaining a terrifying silence, the effect of which was all the more harrowing coming, as it did, so abruptly on the ear-splitting blast.

Now a tremendous spectacle took place on the plateau of the basalt ziggurat. Carried by four gigantic vampire bats, a blue man wearing a truly infernal head-dress floated down out of the luminous sky onto the flat space outside the temple. As his feet touched the ground, the monsters obediently let him go and flew away over the waiting crowd towards the all-encompassing jungle.

By this time O'Shea and his companions had gone a couple of miles into the primeval forest which, to their relief, turned out to be less dense than they had originally feared. There was no underbrush at all. There was a profusion of exotic ferns everywhere, but the trees, of a species completely unknown to them, were far enough apart. Climbing plants with flowers so vivid they were painful to look at snaked their way up damp, almost dripping trunks.

As on the previous evening, O'Shea tried to fire his revolver, but with no greater success.

From time to time there was a rustling suspiciously close to them in the waist-high ferns. Wading unarmed through the treacherous green silence was an anything but enjoyable experience for the three, especially as at every step they were in danger of being attacked by reptiles. So far, however, they had not seen any larger specimens of the animal kingdom. On the other hand, the forest was teeming with climbing salamanders and tree lizards, chameleon-like creatures scarcely distinguishable from their surroundings, but which scurried up and down the centuries-old trunks in eerie silence.

Eventually they heard a loud gurgling, swirling, roaring noise and soon found themselves beside a fairly wide, fast-flowing river, entirely enclosed beneath the canopy of the colossal trees with the sun trickling through, a tunnel of vege-tation, a canal with ferny banks that sent a shiver down the spine of anyone treading on them: with each step they sank ankle-deep into the viscous mud, and the hothouse atmosphere with its buzz of insects was hardly calculated to raise the morale of the three, either.

'And we're supposed to get across that?' O'Shea swore and wiped the sweat from his forehead with the back of his hand, a pointless gesture since in this infernal forest every movement opened the floodgates of perspiration.

'It'll be just the same over there, perhaps even worse,' said Farrar.

'We could swim for a bit . . .' suggested Billy Tuwap.

'And end up back in the sea,' said Farrar dryly, sending a gobbet of spit in a wide arc into the rushing waters.

'Christ Almighty,' said O'Shea, 'we'd be better off swimming back in this filthy water than crawling through that goddam mouldy green stuff again.'

'And crocodiles?' Farrar threw a small tree trunk into the water.

'That's a risk we'll just have to take,' said O'Shea, but one could tell he was not very happy with the idea.

They tried to keep as close together as possible while they were swimming. The water was even reasonably refreshing, and they soon realised that the river was not heading for the coast, as they had at first thought, but somewhere into the interior, though towards what kind of country they had not the least idea.

The blue man on the flat top of the hill, the shaman of the Nkwyi – that's what he must have been, who else would have himself flown to the scene of his fiendish activities by four bats of the most gigantic proportions? – the shaman of the Nkwyi, then, raised a stone axe and brought it down on an object placed on the altar, that stood out in the open. The object in question was, in fact, a large egg, about the size of an emu's egg, though from this distance it was impossible for the uninitiated to identify. Immediately a tongue of flame shot up into the azure sky, finally disappearing in a black mushroom cloud.

In unison, the assembled Nkwyi broke out into a cry of joy – apparently the experiment, or whatever it was, had been successful. The four bearers got to their feet, picked up their platinum-blonde burden and started to climb the basalt steps.

When, after what one could call a marathon swim, the three noticed that the woodland, through which the river was winding its way, was becoming less and less dense, they climbed up the bank, which was somewhat steeper at this point, and came across, as if by chance, a path which was obviously made by human feet. They decided to follow it. They had no choice, they ought to be glad, indeed call it a piece of good fortune that they had left the river at that particular spot.

The track grew broader and broader, brighter and brighter until eventually, after about an hour, they came to a road, or at least to something that would be called a road in this kind of place, though *not* elsewhere, and it was not long before they saw, shimmering in the heat haze, the city of Nkw, which lay dreaming before them; there is no better way of putting it, it seemed to them like a wild, absurd dream.

The four aboriginal bearers with the cage in which, by now, Millicent Naish was squatting apathetically, had reached the flat top of the basalt ziggurat. Once more they put down their burden and squatted on the ground. The light-blue shaman, who until now had remained motionless, stony-faced, picked up from the bizarre altar an obsidian machete, a truly mega-lithic implement, whirled it round a few times above his immense head-dress, which consisted of petrified shells, ani-mal sinews and tied-on butterflies, each one more dazzlingly colourful than the next, then neatly sliced three, four, five times across the knotted lianas holding the cage in shape. Without a sound the latticework fell apart, leaving Millicent free before the altar. Her tangled silvery blond hair shimmered in the heat of the morning sun, her clothes were torn in many places, one breast, liberated from the grubby cloth of her white safari shirt, shone, her face, and also her arms and legs, bore the signs of the hardships she had been through as well as of the lack of washing facilities.

298

'*Oarrngh!*' said the satanic shaman – could the intentions of this gruesomely grandiose figure be other than fiendish? '*Oarrngh mmmflullwl ahrhkpp nn-nshnl!*'

He had gone up to Millicent, who was infused with unutterable terror, and shouted these words literally in her face. But were they really words? Could these beastly sounds be the vehicle of expression of a human mind? There *must* have been some meaning contained in them . . . think of all the things an LSD user says during his so-called trip which are entirely incomprehensible to the sober observer; but for the addict under the influence of the drug they represent the only adequate expression of an event taking place within the depths of his psyche, which at that moment is probably floating in some other dimension.

The four bearers remained squatting, motionless, heads bowed and fingers in their ears, clearly in order not to hear these sounds, which for them were *even more* terrible. And if one had observed the crowd at the foot of the southern side of the basalt hill, one would have perceived the same phenomenon.

Meanwhile O'Shea, Farrar and the loyal Malay cook had entered what they initially assumed was a ghost town. After passing though a series of streets, they had reached the dark basalt steps at the rear of the ziggurat, a place, that is, from which they could not see the dog-tailed crowd, the bright-blue inhabitants of a completely unsuspected Australia. And even though the unspeakably spine-chilling crescendo of the unison roar could be heard from time to time, they probably assumed it was the primal sound of a forest that seemed out of this world, borne to them on the wind that had arisen.

'A pyramid,' said O'Shea, 'but it can't possibly have been built by human hand . . .'

'Basalt,' said Farrar, scraping his thumbnail across the first step, 'worked basalt! If there aren't any people here now, there must have been some at one time, even if it was a thousand years ago.'

Billy Tuwap, whose expression revealed the beginnings of

an uneasy feeling, looked all round and said, with fear in his voice, 'I've nothing against snakes, nothing against crocodiles, nothing against man-eating apes, but this here's a ghost town and we're right at the centre.'

The two others were silent. To contradict their cook, they felt, would have been unnecessarily boastful.

'The best thing to do is to go up,' said O'Shea. 'At least from the top we'll have a good view of the whole goddam area.'

This overhasty resolve might have been the beginning of the end, but, as so often in life, things fortunately turned out differently.

'*Oarrngh mmmflullwl ahrhkpp nn-nshnl!*'

Millicent Naish, seized with icy terror at the incantatory sounds issuing from the lips of the long-toothed shaman, sounds which she did not understand, could not possibly understand, but whose meaning yet entered her subconscious, suddenly began to run, as if in a nightmare, to run towards the temple, round the temple, down the steps at the back, without thinking, without noticing how dangerously steep they were, straight into what she at first thought was a mirage sent to mock her, straight into the arms of the three dumbfounded pyramid-climbers.

O'Shea, Farrar and Tuwap had already completed a third of their mountaineering challenge.

Now they could also see the shaman in an epileptic rage and his four acolytes hurtling down the basalt steps like beasts of prey. The reunited survivors of the *Archipelagus* seemed lost. Closer and closer came the light-blue cloud, the fiendish product of antediluvian depravity. But in the ensuing clash the attackers had reckoned without the agility of the brave Malay. Tuwap, who – no one had even suspected it – turned out to be a san-ikwong fighter of quite colossal proportions, sent the charging shaman flying over his shoulder so that his head with its diabolical get-up smashed into one of the dark steps, killing him instantly. The next attackers slumped to the ground, felled by the precise kidney punches of O'Shea and

300

Farrar, and the rest, seeing their high shaman or whatever he was lying in an immense pool of blood, fled back up the steps.

Their escape through the deserted town – all the people, as you will remember, had gathered in a dense crowd on the southern side of the ziggurat – was perhaps the easiest part of this grotesque adventure. The pursuers they were afraid of did not appear. Once they reached the river they threw themselves straight into the water, which, though warm, was still refreshing, swam briskly for long stretches, rested a few times at convenient spots on the bank, ate the fruits they found in abundance, and reached the breakers of the Gulf towards evening. It so happened that, for a variety of reasons – life does throw up the strangest coincidences – a unit of marines had just disembarked from a cruiser of the Australian navy. They took the exhausted survivors on board. Once more the fiery red disc of the sun sank below the western horizon of the immense oceanic desert, which means life and adventure to so many.

The lights went on and the audience at the film *In the Gulf of Carpentaria* left the cinema by the two rear exits. It was around eleven o'clock in the evening and the rain was pouring down in torrents on Milan; you could hardly see the street lights, such was the deluge streaming down out of the darkness of the opened heavens.

The couple beneath the huge umbrella had reached the park, where the broad branches of the plane trees offered a little more protection from the cloudburst.

'What do you think the blue savages were going to do to Millicent Naish?' Francesca, the nursery-school teacher, asked her companion, whom she had first met just three hours ago in the foyer of the *Cinema Gardenia*.

'Oh, I can tell you that, no bother,' he said, revealing his long white teeth, '*Oarrngh mmmflullwl ahrhkpp nn-nshnl!*'

It was a terrifying sight as he tossed the large umbrella onto the waterlogged, leaf-strewn gravel path . . .

Journey through the Night

Jakov Lind

If you look back, what do you see? Nothing at all. And if you look in front? Even less. That's right. That's the way things are.

It was three o'clock in the morning and it was raining. The train didn't stop anywhere. There were some lights somewhere outside, but it was impossible to say for sure whether they were living rooms or stars.

The railway track was a track – but why shouldn't there be one in the clouds?

Paris was somewhere at the end of the journey. Which Paris? The earthly city, with cafés, green buses, fountains and dirty plaster walls? Or the heavenly city? Bathrooms with fitted carpets and views of the Bois de Boulogne?

In the blue light the man sitting next to me looked even paler. His nose was straight, his lips thin, his teeth excessively small. His hair was slicked back, like a seal's. He ought to have a moustache. He could balance things on his nose. And under his clothes he's wet. Why doesn't he show his tusks?

After 'That's the way things are,' he said nothing. He'd disposed of the matter. Now he's smoking.

His skin is grey, that much is obvious, and it's taut, if he scratches himself it'll tear. Where to look? He's just got his face and his suitcase. What's he got in his suitcase? Tools? Saw, hammer and chisel? Perhaps a drill as well? Why would he need a drill? To bore holes in skulls? They drink beer out of them. They get painted when they're empty. Will he paint my face? What colours? With water colours or oil paints? And what for? Children play with empty eggshells at Easter. His with skulls.

Well then, he said in non-committal tones, stubbing out his

cigarette. He rubbed it out, it scraped on the aluminium. Well then, how about it?

I don't know, I said. Can't make up my mind. Has the man no sense of irony?

Perhaps you're not tough enough, he said. Make up your mind now, in half an hour you'll be asleep anyway, and then I can do whatever I want.

I'm not going to sleep tonight, I said, you've warned me.

Warning makes no difference, he said. Between three and four everyone's as good as dead. You're an educated man, you ought to know that.

Knowing's one thing, but I can control myself.

Between three and four, said the man, rubbing the moustache he ought to have, we're all in the plastic bag, hearing nothing and seeing nothing. We all die. Dying's a rest, after four we wake up again and things continue. Otherwise people couldn't stand it so long.

I don't believe a word you're saying. You can't saw me up.

I can't eat you the way you are, he said. Sawing's essential. First your legs, then your arms, then your head. One thing at a time.

What do you do with the eyes?

Lick them.

Can you digest ears or do they have bones in?

Not bones, but they're tough. I don't eat everything. What do you take me for, a pig?

A seal, I thought.

That's nearer the mark. So he admitted it. A seal. I knew it. He's a seal. How come he speaks German, then? Seals speak Danish and we can't understand them.

How come you don't speak Danish?

I was born in St Pölten in Lower Austria. They didn't speak Danish there. Excuses, of course, excuses, excuses. Perhaps he is from St Pölten, there are supposed to be people like that round there.

And you live in France?

That's neither here nor there, as far as you're concerned.

You'll be gone in half an hour. Knowledge is only useful when you've got a future ahead of you. In your situation . . .

He's mad, of course, but what can you do? He's locked the compartment – where did the fellow get the key? – Paris will never come. He chose the right weather. You can't see anything and it's raining, of course he can kill me. If you're afraid, you have to make yourself speak. Would you describe it again, please. That please will flatter his vanity. Murderers are sick and sick people are vain. The please does the trick.

Well, first there's the mallet, he said. It was just like at school. Stupid pupils have to have everything explained twice. Stupidity's another kind of fear, teachers give smacks and marks.

Then, after the mallet, there's the razor, you have to let the blood out, at least most of it, you get enough of the stuff smeared round your mouth when you eat the liver as it is. And then it's the saw.

Do you cut off the legs at the thigh or the knee?

Mostly the thigh, sometimes the knee. At the knee if I have time.

And the arms?

Never at the elbow, always at the shoulder.

Why?

Don't ask me, perhaps it's just habit. There's not much flesh on the lower arm, none at all on yours, but still, it looks better when it's there. I mean, just think of eating a chicken leg.

The man was right.

A cannibal knows how to eat people.

Do you use spices?

Only salt. Human flesh is sweet, you'll know that, and who likes eating sweet flesh.

He opened his suitcase. No, I screamed, I'm not asleep yet.

No need to be afraid, scaredy-cat, I just wanted to show you I'm not joking. He rummaged round among his tools. There really were only five in the case, just lying there, loose. It was a small case. Like a doctor's, but their instruments are attached to the lid, which has a velvet lining. Here they were just lying on the bottom. Wooden mallet, saw, drill, chisel and pliers. Simple carpenter's tools. There was a cloth as well. The salt cellar was wrapped up in the cloth. A simple glass salt cellar like you see on the table in cheap restaurants. He stole that from somewhere, I said to myself. He's a thief.

He stuck the salt cellar under my nose. There was salt in it. He poured some salt out into my hand. Taste it, he said, top-quality table salt. He saw the annoyance on my face, I was speechless. He laughed. His tiny teeth were repulsive.

Yes, he said with another laugh, I bet you'd prefer to be salted alive than eaten dead.

He closed his case and lit another cigarette. It was half past three. The train wasn't just going, it was flying, but there still won't be Paris at the end, neither the earthly nor the heavenly city. I was trapped. Death comes to everyone. Is the way you die really so important? You can be run over, you can be shot by accident, you can have a heart attack, if you live to be old enough, or you can die of lung cancer, which is very wide-spread today. People kick the bucket one way or another. Why not being eaten by a madman in the Nice-Paris express?

All is vanity, simply vanity, of course. We have to die, it's just that we don't want to. We don't have to live, but we want to. The only things that are important are things that are necessary. Big fish eat little fish, the lark eats the worm and still its song is beautiful, cats eat mice and no one has ever killed a cat for it – everything eats everything to stay alive, people eat people, what's unnatural about that? Does it hurt more if you can say, 'That hurts'? Animals don't cry, people cry when a relative dies, but is there any reason to cry at your own death? Do you like yourself that much? Then it's vanity. You aren't heartbroken at your own death. That's the way things are.

I felt a warm glow. Here's a madman, he aims to eat me up. At least he has an aim. What's my aim in life? Not to eat anyone up, is that as honourable? What's left if you don't want to do what you definitely ought to?

If you don't do the disgusting thing, what happens to your disgust? It sticks in your throat. Nothing sticks in the throat of the man from St Pölten. He swallows.

A soft voice said, and it sounded almost tender, There, you see, you're getting sleepy, that comes from thinking. What is there for you in Paris, anyway? Paris is just another city. Who do you need and who needs you? You're going to Paris. So what? Sex and drink don't make people any happier. Not to mention work. You get nothing out of money. And out of life you get shit all. Off you go to sleep now. You won't wake up, that I can promise you.

But I don't want to die, I whisper. Not yet. I want to go to Paris and. . . . walk around.

Walk round Paris? Oh, great. You'll just get tired. There's enough people window-shopping anyway. The restaurants are crowded. The brothels too. You'll just be *de trop* in Paris. Do me a favour and get to sleep. This night's not going to last for ever, and it means I'll have to gulp everything down so quickly you'll give me stomach-ache.

I have to eat you up. In the first place I'm hungry, and in the second I like you. I told you straight away I liked you, and you thought I was a queer. But now you know. I'm a simple cannibal. It's not a profession, it's a need. Come on, don't you see, you've got a purpose, your life has a purpose. And it's all because of me it has a purpose. You think it was pure chance you got into the compartment where I was? Don't you believe it. There's no such thing as chance. I watched you walk all along the platform in Nice. Then you got into my compartment, mine, of all compartments. Because I'm so handsome? Not at all. Is a seal handsome? You came into my compartment because you knew there'd be some action here.

Very quietly he opened his little case. He took out the mallet and closed the case. He held the mallet in his hand.

Shall we get on with it? he said.

In a moment, I said, in a moment. And suddenly I stood up. God knows how, but I was on my feet and stretching out my arm. The thin wire tore, the lead seal came off, the train hissed and squealed. There were screams in the next compartment. Then it stopped. The man from St Pölten hastily slipped the mallet back into his case, took his coat and was at the door in no time at all. He opened it and looked round. I feel sorry for

306

you, he said. This nonsense will cost you a fine of ten thousand francs, you fool, you'll have no choice but to walk round Paris now.

People pushed into the compartment. A guard and a policeman appeared. Two soldiers and a pregnant woman shook their fists at me.

The seal from St Pölten was already outside, just below my window. He shouted something. I opened the window. You've made a complete fool of yourself, he yelled, for your whole life. And a person like that insists on staying alive. He spat, shrugged his shoulders, carefully climbed down the embankment, holding his little case in his right hand, and disappeared into the darkness. Like a country doctor hurrying to a confinement.

The Unmasking of the Briefly
Sketched Gentlemen

Gerhard Amanshauser

For a baby not to bawl is a clear sign of a lack of vital energy,
writes a well-known paediatrician, for crying is a baby's physical exercise. The Protestant nurse knew that, but she said
nothing to the mother, who anyway suspected some sort of
abnormality would appear. Actually, she had been surprised
by the baby's complete conformity with the standard model
you see on posters everywhere. Wasn't there a finger missing
somewhere, a toe? Even if she hadn't gone for an all-out
abortion, a lot of things had been done that were against the
guidelines: knocking back strong drinks or even certain chem-
icals, doing violent ballet steps, indulging in bizarre fantasies
and childish incantations – water under the bridge, as you
might say. Still, it was funny when you thought how others
stuck to the rules and now and then some monstrosity would
emerge, as if further proof were needed of what the cosmos
thinks of our laws.

That young physics teacher she'd met at the fancy dress
ball, the one who'd kept going on about the cosmos (whatever that was), as if she'd be impressed by it, could he be the
father? The date in question was pretty definite, the day of
that party in the abandoned warehouse, but after a party like
that it was impossible to say for sure who was the father. And
later on, when the first individual features began to emerge
from the stereotype infant, at best it would be a guessing
game.

'He's so remarkably quiet,' said the young mother to the
Protestant nurse, as she carried the child past the inscription,
All things that appear on earth must first go past God, back into the
room, 'and such a funny yellow colour.' The next bed was
surrounded by a whole forest of flowers, like a death-bed, and

in it, by way of contrast, was a corpulent woman who was constantly being visited by whole groups, poked by podgy arms, snowed under with grins and encircled with tongues and jaws in unceasing motion. Whilst the flowers in the bouquets and pots, as if under the influence of toxic fumes, were starting to droop and the first signs of decay were appearing on the aristocratic tips of the leaves, the fat woman came more and more to life, took her bawling infant to her spherical breasts, where it drank furiously, laughed with the nurses or the doctor and enriched her vocabulary with hospital jargon, proudly dwelling on every detail of her bodily functions.

The silent, yellowish child, on the other hand, suckled so weakly, so apathetically, that it had to be artificially fed; it would wrinkle its forehead like an old man and the only response that could be elicited from it was a weary blink. No one came to visit the bed where the young mother in her black night-dress scarcely moved, just occasionally lifted up her white-powdered face and pushed aside her long strands of hair with sharp fingernails to stare into space. Clouds of suspicion drifted towards her from all sides: no father to be seen; excesses had got their all-too-visible comeuppance, resulting in an unfortunate situation that aroused nothing but smug gloating.

'Sister, where do those fibres at the corner of its eyes come from? And it always has fibres like that at the corners of its mouth too.'

'Oh, they're nothing to worry about.'

'I'm convinced it can focus. It follows my movements with its eyes.'

'Impossible.'

When she went for a walk in the corridor outside, between the deathly white of the walls, doors and trolleys, between paintings representing stuffed mothers or crucified flowers, she had the feeling she'd been condemned to prison for life. She picked up a book lying on the table and opened it. The Bible! She flung it back onto the table as if it were poisoned.

It was a relief to get out of the hospital and escape the sister's care. Every gesture of assistance there was tied to

309

unspoken conditions which built up into a deposit of all-embracing terror in invisible chambers. But the house in the suburbs to which she returned with the child was empty. There were things here you could tell hadn't been used for ages. Still lying in the hall were two suitcases, coats and bags, things that had been recovered from the wrecked car in which her parents had died. For months now she hadn't been able to bring herself to touch them, to open the cases, even to dust them. She didn't need a third of the things her mother had used in the house. It was out of respect for the memory of her parents that she left their bedroom untouched, didn't even go into it. She'd never liked bedrooms and she found all these double beds ridiculous, completely absurd. Thus parts of the house, and the furnishings, sank into oblivion, slowly covered themselves in dust and abandoned their less compact parts to the small, inconspicuous creatures which were already starting to riddle them with holes and passageways, spread out their nets in the airspace and stake out their territories.

Now the child had started to make occasional noises, which could be taken for crying, only they were about an octave too deep and had a strangely hollow sound. Taken together with its wrinkled brow and bald head, they made it seem like a shrunken old man at death's door. But the doctor assured her its heart-beat was strong and there was no question of debility. He seemed unwilling to admit that the odd fibres that formed at the corners of the baby's eyes and mouth were fibres, explaining them away as either secretions or traces of milk, and he simply laughed at the mother when she tried to tell him how little of the latter she produced. He, too, assured her the infant could not focus, even though the mother had repeatedly observed its eyes following her from beneath its lashes, which, in contrast to its bare head, were unusually long.

'There are exceptions,' she said.

'Not in this case,' explained the doctor, who always seemed to manage to avoid looking straight at the child and therefore not to see anything he could not explain. Printed on the products the child needed were almost identical pictures of babies that seemed to be somehow related in form to young piglets. Perhaps they represented the images that people, and therefore also the doctor, had decided to see when they looked at an infant.

The mother, on the other hand, had the impression the child was departing more and more from this model, and in ways that were disturbing. Its cries or, rather, the plaintive moans it sometimes emitted, were not spontaneous, the child had obviously learnt to use them to achieve certain ends. For example, it seemed to like the noise of the radio; if it was switched off, it would start to moan, when it was switched back on, it would quieten down. It could lie for hours beside the noisy radio without falling asleep, though as it always kept its eyes half closed, it was impossible to say for sure whether it was actually awake or not. Once it was lying so that it could look out of the window and the mother thought she could see its eyeballs flicking back and forward in the crack between its lids as cars drove past,

But that was not all. At night, when the baby was in the adjoining room, it never cried, as one would have expected, but made movements which stopped immediately the mother came in. Sometimes its cradle was still rocking.

The child – at least that was how it seemed to her – was developing a life of its own which it was trying to hide from her. Even if it was too early to assume it had thought processes of its own, it certainly seemed to have alien instincts which were guiding it towards some unknown existence. Since whatever hints she dropped about this were dismissed by the doctor in a manner that was nothing short of brutal, this idea, that she shared with no one, fixed itself at the back of her mind, and sometimes she would smile with the stubborn pride of one who, surrounded by the blind who refused to be persuaded, was the sole possessor of the truth.

Whereas at first she had kept the baby under close observation, she now quite often gave it the opportunity to pursue its secret purposes, and just nodded when she heard its noises in the adjoining room at night, a rapid pattering, for example, a shuffling or knocking. She thought it likely it had reached the stage where it could climb out of its basket alone and get around carefully on all fours.

Just as she kept herself under control and showed no reaction to the child, even if that meant a certain coolness vis-à-vis its feigned helplessness was unavoidable, she was careful to observe all the proprieties in the streets and shops. She, who had previously been known for her dissolute lifestyle, achieved an astonishing mastery in this. The precision with which she moved through her surroundings had a narcotic effect on her. She heard the expected words emerge from her lips as if there were some highly efficient machine inside her producing them; it just needed a touch to set it working. The game of conformity fascinated her much more than her previous unconventionality. People appeared to conclude she had finally come to her senses.

To her amazement, she realised that the way of life of these people was nothing more than an indeterminate fiction, casually knotted together at particular points that were used again and again. With four or five remarks and a couple of facial expressions, she had mastered it with no problem at all. In the morning she would listen for the slamming of car doors and engines starting up, when various men, whom she called briefly sketched gentlemen, set off for randomly distributed, haphazard districts to pursue their salaries so they could keep up the façades in which the light from TV sets flickered in the evening. When she saw ties and cuff-links, she felt like laughing out loud because they made her think of the constant restoration of connections, which reproduced themselves in deadly earnest. Brassières and suspender belts also aroused her amusement, in fact anything that had to be hooked or fastened together. On television, which gave her a new kind of pleasure, these objects that were constantly being unbuttoned then done up again appeared a second time, and there you could see that corpses fell out of them. It kept on making her laugh. Everywhere these people had concealed corpses, which she called dolls, and when one of them tumbled out again, out of an open car door for example, she would shout, 'Dolly!'

But she liked watching other series as well. *The Mysteries of the Cosmos* for example. She was fascinated by shining objects moving through huge black spaces. They reminded her of the drunk physics teacher at the fancy dress ball who had kept on talking to her about alien galaxies, as if he were asking her to fish herself a few compliments out of the immense void, since now any others just seemed ridiculous. And when you thought about it, a fancy dress ball was a not inappropriate place to imagine strange worlds and beings.

The only thing she found unpleasant was that in her dreams she always went back to the same places with the same circumstances, as if her dream life were starting to assume a similar, brief yet plausible consistency to her daytime existence. Since she had become aware of the threadbare texture of daytime existence, suggestions had the power, provided they repeated themselves and intertwined in certain patterns, to penetrate the cracks yawning everywhere in everyday life. These pieces of black crepe (that was her name for the night-time shapes that were trying to infiltrate the daylight hours) did bother her a little, and she would often wave her hand to shoo them away, saying, 'Off you go.'

It was not surprising that the child, having a life of its own, should leave more and more traces of this the stronger it grew. But who would have thought that the yellowish fibres, which the doctor had dismissed as secretions of no significance, should more and more take on the character of small growths or tufts? There was constantly something of that kind to wipe off, hanging from the edge of its cot for example or, more recently, stretched across to other pieces of furniture. In principle she had nothing against the child going over to producing things of its own. She didn't find the strangeness of them disturbing, but the fibres, even if they were gossamer-thin, almost completely insubstantial, gave her the feeling of something unclean. At the same time the moths had spread in great numbers from the uninhabited parts of the house, so that those whitish structures formed everywhere on the materials, causing the fabric to split.

Almost every day she went out for a walk with the child to

the so-called air-raid-shelter pond, a left-over from the last war where there were a few benches beside empty cable drums and tar barrels; some rushes had grown there too. The child stayed perfectly quiet on these expeditions. She just left it in the pram and could have read for hours, except that recently she had discovered holes and crevices between the words which she immediately had to fill with her own ideas until she was fed up with patching up the makeshift constructs.

Once, after she had left the pram for a while, she came back to find it empty. Without thinking, she turned towards the main square and called out in a loud voice to a policeman who was going round in circles on his bicycle there. What madness, to appeal to a policeman! The next moment she heard rustling and splashing noises behind her and when she whipped round she saw the pram was wobbling. The child was back in it, but dripping wet and with bits of aquatic plants in its eyelashes.

A shadow fell across the pram. The policeman was looking over her shoulder, staring at the child. She said, 'It slipped out of the pond and back under its blanket.' Slack-jawed, the policeman surveyed the trembling woman. Slowly, one feature after another, his expression of professional obtuseness changed into one of ditto cunning. His eyes dilated and began to prophesy. He suddenly smelt of beer. At once she realised she had made a crucial error. Her mastery of adaptation had deserted her.

From now on she was pushed and shoved, interviewed and interned, she was a load that was being transported. The terminus was an institution the nature of which she knew perfectly well, even though a doctor she thought was weak in the head tried to convince her of all sorts of things, especially that he had nothing to do with the police, to which her only reply was a repeated smile. She quietly disposed of the medicines she was given. She knew that everything she had discovered was to be hushed up and that they were trying to drug her because she was on the track of the briefly sketched gentlemen. In order to neutralize her child, in which an unknown

314

power was manifest, they had handed it over to the feeble-minded Protestant nurse. They openly admitted that.

But for her the walls they had surrounded her with were not a serious obstacle. She had long since noticed how, with their whole existence, flies and ants made a mockery of a dungeon that was piled up in such a primitive manner. They were ubiquitous witnesses and only brief minds thought they could be ignored. The institutions of these gentlemen were like the stage set of a castle she'd once seen in the theatre, in a famous play of which only one thing had remained in her mind, the solid stone blocks that quivered at every breath of air.

As well as that there were lots of pigeons on the tin covering the window-ledges: born messengers. You only needed to select one which gave itself away by its nervous fluttering; it could carry not only messages but a whole consciousness.

Thus they had not been able to conceal from her that parts of the city had already been abandoned. Of course, in certain show streets they tried to create the impression of packed life by special noise effects, traffic jams, crashes and the like. Neon signs proclaimed the vitality of the city while various suburbs were being undermined by foreign troops, or even occupied and filled in with concrete; others were left to decay. Whole blocks, whole districts were given over to the pigeons. With their shit, mixed with rain, they had started to draw the mysteries of the cosmos on ledges, ornamental plaster-work and the dented roofs of burnt-out or shot-up cars.

The Protestant nurse looking after the child watched the television every evening, and since she had noticed that the changing lights fascinated it, she placed its basket in a suitable position. The child's eyes seemed to move feebly beneath its half-closed lids as it read, on the flickering screen, messages to itself of which the people who organised television had not the faintest idea. If the nurse tried to put the child in the dark, it would start emitting the dull moaning that was so imperious and only stopped when its corresponding wish had been fulfilled. So the nurse had got into the habit of placing the child beside her in front of the television. Sometimes a pigeon would scratch at the window. Waking or sleeping, the two unequal viewers would spend hours with shimmers of blue over their faces, until finally the picture went off.

When the square of brightness rapidly became smaller and disappeared out into the black of the cosmos, it was life itself going out for the nurse; but each time the child fell asleep unprotesting and was trundled into its room. The nurse went to bed, alone, as best corresponded to her physical and mental disposition, and hid underneath the eiderdown, never forgetting to murmur the Our Father which lacks the Ave Maria.

As the days (weeks?) slipped past, mould-like adhesions gradually formed on the iron boot-scraper outside the front door, and if passers-by let their eyes follow these growths, they saw whitish structures, recalling lines of saltpetre on masonry, spreading radially from the house, as if some explosion in the interior had squeezed them out through the walls. At certain points ganglion-like stars had formed, covering the damp earth. 'Fungi?' a voice asked, and a nose could be heard testing the air.

Eventually the physics teacher appeared out of the fog. His loud ringing and knocking was unanswered. He gave the front door a kick, but it was only a perfunctory effort, he certainly didn't put his full strength into it. To his amazement, it gave way and he fell into the building with it. It wasn't a hard fall, it just made a soft, dull thud, as if he were falling onto cotton-wool. After he had picked himself up, he was shocked at the sight of the staircase, which was filled with a network of whitish filaments, completely alienating it from its original purpose. As with the nests of certain ichneumon wasps, only a hundred times enlarged, the fibres formed a round tunnel leading in. The physics teacher went along it into the interior. Soon the network of bizarre strands and knots opened out and the old outlines of the stairs reappeared, overgrown and gnawed away, like a house that had spent centuries in an alien element. A lacy tangle on the wall probably concealed the horns of a hunting trophy and another place, where many threads appeared to have plugged themselves in, as if to obtain power, was probably the electricity meter. It seemed as if these

316

growths could make use of anything, though to ends which had nothing to do with the original purpose of the object.

The physics teacher heard a rattling and crackling above him, which he assumed came from a malfunctioning television. It was obviously also the source of the confused shafts of light that were issuing through a gaping door onto the landing and shining down the stairs. Seeing the reflection of this light on the interlaced tendrils reminded him of the decor at a fancy dress ball he had once wandered round, already drunk and talking gibberish, with a girl with long hair. He stumbled, grabbed onto something and received a deep cut on his index finger from a sharp object hidden beneath the growth.

When he got up there, his handkerchief wrapped round his finger, he saw through the crack of the door a whitewashed armchair on which the corpse of the Protestant nurse hung, sewn into her surroundings, so to speak: whitish threads came from her limbs or sprouted there, one would have even thought this whole gangliar system had been put forth by the substance of her flesh as it melted. Certain parts of her body looked used up, so that dry bits of the skeleton lay bare. And since the child, which had threads and filaments growing out of its basket, looked similar, it seemed as if, nourished by these two bodies, a kind of loosely connected, gigantic brain had formed which was taking possession of the house bit by bit. The bodies did not give the impression of deterioration or decay; on the contrary, alienated from their human form, they had become working components of this gangliar system, in the branches of which the light from the television was climbing around.

The physics teacher, who at first could not see the screen from the doorway, noticed that the crackling noises, which initially reminded him of interference, followed a certain rhythm. He moved forward on his knees until he could see the picture. As previously with the sound, he initially assumed the set had long since broken down and was only producing cascades of glittering snow which poured down the screen at random. But then he realised there was a certain regularity in the cascades. To his astonishment he recognised the turbulence of a spiral nebula.

And then, while he was observing this phenomenon, which was bound to fascinate any physicist, he lost his balance and, now with an open, bleeding wound, toppled sideways onto a table half covered in mildew.

The last thing he heard might have been the scrape of a pigeon's feet on the tin over the window-ledge before it rose up with a flutter of wings and flew off into the fog.

At the World's End

Hannelore Valencak

They met again at the world's end, where the smooth, black cliffs plunge down to the sea, at the place where the shades of the dead meet before they finally detach themselves from the earth, where they give each other one last smile, or one last word in that familiar, ponderous language they will soon have to discard and forget.

The shade of a very young man stood there on an over-hanging rock, staring down into the depths from which plumes of steam drifted up out of the huge geysers. Clouds passed though his body and storm-winds tugged at his hair.

He seemed to be waiting for something, for he hesitated to place his foot on the narrow path leading down to the shore. And when a second shade approached across the cliff, he turned round and glided to its side.

The second shade looked at him out of lifeless eyes, then a gleam of recognition passed across his features. 'Now I remember. You came to see me yesterday.'

'Yesterday?' asked the first shade, drawing out the strange word. He already existed half in a different space and the concepts of time and the past had become empty vessels to him.

'That's right, yesterday,' insisted the second shade. He had only just lost his life and not completely detached himself from the earth. His gestures were still lively and purposeful. He still had the freshness of the living world about him. 'Cigarette?' he asked, then waved the question away. 'Sorry, I forgot where I am. I'm still thinking back to my hearty break-fast, to the strong coffee, and I felt like a smoke. You can believe me when I say you came to see me yesterday, even if that doesn't mean anything to you any more. You were a young actor and you read for me. I should have encouraged you because you had exceptional talent, but I sent you away. Why? Jealousy, probably. You were so young.

This morning I read about your death in the newspaper. No one reproached me, I didn't even reproach myself. You wouldn't believe the excuses you can think up when your conscience starts getting uncomfortable. I managed to forget about you for the whole of the morning. It was only at mid-day, when I was driving my car, that I thought of you again, and then there were no more excuses. I don't know why I took my hands off the wheel, and I didn't have any time left to think about it. The last thing I saw was a woman's smile on the poster on the wall in front of me, a wheel of fire spinning round and then this twilight, this mist I'm gradually getting used to. And now I'm here so you can reproach me. I've brought all my remorse. Do you want it? I'll give it to you.'

The shade of the young man slowly looked up. A distant, painful memory stirred within him, the feeling of a great disappointment and humiliation, then the image of a bridge, a balustrade, the silent flow of water, a fall and release, afterwards the path to this place. Now he knew what he had been wait-ing for.

'I give you all my bitterness,' he said. 'Take it from me and cast it into the sea.'

They held out their hands towards each other, but it was too late for contact. Neither understood what the other was giving him. The last traces of humanity slipped from them and dissipated. 'We must go,' they murmured, almost simul-taneously, and the shade of the young actor tried to let the one who had once been his ideal go first. But the other said, 'You first,' and neither felt it was unfitting. They made their way down, got into the boat and the mute, dark ferryman rowed them out.

The Sewermaster

Peter von Tramin

When I left my house that evening a man came up to me who was wearing dark glasses despite the mist and overcast sky. He was small and was wearing a black plastic raincoat glistening with the damp.

'You,' he asked – though from the tone of voice it was more of a statement of fact – holding me by the upper arm in a surprisingly powerful grip, 'you have keen powers of observation?'

Now I have always tended to suffer from nightmares, but years of experience have taught me to be aware that something is a dream, even while I am dreaming. With an amused smile on my lips, I go along with the confused plans, demands and actions of the imaginary creatures that people my sleep, plunge cheerfully into the abyss and make not the slightest attempt to run away from the fiend with the club. If the situation should get too unpleasant, however, I simply have to say, 'It's only a dream,' and the phantasms immediately fade away and I wake up.

When I saw that the stranger in front of me had the forked tongue of a snake I started to enjoy the situation. 'That is correct,' I said in an amused tone, 'I have extraordinarily sharp powers of observation.'

'That is good,' said the stranger with a sigh of relief, 'that is very good, sir. I almost feared you were not the man I was looking for.'

There was nothing to say to that, so I decided to go along with the man, who hurriedly drew me away from the house entrance. He took me to an allnight café, where he appeared to be known. At least the waitress greeted him with a polite, 'Good evening, Sewermaster,' and immediately showed us, without being asked, to an alcove which was partly concealed from view by a curtain of glass beads.

The little man did not take off his coat, but ordered one bottle of beer and pulled the glove off his free hand with his teeth. I saw that it had webs reaching almost to the tips of his fingers, which ended in sharp claws.

He poured the beer into a glass and pushed it over to me. He did not have a drink himself.

'Do you think you could let go of my arm, Mr Sewermaster?' I asked. 'Your grip is exceedingly painful.'

The stranger quickly let go. 'You must excuse me,' he said, 'it's almost become a habit.'

I took a sip of beer and gave him a questioning look.

'You live,' the stranger started, 'you live on the second floor of number 15?'

'Correct.'

'And,' he went on, 'and you are in the habit of sitting by your window at night looking down into the street. Would you be so kind, so exceedingly kind, as to tell me what you observe?'

'Well,' I replied, 'all I can really see is a portion of the pavement opposite my flat. There is an advertisement hoarding beyond it and a pillar covered in posters on this side.

'And what,' inquired my companion, his forked tongue nervously playing between his uncommonly sharp, white teeth, 'and what is so interesting about that view to make you spend half the night sitting by the window staring out?'

'Mainly the fact that people sometimes pass by.'

The stranger nervously adjusted his glasses. Despite the dark lenses, I could see his eyes. They were lidless, like fishes' eyes, and had round, staring pupils. 'Would it not,' he said with an urgency that was almost vehement, 'would it not be much more satisfactory for you, sir, to pursue your observations by day? Apart from the fact that the light is better, you would have a much wider choice of material to study.'

'Excuse me for interrupting, Mr Sewermaster, but I'm not interested in this, what I would call banal material. It is some-

322

thing quite different that I find so out-of-the-ordinary and remarkable. I presume I would not be far wrong in thinking that it is the occurrence of this something quite different to which I owe the honour of your acquaintance?'

It amused me to observe his embarrassment. He repeatedly licked his colourless lips, during which operation his forked tongue performed bizarre, flickering acrobatics, and rubbed his short, button-like chin with the palm of his hand, which, oddly enough, was covered in hair.

'And what out-of-the-ordinary occurrences,' he finally managed to get out, but with difficulty, his Adam's apple jerking wildly, 'what out-of-the-ordinary occurrences are you referring to, sir?'

Very content with the effect of my words, I leant back and took a long draught of beer. This dream was starting to get interesting.

'Well,' I said, wiping my moustache, 'it is the disappearance of several nocturnal passers-by to which I am referring. During the past month,' I said, not without a certain pride in the almost scientific meticulousness with which I had conducted my observations, 'I have seen no fewer than nine people go past the advertising pillar outside my window. Though 'go past' is not quite the right word. I saw them disappear behind the pillar, but they did not reappear on the other side, however long I waited.'

The Sewermaster looked up sharply. I thought I observed in his fixed, fishy eyes, which the dark glasses only partly concealed, a look of extreme desperation.

'And what,' he croaked in a strangled voice, whilst his hands casually crushed a solid brass ashtray on the table, 'and what do you conclude from that?'

'That the pillar conceals a concealed entrance to the city's sewers.'

'And why,' my companion asked – his voice, though cautiously muted, cracked and he tore the ashtray into tiny pieces, a feat he performed quite unconsciously, almost, one might say, absent-mindedly – 'and why do you think those nine people went down through the pillar into the city's sewers?'

323

'Anything I said about that would be pure conjecture,' I observed reflectively.

'Please,' said the stranger, convulsively clasping and unclasping his hands which, having competed the destruction of the ashtray, were now once more unoccupied, 'please,' he said in uncommonly urgent tones, as if much depended on what I said, 'please,' he repeated, 'would you be so good as to do just that.'

'Well, then,' I said, clearing my throat. I felt uncomfortable. It is not my way to express vague conjectures which I myself am not prepared to acknowledge as undisputed fact. 'Well, I imagine there may be a secret society that goes about its business under the cloak of darkness in the labyrinth of more or less unexplored passages and sewers beneath the Old Town. Perhaps,' I went on, watching the Sewermaster with a certain unease as his uncommonly sharp fingernails bored a hole in the table, 'it is a mystical society of religious enthusiasts who carry out strange rituals in the dark beneath our streets.'

Strangely, these words had the effect of completely dispersing the concern, of which he had previously made such a show.

'There,' he said with suppressed rejoicing in his voice, while an expression of extreme relief appeared on his pale features, 'there you have hit the nail on the head.' He left the hole in the table unfinished and placed both hands on my shoulders. 'And doubtless,' he went on, his sharp claws boring almost painfully into my flesh, 'doubtless you will be very interested to find out what those mysterious rituals are like?'

'Well,' I stammered in alarm, for I could not fail to note the menacing undertone in the question, 'well, I could imagine the society would not be at all happy to have an outsider observing its meetings.'

'That conjecture,' the Sewermaster replied, refilling my glass with inexplicable enthusiasm, 'that conjecture is also correct. Except that it does not extend to a man like you, whose keen powers of observation could be so uncommonly useful for our society that I feel I simply must propose that you become a member of our lodge.'

I was flattered. But I had reservations. Especially as regarded the aims and intentions of that strange society. I had the feeling they might perhaps be contrary to my own beliefs.

However, after the Sewermaster had assured me the goals of the society were entirely consistent with our constitution and in no way ran counter to the established religion of the land, and that, what is more, it insisted on good breeding, perfect manners, irreproachable morals and sensitivity to culture in its members, I agreed, provided I was by that not committing myself to anything, to accompany my strange companion to the meeting place of the mysterious lodge, where I would be further enlightened.

Now that my reservations had been dispelled, we set off. The Sewermaster paid the waitress with a coin which, as a joke, he bent at right angles in his fingers. Then we went out into the night, into the deserted street. Immediately he set about nudging me, propelling me in front of him with jaunty impatience, sometimes hopping on one foot or giggling as he rubbed his hands, humming shrill, incoherent tunes to himself, even trying the occasional dance-step, the effect of which was odd and childish. I soon began to find his antics unbearable. In his maniac high spirits, he kept pushing me so violently I stumbled more than once and almost fell over several times. The sensible thing to do seemed to be to wake up from this unlikely dream or simply to walk away from the Sewermaster. A friend coming home late could see me in his company, something I would have found extremely embarrassing. On the other hand I was very keen to be introduced to this secret society and become acquainted with their remarkable customs.

'If you don't mind my asking,' I said in an attempt to distract my companion from his eccentric caperings, 'how is it that you have a forked tongue? To inquire about only one of your – mmmm – physical peculiarities.'

I thought that such an impolite question would make him forget his embarrassing antics and I was not mistaken.

The Sewermaster halted in his tracks. He was a few steps in front and now he turned round and scuttled up to me with such a menacing expression on his face that the sudden shock almost made my hair stand on end. But he recovered his composure and his teeth, bared in fury, vanished behind lips which twisted in a smile.

'And how is it,' he murmured, half an inch of the subject of our conversation shooting out several times between his lips, 'and how is it, sir, that your tongue only has one tip?'

I had no answer to that. I was glad to see that by this time we had reached our destination, the pillar.

With a movement that was so rapid I could not follow it with my eyes, the Sewermaster opened a door which fitted so neatly it was invisible among the colourful posters pasted on the pillar. What I did notice when I had a closer look, however, was a hole in the picture of one of the adverts, allowing someone standing inside a view out.

As I made to follow, the Sewermaster gestured me back. 'No,' he insisted with a shake of the head, 'no, we must follow the traditional ritual, it's a little habit of mine. I shut myself in here, you go back to the corner, then walk to the pillar and past it as if you knew nothing. I will open the door and,' he bared his pointed teeth in an exceedingly unpleasant manner, 'formally invite you to enter.'

Though a little surprised, I agreed and followed his instructions precisely. I had almost passed the secret door and was beginning to suspect the Sewermaster had played a joke on me, when the flap suddenly shot open, two steely hands were placed round my neck and I was dragged inside the pillar. Before I even had time to think, he had flung me against a wall and, with lightning movements that betrayed years of practice, chained me to an iron frame. Then he turned a handle, setting the frame, which was in the form of an X, rotating on its axis, so that my feet went up and I was left hanging head down. My hair was trailing in some sticky, half-dried fluid on the ground, and my eyes almost leapt out of their sockets when I realised it was coagulated blood. It had trickled along a dark channel to a circular opening in the ground in which the top rung of a rusty iron ladder could be seen leading down into the shaft, out of which rose the fetid fumes of the sewers. The scene was dimly lit by an oil lamp, and to my inexpressible horror I saw in its light that the Sewermaster had drawn a long, gleaming, uncommonly sharp-looking knife. Holding it, he squatted down in front of me.

'I do very much regret,' he said, rocking back and forwards on his heels, 'I do very much regret having to disappoint you like this. It is true that there is a secret society that goes about its business down here in the sewers, but the men and women whose disappearance you, sir, were unfortunate enough to witness, do not belong to it. There are only a few of us who lurk in the advertising pillars of this city –'

I tried to scream, but like lightning his hand was over my mouth.

'– waiting for prey when we're hungry.'

His hand pulled my head down, presenting my neck to his knife, the sharp edge of which touched my throat. Out of my mind with fear, I jerked and the steel slit the skin. I felt a drop of warm blood run down my neck and onto my chin.

Enough was enough. I couldn't stand it any longer. I had to wake up.

'It's only a dream,' I shouted, almost bursting my lungs in the process. The Sewermaster's terrible grip turned the words into a groan.

But the fiend understood and shook his head with a grin. 'That,' he said with such an undreamlike smacking of the lips that the awful truth dawned on me in a flash, 'that is a mistake many have made before you, sir.'

Then he cut my throat.

Funeral Meats

Peter Marginter

Since so many people die in this city, supposedly one every four-fourteenths of a minute, and since everything has to have its proper place, most of them are buried in the one big cemetery, making them easier to find, if anyone should want to look for them, using alphabetic lists and numbers and maps and signposts. There's always plenty going on in such a large cemetery. The average burial lasts all of three-quarters of an hour, so, assuming the statistic about the four-fourteenths of a minute is accurate, that must mean there are ten funerals going on at any one time. In fact there are more, since people die at any of the twenty-four hours, while they are only buried during the day. In winter, when the days are short, it's no simple task for the cemetery managers to route the funeral processions so that they don't get in each other's way. So-called 'transverse intersections' are sometimes unavoidable and after them mourners often discover too late – or not at all – that they are at the wrong funeral. Indeed, it is claimed that more than one body has ended up in the wrong grave because after a 'transverse intersection' the pall-bearers followed the wrong cortège leader. These leaders, particularly dignified-looking gentlemen in black cocked hats, never look round and so have no idea who is following them. It has often happened that in the jostling a funeral procession lost sight of its leader several times, each time having to return to the starting point, while a whole row of cortège leaders was lined up beside the open grave.

This confusion was to prove fateful for Alfred B.

Alfred B, the work-shy offspring of a respectable but impoverished family, lived off his naturally mournful expression. Every morning he went through the long list that was pinned up on the notice-board outside the cemetery manager's office, and noted a few promising funerals in his diary. Punctually and with measured tread, he would make his way to the mortuary in question, where initially he would mingle unobtrusively with the mourners, keeping a sharp ear open for the quiet conversations of those around. Once the short service of blessing was over he was usually in a position to take part in the discussions himself. With practised eye he would select, from among those present, the person he would walk beside to the grave, a person, as far as possible, who did not quite belong to the close circle of the deceased's friends, and was consequently happy to find someone whom they could tell how well they had known Mr, Mrs, Miss or even Ms X. During the funeral orations at the grave-side, Alfred would gradually edge closer to the relatives, not those most immediately involved, they were too preoccupied with their own grief, but those for whom the funeral was a kind of solemn family gathering. He would express his sorrow at the loss of his old friend or the lady of his acquaintance he had so much admired, recalling, with tears in his eyes, times they had spent together. His 'we were in the army together' was a virtuoso performance and he had saved countless lives that were now finally lost. Yes, there's nothing that binds men together like having faced danger side by side. They hadn't seen much of each other in recent years, work you know, been abroad. And now it was too late. A tear would creep down his cheek and be wiped away in a gesture of quiet embarrassment.

The closer relatives were the most difficult hurdle to surmount. With them, who had quite commonly been in fact less close to the deceased than a really good friend, he had first to overcome the petty, almost unconscious jealousy directed towards him. Once that was accomplished, he could be so bold as to ask to be introduced to the immediate family. It would be intruding on their grief, he knew, but he had always regretted not knowing those who came first in his dear friend's affections. This request had a double effect. His implied admission that blood was, after all, thicker than the water of friendship, cleared away the last jealous misgivings, at the same time bringing him to his goal. Now he would patiently wait for the end of the ceremony, when his patron would introduce him to the chief mourners. His desire to hear more about poor X was well-nigh insatiable and coincided with the need the bereaved felt to honour his or her memory. It was quite natural that the charming stranger should be invited to the subsequent meal. That was all Alfred, ever modest in his requirements, could wish. They often asked him if he would not like some small memento, some item from the deceased's personal possessions. Or did he have a use for any of his clothes? Alfred did not say no, was both delighted and deeply moved as he expressed his thanks. The things he came by in this manner were not particularly valuable, mainly walking sticks and paper-knives, but Alfred knew where he could dispose of them. He never forgot to ask for a photograph of his late friend. This touching request was always granted and also hinted at the idea of a memento when that had not already been suggested. Alfred stuck these pictures in an album, meticulously noting underneath them what he had to thank the person portrayed for.

Of course, not every funeral passed off in this ideal manner. It was not always easy to choose the right one from the many on offer. Names and titles were clues, but they did not tell one everything. They were sufficient to cross off certain funerals from the outset, for example those of very high-born or very rich people, whose nearest and dearest never bothered to conceal their instinctive antipathy to acquaintances unbefitting the deceased's rank and station. Anyway, instead of the hearty feast, they at most provided a mourning cocktail, to say nothing of souvenirs. From that kind of people there was not even so much as a moustache-trainer to be had. To be avoided were also the working classes, whatever their financial status. A man like Alfred, who could not, indeed would not, disguise his family background and education, would only have aroused suspicion. Here the names were not much help, nor the standard of the funeral. That it would be at most out of sociological interest that Alfred would accompany a pauper, whose coffin was transported on a trolley pushed by a single cemetery attendant, to his final resting place, is understandable. But what should he make of a Herr Krachler or a Frau Prikopa with a middle-of-the-range funeral? It called for a personal inspection, and it was fortunate that the previous burgomaster had had the various mortuaries brought together in a small number of appropriately dignified buildings. This allowed Alfred, hovering on the threshold as if unacquainted with the topography of the place, to establish with a brief glance at those present whether it looked promising, or whether he should quietly continue on his way until he found representatives of the better-off middle classes, with whom his best chances lay.

The risks were greatest with female funerals. Basically there was no need for Alfred to attend them, he did so more out of a sense of artistic pride.

When talking to cemetery officials, he would often point out that respect for the dead, if nothing else, required that the obituary notices, which would indicate the deceased's background, should be displayed on the cemetery board. This suggestion, however, was never taken up by the authorities; why should he, of all people, who appeared so often as a mourner, need more precise information? But it is by no means certain that he really desired something like that, which would have made his assignment easier. For the artist, whom we can see here as the complementary counterpart to the official, the attraction of a task grows with the uncertainty as to whether he will be able to carry it out, and in this respect Alfred had to be considered an artist. The risk was great and the outcome remained uncertain until he had taken his modest, but accepted place at the table. On some days nothing worked at all, while on others he was passing over dishes because his stomach was still full from the previous meal, which he had enjoyed only a few hours ago.

Thus the years passed. What is there to say? We can only shake our heads, along with all right-thinking citizens, at the mental and physical exertions to which a person will descend to avoid at all costs taking proper employment or doing anything we understand by honest work.

One mild and cloudless spring day, after death had brought in a rich harvest, Alfred joined a particularly promising funeral procession heading for Burial Plot 80796e, on Side Avenue 7 of Section F (north); or, to use his professional jargon, 'climbed aboard a well-stocked cold-meat wagon.' In the handsome coffin with its bronze-finish cardboard ornaments were the mortal remains of a small lemonade manufacturer who, in the face of stiff competition from his powerful rivals, had managed to keep his head above water, commercially speaking, into ripe old age, much to his own enjoyment and the detriment of his heirs. Alfred had talked to some of his former employees and come to the conclusion that with just a modicum of good luck his programme should run like clockwork. There was a large number of mourners, since the late factory owner had been a philanthropist of the old-fashioned kind, one of those, that is, who simply helped people in need without having to make it part of a sales pro-motion; he was also a keen patron of the arts who in many amateur groups had defended the muses against the moderns bent on raping them. From Alfred's experience a large gather-ing was always the better bet, since a sparse group of sorrowful faces indicated that the deceased, relatives apart, had had only a few friends, and those particularly intimate. Alfred, as a war-time comrade of the lemonade manufacturer, was treated with diffident respect by those around him. The nephews and nieces following the van, which purred along at a leisurely pace, enveloping their black-clad legs in pungent little clouds of petrol fumes, were all said to be comfortably off and forward-looking; it was assumed they would want to dispose of their late lamented uncle's personal and household effects as quickly as his lemonade factory. In his pocket Alfred had a list of items he urgently required, at the top of which was a new winter coat. The meal, as he had also already established, was to be held in the Black Lion Hotel, renowned for its simple but substantial fare.

In the broad thoroughfare separating Sections C and D another procession could be seen approaching from the opposite direction. Most of the mourners, who visited the cemetery only rarely, if at all, thought nothing of it, many not even noticing, being immersed in conversation or grief, or unable to see over the person in front. Alfred was not concerned either. The generous proportions of the avenue, lined on either side with splendid monuments, were sufficient to allow two state funerals to pass comfortably. When they turned off to the right before reaching the procession coming in the opposite direction, all danger seemed past. The chaos that then ensued behind the memorial to Dr Girowetz, a former speaker of the regional parliament, was, therefore, all the greater. As it turned out – too late, unfortunately – the other procession had also branched off, in order to take a short cut in a north-easterly direction. Alfred's lemonade manufacturer had to go to the north-west.

Such short cuts were common on busy days. They avoided the intersections of the major avenues, at the same time revealing to the public various idyllic corners of the cemetery, often familiar to the gardeners alone, whose job satisfaction was slightly increased if they felt they could count on the fruits of their labours coming to the notice of a human eye at some point. Alfred had often mused on the paradoxical silence that reigned in the cemetery, despite the fact that it was teeming with activity, and he loved those secluded places, which were perhaps rediscovered by the odd visitor on All Soul's Day, even though they were no more than a few dozen steps from the crowded paths.

The catastrophe occurred in one of these out-of-the-way spots. Both processions had stretched out because the paths between the graves were too narrow to allow more than single file. Alfred, who was trying to keep close behind his latest informant, was already becoming concerned about the increasing crush when he suddenly saw, either side of an alabaster angel extinguishing its torch, two crucifixes swaying above the crowd in front of him. Like a soldier clinging to his regiment's flag in the tumult of battle, Alfred fixed his gaze on the black crepe of what he assumed was the lemonade manufacturer's crucifix. He was mistaken, as were many others. They had all known the old gentleman, of course, but hardly knew each other, and the bereaved family not at all, despite everything they knew about them.

The disaster took its course. Soon they had reached the open grave. The priest said the prayers and a few heartfelt words about the deceased which would have fitted any deceased. Alfred had worked his way to the presumed nephews, who were standing with the veiled nieces by the mound of freshly dug earth, some of them already receiving handshakes of condolence. A youngish man who was standing somewhat to one side seemed the right person for Alfred. Mourners who, either from shyness or a dislike of empty ceremony, avoided the hand-shaking were almost always worth while talking to.

'Might I make a request?' Alfred's grief led him to disregard normal formalities, but the mute question in his raised eye-brows also contained an implicit apology. 'Alfred B., by the way.'

'Pleased to meet you – Kurzmann.'

Alfred was told that Herr Kurzmann was not actually related to the deceased. 'He'd been a fatherly friend.'

'Ah yes, he was that to many. When I think back to those long winter weeks we spent side by side in the trenches . . . We shared everything, everything: bread, cigarettes, schnapps. Was he still smoking at the end?'

'He never smoked.'

'Oh. He did then, but those were exceptional circum-stances. I really regret that we lost sight of each other. It was only a few weeks before he died that we happened to meet, by chance in the street. We went to a café together and talked about old times, and a bit about new times, too. What was the cause of death? it came so suddenly?'

'A weak heart.'

'A weak heart? Death can come quickly then. But I think he must have suspected it.'

'You think so?'

'I wouldn't be at all surprised. I tried to get him to have an espresso, but he said no, not an espresso, that's poison for me. I laughed at him, but he had a vermouth.'

'He did? But he hated vermouth.'

'Really? Perhaps it was a sherry, then, or something like that. He didn't enjoy the stuff anyway.'

Cautiously Alfred worked his way round to the request he had not yet made. He was glad there were so many people who insisted on shaking the bereaved family's hands, for this Herr Kurzmann had turned out to be an unexpectedly awkward customer, monosyllabic and suspicious. Also, only the most general outlines of the picture of the dead man Alfred had put together, like a mosaic, from various remarks appeared to correspond to the reality. At least Herr Kurzmann immediately expressed his willingness to introduce him to the widow. Alfred, who had somehow got the idea the lemonade manufacturer had been an old bachelor, thanked God for saving him from a disastrous faux pas. Herr Kurzmann went over to one of the black-veiled ladies and whispered something in her ear.

When, finally, the last of the condolences had been expressed, the lady turned round and came over to Alfred, who was chatting to Herr Kurzmann about the advantages of cremation. Alfred bent over a tired hand on which a variety of different perfumes mingled.

'I hear you knew my Teddy,' the widow whispered in a voice choked with tears.

'I didn't know him half as well as I would like to have.' At times Alfred could be disarmingly frank. 'But I would be delighted to hear more about him. It's been a long, long time since Teddy and I . . .'

The lady gave an understanding nod and invited Alfred to accompany her home, where she would love to talk to a man who had known Teddy during the war. Herr Kurzmann drove the car.

It was a very expensive limousine, with plenty of chrome and leather and even more horse power. Alfred had never travelled in such luxury before. He sat in the back beside the lady who, as he had suspected, turned out to be beautiful into the bargain, and made an honest attempt to demonstrate his interest in good old Teddy. Outside, the last houses of the suburbs flashed by.

'A house in the country, I've always dreamt of that,' sighed Alfred.

The lady concurred. 'Just like us.'

'Just like good old Teddy,' sighed Alfred.

'May I offer you a sweet,' the lady asked. 'Teddy's favourites.'

'May I?' said Alfred, popping one of the horrible sweet things in his mouth. He was soon overcome with a pleasant tiredness.

'Are you sleepy?' asked the lady.

'Incredibly,' Alfred yawned.

'Just like good old Teddy,' the lady declared. 'It's the sweets. A good job he didn't eat all of them. You knew too much, Herr B., and asked too many questions. Shall we let him out here, Max? We have to get back, the guests will be sure to be waiting for me. If we don't, he'll die on us here in the car. Max?'

Herr Kurzmann stopped and opened the door. Alfred got out and, supported by Herr Kurzmann and pushed by the lady, tumbled down the deserted rubbish tip until he came to rest on a pile of rusty bed-springs. The last thing he heard was the squeal of the tyres and the roar of the engine as the car turned and drove off, then a hot, burning sensation starting out from his heart engulfed the whole world and extinguished it.

Incident in St Wolfgang

Peter Daniel Wolfkind

It was a gloomy day. The lake was rough. Not many people swimming. A lot of sailing boats were out. The road into St Wolfgang was jampacked with cars. I drove very slowly. I could see the soft contours of the old church even when I was still a good way away.

The radiant white of its plaster seemed to have grown duller since my last visit. The car parks were full. I drove slowly round the narrow streets of St Wolfgang. They were crowded with pedestrians. I got many angry looks. Women pulled their children out of the way. Others walked on with pointed slowness in front of the car. I turned off into a side street. It went up steeply. It was empty. The surface potholed. A mouldering wall guarded the drop. There were large cracks in it. Just before a hairpin bend the street became wider. I drove up close against the mouldy wall and parked the car.

I walked slowly back down into the town. There was a stiff breeze blowing. I stumbled on loose cobblestones. In the streets below, the stream of cars and pedestrians was washing at the houses up to their flower-bedecked window-sills.

I went up the few steps to the church. People were crowding round the headphones through which, after inserting a few coins, they could hear the history of the twelfth-century church and the town. I went down the arcades surrounding the church. Under one of the round arches in the grey wall I stopped. I was alone. I looked down at the lake. A gust of wind seemed to go right through me. It was very chilly. The wind cut the surface of the lake up into lots of small waves. Each one of them had its own grubby white crest. The little waves broke up the reflections. The grey of the arcades and the grubby white of the church tower mingled with the dull colour of the waves. In the shattered mirror of the lake the church appeared like a shapeless lump of dough. I looked for my own reflection. Raised my arm, made furious movements. But I could not see myself.

It was one o'clock. I wanted something to eat. I went to the steps leading down into the town. The grey of the wall dissolved in the bright colours of the tourists. I pushed my way through the streets to the inn where I normally eat. All the tables were taken. I went out again.

I drifted through the streets with the stream of people. The entrances to the restaurants were packed. Some were forcing their way in. Others pouring out. The air in the dining rooms was oppressive. I couldn't find a seat. It would be a while before one was free, I was told again and again by sweating waitresses.

I came to the deserted lake shore. The wind was billowing out the grey sails of the far-off boats. There was an inn. It had flowers in the boxes on the window-sills of the upper floors. Bits of plaster were lying around on the cobbles. A large piece had fallen off from the front of the doorway. The dark, vaulted entrance was empty. Beside it was a small door with 'To the Dining Room' written on it. It led to a huge verandah where just a few people were eating. It was stuffy. Someone coughed. It was the waiter. He was leaning forward on a seat next to the serving table and smoking. He ignored me. There was one table still free by the window. I sat down. I felt a cold draught on my left shoulder and my left arm. The window beside me was open a little. I wondered whether to close the window. In many places the dull brown paint was peeling off. You could see the split wood underneath. I heard the waiter coughing. All the time I could feel the cold draught on my left shoulder and my left arm. I left the window open. The air in the room was stale enough as it was. There was a huge set of antlers over the little doorway. The dark sockets in the yellow bone were fixed on me. I turned away. My view of the choppy water was hindered by people walking past. I saw the lake between their arms and bellies. Now and then a sailing boat. A grubby steamboat by the shore. There were stains on the table-cloth.

The wind was pushing the trailing tendril of a flower in through the window. The cold draught was becoming unbearable. I decided to see if I could get another table. When I looked up, the waiter was standing there. His shoulders were hunched up. His eyes bulged in their sockets. His jacket was grubby. Without a word he handed me the dog-eared menu. Many items had been crossed off. Others added in scarcely legible handwriting. He stood by my table, staring at me. His presence made me uncomfortable. I would have preferred to read the menu in peace. I ordered trout and red wine. The waiter snatched the menu up from the table and went. I heard him coughing again. A pale girl brought the red wine. It tasted of mould. I had to wait a long time for my food. The draught did not stop. I was afraid I might catch cold. The waiter kept on coughing. In a strained voice he gave orders to the pale girl. She brought the trout. She set it down clumsily on my table. A few drops of melted butter fell onto the stained table-cloth. 'Get out of the way!' he shouted and made heavy weather of placing the fish before me. He only used his left hand. 'Enjoy your meal,' he wheezed. He sat down by the serving table again and smoked. The trout had a strong smell of fish. Raised in a tub, I thought. Its flesh was grey. It tasted stale. A strong gust of wind blew the window almost fully open. I stood up and closed it. I just managed to suppress a cry of pain. I felt a violent stabbing in my left shoulder and my left arm. I sat there without moving for a long time. I hoped the pain would go away. It didn't. I continued eating. It took great self-control. By this time the trout was cold. The waiter was sitting in the background, smoking and coughing. In closing the window I had trapped the tendril against the top of the window. It was only hanging on by a thread. I heard the waiter stand up. He came towards me. Without a word he leant over my table and pushed the window open again. 'Please leave the window closed. I have pains in my arm and my shoulder from the draught,' I said. The waiter gave me an angry look. 'You don't get pains from fresh air.' He spoke very loudly and in fits and starts. Like someone with asthma. His bulging eyes had gone red.

Conversation at the neighbouring tables went quiet.

He was breathing heavily. With great deliberation he took off his jacket. He threw it over an empty chair with his left hand. The nylon shirt he was wearing underneath his jacket was damp. There was a stench of sweat. I was afraid. I did not know what the waiter was going to do. He tore furiously at the cuff of his right sleeve until the button shot off and rolled across the dark floorboards. He jerked the sleeve up over his right arm. I drew back, horrified.

A woman at the neighbouring table screamed and vomited.

'That's what's hurting you,' wheezed the waiter. 'That's where the pain comes from. You'll feel it often enough from now on. You'll all feel the pain.'

He held up his bare arm with his left hand. It was puffed up like a pasty lump of dough. The skin was broken by wave-like spots. It gave his arm a fungoid look. I could see small, dark openings at the tips of the bumps. Some were crowned with grubby white crusts. His lower arm was grey. As if covered with mould. 'That's what's hurting you,' the waiter groaned again. He squeezed the grey flesh of his diseased lower arm. Milky pus poured out of the dark openings of the wave-like spots. The waiter was getting more and more worked up. In a frenzy, he kept pressing the fluid from his right arm. A little pool had formed in the crook of his right elbow. A drop trickled slowly down to his hand.

There was a smell of vomit.

'That's what it looks like when you're in pain,' he roared and began tearing at the rotting flesh of his lower arm. It came away, layer after layer. Bigger and bigger lumps dropped onto the floorboards. The customers leapt up in horror. Some threw a banknote on the table. Others ran out without paying. I didn't dare move. The waiter was standing close to me. I was afraid a piece of his disintegrating arm would touch me. The serving girl ran up. 'Don't, Papa, don't,' she shouted. She held on tight to his left arm. She was flushed. The waiter stumbled back a few steps. 'Get out of the way,' he shouted again.

I took advantage of the moment and ran, as fast as I could, out into the open. The streets were still thronged with people.

My arm was very painful. I examined it as I went along. The skin of my arm had not changed. I got to my car as quickly as I could. Hurriedly I unlocked the door. As I got in my left sleeve touched the mouldy wall. I tried to brush the mould off my sleeve. But the deposit on my sleeve was tough and was soon sticking to my right hand. I didn't have a handkerchief on me to wipe myself down. I started the car and touched the instruments with my soiled right hand. This put mould on the steering wheel and gear lever. It was only with difficulty that I managed to get out of the crowded town. The pain in my left shoulder and my left arm made driving difficult. It wasn't until much later, when I was well away from St, Wolfgang, that it gradually eased. The sticky mould dried up and dropped off from my hand and sleeve in little lumps. From the steering wheel and gear lever as well.

The Journey to the World's End

Barbara Frischmuth

So there she sat and it wasn't funny. The long clothes round her body, a straw hat on her head. That was the way she looked when she wasn't in the mood for anything.

There was the philosophy book she'd been reading, lying by the water, and next to it the woollen jacket she'd been knitting. The half-empty bag of popcorn, the sweet kind, caramel flavour, and the can of apple juice.

She had been young for so long it didn't mean anything to her any more. Come on, she said to the secret soulmate she talked to, there's no need to sulk just because you've deprived me of your voice again today. And she went on waiting, as was only right and proper. There was nothing she was so good at as waiting.

D'you know, she said to Osman, the son of the boat-builder, I've waited long enough. If only I hadn't got so used to it. Her bare toes played with the pebbles in the water, the wind stuck its hand up her long skirt, making it billow out at the hips, then got inside her blouse from the other side. The waves were still small, and the sun shone brightly between the clouds as they crossed the sky.

Can you tell me why I never learnt to swim? She dipped one foot up to her ankle in the water, which wasn't all that cold. I could even go for a swim in the nude here.

The wind leafed through the philosophy book, then went off with the half-empty bag of caramel popcorn.

I gave you everything you need to listen to me. She picked up the jacket, wound the wool over her finger and started knitting.

I really went to a lot of trouble not to bore you. I don't want to complain about all the years with you, but are we going to grow old together like this?

She stopped knitting, letting the wool slip off her finger. I've spent long enough imagining you'd come one day to fetch me, drag me away from here, by the hair if need be, and I'd know what was happening. But all that came were the parcels from the mail-order stores, the books and the travel brochures. All by post.

So that will remain, she said with the same waiting in her voice as always. And she watched her hat the wind had taken off her head and carried out onto the water. Her hair came undone and blew back over her shoulders towards the land. The hat was lifted up by the waves and bowed in one last greeting. She waved to it.

I went to a lot of trouble over everything. Your looks, your voice, your character. Even your education. She picked up the philosophy book and carefully let it slide into the water.

The waves wetted it, but tried to push it back onto land. Even this jacket. It's too big for me. She took the needles out and threw them, like tiny spears, far out into the water. They glittered and sank. The waves accepted the ball of wool and she just had to hold onto her knitting until the pull of the water had unravelled it.

I've never been able to quench my thirst. She drank up the apple juice and threw the can a long way away. I can imagine even the desert wouldn't have dried me out as much as my life.

She had stood up and had both her feet in the water.

There's one more thing I have to ask you. Why have you never put in an appearance? The impetuous wind tore the words from her lips and she made her hands into a funnel. Why?

And for the first time in their life together, Osman, the son of the boat-builder, replied.

Because you never looked for me.

Why?

You always just waited, never looked for me.

For a brief moment her heart forgot to beat. Then she asked, in such a quiet voice only Osman, the son of the boat-builder, could understand, Where? Where should I look for you?

Everywhere, said Osman.

Where? The water already came up to her hips. The hem of her long skirt had risen.

Here! Osman's voice seemed to come from the depths. She thought she could even see the air bubbles in which it rose to the surface.

Then her head was under water too and her long journey began. At first she was surprised that moving was just the same under water as on land. Easier, in fact.

She walked on stones and shells, on smooth-scoured sand and green water-plants. And when she looked up, she saw that the water was rather troubled. The light that came through was dim and everything was blurred.

Once I thought I was seeing mud in bloom. I was bending over a stream to scoop up some water. I saw little star-shaped flowers hanging in the mud. I was overjoyed. A miracle, it seemed to me. Until I knocked my head against the branches of the elder bush above me and even more star-shaped flowers drifted down into the water.

She moved effortlessly. She even walked through the cling-ing tendrils of the few plants close to the edge as if through a meadow with tall grass.

Why did it never occur to me to go looking for you? She waved away an inquisitive fish which had refused to give way even when she was close enough to stroke it with her eyelashes. It turned round in a flash and its tail touched her forehead. She moved her hand as if to wipe off its touch.

The first time I talked about you in my sleep, my sister told my mother. She couldn't make head nor tail of it, but I had to stay at home when my sister went out dancing. And when I went on talking about you at night, my sister was given a room of her own, which she kept until she went to live with Tim and married him. By that time, however, she'd already been carrying Tom for a few months

Sometimes my mother slept with me at night, to find out who you were. But as the years passed and I never said to her, That's him! she abandoned the hopes she'd placed on you.

The water must have been very deep at this point, or was it

344

dark already? She felt fresh and was not, as usual, looking forward to sleep long before it was time to go to bed. The spark of hope that Osman, the son of the boat-builder, had aroused in her was flickering into life and lit a path for her courage through the water.

Perhaps it was just chance that I gave you a name so early on. But my longing was so great, no other name could fulfil it. I can't say I never doubted you. But after that I just loved you more and more.

It wasn't so easy now to find a way through the dark water. She didn't want to end up going round in circles looking for Osman. She had the feeling the water was pushing her in a particular direction. Had she got to a place where a river flowed into the sea?

Whenever I thought, There you are at last, in disguise, but it's you, it was too soon. The moment I realised my mistake, I felt cold, and I went cold, and that was the end of it.

My mother was getting more and more desperate. What's the matter with you? she said. You're not ugly, you don't smell, you're not quarrelsome. Why can't you be so nice to a man he'll never want to leave you?

I said nothing and sat on the verandah with a book. The apple trees were in blossom in the garden and I liked being there. It was only with you I wanted to be somewhere else . . . even in the desert.

When I had finished school, they asked me what I wanted to do. Go on going to school, I said. I want to learn how to handle words.

The first time I stood in front of the children to explain something to them, I was lost for precisely those words I'd wanted to learn, and I had to start again from the very beginning. I worked everything out in my head, the way I used to when I was a child sitting in the shed for days on end.

I kept on having to yearn my way through a man who showed me a part of you. And I fell for it often enough. So often, in fact, that I heard it said my nocturnal activities were a bad influence on the children. But the children only saw me during the day and not one ever mentioned them.

I never left the house and the garden with the apple trees. Not for any length of time. And my mother got used to the visitors and the laughter, and even to my tears, when I talked of you and she had no idea how to comfort me.

For time to time there was a phosphorescent gleam in the darkness. Fish brushed against her legs, and sometimes she thought she could see, far above, the keel of an even darker boat.

Should I try to drift along with the current? She tried lifting up her legs, first one and then, when nothing happened, both of them and, lo and behold, she was carried along without her feet touching the bottom.

You never stop learning, she said with a smile to a seahorse curiously watching her float along without having to make an effort with her arms or legs. It's even quicker if you do nothing.

Suddenly she saw herself on a tandem with Osman, the son of the boat-builder, cycling through the beautiful city of Alexandria, then out along a narrow path by the desert. Unfortunately she couldn't see his face. He was sitting behind her and she was afraid she'd fall off if she turned round. The wheels would slide on the sand and the pair of them would end up lying there. The farther they rode on their tandem, the wilder grew the blooming all around. The cups of the hibiscus-coloured flowers became so large she was afraid there might be some flesh-eating plants among them and, what was even worse, dream-devouring ones which would leave nothing behind, neither of her, nor of Osman nor the tandem on which they were cycling through the desert.

When she woke up it was a bit lighter on the bottom again and she saw that her legs were still pedalling the tandem. A shoal of smallish fish and a few fat crabs were looking on with interest. My God, she said, the desert . . . didn't I always long to see the desert. And her legs jiggled on a bit, as if remembering.

Of course, I could have written to a travel agent, got on a plane and flown there. But what would I have done, alone

346

in the desert? You're right, perhaps I would have found you sooner.

By now it wasn't just lighter, the consistency of the water was different. Murkier perhaps, not as clear as where she had started out. She watched the fish swimming along with their mouths open, only swallowing from time to time, as if they had had a particularly tasty titbit.

Perhaps I should try to eat something as well. She pushed the water towards her with both hands, so as to get it between her teeth better and then, following her intention, swallowed several times. Who knows whether I need to eat much at all . . . She tried to gather her hair and put it up, but she didn't seem to be able to manage that kind of thing at all.

I wonder if I look very much like Ophelia? She searched through the pockets of her skirt for the little mirror she always carried, because of the children, they always look at you so closely. But then she forgot it and sighed. The children . . . is it time for my class already? Time to teach them something about words I'm not sure about myself? She seemed to hear a school bell ringing in the distance.

Today the children are sure to ask where I am. I'm fine, children . . . I'm on a long journey which looks as if it's going to be interesting. But you can't follow me, not yet. Your skin couldn't stand all this water.

Who was it who stuck the heart on my blouse recently?

It had happened at least once every year that one of the children had fixed a heart to her blouse and she'd gone round with it on for a long time without noticing.

The children love me. Once I even went all the way home with the heart on my back and my mother said I should be ashamed of myself, even the children were alluding to my activities.

And once I almost told the children about you. We were talking about what it would be like going out into the world to seek your fortune. It was a class of smaller children. Some wanted to set off there and then. I suggested they should wait a while. Perhaps their fortune would come straight to them? I wonder if that was what I did wrong? I have as good as never moved from the spot.

Once a man wrote to me who had your name, though he spelt it Ousman. The letter came from Senegal, Ousman had my name from an international exchange office and asked me to send him stamps and photos. When I got a photo of him, the face on it was so black, I couldn't make out his features.

Lost in thought, she strode through the soft mud as if she were looking for something to pin her thoughts to. Sometimes the feeling crept over her that her feet and the bottom were becoming one. Then she would draw up her legs to drift with the current again. She thought she recognised objects people threw in the water, which then sank down slowly, an empty can, its label already gone, pieces of glass . . . and when she had a proper look, she could see something that looked like kitchen scraps, which didn't sink down as far as her because the fish ate them up before they got there.

This time I will find you, she said, and I'll give you enough of my life for us to survive on for a long time.

Her fingers had gone pale and thin, and there were wrinkles along the sides of the tips. She took out her little mirror, but the reflection would not stay still long enough for her to recognise herself.

I wonder if my face's all wrinkled too? She tried to run her fingers over her cheeks, but couldn't feel anything. Perhaps this isn't the right kind of journey. Perhaps, when I've found you, we ought to fly, fly high above the world so we can see that it's round.

Flying, she said, her head held up by the current alone, flying on the back of a bird round the minarets of the beautiful city of Alexandria and then on, up the Nile to Al Qahirah, the Victorious One. Flying over all the mud domes of the city of the dead – a city of the dead where so many living people live – like the beautiful photograph in that book, flying to the citadel and then beyond, on and on . . .

When she opened her eyes again, she saw a figure beside her. She called out to it, but the figure did not answer, it just drifted along beside her, dark and silent. Some people are so immersed in their own destiny, she said, they don't notice when there's someone beside them in the same situation.

Hi! She tried again, but nothing happened.

Trying to move in a specific direction was starting to get a bit strenuous.

Drifting with the current for so long has made me weak.

Then she did manage to give the figure beside her a poke. And when the material simply gave way, she tried to attract the figure's attention by grabbing its sleeve and tugging it. And lo and behold, the garment opened out, without anyone appearing inside it, lifted up its coat tails and was suddenly caught up in another current, less deep than the one she was in, and floated away over her head. She let go of the sleeve and even turned her head to watch the solitary coat as it spread out more and more. Now and then she had the feeling her body too was already tilting backwards a trifle.

Faster and faster, she thought, could that be the momentum you get with time? Walking . . . walking is perhaps best, after all, the most pleasant way. We'll walk together, we have time, plenty of time. We'll walk along the bank, on and on along the bank, in the shade.

The coat was above her again, spread out like a dark cloud over her body, which was still moving along in a horizontal position . . . in the shade of the palm trees and the laden camels, past water carriers and mud huts. We'll watch the great barges on the Nile, none of which will carry an Egyptian princess to her burial chamber any more. We will walk barefoot through the soft dust of the paths and drink tea with the merchants in the shade of their tents. We will listen to the stories and fairly tales, and keep on going up the Nile, on and on . . .

She hardly felt cold now and all at once she had the feeling she wasn't going to be bothered by the cold any more. Incredible how the body can adjust, she said. I know I am cold, but I don't feel it. Will it be the same in the heat on the edge of the desert? I always suffered from the cold, even as a child and now . . . I've not even caught a chill. She tried to sneeze, but couldn't. I wonder what my life might have turned out like if I had managed to hold it back all those years ago? And she watched the bubbles from her laugh rise up.

The Director of the Music Academy was a handsome older gentleman with a fringe of curly hair round a tonsure-like bald patch. He could look at you in such a way that he seldom had to ask for anything, so clearly did his eyes express what he wanted. He wore elegant suits, in the summer natural linen, in the winter grey wool, and it was said he was married to his cello and the young men who went to visit him so often did not count.

One day he came to our house and went in to see my mother. I had no idea why he had come. True, I did play the flute, but if that had been the reason, he could have asked me at the Academy. That was the period when I had to spend a lot of time thinking about myself, so I was sitting in one of the apple trees. It happened to be the one with the table and chairs at the bottom where my mother used to entertain her guests. It had never occurred to me that the Director of the Music Academy would stay for any length of time, and it was only when I saw him and my mother come out with the tray and the coffee pot that I realised what was happening, but by then it was too late to climb down the tree unnoticed.

. . . and that is why, I heard the Director of the Music Academy say to my mother as they sat down beneath me and filled their cups and plates, that is why I wish to repeat the request I made to you before.

My mother didn't seem to know quite what to say to this and bit her cheek in embarrassment.

She has perfect pitch and a beautiful soul, said the Director of the Music Academy.

How do you know about her beautiful soul? my mother ventured to ask.

The Director of the Music Academy raised his eyebrows, thought for a minute and then said, She has never once offended my aesthetic sense. She doesn't bite her nails or chew the ends of her hair like so many girls of her age. She doesn't wear make-up or signal to lovers with her eyes, as you

350

can see girls of even that age do. The posture of her neck is regal and she has never been caught cheating, I asked her class teacher. He brushed a speck of bark off the lapel of his linen suit that I must have knocked down.

How can you love my daughter if you don't know her that well? asked my mother in an attempt to mask her confusion.

I wish to marry your daughter, said the Director of the Music Academy, because she suits me in every respect. Moreover, she is still young enough to be moulded according to my wishes. I assure you, he said with a slight bow, that I will always show due consideration for your daughter's beautiful soul.

That was the moment it happened. I had to sneeze, and so violently I fell out of the tree. So there I lay, giggling like a madwoman from the shock, surrounded by bits of cake, and the coffee had splashed out of his cup and onto the beautiful linen suit of the Director of the Music Academy. When he saw that, he stood up, looked down at his trousers and went pale.

At first my mother froze, but then she pounced on me, dragged me off the table and checked that nothing was broken. Nothing was broken. Apart from my beautiful soul.

It didn't help that I insisted on apologising. The Director of the Music Academy said a formal farewell to my mother. He did not shake my hand, covered as I was in bits of squashed cake. Pity, he said, before he turned to leave, and it was quite clear to me that I was no longer pleasing in his sight, never would be, ever again. And that night, before I went to sleep, I shed a few tears over my beautiful soul.

It's a nice arrangement, she said, being carried along even while you're lying down. That way I can save my energy for when I've found you. I can imagine we'll be pretty tired sometimes after a long walk on the banks of the Nile. And even if we can see the columns of Karnak in the distance, we still won't have arrived. We'll stop there for a while, rest beside the graves of the kings, but we won't have arrived, not by a long chalk. We'll have things to tell each other for years and years, and as long as the river lasts, we will walk together.

The coat was still floating above her. The distance between

them seemed to be staying the same. Now she too was lying in the current, completely horizontal, with her clothes and hair spread out.

My perfect pitch . . . she smiled. I didn't even make something of that. I did sit in the garden of an evening, playing my flute, but that was all. And my voice, my voice wasn't powerful enough. My perfect pitch has never amounted to more than a trick I could perform on request, and sometimes men turned up who thought no end of themselves at the idea of sleeping with a woman with perfect pitch.

Where is this journey going to take me? She tried to turn more onto her side in the current, to see if there might be land at the edge of the water. I will not stop looking for you, even if I have to go to the world's end. One day I will reach the beautiful city of Alexandria and swim up the Nile from there, to Al Qahirah, to Luxor and Karnak, to Abu Simbel and Elephantine Island. By then I will have found you. Only together can we lose ourselves among the headwaters of the Nile. And the desert will be like a yellowish red glow on the horizon, waving to us with sandy winds.

Sometimes I would hide from my lovers because I wanted to finish a book. All my mother could think of doing was to sit and talk to them. She served schnapps and sandwiches, and made conversation about all branches of art, since she would have loved there to be a real artist among them.

But it also sometimes happened that I fell asleep over the book I wanted to finish and my mother just could not bring herself to show the man in question the door, hoping he might be the one who would eventually marry me. The result was that he would get more and more tired and drunk, until he fell asleep on the sofa in her bay window. Once he had reached that stage, she would go looking all over the house until she had found me, bent over my book She roused me and, together with her I had to get the man up into my room. There we would undress him, I lay down beside him and the next morning he was convinced he had spent the night with me.

You ought to marry and have children, my mother would

say during the first years whenever I swapped one lover for another. Later she stopped saying that. And when the question cropped up, she would say, It's better the way it is, given your crazy behaviour.

When she looked down at herself, she saw that she was floating along in her underclothes. The current must have undressed her some time ago, since there was no trace of her skirt. Only her blouse – at least that was her impression – was drifting down, a long way behind her, towards the bottom in a strange spiral.

What's gone is gone. Doesn't matter, my clothes weren't suitable for the desert anyway.

For long stretches she was already dreaming without words and algae and mud caught in her hair without her noticing.

Strange how little not arriving bothers me. The only reason I can imagine is that you've been swimming alongside me all the time.

The water had distended her body and her nails had gone soft and blue.

And with time all that was left were very quiet thoughts inside her, and it went on like that, just as it went on like that for her once she knew that Osman, the son of the boat-builder, was with her, wholly with her. Some time, was the thought inside her, I will surface and see the beautiful city of Alexandria, or not, as the case may be. And she appreciated the increasing lack of feeling in her body, which did not allow the least pain.

So the illness has come to an end, was the thought inside her, that is good. And it felt as if she must surface once more. Her body righted itself and she was drawn up to the surface. Perhaps the beautiful city of Alexandria after all?

But that was just the afterglow of a thought that had faded to complete unconsciousness when her body emerged from the water, frightening to death a few people who were taking a harmless boating trip.

The Epidemic

Marianne Gruber

Her words had a strange undertone. 'I'm saying goodbye now.'

It sounded odd, but meant nothing to him. K. held the receiver in his hand, uncertain what to do, then dialled his mother-in-law, complained, told her to get his wife sorted out, then went back into the vast shed where the machine he operated was.

Items for repair went past him on the conveyer belt. He straightened out legs, removed faulty parts, closed up splits, opened brains.

When someone asked what was the matter, he shrugged his shoulders. His answer was lost in the noise of the machines. The sun was shining through the closed windows of the factory shed. Midday arrived.

Before the conveyor-belt was shut down temporarily for lunch, he was called to the telephone a second time.

'She's not there,' his mother-in-law said. She sounded helpless. 'Women,' he thought. There was always something contrary, something that disrupted the schedule. The day had been planned, had its directions, its targets: a leg to be pinned, two cuts into the abdomen, injections, bandages.

The foreman gave him permission to leave with a pitying nod. Suddenly he started running, ran to his car, drove too fast along the straight stretches, skidded round a bend, took his foot off the accelerator, ran from the car to the house, then eased off again, finally going in with quick, if measured steps.

She wasn't in the house. His mother-in-law had said that. There were a few things scattered around, indicating an erratic route. He bent down over the items and started looking for clues, went in a circle from the living-room to the hall and back to the living-room, went to the bathroom, bedroom, utility room and garden. The garage in the garden was locked. He shook the door, looked for a key, finally had to call on the man next door who happened to be there and knew something about locks and how to open them without keys. Then the garage door gave way too.

She was lying on the back seat of the new car, still warm. She had stopped breathing. He knew about that. *Conveyor-belt emergencies*. Mouth-to-mouth resuscitation. He dragged her out of the car, lay her heavy body down on the concrete and bent over her lips.

It was not the same as usual this time. There was no noise of the motor starting. He kept up the artificial respiration, she was still warm and silent.

'Send for an emergency unit,' he said to his mother-in-law, bending over his wife's body again. He was no longer cool, no longer detached. The emergency unit arrived and took charge of her. He jumped into the vehicle with them. They were poorly equipped. By the time they reached the workshop all hope had gone. The sensitive motors that looked after her could only tolerate a complete stoppage for a very brief period.

They continued to try. 'To give up' was not in their vocabulary. The company specialists arrived. Eventually they too turned away and, without a word, shook his hand. It was all over.

After the end of his shift he went to the pub with some friends and got moderately drunk. They raised their glasses to him, but in silence. No one ordered sandwiches. By now the next shift would be at the conveyor-belt. It was already getting dark when he went home.

The next morning before the shift started he was sitting in the recreation room, not knowing what to do. His bewilderment was beginning to turn to anger. To leave him like that. Why? Blackmail, that's what her death was. Hesitantly, his friends agreed. The word freed them from their own thoughts. Who knows? Why? Whatever for?

He left the factory and began to arrange her funeral. There was a lot to think about, not really to think about, but to choose. Red and blue, carnations or roses, the writing that wasn't the writing on the wall, but was still his writing. Then he went back to the factory and took up his place at the conveyor-belt.

In general they shared K.'s thoughts and views. Their wives were somewhere outside the factory gates, just waiting for the chance to overwhelm them, disturb their plans, break out of their ordered world. They would stop at nothing. Not even suicide.

The following morning a worker at the same conveyor-belt came up to K. He had a black tie on and the same expression K. had had the day before. 'Last night,' said F., 'after I'd told my wife about yours, my wife committed suicide. I don't know why. She didn't say much, although she usually had a lot to say for herself. She asked me what I had to say about the 'business'. Then before we went to sleep she asked me if I had anything to say to her. I turned over on my side and said nothing. You know how it is. That's the way they start when they're looking for an argument. The first thing that struck me in the morning was that breakfast wasn't ready, and then that she was still in bed – I hadn't noticed when I got up. I bent over her, but she was already dead. She must have taken sleeping pills. No thought for the children.'

K. went to his locker and brought out a bottle of brandy. They both had a drink. When the shift began, they stayed there for a while, but then went into the machine shed and were only slightly late getting to the conveyor-belt. The cleaner passed them. She gave them a long, hard look as they went to their places. A morning accident rolled past on the conveyor. Word of the new incident slowly got round the shed, and the neighbouring sheds as well. After the end of their shift K. and F. went to the pub together again. They got moderately drunk. It was already getting dark when they went home.

A few hours later first K., then F. heard the news that, when he got home, B. had found his wife dead. She had cut open an artery. She must have done it immediately after he left for work.

An incredible quantity of blood had come out of her, the amount had surprised him, even though he was not usually surprised by wounds that bled profusely. That same night K., F. and B. made an arrangement and met at B.'s house, which was out in the country and contained neither children nor a dead woman.

From there they went to the factory, where they saw the old cleaner again, who gave them a long, hard look then, without being asked, brought a bottle of brandy and four glasses. K., F. and B. were probably surprised at the fourth glass, but they said nothing. A little later W. came in. He was wearing a black tie and didn't waste words. His wife had also killed herself during the night.

At this point they still tended to regard the incidents in and around the factory as a series of coincidences. Even the experts could find no evidence of any connection. What had happened was tragic, of course, but their work at the conveyor-belt definitely came first. None of them had ever had anything other than this work, these motions, these daily operations, nothing other than the thoughts of what was, the way it was.

As far as K., F., B. and W. were concerned, work not only came first, it was their salvation. *Occupational therapy.* Take your mind off it. Think of something else. Do something meaningful. Sometimes K. broke off working and put his face in his hands, in one of those mute, helpless gestures for which no one else would have found a word either: a silent keeping-yourself-together. These gestures only took up a short time and so only disturbed his work-rhythm imperceptibly, if at all. The way he coped was magnificent and a not inconsiderable support to his colleagues, above all to P., whose turn it was next. His wife threw herself under an express train. After that it was K.2.

When he arrived at the factory with the news, everyone apart from the cleaner was devastated. She went to K. 2 with a glass, which she held to his lips saying, in response to his look of surprise, 'Of course, your wife also . . .'

When the number of suicide wives reached a round dozen,

the Works Committee convened. Coincidences of this type were either uncanny or not coincidences at all. The discussions came to no new findings and no conclusions. Eventually it was decided to leave things as they were and wait and see.

The only difference was the cleaner's new activity. She waited by the factory gates when the shifts changed to welcome the newly widowed workers. They all behaved in exemplary fashion. Only J. departed from the norm. When his wife rang one morning and pleaded with him to come home, she was so terribly afraid, he left the factory at once, only returning after several days. The cleaner was waiting for him at the entrance, but the glass she had ready in her hand sank when she saw him. 'Your wife didn't . . . ?' J. shook his head.

The deaths started to come thick and fast in the neighbouring sheds. One firm of undertakers concentrated entirely on organising funerals for the factory workers at specially reduced rates. Things developed a routine. Now and then one of them got immoderately rather than moderately drunk. The management granted a day's leave of absence for the formalities as an exception rather than the rule. Conjecture was rife in the recreation room as to who would be next, but no bets were made.

J. was threatened with the sack. He kept running away from work and driving home. When he arrived at the factory one morning, the cleaner drank to him, then took up her mop and bucket again.

'You're the last,' she said. 'It's not worth waiting just for you. It could take a long time.'

The days passed. K., F., B., W. and the others worked at the conveyer-belt. The sun shone in through the closed, frosted windows. They straightened out legs, arms as well, closed up splits and opened brains. They spoke little and worked hard. The transporters brought more and more pieces for their conveyer-belt, and more and more quickly. They often had to work overtime.

Overtime had sometimes been necessary in the past as well, but now the workload doubled. That was why J. could not be dismissed. The arrangements were becoming difficult. Many of them had children who had to live with their grandparents. They could only go and see them on their free days, if there were any free days.

Now and then one of them would talk about his wife. She had done some things quite well. It had been quite pleasant while she was still alive, especially on days when she had operated in silence. They might have considered other women, but none were available. People were obviously avoiding the factory employees.

One morning an angry crowd prevented the early shift from going into the street as they tried to leave the premises. The men were driven back into the factory grounds with catcalls and then stones. J. telephoned his wife at once and begged her to come and collect him. The Works Committee convened. The local police station was informed, but the crews of the patrol cars that appeared were exclusively made up of policewomen who strengthened the siege instead of dispersing it. No one was stopped from entering the factory premises, but it was impossible to leave them again.

Despite this all the employees, impelled by an inexplicable sense of solidarity, gathered there, even those who had already gone home, or not yet turned up for their shift. There were no problems with catering for the internees. During the first few days of quarantine books and newspapers were also brought in. The transporters continued to bring fresh work. Those who had children were allowed to send letters, the telephone lines remained open, radio reception functioned as normal.

After a few days, however, there were increasing indications that things were not going to remain as they were. First of all the letters came back: Return to Sender. Then the newspapers stopped being delivered. The men, who had initially accepted the situation with stoical calm, became uneasy. The transporters brought less and less new work, so that hopeless cases were sent through to maintain the same level of employment. One morning the telephone wires were dead, radio reception impossible and the factory gates only opened to bring in food supplies.

J. stood at one of the windows staring out. Right at the back of the crowd surrounding the factory he had seen a hat, a ridiculous thing, like one his wife wore. He had bought it, even though he didn't like it. Maria loved turquoise and green, but so childlike was her delight, he didn't care about the colours.

She was standing far away from him and he had left the conveyor-belt without permission. It ran day and night now, since it could only be switched off from outside and clearly no one could be bothered any more. They no longer had anything to repair. What ran past them were dead bodies, just dead bodies, nothing but dead men.

Then J. saw the hat begin to move and push its way towards the front. He saw her face. It was pale and seemed tired. He waved, although he did not expect her to be able to see him.

Now she was standing in the front row, talking to some of the women. Suddenly she looked up at him. He waved, making elaborate gestures, and called out her name. A colleague walked past behind him. It was K.

'Stop that,' said K., 'it could be misconstrued.' He tried to pull J. away from the window. J. freed himself from his grasp and ran out into the yard.

During his military service he had learnt the Morse code. Later, after he had met Maria, they had turned it into a game, conversing between rooms by knocking on the wall. J. started hammering out their secret words on the factory gate. It was a long time before he received an answer.

'I love you,' came the message in Morse.

'I love you . . .,' then, 'wait, wait, wait . . .'

J. waited. From outside came the noise of machines, diggers, cranes, bulldozers. Something was being built right beside the factory, or perhaps even around it. J. waited all night. Once K. came and then W. and tried to get him to come away. They meant well. Three of them had taken over his work at the conveyor belt so that his absence would not be noticed. After their shift had ended, they came and sat with him. K. even brought some blankets. But suddenly J. could not understand them any more. Towards dawn they left him. Their next shift was about to start. The sun rose over the roofs and a soft tapping could be heard on the gate.

'Are you awake?'

'I am so awake,' J. replied, 'that it hurts.'

'Are you alone?'

'Yes. I am as alone as before I was born.'

Suddenly the door opened. In astonishment J. watched the narrow strip of sunlight appear in the darkness of the yard. Only then did he stand up. Maria was outside. She took him by the hand and tried to pull him away quickly. The door was closed.

'You're the only one,' she said.

J. looked around. They had started to build a high wall round the factory. It was already half finished and the work was continuing at incredible speed.

'What's the point of all this?' J. asked. One of the women in uniform stopped.

'It's to shut the factory in,' she said.

'And then?' asked J.

'Come,' said Maria, but J. held her there. 'What will happen then?' he asked again.

'Nothing,' the woman replied. She did not even smile as she turned away. A funeral cortège drove past, a dozen black vans, the sides of which had been replaced with black glass. Through the gleaming windows J. saw glass coffins. Men. All of them men. Dead.

'Now you've found out after all,' said Maria. 'I had hoped we could get home before you . . .'

'Everything's the other way round out here?' asked J.

'Don't look.' Maria put her arms round him. J. extricated himself from her embrace and followed the vans. They were going at walking pace. Suddenly he stopped and screamed her name. She could feel his mortal anguish.

'We have always betrayed each other as honestly as possible.' He trembled.

'There's another way,' she said. He followed her as if in a dream. She opened out a picture book in front of him. A path led across a green meadow to sky-blue mountains.

361

'Leave everything behind?' he asked. She nodded. He took her by both hands. 'I love you,' he said, 'I truly love you.'

Together, and without looking round, they stepped into the picture book of their unborn children. Someone behind closed it and picked it up carefully.

They talked together for a long time. Late in the night, when they had found all the words again, they lay down side by side.

They slept out in the open, under a starry sky.

My Day

G. F. Jonke

Early morning

The post arrives. The postman brings me a parcel. In the parcel I find: a picture by Hans Staudacher that can be bent slightly since it is stuck onto a thin metal plate, the latest atlas for use in secondary schools, and a book in English sent to me by a writer from Japan whom I know personally but can't remember.

Morning

I go into town and see the city councillor. She is just about to get into her car, probably to drive to the office. I wrote her an angry letter yesterday which will be waiting for her when she gets there. I won't mention it to her just now, I think, instead I'll ask her who the man might be who sent me his book in English from Japan. I go up to the councillor, who is just putting her briefcase, with the files she probably spent all night going through, in the boot. I ask my question and notice there is someone else with her. I know him vaguely, he's called Gunter. The matter seems to interest not only the councillor but Gunter as well, and they come with me to try to get to the bottom of the mystery. The contents of the parcel are examined, Gunter picks up the picture, bends it right round a few times and observes that it is one of the best pictures Hans Staudacher has ever painted. 'People will keep on sending me the latest atlas for use in secondary schools,' I reply. The main problem, the problem of the English book from Japan – really it should be the business of the councillor to deal with it – is simply ignored.

Midday

A walk in the nearby park. Gunter and I climb a huge birch tree, but I climb so high I can't find the way back down and

363

the city councillor, who is sitting on a bench at the bottom, shouts up to ask me why I look so sad, is there anything wrong with me? 'You'll find an angry letter when you get to your office today,' I growl in reply. Then I discover that the birch tree I have climbed is a weeping birch and some branches hang down to the ground like ropes. I immediately grab one of the ropes and a start to let myself slowly down, hand over hand. But then Gunter, who by this time is back at the bottom, goes to the trunk and starts shaking the tree vigorously. 'Stop fooling around,' the councillor shouts to him, but he clearly has not the slightest intention of obeying her, he is obviously enjoying the way the tree is swaying. The birch rope I am hanging from swings back and forward, more and more violently, until I can hold on no longer and fall down, but land in the blanket which some firemen, who have been urgently called to the scene, hold out at the last minute. The councillor finally goes to her office, and Gunter leaves as well.

Afternoon
Soldiers march up, position themselves outside the entrances to the café and forbid people like me to go in. Menacingly, they release the safety catches on their rifles when I come too close and engage the bolts with a resounding clash.

I creep up to one who seems, to judge by the expression on his face, to be slightly more good-natured, well-disposed and understanding, ask 'why carn't oi go t' the caff' and am told the antiques dealers have occupied the media, some of them the press, some the radio and television, and protested against people like me because of unfair competition. That's why people like me carn't go t' the café. The owners of the galleries selling paintings of alpine sunsets, glittering watercourses and mountain huts with appropriate animals, he added, had in the meantime joined in the protest. Pity, I think to myself, I'd have loved to have a glass of *Vintner's Pride* in the café.

Evening
I go to a concert with my grandmother and my mother. A Japanese pianist is playing. Of course we arrive too late, as

usual, the pianist has already begun her programme. We have tickets for the third row, however I don't sit in the seat reserved for me at the end of the row, but on the floor beside it. We are not the last to arrive late, someone else comes after us. I turn round and see that he is Japanese, clearly the boy-friend, brother or husband of the pianist. He makes no attempt at all to be quiet so as to create as little disturbance to the concert as possible, the clatter of his footsteps can be very distinctly heard throughout the concert hall. He comes closer and closer and then sits down on the seat which is actually mine, so that I end up sitting on the floor at his feet. He immediately starts talking, describes a dish he must have just partaken of in a nearby restaurant, saying I simply must pro-cure the recipe for him, he didn't know how to explain to the people in the restaurant what he wanted, being a foreigner they didn't understand him properly but I probably knew exactly how to go about something like that. The thought of the meal the Japanese described arouses such a feeling of delight within me that I immediately start to stamp my feet alternately on the floor at intervals of one second, precisely in time with the piano music the Japanese woman is playing. At this the pianist breaks off playing, gives me and then the Japa-nese beside me an angry look and hisses some incompre-hensible words, probably indicating her intention to abandon the concert on the spot if there is not immediate silence in the auditorium.

During the interval I go to the foyer, meet Gunter and the city councillor, tell them about the Japanese and how he sim-ply sat down in my seat, though, as I explain, I was sitting on the floor beside my seat at the time, so he might well have had the idea the seat was unoccupied, but that is no reason to sit in my seat without so much as a by-your-leave, however much of a foreigner you are and don't know they way things are done here.

Conjecture: perhaps the man has something to do with the book in English from Japan that I received in the post today.

Then, however, I remember the duties of a local inhabitant towards a foreigner and think of the recipe the man absolutely has to have, but it occurs to me that in the end he was not so insistent on his need for the recipe, he just went on and on about it, what he in fact absolutely had to have was a comb, I should help him get a comb as quickly as possible, he had said, any minute now he had to comb his hair. So I go to the snack bar and buy a packet of threes and a comb. The interval crush in the foyer is too much for me, so I go back into the auditorium to take the comb to the Japanese, who has stayed in my seat. But what do I see, hardly have I entered the hall? My aunt, who is about fifty years old, is standing right in the middle, on the rostrum, and I didn't even know she had come to the concert too, I would never have expected to see her here at the concert because she is not in the habit of going to concerts and today of all days she has come to a concert, so there is my roughly fifty-year-old aunt, right in the middle, on the rostrum, stark naked in a wooden trough filled with steaming hot water rubbing down her already somewhat wrinkled body with a sponge, making her breasts wobble like anything, and scarcely has she seen me come into the hall than she drops the sponge with a splash into the steaming water, throws her arms in the air and calls out to me in ringing tones, 'Anselm, bring me a towel at once!!!'

Night
Nothing.

The Thief

Michael Köhlmeier

Do you know the story of Tschawo? No? Then listen.

Now Tschawo was a poor man, everything had been taken from him. That is, he had taken everything from himself: drinking, gambling . . . he stole his whole life from himself. In the end his wife left him. It happened like this:

He says to her, 'Hey, fetch some tobacco.'

She says, 'Let's have the money.'

He says, 'Anyone can fetch tobacco with money.'

So, two hours later she comes back, slaps her hand down on the table and says, 'There, get smoking.'

He says, 'Where's the tobacco?'

She says, 'Anyone can smoke with tobacco.'

And then she leaves him. Tschawo –

Hang on a minute, stay there. The story's not over yet.

So, Tschawo thinks a bit. Then he goes to the town. He wants to see the mayor. But there's a secretary. The secretary wants to know who he is.

'Well, then,' says Tschawo. 'Listen. I'm Tschawo. Yes.'

'Fine,' says the secretary. 'Now write your name down here.' Tschawo has to write his name on the list. 'Then I'll know when it's your turn,' the secretary says.

But Tschawo can't. He can't write and he can't read either. So he says, 'Listen, secretary. The thing is, I've got an unusual name. The way it's written is quite different from the way it reads. It's as if your name was Peter, but you wrote it Paul. D'you see? There'd be no point in my writing it down here.'

The secretary does see and lets him in to see the mayor.

To the mayor Tschawo says, 'I'm the best thief in the world. I imagine you can use someone like me.'

'Mmmm,' says the mayor. 'Prove it.'

'How?'

'Steal the parish priest?'

Tschawo says, 'Give me some expenses.'

Right then. The mayor gives Tschawo some money. With it Tschawo buys twenty live crabs and twenty candles. Then during the night he goes to the church, sticks the candles on the crabs and lights them. Then he hangs onto the bell-rope and the bells ring. And the priest comes running. He rushes into the church. He wants to know what's going on.

Then the priest sees lights moving over the floor. He can't see the crabs underneath the lights. And the priest thinks the lights are the souls at the Last Judgment. So the priest thinks it's the end of the world.

Tschawo stands behind the altar and cries out in a deep voice, 'Kneel down, sinner. Close your eyes, sinner. Crawl on your knees, sinner.'

And the priest does. The priest wants to go to heaven. He kneels down, closes his eyes and crawls on his knees. And crawls straight into Tschawo's potato sack.

Tschawo ties up the sack and takes it to the mayor. 'There you are,' he says, 'one stolen parish priest.'

Hey, wait a minute. There's more.

The mayor says, 'That was good. No buts about it. If you really are the best thief in the world, however, then you must be able to do more than steal a stupid priest from his church.'

'What else must I be able to do?'

'Well, now,' says the mayor, 'you've to steal my wife's nightdress, during the night while she's wearing it, and the wedding ring off her finger.'

'And what if I succeed?'

'Let's say that if you succeed I'll resign and you'll be mayor,' says the mayor. 'And you'll get my beautiful wife into the bargain.'

And Tschawo asks, 'And what if I don't succeed?'

To which the mayor says, 'Quite simple. Then I'll chop your head off.'

So what does Tschawo do? He goes to the graveyard and digs up a dead body. A newly dead body. And during the night he carries it to the mayor's house. Places it underneath the bedroom window. Lifts it up. From inside it looks as if someone is trying to climb in through the bedroom window. It's that Tschawo, the idiot, thinks the mayor, who's lying in bed beside his beautiful wife.

And the mayor says to his wife, 'Do you see that. Just a moment while I sort it out.'

Then Tschawo lifts the dead body a bit higher. Now the head is leaning into the mayor's bedroom.

Then the mayor takes the axe he has ready and chops off the dead man's head. And he says to his wife, 'I think I'd better just nip out and clear up the mess. We don't want the neighbours getting funny ideas.'

After the mayor has gone out of the bedroom, Tschawo comes in through the door, doesn't put the light on and behaves as if he were the mayor. He says to the wife, 'You know, I think I'll do that later. I fancy you first. Take off your nightdress.'

The mayor's wife does that and Tschawo sleeps with her. While he's doing that he also takes her wedding ring off her finger. And then he says, 'Right, now I'll go and clear up outside.'

And just as he gets outside the mayor comes in, at the very same moment, and he says, 'Right, I've cleared up outside. Now I fancy you. Take off your nightdress.'

And his wife says, 'Are you mad? You've just said that and just done that.'

Then Tschawo comes in, switches on the light and produces the nightdress and the ring. He's made mayor, gets the mayor's wife.

Hey, don't go. You haven't heard the end. A story's only finished when Death comes.

Tschawo was a good mayor. Well, a bit corrupt, yes. But otherwise a good mayor. And at the end Death comes for him.

He stands there, does Death, and says to Tschawo, 'It's your turn, Tschawo.'

And Tschawo says, 'But, but – I don't believe you. There must be some mistake.'

Death says, 'No buts about it. You're here on my list.'

And Tschawo says, 'Oh, so that's it. Well, I can explain that. You see the way my name is written is quite different from the way it's spoken. It's as if your name was Peter and you wrote it Paul. It's a case of mistaken identity. Let me see your list, Death.'

Death gives him the list.

Then Tschawo tears the page out of Death's order book and swallows it. – Exactly. And since he didn't die, he'll live for ever, will Tschawo . . .

Now the story's finished. Musicians who travel from village to village used to tell it – or something like it.

Snitto-Snot

Michael Köhlmeier

Fairy tales aren't beautiful, ugliness was invented in them. Fairy tales don't smell nice, stench was invented in them. It was in this fairy tale that stench was invented. Until then it was just called a bad smell.

In the Finnish midgeland lived a young man called Snitto, lazy Snitto. People used to say he had invented laziness. But that's not true, it existed before him. Snitto's favourite occupation was to sit beside the roadside watching. Lazy people always find something to look at. A man came along on a cart. He looked like anyone and everyone, as if he were everyone's father, and he said to Snitto, 'Anything wrong?'

'Nothing,' said Snitto. He could just as well have said, 'No, sir, there's nothing wrong,' but that would have been too much like hard work for his lazy tongue.

'Looking for work?' asked Tomdickorharry.

'Only very easy work,' said Snitto.

'Jump up then,' said the man.

Off they went to the man's farm and in no time at all Snitto was sitting at a large stone table in a large stone room.

'What now?' asked Snitto who, though lazy, was a pleasant enough fellow, a handsome one at any rate.

'Now,' said the man, 'comes the work.'

He put a silver thaler down on the table beside Snitto's hand. 'Take the coin and hit the table with it. Go on.'

Snitto did so, and there were two silver thalers. He did it again and there were three.

'Does it keep doing that?' asked Snitto.

'It keeps doing that,' said the man.

'And that's my work?'

'That's your work.'

'And apart from that?'

'Apart from that you're not allowed to stand up, you're not allowed to wipe your nose, the snot will run out and you're not allowed to do anything about it, and you have to pass water where you're sitting and you're not allowed to mop it up, and even your number twos you have to leave down there and you're not allowed to wipe or clean up and you'll be fed and are not allowed to wash and it's for three years.'

Snitto understood that, it wasn't difficult to understand. But to do it was difficult, you just try!

So there sat Snitto, with the snot running down, hitting the table with one coin after another, and when three years were almost up the stone room was full of silver thalers and filth, and in the middle of it sat Snitto, black with filth, with flies on his face, and only occasionally taking a coin and hitting the table with it, for there was a danger Snitto might suffocate in thalers and filth. And he was no longer hitting the table with coins out of greed, but just to pass the time, for he thought time passed a little more quickly if it was chopped up into pieces with thaler-taps.

Nearby lived a man who no longer had a wife but three daughters who were called the First, the Second and the Third. The First was the oldest, and so on. The man was in debt and said to the First, 'I know there's a man living on the neighbouring farm who has a lot of money. Go and ask him if he'll make us a loan.'

The First went and when she entered the stone room she smelt a stench that had not existed before, until then there had only been bad smells. She breathed through her mouth and said, 'Can I have some money?'

'Yes', said Snitto, 'as much as you like. But you have to give me a kiss.'

She couldn't. 'Anyone who stinks like that,' she said, 'could die and no one would shed a tear.'

At home she said, 'I couldn't.'

'Stupid girl,' said the Second, 'father's going to lose everything.'

She went, and the same thing happened. 'Anyone who

372

stinks like that,' she said, 'could die and no one would shed a tear.'

And the Third, the youngest, cried, 'Does he really stink like that?! Does he really look like that?! Do I have to? Do I really have to?'

'Yes,' they said, 'you have to.'

The youngest daughter took soap and water with her, and sweet-smelling oil. And she went into the foul, stinking room where Snitto was sitting, sunk in a mound of filth and silver, and said, 'I want a loan.'

'And I want a kiss,' said Snitto. And he got one. The youngest daughter even forgot to wash her mouth with soap and water and sweet-smelling oil when she was outside. She carted off as many thalers as she could carry and her father was saved.

Then the three years were up and the man who looked like everyone's father and was actually the devil came and said, 'Haven't I got your soul?'

'No,' said Snitto, 'not that.'

'Then I'll wash you,' said the devil. Three hours for his skin, three hours for his hair, three hours for his teeth. And the devil dressed him in fine clothes and said, 'Go and ask for the hand of the youngest daughter.'

It was the First who opened the door and she wanted him for herself. 'You stink,' said Snitto. 'Anyone who stinks like that could die and no one would shed a tear.'

The Second showed him into the parlour. He said exactly the same to her.

But the Third, whom he called the youngest daughter, he took in his arms and there were wedding bells.

The devil also got something. 'I had hoped for a soul,' he said, 'and got two. But out of respect for you, Snitto, I shan't allow them to hang themselves in your house.'

So the devil found another house, and the First and the Second were so furious they hanged themselves because they couldn't marry handsome, pleasant Snitto, the inventor of stench.

This story, or something like it, was told in Finland.

373

The Trouble with Time Travel

Martin Auer

'What strikes me when I read all this speculation about time travel,' said Vladimir, 'is that some problems are never touched on at all. For example, the problem of arrival. If you arrive in a different time, then there's only one way you can do it: *suddenly*. A moment ago you weren't there, now you are. So you'd be arriving at an infinitely high speed, even if it's not quite clear from which direction. But that would mean that a collision with even the lightest of atoms would be fatal. I'm a pilot, not a physicist, but I imagine if you were to collide with an atom at an infinite speed, an infinite amount of energy would be released and everything would explode. And I mean *everything*. Even intergalactic space is not so empty that I would risk it.

And that brings me to the second problem no one appears to have thought about: space. I just cannot imagine how, if you're going to travel through time, you can determine the *place* where you'll land. You see, it's time that holds us in space, time alone that defines space. To put it another way: we're *here* because immediately before we were in a *similar* place. Nothing stays the same. While we're sitting here in this bar, the walls all around are slowly rotting away, even if they are made of non-degradable aluminium. There are atoms decaying, there's the constant bombardment by radiation, people are coming and going, leaving behind the vapours their bodies give off, the air is being shifted round by the ventilation system, though I think they ought to turn the thing up a bit, and so on. And all the time the planet's revolving round its sun, the sun is travelling round the centre of the galaxy, and the galaxy's moving round God knows what, and anyway, as we all know, the whole universe is flying apart in all directions and at one hell of a speed. The point is, space is different all the time, and, if truth be told, we're not in the place we were a moment ago any more. That *place* no longer exists.

Even if I only want to take a tiny jump in time, say ten minutes into the future because I want to see if Hopalong's going to cut his forehead open when he gets so pissed he slumps onto the table, I still have to somehow extricate myself from time. But if I do manage to get outside time, how do I get my time machine to stay in this *place*?

The planet's gravity field can't hold me, if I'm outside time. Everyone knows gravity needs time to attract me, or, to look at it from the other side, that I need time to overcome it. The same is true of the force of inertia. As long as I'm in time, my body puts up resistance to every change in its state of motion. But outside time there is no motion, no state of motion, even less a change in the state of motion, to say nothing of resistance to it.

So, how can I programme my time machine to stay *here*?

While I stay *here*, the bar will keep revolving and disappear from under my feet, the whole planet'll vanish into the distance at a great lick, the solar system, the galaxy – all depending on what it is I'm 'standing still' in relation to. I have the feeling that as soon as I step outside time, if only for a moment (for what kind of *moment*, if I'm outside time?), then it's a matter of pure chance where I reappear in time. Because there's no such thing as absolute space, because there's no fixed point in space I could hold on to 'while' I'm outside time.'

'Hmm,' said Tinhead – so called from his artificial frontal bone – reflectively. 'But if we could solve that problem, then we could use time machines to travel through space at any speed we liked. I could, say, just hop over to old Ma Goddam's cathouse. It's three hours away from here, but if I also travelled back in time three hours, I'd be there in literally no time at all, and without any hassle.'

'You'd even be here and in the whorehouse simultaneously, and at all the infinite number of points in between.'

'Well if I had a time machine,' Hopalong's rumbling voice

came from somewhere under the aluminium table-top, 'I'd go to Ginger at Ma Goddam's, and I'd get there yesterday evening, at nine o'clock precisely, and I'd screw the arse off her for an hour. At ten o'clock I'd hop into my time machine and travel back to nine o'clock again, so that simultaneously I could give it her from . . .'

'Okay man, okay. I think we all get the idea.'

'No you don't. I wouldn't just duplicate myself, I'd . . .'

'You'd do nothing of the sort. One of you's more than enough. Ginger would throw up the moment a duplicate appeared, so you can scrub all plans in that direction, sonny boy.'

'You just don't understand me,' Hopalong muttered, slipping even farther under the table.

'The question that concerns me above all,' Vladimir went on after the interruption, 'is this: if I step outside time, what will hold *me* together? It's only temporal continuity that gives me my sense of identity or, if Popol insists, the illusion of a sense of identity. If I step outside time and then step back in somewhere else, am I then still *me*? That's what I ask myself.'

A leaden silence was the only answer Vladimir received to his question. But then Popol the Aged said, 'I arrived in Kruun about a year after they had invented time travel there. I've no idea whether they'd asked themselves any of the questions Vladimir has been airing here – or now – or here *and* now, I suppose I should say. It worked, and that was that. One of the first things I saw there was a demonstration outside the Kruun Historical Museum. Young people, mostly students of course, were demonstrating against what they called the plundering of Kruun's history. Kruun is not dissimilar to Earth. Naturally they don't have sphinxes or Venus de Milos there, but I'll explain the matter in terms of Mama Earth to make it easier for you to understand. The company that had the initial monopoly on the time machine patent launched the thing with a spectacular advertising gimmick: 'What did the Venus de Milo look like when she still had arms?' Then they sent off an expedition which followed the history of the statue back into the past, all the way to the sculptor's workshop. There they bought it from him and took it with them back to their own time, where they installed it next to the one with its arms broken off that everyone knows. You'll have seen the photo of the two statues, it was in the papers all over the universe.

"But how can that be possible?" some people said. "If they've brought the Venus de Milo here from the past, then it was never lost, it's arms were never broken off, and it couldn't have been found on Melos in 1820. How can it be here at all?"

"But you can *see* it! There it is!" said the company's PR men, and there was no answer to that. Soon after, the market in antiques went haywire. Greek vases, Roman swords, Celtic spears, you name it, you could get it. The prices were horrendous, but the goods were brand new.

Before long the artists and craftsmen of all ages were spending all their time working for what for them was posterity. The Teutons spent their booze-ups lying on straw because their bearskins had disappeared into the future – until, that is, the dealers started supplying them with car-seat covers in orange PVC velours from the 1970s. And instead of beer and mead, they were soon swigging Synthecola with aspirin because the purchasers of their bearskins naturally also wanted authentic drinks from the period to go with them.

And that's the way it was in all periods. The Viennese Biedermeier family ate off tables made out of tea-chests, Aztec priests dumped the hearts of their victims in plastic buckets. There was soon a firm employed in dismantling the sphinx stone by stone, beginning with its nose, and transferring it into the future.

And then came the package tours. A few highbrows wanted to experience Shakespeare's plays live at the Globe, or the tragedies of Sophocles in ancient Athens, but the most popular by far were trips to see the gladiators in ancient Rome, bullfights in Seville at the beginning of the nineteenth century, niggers being lynched in the USA, and football hooligans in the later twentieth century. Tours of the three World Wars were also in great demand.

Eventually they started bringing the best gladiators from

Rome into the present and getting them to fight against mammoths and dinosaurs, which had been transported from various geological periods. The authorities did actually soon ban them, but the entrepreneurs just transferred them to the tertiary period, or to the twentieth century, when people weren't so wimpish.

And there was big business in dead babies. Mothers whose children had died couldn't wait for the chance to travel back into the past and see their babies again. They went back a few years and watched themselves changing nappies. That was relatively harmless. The problems started when they wanted to kiss and cuddle their little darlings. The kids went half mad with fright when a second mother – and one who in some inexplicable way had aged – suddenly appeared and clasped them to their bosom. Some children never recovered from the shock and died even younger. Then, of course, there were cases where the mothers simply flipped their lids and tried to abduct their children and bring them back to the present. The courts were swamped with the number of cases that caused.

There were even more people who travelled back to see their dead dogs and cats. Many got bitten for their pains.

Just as many tried to use time travel to solve their sexual problems. And I'm not just referring to the fat cats who had famous whores like Rosemarie Nitribitt or Christine Keeler brought to the present for them, or engaged Salome to do a striptease. People whose lovers had left them went back to happier times to vie with their formers selves for the favours of the object of their affections. Married couples who felt the magic had gone out of their relationship no longer took a second honeymoon to try and save their marriage, but travelled back to their original honeymoon, to relive their days of wedded bliss. Can you imagine on your wedding night a paunchy middle-aged couple in Bermuda shorts and sunglasses suddenly appearing from the wardrobe and saying, "Hi, we're your future!"

The hotels shut up their honeymoon suites and reverted to letting single rooms to travelling salesmen because they were fed up to the back teeth with all the double suicides and the hordes of policemen constantly tramping through the building.

But why limit oneself to the past? Trips to the future opened up undreamt-of opportunities. Firms shut down their R & D sections and simply brought inventions and new developments back from the future. They bought them or just stole them, in the latter case especially from those enlightened ages that had abolished money. And at the same time, naturally, they headhunted specialists who could handle the technology from the future. One after another the universities closed down, then all the schools apart from primary schools. No one bothered to learn anything any more. There was no point: without future know-how you had no chance of landing anything but a dead-end job. The one possibility was to get a place at a university in the future, but only very few managed to reach the standard of future entrance qualifications.

It was the same in the arts and the entertainment industry. Soon the only thing pop music companies were doing was sending out expeditions to the future to supply an insatiable public with next year's hits, or those of the year after, of the next decade, the next century. The natural consequence was that two, ten or a hundred years later no one wanted to hear such tired old numbers, so that quite different songs, often in completely different styles, made the charts – only, of course, to be immediately transported back to be sold to the disc-buying public as the *real* hits of the future. The musicians of the future soon got fed up with finding that all their most successful numbers immediately turned out to be ancient hits from the last century. The best among them fled to other epochs, which led to some surprising new developments in Gregorian chant and the Indian raga.

When I left Kruun after I'd finished my business there – given the circumstances, it was difficult to say exactly how long my stay had actually lasted – the situation was that the opponents of time travel had a small majority, and that it was about to be banned. Those in favour of time travel merely shrugged their shoulders and said that in that case they would simply stay in the time *before* the ban. That led to a fierce debate among its opponents as to whether it was morally justified to declare a *retrospective* ban on time travel, and if so, how to make it effective. Eventually the suggestion was made that the whole confusing epoch should somehow be chucked out of the time continuum. I quickly made my departure before they did something that might mean I had never been on Kruun. After all, I'd done some big deals on Kruun, and didn't intend to lose my profit.'

In the Sand

Barbara Neuwirth

> There people walk in such a way their clothes
> become quite slender, there they hold their
> heads so high each one must see the other, there
> children never cry; but no one laughs either.

The approach to the plain is bordered by the most mighty
peaks. A hundred metres high and more, they are like battlements guarding the yellow sunrises. The cold wind sweeps
down the slopes like a pack of wolves and woe betide anyone
who leaves their house before the morning brings its warmth.
On some days, when the storm refuses to die down, iron-red
sand dims the daylight. Then stones fly through the air, slashing at the plaster on the houses.

To each house one room. To each room just one person.
And far away another house, another room, another person.

The traveller is looked after by the natives, she is given food
and neutral ground to sleep on. The visitor house, the place is
called, similar to the others yet different: for there in that night
lovers meet / to talk or make love / as it says in the old texts.
The place where time is not. For ever and ever. And beyond
understanding.

The pointed domes above the rooms have been made from
branches and spread with mortar, grey crouching on red, like
elephant skin. But it is a long time since there were any trees
on this plain, saltlicking tamarisks and acacias creep into the
depressions and bow down behind piles of stones.

/The graves,/ certainly, are one of the strangest aspects of
the customs of those people. Whenever one dies they do not
gather, but seem to flee. Just one stays. Perhaps it is the one
who loved the dead person most of all, perhaps one who had

nothing to do with them, what the truth of it is I don't know. The dead person is taken out into the open country, to a place where there is nothing but tears. They are laid down with their face to the ground and arms and legs spread out, almost making them like a cross. The body is enclosed in stones, painstakingly collected, they rise up over its back and when it is completely covered, the work is done. The master of ceremonies goes. No prayer, no service detains the people at the place of the dead. The dead person's house becomes a visitor house until a child leaves its mother and needs somewhere to be alone.

The language of this tall people is loud and violent, a shock on first hearing, so unsuited to the calm faces do the harsh sibilants seem. Apparently they use different words for love, but they do not fall in love with strangers and I did not hear those words.

Hospitality for three days, then leave. An awakening as never before and no one left there. And the wells dried up. And the wind a frenzy of red. (And alone.) That is how they indicate the end of their hospitality to strangers. The herds of sheep have moved on, the dogs among them like sacred wolves, the shepherd in front with his long crook.

Only the track in the sand to follow them.

The wind drives everything before it down the slopes, but the traveller must go up into the mountains and pin the wind to her shoulders to get home. A hundred metres high and more the ranges tower up above her, and soon the ranges will be behind her, or between her and the sand. The sand.

The Furnished Room

Barbara Neuwirth

The bare wood shone black in the light from the bulb. The night threw cats off the wall. They scattered with yowls of protest and leapt out of the window. When the moon was sad, it told lies. The fragrance of lilac warmed the night.

The book still lay open and it had an air of wisdom or culture, even though no one was looking at the characters. Dust had settled on the open pages. It had no qualms about covering the black print and gilt borders. It was a valuable book. Whenever the wind sniffed round the room, the motes danced over the rough paper.

The light bulb gave off a dull glow, but it was still a wasted effort. No one came into the room.

Perhaps the woman who lived there had gone away, perhaps she was dead . . . she had not come into the room for some considerable time, and the bulb had been shining over the round table ever since the moment she had left the room with her short, pitter-patter steps. During the day no one saw it, it was too weak to attract notice. But at night the cats saw it and they avoided the light. Wailing, they fell off the wall and dashed to the window. They jumped into the lilac bush and sang a song to the moon. Sometimes they squabbled over the best branches. Their song came plaintively from their lips, for the moon was telling lies for sadness.

The little girl behind the chest of drawers was wearing a frilly white dress. She was holding a ball with coloured stripes. When it slipped out of her fingers and rolled away, she ran after it and picked it up again. Then she clutched it to her chest and looked up at the light bulb. In the past she had had visitors, every day, or at least almost. Now no one came any more, she had put on her pretty dress for nothing. What had happened to constancy?

Annoyed at the continual changes in temperature, the wood creaked and little cracks spread all over the velvety surface. In the past it had been rubbed down with liquid furniture polish once a week. That had made the wood gleam.

Once it rained in the evening. Heavy storm clouds had appeared, licking at the sun. They ate up the light and set off a whirlwind which sucked the curtain out of the room. The rings jangled on the rail. There was a sudden cloud-burst and in a few seconds the curtain was dripping wet, making a puddle below the window. Then the wind died away. It stroked its chin contentedly and uncovered the setting sun, which took an embarrassed peek into the room, then disappeared behind the turquoise hills without having dried the puddle of rain. The chest of drawers swayed anxiously in the damp atmosphere. The little girl took care not to move. The cats took big jumps so as not to get their paws wet.

The next day the house owner came with the new tenant. She came into the room and switched off the light. She gave the damp patch on the parquet floor an irritated glance.

'You'll like the room,' she said. The new tenant did not dare contradict her.

'Yesterday's storm must have blown the window open, but of course that can't happen if you close it properly.'

The new tenant nodded agreement.

'Right then, I'll leave you in your new room, my dear. I think it'll be best if you pay the rent on the last day of the month, in advance.' With a businesslike turn of the body, she left the room. The new tenant looked round, uncertain what to do next. She sat down on the velvet couch and the springs squeaked indignantly at the weight.

No, she did not feel at home here, the furniture was so dark and heavy, stolid, full of memories. The wallpaper with the cats struck her as too busy, the picture with the affected-looking girl as kitschy. This was no place for her, everything was already filled with others, even the air coming in through

384

the open window was part of another, indefinable feeling that had completely permeated the room.

She stood up and went to the window. Drawing the damp curtain aside, she leant over the window-ledge and looked out. Opposite loomed the menacing, windowless façade of a warehouse. Above it stretched a freshly washed sky, while below was the loud and aggressive uproar of the morning traffic. When she looked out of the window she could imagine feeling at home here. When, however, she pulled her head back inside and the curtain fell over the opening, dimming the activity outside, she was once more gripped with unease and felt unhappy and lonely.

She wished she was back home with her family, the woods and water. What substitute was the asphalt of the streets for the smooth expanse of lake, the buildings for the boundlessness of the landscape. How could the room give her the freedom she had dreamt of, at home, shut up with her brothers and sisters in a small room that had just enough space for them to sleep in. All the dreams that had sent her off to the city had been different. They had tasted of freedom, freedom on her lips, in her eyes, in her ears. She had laughed, and cried too, in her dreams, according to how she felt, but never in her imaginings had she been disheartened, apprehensive, void of all hope. This was not the place of her dreams. Her work was neither interesting nor well paid. The people she worked with were ugly, twisted in their faces and in their behaviour. And she was to live in this room, alone and lonely, an intruder among the memories of others who had lived here before her. There was no one here she could love. Who would even think of being loved by her? The smiling man she had seen at the station, perhaps, the man with the beautiful woman on his arm? He hadn't been smiling at her, of course, but at his companion.

Sadly she got up and went to fetch some water from the corridor. It smelt musty out there.

She spent the whole evening staring out of the open window. The air was stuffy and close again, and she lay down on the couch, exhausted. Whether it was the moon that disturbed her, or perhaps the soft footsteps she thought she could hear, whether it was the destruction of her fantasies by banal reality, whatever it was, she could not sleep and felt shattered as she left the room with her short, weary steps the next morning.

That evening she stood outside the door to her room for a few minutes before putting the key in the lock. She thought she could hear noises, wood being dragged over the parquet floor and the curtain rings jangling on the rail. But there was no one in the room, nothing was changed, everything looked the way it had been when she went out in the morning. Exhausted, she dropped onto the bed and fell asleep without getting undressed. Some time after midnight she woke up, convinced she was not alone in the room. She heard the rustle of some stiff material and the sound of an elastic object bouncing several times. She lay stretched out on the bed, not daring to move. Whoever it was, she didn't want them to realise she was awake. She was sweating and her clothes stuck to her limbs. In her fear, she tried to hold her breath, but it meant that each breath she took sounded loud and wheezing so that she started to sob from fear of the unknown.

When, at last, day broke, the light of the distant sun showed her that she was alone in the room, that no one was threatening her.

She got up and, teeth chattering, went to fetch a basin of water from the corridor to wash herself. She sat down at the round inlaid table and tried, in vain, to collect her thoughts. Finally she went to work.

That evening she was sure she had drawn the curtain back in the morning, although now it was covering almost the whole of the window. Furiously she pushed it aside and looked down at the tired, wilting lilac. Not even that was green in this city. She did not switch off the light, out of fear of whatever might be waiting for her in the dark. The bulb gave out its weak, sickly light, which stopped the darkness from attaching its suckers everywhere. And yet, scarcely had she reached the boundary between waking and dreaming, than she realised the light could not prevent the others from taking up their places. Although there was no one to be seen, she could hear the soft steps of the paws, the rustling of the dress and the bouncing of the ball. From the lilac bush came the multiple song of the cats who had gathered outside the house.

She slipped out of bed and her movements did not expunge those of the others, who were now brazenly taking over the room, even in her presence. With short, stiff steps, she went over to the window to look at the lilac bush. The cats were sitting there, congregated in harmony. Cautiously she sat on the window-ledge and swung her legs over. The cats turned their heads and watched her unconcernedly. Their green and yellow eyes were wide open, but they showed no sign of interest.

There was no affection here. Was freedom possible at all under these circumstances? And what should that freedom be like? She had had a dream, a dream of success, happiness and love she had called freedom. Now she no longer knew whether that really could be freedom. It was probably something quite different, something she had not understood. Perhaps it was simply the opportunity to make every decision, never mind what the consequences would be. Here and now. Not to go back into the room but to push herself off from the window, float down to the lilac bush and do the same as the cats, who were singing to the moon. The lying moon.

The bare wood of the chest of drawers shone black in the light from the weak bulb. The night threw cats off the wall. They scattered with yowls of protest and leapt out of the window. The girl in the frilly dress ran after the ball with its coloured stripes which had slipped out of her hands. With a sigh, she returned to her place behind the chest of drawers. No one had come to see her.

The night rain had soaked the curtain, making a long puddle underneath. The next day the house owner came with the new tenant. She came into the room and switched off the light. She gave the damp patch on the parquet floor an irritated glance.

'You'll like the room,' she promised. The new tenant did not dare contradict her.

387

Extracts from
Novak: A Grotesque

Günther Kaip

It gave Novak a great sense of satisfaction whenever he came across his name in the newspaper during his daily hour in the coffee house.

'Aha,' he would think, 'I'm not alone, there's two of us,' and his mood would undergo a dramatic improvement. Taking heart, he would order his next coffee and resolve to remain a Novak.

'I am Novak,' he said to the waiter, who bent down and regarded him with amazement. 'Don't hold it against me. And no recrimination, I won't have it,' he added, when he noticed the waiter grimace in disgust and throw up. That attracted the attention of all the customers, of course, and they immediately got up and fled from the coffee house.

The only one to remain seated was a young woman with butterflies soaring up from her blond hair.

Novak nodded to her and stood up, pushing aside the waiter, who was writhing in guilt on the floor, racked by uncontrollable sobbing. Novak was a regular, after all. For years his newspaper rustling and thoughtful look had contributed to the stability of the coffee house, giving him the right to preferential treatment. But Novak had no intention of insisting on that now. He freed himself from the waiter's hands, which were clamped round his ankles.

'Outrageous,' hissed Novak, sensing the hot breath of a revolutionary attitude. It stiffened his neck muscles, straightened his posture, and with a spring in his step he walked over the the young woman's table. His heart turned a somersault as he looked into the green shimmer of her eyes.

'I love you, miss,' he said in the excited tones of a

revolutionary, for love is revolution, Novak realised. 'I have always loved you.'

The young woman shook her head and looked down at her lap in which a man's head was rolling to and fro.

'He stepped on a butterfly,' she whispered. 'Help me, if you really love me,' she said, pointing to a cushion beside her.

She grasped Novak's hands. In that moment he loved her even more, picked up the cushion and pressed it as firmly as he could down onto her lap.

'He hasn't even combed his hair,' Novak panted. He increased the pressure, feeling himself a man.

'This doesn't happen every day,' he muttered, ignoring the wheezes coming from head. Novak started to sweat, drops were running down his forehead and falling straight into the hands of the young woman, who had formed them into a cup.

It lasted five minutes and Novak only released the cushion when silence reigned and the man's limbs had stopped twitching.

'Thank you,' said the young woman, standing up. She looked sadly at the lifeless body under the table. She was trembling all over and put her hand on the place on her chest where her heart was beating.

'Now she means me,' thought Novak, and moved one step closer.

'We'll see each other tomorrow. Be on time,' said the young woman as she passed between the rows of tables on her way to the door, which Novak, a gentleman of the old school, held open for her.

Proudly he walked back to his table and opened a newspaper. On the second page he came across a Novak who had escaped after a bank robbery.

'Aha! That's a good sign,' he cried, looking absent-mindedly at the waiter, who had crawled on all fours to the kitchen and was lying there, motionless.

Novak leapt up, danced round the tables, through the coffee house out into the street and then – two hours had passed – around his wife, who watched her husband with a shake of the head but a smile on her face.

'Magnificent,' she said and put on her coat to go out. She stood in the open doorway looking in astonishment at Novak, who was running across the ceiling, clapping his hands and giving her encouraging winks.

Nothing could stop him now. He tried his hand at somersaults, attempted elaborate pirouettes, keeping his balance securely, jumped from the wardrobe to the glass-fronted cabinet, slid across the walls and finished off with a spin.

'Magnificent,' she murmured, unsure whether, under the circumstances, she should go out. But the thought that she could bring him back a present commensurate with the event sent her tripping down the stairs.

Novak leant against the wall, panting. He thought of the young woman and realised he had not asked her name.

'That was a mistake, unforgivable,' he muttered and went to look in the mirror.

'But I know you,' Novak said to his mirror image, which had its eyes closed. 'You're refusing to look at me,' he shouted and prepared to attack.

Suddenly his mirror image wobbled and toppled into his arms without warning. It was heavy, infinitely heavy, and Novak simply dropped it on the floor, where it shattered.

With difficulty he made it to the living room. Once more the sweat was dripping from his forehead, but there was no young woman here to catch the drops. Novak lay down on the floor and cried.

In his mind's eye he saw the young woman and his colleagues at work. They were whispering and giving him pitiful looks.

'And everything started so well,' thought Novak. 'It's just not fair.'

He stretched out his hands towards the young woman, but all he grasped was the empty air. When he opened his eyes, he gave a start. The room was crowded with people. They stepped aside, making a corridor along which his wife came towards Novak. She was laughing and waving a bunch of flowers in her left hand.

'For you, darling. Just for you,' said his wife, then turned to the young woman, threw her arms round her and kissed her.

Novak tried to sit up while the couple separated and turned towards him. The young woman ran her fingers through his hair and whispered, 'You're tired . . . go to sleep . . . remember our rendezvous.'

'Of course. You're quite right,' he meant to reply, but his eyes fell shut and he sank into the young woman's soft voice.

★

The passageway was dark and damp. The floor consisted of bare earth. There was a musty smell. Novak felt his way forward by the light of his torch, cursing himself for promising his wife he'd tidy up their cellar. Cobwebs clung to his face. The ground sloped slightly downward.

Pipes as thick as his arm ran along the walls, dripping. The bricks were covered in mould.

Novak reached the end of the passage and opened the door to their cellar space. It took minutes for his eyes to adjust to the darkness. He went in.

He remembered the room as smaller, not so rocky and cavernous, not so neat and tidy. Along the rear wall was a tarpaulin covering objects lying under it. Novak could hear his own breathing change to a high-pitched whistling.

'This is not normal,' he said out loud and ducked beneath the echo of his voice coming at him from all sides.

Cautiously he went over to the tarpaulin and tore it aside. Underneath Novak had expected spiders and other insect life, perhaps a dead rat.

But lying there, packed close together, were rigid bodies, the bodies of schoolmates, colleagues and acquaintances whom he had forgotten because they were not important to him.

They turned their eyes towards him, dead and empty eyes. They ground their teeth and stuck out their tongues. Novak panicked and ran into the cellar walls from which lumps of plaster fell off. Their eyes boring into his back, he desperately tried to find the way out.

'But they're dead. Dead and buried long ago,' he said, trying to raise his spirits as he tripped over objects on the floor.

When he looked at the bodies again he noticed a change in their gestures and expressions. They were grinning and beckoning him over. A few even stood up, but collapsed as soon as they were upright and crumbled into piles of dust.

Novak took a step towards them, a stick in his hands, ready to hit out, but dropped it at once, pulled trumpets and drums out of his head and put on a deafening concert. The floor swayed, the wine bottles in the rack clinked, the cellar door tugged at its hinges, the torch went on and off, fell out of his hand and smashed to pieces against one of the walls.

Then, when Novak was sure his voice could not be heard above the tumult, he started to scream and jumped into one of the piles of sand, thrusting the stick into it. He spread the dust into every corner of the cellar and covered himself in it. He rolled on the floor, kicking his legs in the air, stood up, knocked over some stacked-up planks, smashed bottles of wine and only stopped when the swirling dust had settled.

Novak spread out the tarpaulin and covered the whole of the cellar floor with it.

'The shroud,' he said, picked up his torch, which was undamaged, immediately found the way out, locked the door and followed the beam of light, which was hurrying on ahead. The ground sloped slightly upward. There was a musty smell.

In the courtyard Novak brushed the dust off his shirt and trousers, threw the key into the bin and went to the stairs, where he met the caretaker, who gave him a friendly *hello*. Novak did not notice her, but went on up the stairs, trusting that his apartment lay within reach.

★

The lamps over the bar were switched on when Novak ordered his fifth whisky. He was the only customer in the place and kept nodding to the barman's stories, saying *yes, hm,* or *'s that so?*

Novak had had too much to drink and found it difficult to keep his balance. In addition, he was desperately trying to find a story that had once happened to him. To loosen up his memory, he rotated his head, stretched his back up straight until the vertebra cracked and swung his arms round in the air.

He wanted something he could use to counter the barman, anecdotes from his life, but nothing occurred to Novak that would have been worth mentioning, whilst the barman talked and talked, piled story upon story, watching Novak's contortions with a smile. He was just lowering his voice and rolling his eyes when Novak broke off his exercises, leant over the bar and shouted:

'This lust for stories, at best it's two or three things that have happened to a person, if at all!'

The barman looked up in surprise and fell silent at the sight of Novak clenching his hands into fists.

'Those are just standard samples of experience, not stories. That's enough!'

Novak's voice ended in a squawk. He downed his whisky in one gulp, banged the glass on the bar and slipped off his stool.

He intended to leave the place as quickly as possible, but when he heard steps and the crash of the toilet door shutting, he turned round and went back. The barman had disappeared. From the toilet came the dull thud of some object and shrill laughter.

'Strange,' thought Novak, hurried to the toilet door and opened it cautiously. In the middle of the blue-tiled floor of the urinal lay the barman with his knees drawn up and holding his stomach with both hands. Beside him sat a transparent figure with a piece of paper fixed to its chest. On it was written in large letters: *I am his story. Ahoy! Ahoy!*

It was regarding Novak attentively.

'He was lying,' it said in earnest tones, pointing to the barman. It was writing in a notebook with a pencil, filling page after page with neat writing, while beside it the barman kept on groaning. Ignoring him, the figure rose and looked down at the barman, who was trying to lift his head.

It pointed at him, smiled and went over to Novak. It

seemed surprised that he was still there looking at the barman, who was lying still.

'Can't you see you're in the way. Go now,' it whispered. Its face, with a terrifyingly resolute expression, was coming closer, already it was stretching out its arms towards Novak, who fled, slamming the toilet door behind him, out into the street, not stopping until the door of the bar was nothing but a tiny black rectangle.

He leant against the wall of a house and looked back, since he was afraid the figure might follow him. After nothing had happened for a few minutes he decided to go home. He staggered at every step.

In spite of everything, he envied the barman his story, a story that belonged to him alone, even if it obviously did have a tendency to violence.

Novak kept stopping in his tracks and turning round, hoping to discover his own story. But there was nothing there.

It was depressing, and if Novak hadn't learnt to control himself, he would have sunk to the ground and surrendered to unrestrained weeping.

'You just have to make a start. But how?' he thought.

Perhaps his own story would have comforted him, or told him jokes to cheer him up. That would have calmed Novak down.

As it was, he walked straight past his house and out of the town, obsessed with the idea of finding his own story.

Yet all he had to do was to feel his left shoulder. There sat a figure busily writing in its notebook.

★

Novak could never claim that he was treated with consideration on his way to work. People, and there were a lot of them, stepped over him when he fell down, trampled on his stomach or shoved him without warning off the pavement and into the path of buses, which almost cost him his life every time. On seeing him, women pushing prams crossed over to the other side and the infants shook their fist at him.

But the most unbearable, as far as he was concerned, were those who simply dissolved into thin air before his eyes.

And Novak was such a harmless person. His colleagues at the office ignored this trait, squeezing tears of resignation and desperation out of his face and collecting his saline discharges in their teacups.

During the lunch break he attempted to get a meal.

'But you can't take the place away from someone else, a strong young man like you,' he heard the waiters say when he asked to be allowed to have a meal. 'A little more restraint, if you please. You're not the only person in the world.'

They were right, of course, even if he did think it was going a bit far to throw him out of the restaurant onto the pavement every time.

'Nevertheless, one day I'll be lucky,' Novak thought as he crossed the street and hurried up the steps to the office.

There his boss was waiting, arms crossed. He was angry, Novak could tell that at first glance, very angry even, for he was hovering an inch above the ground.

'Too late,' he roared and pushed Novak so violently against the doorpost that he lost consciousness and sank down onto the parquet floor.

After that excitement he deserved a rest, all his colleagues were agreed on that, patted him on the shoulder, set him down at his desk and brought him their files with concerned looks on their faces. They stroked his hair, whispered encouragement and assured him they held him in high regard.

That usually lasted for five minutes, five minutes of balm for Novak, who recovered consciousness during these blandishments, so that his colleagues could go back to their card game with their minds at rest.

Novak frequently interrupted his work on the account books to feel his head, which had not suffered any damage. He made an effort to cheer his colleagues up with jokes, but they didn't notice, since the card game demanded their full attention.

After work Novak went out into the street whistling. He had got through a working day without serious damage, he still had arms and his head, which swayed in time with his steps.

Naturally that was a provocation, and a number of those hurrying past had to turn back to hit the smile, that early-evening irritation which was beyond forgiveness.

Novak accepted it, he understood his fellow men, whom he had brought into a dreadful situation with his lack of consideration.

'After all, I'm part of society, I don't live alone,' he thought, protecting his face, which was wet with blood, frightening some of those coming towards him. Others, for their part, kneaded his skullbones, pulled his cheeks tight or stretched them out and twisted his ears until they were satisfied with the result.

'Thanks,' Novak shouted after them, for he appreciated the fact that they had sacrificed valuable time for him.

And he would have gone on his way in carefree mood, had it not been for the pain, the white-hot pain that brought the tears to his eyes.

'Even that will change,' thought Novak, and looked straight ahead, glad that that thought had occurred to him.

*

'Good morning,' said Novak to his wife before sitting down at the breakfast table. That was at six o'clock.

He bit firmly into a roll.

'Tastes good,' he said to his wife, without raising his eyes. He chewed slowly, methodically.

His eating tackle was well serviced, the daily paper had reached eye-level and rustled as he turned the page. That was at 6.30.

'The jam, please,' he said to his wife, starting with a shock of surprise when he noticed his wife wasn't there. That was at 6.43.

One minute later he had so far recovered that he could immerse himself in the newspaper again. Now he was reading more quickly, not concentrating. That lasted from 6.45 until 6.49.

Suddenly he jumped up, ran round to the other side of the table and went to the balcony door. The sun was saying its morning litany, the heavens were intact. Crows were flying with tape measures to put figures on the distances.

'That's nice,' murmured Novak, impressed, stepping to one side as a high-speed train thundered past and disappeared into the bedroom. That was at 6.54.

Normally at this time Novak had finished his breakfast, the folded newspaper lay on top of his sandwiches in his briefcase and his wife was standing by the door to kiss him good-bye. But something had gone wrong.

Novak scratched his head to facilitate thinking. However, as he touched one spot on the back, his whole head fell off his body straight into his lap. Novak looked down at it in astonishment, but immediately pulled himself together since recently it had often happened that his limbs broke off or he left a hand on his desk in the office.

But today was the first time for his head, and he needed that. There would be problems if he started going round headless.

'It was probably already loose,' thought Novak, to calm himself down, and looked at the clock. It was 7.05. That irritated him.

'Such a little thing and I'll be late for the office,' he thought.

Resolutely he pressed his head onto his neck, jumped up onto his two feet and hurried to the front door. His wife was leaning against the doorframe.

'Well, where on earth did she come from?' he muttered.

With a smile, he went up to his wife, spread out his arms and kissed her so clumsily on the lips that his head slipped onto his left shoulder.

'Comedian!' his wife called out after him as he hurried down the stairs, blushing as he straightened up his head.

★

397

Transparent webs formed between Novak's fingers. They tore, fluttering in the wind as his hands rose up and, fingers splayed, placed themselves on his face. Novak lost his balance. His right arm flailed around in the air, his trunk swayed to the left and right, whilst his legs tried to run away. There was no one at all to be seen, which was unusual on this Saturday morning.

'Something must have happened,' thought Novak.

The shops were shut, barricaded with planks of wood and crouching down behind rolls of barbed wire. The queasy feeling Novak had had in his stomach since wakening from a death-like sleep increased and slowly spread throughout his body.

That was inconvenient, as he had prepared himself for a pleasant day devoted entirely to himself. After all, he had come to an understanding of many things, had both feet on the ground and had removed all obstacles, broadening the scope of his mental perspective. In a word, he embodied hope.

His body became weightless and hovered above the asphalt. He rose higher, as if he were being pulled up through the air on a rope.

'Is there more?' murmured Novak in astonishment. He was sure that in a few seconds he would wake up in bed, alone, as his wife was away, with the sound of the alarm-clock in his ear and the warm rays of the morning sun on his face.

At that moment his legs fell off his body onto the street, as did his arms, which flailed around in the air until shortly before hitting the ground. It tickled, and Novak looked in astonishment at the stumps of his arms and legs, which were not bleeding. The index and middle fingers of the right arm he had lost spread out in a V, V for Victory.

His head was in its proper place and covered in sweat; his shirt was sticking to his skin and the coat he had bought yesterday was fluttering in the wind sweeping through the town.

'That's not fair,' he shouted, when he finally realised it wasn't a dream and he had really been on his way to the supermarket to do his weekend shopping.

'What a time for this to happen to me,' he panted. His

voice echoed down the ravines between the tall buildings and the roaring of the wind became so loud it hurt his ears.

Things that had been far away now seemed close to his ear: the jangle of the tram below him, the stuttering engine of a car, the sudden cry of a child in a park, the rustle of a mac-intosh, glass shattering, the town hall clock ticking a mile away, a telephone ringing, a computer humming as it was switched on, fat sizzling in a frying pan.

Every sound, every noise was an explosion and startled Novak, who was flying up and down the street. Sometimes he dropped down in an air pocket, but before he hit the ground he was caught on an upcurrent which flung him back into the sky.

Suddenly it was silent and down on the footpath – he happened to be flying along the gutter of a house – he recog-nised his wife, Tamara, Kurt, Georg, the caretaker and her husband. They had linked arms and were crossing the street in close formation.

'You're staying, aren't you?' they called out to Novak.

Directly below him, outside a cake shop, Brustbein was just picking up one of his wife's white gloves.

'Come on,' she too shouted up at Novak.

'And hurry up, if I may make so bold,' added Brustbein.

'Come on, never say die!' They were all trying to spur him on and clapped their hands in time. 'Don't be afraid.'

'But it's too early,' thought Novak, who had allowed him-self to be distracted and only just managed to avoid a pigeon crossing his flight path.

'Bravo!' came the cry from the street below. Novak felt flattered and performed a few somersaults in the air, though because of his lack of arms the sleeves of his coat slapped him round the ears.

'Are we going for a meal?' he shouted when he had his flight under control once more. 'Or to the zoo? Perhaps to the fairground? You decide, I'll go along with whatever you want,' Novak shouted, but he realised they couldn't hear him, for they went into a restaurant while he was flying through the air, while birds darkened the skies, while huge clouds of dust rose from the streets, while bricks slowly floated up like balloons and disappeared in the black of the sky.

Novak pumped air into his lungs, pulled his head in and tried to become as small as one of the birds that accompanied him up here, hoping to lose all memory, all thought of his future, simply to be there, whatever might happen to him, and he felt feathers growing under his shirt, and in his chest was a bird's heart, transparent and warm, beating like mad.

But suddenly his flight came to an abrupt halt, he crashed into the air, simply got stuck, and when he panicked and looked down he saw the barman with his story on his shoulder. They were both watching Novak and whispering to each other while the barman held up a long pole on which an old man was balancing, arms outspread.

'You can't do anything without a pole,' the man called up sadly to Novak, who was still stuck above the street, on a level with the sixth storey. The old man jumped down onto the street, broke the pole the barman had dropped and disappeared round the corner.

'Please stay,' Novak called after him, whilst the barman, with his story sitting on his shoulder busy writing in a notepad, followed the old man.

Meanwhile Novak's wife, Tamara, Kurt, Georg, Frau and Herr Brustbein, the caretaker and her husband had come out of the restaurant. They were in a good mood and looked up at the sky.

'Where is he? He can't even wait for us,' they said, 'how selfish can you get.'

'Here I am,' shouted Novak, but he was caught in a gust of wind. With his last reserves of strength he managed to hold on to a gutter. When he looked down he saw the young woman from the coffee house. Butterflies were fluttering up to him from her hair.

'There, it worked out after all,' thought Novak and forgot his precarious situation for a moment when the young woman saw him and shouted up to him, 'There you are at last!' and he shouted back, 'Of course,' and suddenly the gutter broke away from its fixing, a gust of wind flung him high into the air and carried him out of the town, towards the horizon. No longer was Novak pushing it away from him, now it was zooming towards him.

The End

Austrian Literature from Dedalus

Work by some of the authors in *The Dedalus Book of Austrian Fantasy:1890–2000* has been featured in the Dedalus European Classics and Decadence from Dedalus series.

The Dedalus Book of German Decadence –
  editor R. Furness £9.99
The Other Side – Alfred Kubin £9.99
The Road to Darkness – Paul Leppin £7.99
The Angel of the West Window –
  Gustav Meyrink £9.99
The Golem – Gustav Meyrink £6.99
The Green Face – Gustav Meyrink £7.99
The Opal (& other stories) – Gustav Meyrink £7.99
Walpurgisnacht – Gustav Meyrink £6.99
The White Dominican – Gustav Meyrink £6.99
The Maimed – Hermann Ungar £6.99

Forthcoming titles include:

The Class – Hermann Ungar £7.99

For full description of these titles visit our website dedalus-books.com, click on catalogue and then Dedalus European Classics and Decadence from Dedalus. All Dedalus titles can be ordered from your local bookshop or can be obtained from Dedalus directly by writing to:

Cash sales, Dedalus Limited, Langford Lodge,
St Judith's Lane, Sawtry, Cambs, PE28 5XE

The Golem – Gustav Meyrink

'Gustav Meyrink uses this legend in a dream-like setting on the Other Side of the Mirror and he has invested it with a horror so palpable that it has remained in my memory all these years.'

Jorge Luis Borges

'A superbly atmospheric story set in the old Prague ghetto featuring the Golem, a kind of rabbinical Frankenstein's monster, which manifests every 33 years in a room without a door. Stranger still, it seems to have the same face as the narrator. Made into a film in 1920, this extraordinary book combines the uncanny psychology of doppelganger stories with expressionism and more than a little melodrama . . . Meyrink's old Prague – like Dickens's London – is one of the great creation of city writing, an eerie, claustrophobic and fantastical underworld where anything can happen.'

Phil Baker in The Sunday Times

'A remarkable work of horror, half-way between *Dr Jekyll and Mr Hyde* and *Frankenstein*.'

The Observer

£6.99   ISBN 1 873982 91 7   262p   B.Format

Walpurgisnacht – Gustav Meyrink

It is 1917. Europe is torn apart by war, Russia in the grip of revolution, the Austro-Hungarian Empire on the brink of collapse. It is Walpurgisnacht, springtime pagan festival of unbridled desire. In this volcanic atmosphere, in a Prague of splendour and decay, the rabble prepare to storm the hilltop castle, and Dr Thaddaeus Halberd, once the court physician, mourns his lost youth. Phantasmagorical prose, energetically translated, marvellously evokes past and present, personal and political, a devastated world.

The Times

£6.99   ISBN 1 873982 50 X   192p   B.Format

The Angel of the West Window – Gustav Meyrink

'The narrator believes he is becoming possessed by the spirit of his ancestor John Dee. The adventures of Dee and his disreputable colleague, an earless rogue called Edmund Kelley, form a rollicking 16th century variant on Butch Cassidy and the Sundance Kid as they con their way across Europe in a flurry of alchemy and conjured spirits. At one point, Kelley even persuades Dee that the success of an occult enterprise depends on his sleeping with Dee's wife. Past, present, and assorted supernatural dimensions become intertwined in this odd and thoroughly diverting tale.'

Anne Billson in The Times

£9.99   ISBN 0 946626 65 0   421p   B.Format

The Maimed – Hermann Ungar

What is with these Czechs? It is not just Kafka: they all seem
to be obsessed with the idea of forces acting against them,
forces of motiveless malevolence. Franz Polzer is that quintessentially 1920s creation, the tormented bank clerk. His
outer life is pristine, his inner one deeply unhygienic: fears of
disorder plague him and when his landlady, Frau Polger,
begins to make unmistakably sexual advances to him, his mind
buckles into a state of helpless paranoia. Nor is that all: his best
friend, Karl Fanta, is dying slowly of a hideous wasting disease
which unsettles his reason. Everyone is drowning in a desperate search for security. The destinies of Franz, his landlady,
Karl and a mysterious male nurse converge in a denouement
of madness and murder. Somewhere Polzer knows that whatever it is, it's not his fault, but he can never find the words:
the text seems to hint that a sense of guilt is preferable to
bewilderment. Polzer himself is a profoundly poignant figure:
one of the novel's most moving moments has Frau Polger
throw out the picture of St Francis which Polzer had always
treasured: "It's just that he was always on the wall above my
bed".'

Murrough O'Brien in The Independent on Sunday

£6.99   ISBN 1 903517 10 9   210p   B.Format

The Others – Alfred Kubin

Expressionist illustrator Kubin wrote this fascinating curio, his only literary work in 1908. A town named Pearl, assembled and presided over by the aptly named Patera, is the setting for his hallucinatory vision of a society founded on instinct over reason. Culminating apocalyptically – plagues of insects, mountains of corpses and orgies in the street – it is worth reading for its dizzying surrealism alone. Though ostensibly a gothic macabre fantasy, it is tempting to read *The Other Side* as a satire on the reactionary, idealist utopianism evident in German thought in the early twentieth century, highly prescient in its gloom, given later developments. The language often suggests Nietsche. The inevitable collapse of Patera's creation is lent added horror by hindsight. Kubin's depiction of absurd bureaucracy is strongly reminiscent of Kafka's *The Trial*, and his flawed utopia, situated next to a settlement of supposed savages, brings to mind Huxley's *Brave New World*; it precedes both novels, and this superb new translation could demonstrate its influence on subsequent modern literature.

Kieron Pim in Time Out

£9.99   ISBN 1 873982 69 0   249p   B.Format